P. C. M. Vandermeer

FAR BEYOND THE MOON

A Queer Cosmic Body Horror Monster Romance

Impressum

Bibliografische Information der Deutschen Nationalbibliothek:
Die Deutsche Nationalbibliothek verzeichnet diese Publikation in der
Deutschen Nationalbibliografie; detaillierte bibliografische Daten
sind im Internet über http://dnb.dnb.de abrufbar.

E-Mail: pcm.vandermeer@web.de
Website with TWs: pcm-vandermeer.carrd.co

cover designed using an image by @juliakadel on unsplash.com

Herstellung und Verlag: BoD – Books on Demand, Norderstedt

ISBN: 978-3-7568-6283-2

To anyone in need of a hug.

You are not alone.

CHAPTERS

DISCLAIMER

This novel contains sexual and potentially re-traumatizing content. Please see if the read would be safe for you, as this book contains discussions, scenes, and/or mentions of:

- paranormal romance and sex, including tentacle sex
- body horror and body dysmorphia
- past abuse and rape
- homophobia and homophobic language
- racism and racist language
- eating disorders
- mental illness, self-harm, and suicidality
- physical, emotional, sexual and mental violence (not between the main characters)

All sexual acts between the main characters are consensual. Further content warnings for this novel could potentially spoil the story; they can be found at the end of the book on p. 411.

While writing "Far Beyond The Moon" has had a positive effect on my personal healing journey, all survivors experience and process their history differently. This novel, and by extension I, do not claim to represent with universal validity how trauma affects people in their everyday life. The same applies to the exploration of queerness and queer trauma – queer people are not a monolith. If you are currently struggling yourself, do not hesitate to seek help, for example with mental health professionals or anonymous aid centers.

SHIMMER

THE MARCH AIR is still chilly, as though it had not yet fully woken from the night. Dew from trees sheens the streets of Hillsburg, Massachusetts, once a picturesque smalltown with houses made of wood, bricks, and honest American work. Now the doorframes are shabby and the windows impervious from dirt or taped newspapers. No children buying donuts on Main Street, no cat rushing through the matutinal emptiness. Even the gas station by the southern town sign has been abandoned years ago.

The reason Hillsburg has turned into a ghost town is located on 27 West Street, in a parallel road to Main. From every crack of this red brick building's third floor, a pink shimmer overtakes the golden rays of the morning sun. Everchanging, everlasting. It shines as though refracted by a crystal, if said crystal was constantly changing its form and composition.

Not once in the past fourteen years has the light vanished. It attracts tourists and scientists from around the world and, more importantly, MIT. And so, West Street has been continuously filled with metal tables and plastic tents in the place of abandoned pickup trucks. Electronic receptors and measuring equipment keep growing in it like a tech jungle. In-between the instruments and flying papers, humans scurry through the site, day and night. Some are dressed entirely in white protective clothing, some in the pajamas they took to camp here.

This is the scene that Colin Waverford arrives to. He is a young MIT student determined to impress his old MIT teacher, Professor Wong, head of the Hillsburg Project that observes and studies the anomaly on West Street.

Further behind him follows a smaller figure, packed away into a dark blue coat to keep the spring cold out. Every step makes her kinky head of hair bop with energy. It is fellow student Allison Birk. Her brown eyes are glued to the same spot as his, though for different reasons.

Colin Waverford shields his eyes with a hand. "Whoah." It truly is a pink shimmer, irradiating through the windows and all the tiny holes in the roof. And it was true, even the joints between the brick stones are corrugated. As though a painter had used too much water; no straight lines to be seen.

"Incredible, isn't it?" Allison asks him.

"I mean, I'm *looking* at it," Colin says as though his perception was the be-all and end-all of scientific discovery. He turns to look at his fellow student. "I've only seen the videos in the prep cloud."

She sniffs away the chilly air tickling her nose. "I feel you. Nothing could ever prep you for the real thing."

"I know the radiation levels only go crazy inside the building, but it's still so weird standing here without any protection. It's so very weird."

"That's 27 West Street for you." She gives him a smile. "I'm Allison. Welcome to the Hillsburg Haunted House."

"Colin." He shakes her hand with an uneasy look. "Is that a thing? The Haunted House?"

3

"It's what my friends and I dubbed the place."

Colin looks around. "I'll try to do better than my predecessors."

"Up to you now."

The comment, though spoken in amity, makes Colin rub his hands. "The fact that Professor Wong chose to email me is the biggest encouragement. I mean, that's gotta count for something, right?"

Allison just smiles. The main concern and function of Mikaela Wong is the founding for this project, granted to her by the MIT, which Allison depends on to solve the mystery of the Shimmer. Instead of telling him that, she hands Colin the only thing he needs right now. "Here's your manual. With all things that weren't in the cloud." She straightens her back. "Professor Wong's briefing told you what to look for when studying the energy field. And this will tell you *who*."

He gives her a funny look. "Who to look for?"

"Yes."

"Okay?"

"Thank you for joining the project. Make yourself comfortable over there for now." "Will do." As he walks toward the tent Allison had pointed him to, Colin flips through the pages, stapled together and, from the looks of their corners, already having been passed through many hands. He wonders if that meant anything.

Allison walks in the opposite direction, to the biggest table set up in West Street, the monitoring station. Bent over it is a woman who could make a gargoyle look friendly if it stood next to her.

"Good morning."

"Morning, Miss Birk." Allison sets down her bag to join the professor behind the notes and headphones on her metal table. There, she asks her usual question: "Anything new?"

Wong sighs and scribbles another note. "A fucking bird almost flew into my receptor. Other than that, business as usual."

Allison laughs. "A bird?" Her hopeful eyes dart to the sky. It was exceptionally blue this morning. Or maybe that was just the contrast against the pink light. She could never be sure. "You mean they're returning this year?" she asks.

"It's spring after all." Wong glances at her. "But the readings remain unchanged. To be honest, I would not get my hopes up." She practically lives here by now, she knows these numbers like they're her children.

Allison continues studying the sky. "But all animals had left this area. Maybe something's about to change that we can't register yet."

"We'll keep monitoring," Wong says with a considerate nod. "You wanna take a look at the EMS?"

"Yes, right away."

"Oh, Miss Birk, you know what? Go get a coffee first, you just arrived."

"Actually – I'm sorry, Allison?" That is Colin Waverford, waving carefully to Allison after quietly greeting their professor. The manual serves as an extension of his arm. Allison gives those pages to their assistants only upon arrival, so that they would not send her defamatory emails and jump off the project before even coming to Hillsburg. With Colin confronting her now, it would be all the same though. Presumably.

"Can I talk to you for a moment?"

A nod from Wong allows Allison to join him on his way behind the logistics tent, where he turns around to give her a condescending look. "I mean no disrespect. But I've read through your 'manual'."

Against her hopes, Allison crossing her arms fails to steady her tone. "Hardly. I just gave it you."

He looks around and lowers his voice as he leans into her personal space. "You're convinced this energy field is connected to a... personal tragedy of yours?"

Allison stares at him. Sits it out. Wait for it...

"I may be outta line here, but this looks really unprofessional."

She sighs and turns away with a laugh of disappointment. It's way too early in the morning for this kind of talk.

"Does Professor Wong know of your personal meddling with her studies?"

"This 'personal meddling' is the reason she's here at all. She's here because I've brought the Shimmer to her attention."

"Unbelievable. Oh my God, the audacity! You can tell that to yourself–"

"I do," Allison says, calmer than she expected. "Because it's the truth."

"That tells me everything." Colin holds out the manual. "You do realize all those reports of people claiming they saw 'eldritch abominations' roam this town were a tourism ploy, right? In Massachusetts, around Halloween?"

"Those reports align perfectly with the possible time window of my father's disappearance," Allison lets him know, snapping the pages from his hands.

Colin's face contorts into a pitifully disingenuous grin. "Listen, I'm sorry your father went missing. Fourteen years is a goddamn long time. But you need to put two and two together. I'm sorry, someone has to say it! It may be hard for you to see it now, 'cause you've been spinning all these theories for so long, apparently, or watched too many melodramas but – let me get this straight. Your parents get divorced, half a year later someone dies in a gruesome car crash, and the last person they talked to was your father. Shortly after that your mother and your grandmother die in hospitals, sharing almost exactly the same symptoms, and your father 'goes missing' after saying something vaguely ominous to you. I mean – don't you see what happened here?"

Allison shifts, her sneakers wet from the muddy streets. She would be lying if she said this possibility had never crossed her mind. But she has dismissed it years ago. Slowly, she says, "If you're insinuating my father is a runaway murderer…"

Colin leans back. "Right. It's easier to believe he got sucked into some portal or whisked away by a monster or so." He gestures vaguely at the pages. "Or 'hate-crimed'. Grow up."

Allison nods her anger away.

"Yeah. For real." Colin shakes his head as he leaves. "No wonder there's no credit points for this shit."

"Would you still like to contribute to this shit?" Wong asks from around the corner.

"Professor! Yes – what would you like me to do?"

"Scavenge this street. There's a rake over there. Start making yourself useful."

Once Colin Waverford's steps are inaudible, Allison returns to the observer station. Numb. As though by cue, her eyes wander to the Shimmer. Everchanging, everlasting. This is where her dad had lived, in this dark hole of an apartment, before every trace of him vanished from this world with not a soul to care for where he went until Allison was old enough to understand. His blue pickup truck was towed away only when the science camp had settled here two years ago. It has been one of the last cars in Hillsburg to go, after more and more people left, fearful of the pink light and its power. 'It drives you mad', says the urban legend. 'It pulls you apart. It's the most dangerous place on Earth. It's just fun to look at. It fills the area with enough vitamin D so serve hundreds but also gives you sci-fi cancer. It's too strange to even look at. It's impossible to describe.'

'It's unbearable to be near.'

Allison puts her arms around herself like a shield.

Next to her, Wong is observant but tight-lipped as always: "Maybe we should finally separate the personal research from the particle physics."

Allison suppresses her tears. "Yes," she says. "I will continue that part of the project on my own. I'm sorry."

A bird flies over the building. A lone sparrow? Even stretching its wings only once makes it soar higher. Its simple shape up in the sky looks like the cartoon birds Allison has drawn on that picture all those years ago. A drawing of her and her father at the shelter, with all their favorite dogs. It was supposed to be his Christmas present. He disappeared before he got it.

She still has it, safely packed away in her most precious file. And by God, she'll gift it to him someday. "I'll find someone new for the UV readings," Allison says, her voice firmer now, and goes to check on the EMS.

Wong softens as she passes her by. "Make sure to order that Waverford around as often as possible, as long as he's still here. I could never stand that guy. Should be the perfect candidate for those pain-in-the-ass FBI questionaries."

Allison snorts and smiles over her shoulder.

Wong gives her an encouraging nod. "You go get yourself a coffee and carry on, Miss Birk."

Allison thanks her and, indeed, carries on with daily business on Hillsburg Project. Scanning for changes, looking for signs. Trying to make sense of this crazy place.

But her peer's words sting all day. The 'vaguely ominous' parting of her father, that Colin Waverford has twisted into something sinister, is exactly what makes Allison so sure she can find him. Possibly even makes her the only one able to find him. All of this – his deteriorating health, their last interaction, his disappearance, the deaths, the Shimmer – it cannot be a coincidence. For years, she has single-handedly been collecting information and data, calculated formulas, arranged interviews, investigated all on her own, and she is sure it will have been worth her while one day. She just mustn't give up hope.

The biggest clue that Allison Birk was indeed somehow personally connected to the anomaly has not yet made it into her manual though. She just cannot quite believe, with so many having ascended the stairs to the third floor, stepping into the warped rooms, screaming at the light they saw inside the energy flames, that she should be the only one who has ever come out of it alive.

ENCOUNTER

BEFORE HILLSBURG PROJECT, indeed before any of the events that would lead up to the pink shimmer in 27 West Street, a creature crossed the sky above the forest just outside of town. Resembling a whale but mostly invisible to the human eye. Gone just as suddenly as it has appeared.

Below those clouds and trees, a shadow crashed and crawled across the ground. No, not a shadow – a piece of flesh. And bones and hair, just as dark as the forest itself. It is breathing. Yes, it is very much alive. But not home.

This does not belong here, the world whispers.

But whereto?

What's home used to be but a leap away. Now it seems unreachable.

Orientation. Beneath it is a solid ground. To its sides, large trees reach high into the air. Not whispering but crying. Oh, the rain. The water makes the ground so slippery. Just the water? No, it is blood, too.

A helpless trill echoes through the forest. To outrun one's enemies, one must run. The creature summons its strength to move forward, or maybe just to form a shape that would make it easier to advance on the physical ground instead of trying to leap through the fabric of this dimension. But the cold and all the water stifle it. Oh, *the cold* – it crawls into its skin, making itself a terrible home.

Faster, quick! Or should it wait for all those solid forms to change this trap? Just when will they transform?

The threat of the hunters is close. They are now here, too, so far from home. Their smell of decay reeks through all the water falling from the sky.

But nothing changes. Nothing moves constantly. No twirling forms, no swirls or spikes of transformation, no glimmers that illuminate the darkness.

But steps flying closer and closer.

The creature realizes it cannot not wait any longer if it wants to survive. It heaves itself forward, willing to transform itself if everything around it stayed so, so solid. It will need to reassemble all its power to open a rift and leap back home.

At least the big one was in safety, it thinks. The one it ought to protect. She would be able to continue her migratory route.

But its own wounds are deep. It is not as careful as it has once been. Yes, it has been careless, taking on so many hunters at the same time.

Perhaps assuming solid shapes could stop the bleeding, it muses.

Birds fly up at the boom of bones cracking through the night. Or are those branches snapping under its weight? Curls of flesh shove them away, but they tear right through it.

It hurts…!

The creature cries in pain as it crawls forward, over the thorny ground piercing its flesh.

It is now more obvious than ever that it is alone. No one will come to its aid. But that is only logical.

A guardian needs no saving.

Behind it, trees fall down, splashing into deep shadows. The hunters' breaths are like a storm upon this Earth. Oh, but it is not too late for running now if it just tries again – once more!

Make haste! Fly!

This persecution drama goes unseen but not unheard by Jeffrey Hobson. Jeffrey is coming home late now, having just driven his daughter to a friends' party out of town. His truck's windshield wipers squeak helplessly against the pouring masses of rain hammering onto the old car. Even the highest setting can't clear the vision. Shitty weather, and even shittier weather to spend the night out of town, Jeffrey thinks. If he's honest with himself, he can't make head or tail of that Dylan. He doesn't like that. Gives him a bad feeling in his gut. Missy knows what she's doing though, she always has. And Barbara will laugh at him if he comes to bed tonight with a frown on his face. He is now in the stage of fatherhood he has always dreaded the most. He knows he should simply trust Missy. She knows what she's doing.

Yet again, Jeffrey's train of thought is interrupted by those weird-ass sounds coming from the forest. "What the..." He cranes his neck to look out the window, but you can't see shit in the darkness.

They don't log trees in the night, do they, Jeffrey thinks. Especially not during a thunderstorm. Maybe it's two bears fighting? They're coming back, right? Somewhere he read that Black Bears may be moving East, if he remembers correctly.

Another boom – "Jesus!"

The car slows down and drives without gas for a few moments as his foot jerks upwards. Jeffrey rolls back his shoulders. That was loud – he must be driving past them right now! Or right under a storm cloud, from the sounds of it.

13

To not jump at the next crash yet again, he turns up the volume of the radio. After a few seconds he regrets it already. Is everything past ten just the clubbing stuff? He groans and turns it off. He'd rather listen to the rain. The heartland rock CD is still in the office, ever since Barbara wanted to copy it to the computer. He really needs to light a stick of dynamite under that woman's butt. Copying a CD can't take that long, right?

Ah, to hell with it. He gives the radio another try, looking at the glowing green digits of his console instead of the street for not even two seconds.

A tremendous rumble – a resistance – stops the truck on its way, and the entire windshield blackens. Jeffrey slams the brakes. His chest fills with heavy breaths, fingers digging into the wheel as the furry thing slides down the car.

It doesn't move. Jeffrey pauses, swallows.

Wow, roadkill is just what would make this day perfect.

He hurries to the hood and looks at what the yellow headlights illuminate. It is furry, all right, and black, but not a bear.

"Aw, shit." Jeffrey rubs his forehead, stepping back and forward again. Did he just run over a dog?

Its belly is moving, meaning it's breathing. But drops of blood from the hood prove just how badly it must be injured. The rain washes it away already.

Jeffrey curses as he carries the animal to the back of the truck. If Barbara hadn't taken the gun, he would've put the poor creature out of its misery right here and now. Then again, he couldn't just shoot someone's dog, right? Or is it a wolf? It doesn't wear a collar.

Jeffrey pants, grabbing the wet cargo area with calloused hands as he looks around the dark forest. "Hello? Anyone?" He tries the other side. "Anyone? A dog owner here?"

He walks around the car to honk. No response. Just more rain, it seems. Jesus, he should get home, he's soaked already. If he can't deliver the poor thing, he should drive it to a vet. He won't let the cops shoot it. Isn't there a dog shelter by Hillsburg? He'll just take the road through town and drop the animal there. They definitely have a vet. Maybe not at this hour, but there's always on-call duty, right?

Jeffrey rubs drops of rain from his face. If you don't hurry up, he thinks, they won't need to put it down anymore.

The twenty-two minutes it takes him from here to Hillsburg are among the longest of his life. Jeffrey needs to actively remind himself to not look into the rearview mirror too often. "We're gonna be there real soon, it's gonna be all right, buddy," he says, though more to himself than the dog. There is blood on his hands, and on the wheel now, too. Barbara will know how to clean it.

Hillsburg is pretty in daylight, and usually the picturebook-like facades down Main Street lighten up Jeffrey's mood whenever he passes through. It's like a fairytale. Even at nighttime, with all those sparkles from inside the houses, shops, and string of lights.

But right now it's pure agony to drive down this good old American street with a half-dead dog in the back of his truck.

Getting to the shelter feels like ages. After Hillsburg, there is not much else but dark hills and forests. Just when Jeffrey thinks he may have remembered the shelter wrongly, a cheap sign with a dog illustration tells him to turn right.

The parking lot is illuminated by two streetlights that show Jeffrey his deed in all its misery when he grabs the dog from the cargo area. The black fur is sticky with dried blood already. It is still breathing though. And whining.

"Shit. Come on, buddy."

The dog shelter, a bungalow-looking building from the seventies, painted orange near the foundations, is dark except for the window in the main door. Jeffrey stumbles there – warm fluid is running down his trembling arms. This thing is damn heavy. Jesus Christ, hopefully there's someone here. Without a phone, the only alternative is to ring someone's door and ask for a gun.

With no hands free to ring, Jeffrey simply calls, "Hello? I have an emergency here! An injured dog!"

After a surprisingly short amount of time, the door buzzes and slowly opens via an electronic mechanism. It has been activated by the broad-shouldered nightshift volunteer behind the counter, walking toward Jeffrey with worried eyes from behind his thick glasses.

That is Christopher Ennington.

"This way please, sir," he says right away and points to the corridor.

"I ran it over," Jeffrey confesses as he carries the animal to the examination room. It smells in here. Dogs bark from their kennels in another room. Jeffrey feels like he disrupted these poor creatures' nighttime peace.

How will he explain all this to Barbara?

"Please lay him down here," the volunteer says with a gesture toward the metal table in the middle of the room, pain meds already in his hands. "I'm gonna call Doctor Miller, our veterinarian."

There, they have a vet.

"Thank you."

Urgh, the smell in here is unbearable. And the bright neon lights in this room are unforgiving. Jeffrey now sees that the poor thing, though still breathing, has a gaping wound in pinks and reds reaching from its chest down under its belly all the way to the tail. Its right front leg looks like a child could tug it off. And those claws – they're not supposed to be so twisted.

Jeffrey looks away. "It was on Church Road, half an hour ago," he manages to say.

"All right." The volunteer opens the thing's giant muzzle to put the analgesics down its throat like it's second nature. Then he hovers over it with a hand on its ribcage and a blinking device. "Thank you for bringing him here. I, um, didn't get a hold of our vet. Usually we have good reception here. I'm gonna try again in a minute."

Jeffrey swallows, glancing at the dog once more. "Jesus, I feel so damn sorry for 'im. Took my eyes off the road for, like, a millisecond. He must've run straight into me."

The volunteer's face hardens. "A car accident doesn't cause this kind of wound."

"I thought of bears," Jeffrey says and sniffs. "Or wolves, possibly. Could he be a wolf? Hurt in a fight, y'know?"

"Never seen one like this. So pitch-black."

"My uncle, he, err – he had a large dog like that. A Belgian shepherd, I think."

The volunteer shakes his head, deep in thought. "He's too big to be a shepherd."

"Maybe it's a crossbreed or hybrid. Hell if I know. One of those fashionable new breeds."

The volunteer straightens up and gives Jeffrey a weary smile. The indication that he smiles already calms Jeffrey down. They know what they're doing here.

"It's not important anyway. An animal is an animal. We'll treat him as best as we can. I'll keep checking for a microchip. If he is a dog, we can contact his owners that way."

Jeffrey nods and rubs his forehead. His face must be red with blood by now. "If you don't mind," he says, "I'd like to go home. But in case he makes it…"

"Write down your telephone number at the front desk," the volunteer says with a friendly face. "We'll get in touch with you and let you know."

"All right. All right, thank you."

"Thank you, sir. Goodnight."

"Yeah, goodnight."

The dog's right paw shakes as the door falls shut. Christopher hovers by his side, watching his ears fold backwards. He whines, eyes shut.

The sounds agitate the other dogs in their kennels.

Christopher exhales through his nose. "Shh... easy, big guy. You're in safety now."

The dog lets out an anguished cry. His nose works hard. His muzzle opens to bring more air into his lungs, revealing fangs like Christopher has never seen in his life.

The whines grow shallower and higher.

"I know, I know," Christopher whispers. "It's scary. Pain-killers can only do so much. But I can't put you to sleep in your state." He swallows and runs an unsure hand over the black coat. It's clotty with dirt. "No matter how this goes, we will help you. You're safe here." He raises the scanner anew. "Now, where is your microchip? We can see and phone your parents that way, you know? Hm?"

The caresses over his side do calm the dog down. Eyes still closed, he presses his head against Christopher's arm. Searching for contact.

"Yes, I'm here," Christopher smiles. "I won't go anywhere." He puts away the chip scanner and instead looks to the bowls by the door.

"Are you thirsty? You wanna try drinking something? C'mon..."

Though his arms are weak, Christopher manages to help the dog raise its heavy head as best as he can. But the pain is too sharp. Eventually, he does not leave his side to get water out of fear the dog would fall off the table then. Instead, Christopher reaches into the pocket of the jacket that showed him as a Helping Paw volunteer. "I doubt you wanna eat, but I don't know… This is really tasty," he says and unscrews a tube of liverwurst paste.

The dog sniffs it but does not lick or eat it, as expected. Christopher sighs and strokes his heavy head. It *is* a giant dog. He tickles his ears. "You must be frightened. Hm, buster?" He strokes the fluffy neck, and once more, the dog leans into this touch. The motion shoots a terrible thought through Christopher's head – maybe this is the last warm interaction this creature will ever feel.

"I'm gonna call the doctor again, okay?" He leaves another voice mail, just to be sure. The dog's wound twitches funnily.

"I know it's pouring, but please hurry," Christopher begs into the phone. "Just… drive carefully."

The wind does howl louder now, and as though to respond to it, the dog snarls. Weak but full of intent.

"It's just the weather. I won't hurt you either," Christopher promises him. In such situations, he is convinced talking to dogs like this actually helps. But he still needs to read the body language signs. He should back away.

As he does, the lights above the table flicker.

Looking upwards, Christopher returns to the medicine cabinet. He will try and not appear confrontational toward this animal until Stephanie gets here. But simultaneously, he wants to make sure to keep an eye on their patient.

Who owns a dog like that, Christopher wonders. With legs this long, he must have hip or back problems. Or both. And the claws haven't been cut in years, it seems. No microchip either.

Christopher closes his eyes and takes a deep breath. Maybe this is one of those nights of death.

The dog cries.

"Keep calm. Things are gonna be all right," Christopher says, trying to steady his voice. Of course, the dog does not still after these words. "I can give you more painkillers," he offers half-heartedly. "But if you're not in the mood for liverwurst I doubt you'll swallow any more pills," he sighs, pushing his glasses further up his nose. "I can try and clean the wound around your leg. Unpleasant but necessary in case we need to amputate it. That's not as bad as it sounds. You'll see."

Careful not to move too quickly, Christopher collects the disinfectant, a cotton swab, and some bandages. His motions are automated. He does not want his thoughts to run wild again. Just keep breathing. Easier for dogs to stay calm when you're unagitated, too.

When he turns around with a quiet "okay, big guy", he finds the dog has opened his eyes, lying dead still. "Watching me?" Christopher asks in that baby voice all humans use when talking to animals. "Are you watchin' me? I have this fluffy ball of cotton right here," he says and holds the swab up to his eyes. "This is the disinfectant. Decidedly more unpleasant than cotton."

He carefully places a hand on the dog's pulsating neck to keep him in place as he lets the damped swab ghost over the pink flesh above the foreleg.

The dog stills entirely. But doesn't attack.

"Oh. You see? It's not bad at all. Thank you for trusting me," Christopher says. He continues to talk throughout the process of cleaning away little crumbs of dirt and blood from the wound. He also finds what looks like a twig. One that seemingly has no end when Christopher pulls it from between the bloody muscles. It cracks into two before he can get the entire thing out.

"Oh my God…" Christopher swallows, standing up to throw it into the trash. "You did run through the woods. Jesus Christ."

The smell of copper fills the air.

His senses alert, he squats by the table. The dog has started panting. "You're doing amazing. Good boy. Just let me…"

Christopher searches and finds the broken twig. It stabs into the soft flesh of the belly as the dog breathes, spilling blood. Christopher whispers nonsense words for distraction as he sinks his hands inside. "Good boy…"

Slowly, he pulls and shoves at the twig, careful not break it this time around – but blood keeps spilling as he pulls it outside, pooling on the table before pouring onto the tiles. It never crosses Christopher's mind to just keep the thing inside. Because the supposed twig is a full-on branch, complete with fall leaves and moss, about as broad as a man's arm. That alone is distracting. In addition, the dog does not fight back against the action, just whines as Christopher pulls the entire branch out, elbow-deep inside his body.

He throws it to the ground with a thud. The leaves rustle on impact.

Christopher's lungs strain with exhaustion. "Oh my God." He looks at the dog in horror, wondering just how an adnate branch the size of a bicycle got inside this animal. He must have been attacked and then fallen straight onto this branch as he fled. Yes, that sounds right, Christopher thinks. All that, *plus* the car accident – "Good boy," is all he can say.

Eyes empty, he staggers around the table to resume the disinfection.

The warning growl hits him not before but during the dog's attack. He shoves Christopher away with his giant head – it must have been the head, although it felt like a pair of arms –

making him fall backwards onto the tiles. They're surprisingly warm. Or is that…?

"Ah! Fuck…" Christopher holds his dizzy head. The tips of his fingers are red, well, because his entire arm is red. Or are their bloods different shades?

Vertigo makes it hard to stand, but he manages to pull himself up by the medicine cabinet, from where he observes the dog snarling on the table. While pressing a swab to the back of his own head, Christopher keeps looking at him until flickering lights snap him out of it. He should prepare everything for Stephanie, for surgery or euthanasia alike. Best to be prepared.

His shoulders sink at that thought. Much like his heart. The back of his head stings. He had thought tonight would be quiet for once. Just him, the dogs, and the rain pattering onto the roof like drops of peace. Surely it must be a sign that when he prays for a night of calmness, he gets to put down roadkill. Roadkill that now croaks with blood spilling out of his belly. And it's Christopher's fault –

It's always like that, isn't it?

The lights keep flickering, dizzying. God, why tonight? Bad timing. The charity sale is next week, and the neon tube has never made trouble before. Maybe it's the storm.

But the storm would not shake the building. With the force of a squall, Christopher falls into the cabinet. His glasses slither away, instruments clatter dangerously over the desk, the floor. Thunder rumbles above the roof.

Don't earthquakes announce themselves with little shakes at first? Or is this a surprise hurricane? As Christopher still tries to orientate himself, he hears crackles from behind. A look over his hurting shoulder reveals the dog standing up under the flickering lights – only he's not standing up. His left legs grow taller and taller until he's positioned upright again.

"Hey," Christopher begins. He wants to help him calm down, but the senseless words get stuck in his throat when he watches the loose front leg fall off. It smacks onto the tiles with an ugly sound, taking loads of pink flesh and bones with it.

As he is falling apart, the dog stares at the ceiling, teeth bared and eyes wide opened. They seem to multiply, more and more pink holes opening along his head. Eating away his ears. His throat.

Instinctively, Christopher steps forward, wanting to put him back together. "It's fine," he breathes, overwhelmed with the situation. "You're gonna be okay. It's only the weather."

He raises his trembling hands, on the one side to reach the animal, on the other to keep it at arm's length should it attack him. When he reaches toward the big wound to stuff all the flesh back inside, he almost burns himself. Hot blood runs down his hands and arms – does it glitter? Or waver?

Jesus Christ, is his head so fucked already?

Christopher curses and pulls away, his head grazing a sharp fang as he does. Through flickering lights, he watches the dog pick up the severed pieces from the ground. With his teeth? His claws? To Christopher, it looked like an octopus' tentacles. They leave the branch where it is. And twist the leg until is it gone, absorbed, if Christopher sees correctly. But he can't. No dog can absorb severed limps back into itself.

Where are his glasses?

The dog reaches around the table legs, descending.

Holding his burning arms, Christopher blinks through the pain to keep track of what's happening. He cannot let him run away. He would never survive outside in this state.

He looks over his shoulder to check the door. It is closed.

"Stay here," Christopher breathes, missing the commanding tone entirely.

The dog's next grunt – not snarl – shakes the entire room. The rumble makes Christopher fall down – his ears ring – but he needs to keep an eye on him. It's like his vision is blurred, seeing all sorts of twisted forms distorting the room, as though through invisible flames. And his arms *burn*…!

In the hopes of chasing the pain away, Christopher presses his eyes shut and screams. His lungs are flaming. He hopes that burnt smell is not coming from his own body. Coughing, he manages to roll to his side, to get back on his feet.

"You're gonna be fine," he gasps and turns around. In front of him, the dog is rearing up. His vibrating grunt continues, which is weird, because Christopher cannot make out a muzzle anymore. Or a mouth of any sort for that matter. Just eyes and tendrils and dripping flesh, pink, red, brown, then ink-black as though it's been burned despite its wetness, without any particular shape to make out. Like a flower blossoming upside-down, the shape splits open at the sides. Fleshy petals curl back into it, twitching, flickering. Always moving.

It's a display of utter chaos.

"You need to let me help you, please!" Christopher calls in desperation.

He reaches out again. The next impact is not as hot but still wet. Something shatters – the table? – and throws Christopher back to the ground, covered in blood. No, not blood –

He gasps, rushing to get off the floor. It's slime. Pink and warm, everywhere. The lights stop flickering, and the room seems to have stopped shaking. It allows Christopher to find his footing despite the slippery tiles. Full of reds and pinks. His once white sports shoes are covered in the strange fluid, as are his clothes, his arms, indeed all over his face – it drips off him in long strings when he raises his hand to look at it, mixing with red blood. What he thinks is a result of his bad eyesight actually glitters and distorts. But he blames it on himself.

And it is suddenly quiet. Just him and the night.

"What…?"

Oh, idiot! Don't look at yourself, look after the dog!

Almost stumbling over the blood-coated branch, Christopher rushes from the exam room to the corridor, crashing against the doorframe as he does. He blinks – oh, the entrails got into his eyes, too, those must be entrails – and now the other dogs are barking again. They're still here then.

No sight of the big black one though. No blood or traces in the corridors.

Christopher takes a deep breath, realizing only now how badly his scarred lungs needed the air. He trembles, falling, but before his head slams against the nearest wall, a pair of arms supports him.

"Chris! Oh my God, what happened?"

"The dog," Christopher presses out from the floor he's sliding onto. "Was there a dog running? In the parking lot?"

"No? The dog you called me for? That ran into a car?" Stephanie grimaces. "Are you bleeding? What's this stuff?"

Christopher pants, helpless – he doesn't know. He knows nothing of anatomy, neither human nor canine. "He had a branch in his stomach. I think he was sick," he tells her through labored breaths.

"Yeah, sick, all right," she murmurs, shaking her hand to get rid of the slime.

Christopher looks at her through empty eyes, lips parted in exhaustion. Sweat mixes with the fluid on his face. "He ran away before you came here. I'm sorry. I couldn't keep him here."

"Were the doors not closed?"

Panting, Christopher searches his memory. He did close them, didn't he? Or has this one been open when he stumbled through it just now?

"Yeah, whatever, Chris," Stephanie says tonelessly. She doesn't look at him when she adds, "Not funny. What kind of a fucked-up party trick is this?"

Christopher gasps for air. "No, no! It was real! It was a real dog, a man brought him in here." His vision blurs. "I'm not tricking you, I swear! I'm sorry–"

"Okay, it's fine!"

After that yell, Stephanie studies him for a while. From under her coat sparkles the outfit she has worn for this Saturday evening that Christopher just ruined for her. She smells of sparkling wine. He wishes she would speak again, or just let him sit here.

"Fine," she repeats after a terribly long time. "It's fine. I can take it from here and look after the others. And clean up. You can go home, Chris. Get some sleep."

The poisonous tint of frustration in her calm voice does not escape Christopher, no matter how battered he is. "I'm really sorry. I screwed up," he whispers. Tears complete the mess on his face. Mentioning the earthquake and light problems now would only sound like a bad excuse, he thinks. The pain of his arms and head has him in its tight grip now. His clothes stick to him like a second skin. He sits motionless behind his wheel for a quarter-hour before starting the engine.

This is right, he should get the hell out of here, he thinks. His panic made that poor animal lose so much blood, that his boss now has to clean up – he does not deserve to be at a dog shelter.

Christopher often has thoughts like these. The extraordinariness of what he just witnessed is entirely lost on him, in favor of just being another one of his mistakes. That happens rather often. When there is nothing more to hold onto, he punishes himself for whatever he thought was his fault. He will do so tonight too, and the next days, while Doctor Stephanie Miller will soon forget about the whole thing. Punishment means re-taking control. Being at the helm of the body he's living in. And it's just convenient to cut your thighs when you're already in the shower; two birds with one stone, that's what Christopher thinks. He thinks about that rather than the surreal pink fluid washing into the drain.

It is needless to say he cannot sleep that night. His head throbs. An innocent being will have died in the storm because of his failure, he thinks. Because he wanted to be lazy tonight. Because he is a despicable person, who deserves to be yelled at, he thinks, and who has never prepared for the case of an earthquake in Hillsburg, Massachusetts.

Christopher often has thoughts like these.

SPINNER

THE SUNRAYS ON Monday morning are kinder than the entire weekend has been. Christopher realizes the irony in liking Monday, the time everyone returns to the bleak working world and universally hates it. Christopher looks forward to the routine. Going to work on Monday gives him a productive distraction.

Because, and Christopher knows this, cutting his thighs is not particularly helpful. It is an outlet for the immense pressure that creeps out of his mind's shadows. Physically hurting himself has become an effective technique in temporarily regaining control. But Christopher would not call that 'helpful'. It's a means to an end.

It has worked reliably well this weekend though.

Really, Saturday night has been quite uneventful after his dramatic shower, at least in his view. No crying or actively hurting himself afterwards. Just lying in bed, staring at the ceiling. Existing in a small box and hoping that it won't implode before his train of thought reaches the Monday station.

Monday. Transfer here.

Though the pressure of having to leave his home for social performance weighs heavily on Christopher, he likes it better this way. He likes getting dressed and packing something to eat, and planning on actually eating it, because that's what you do in the company of your colleagues during lunch break.

He also likes the rush of air outside. The wet streets, lazily reflecting whatever light fell onto them. He likes the air smelling of rain and the golden September colors on the trees. He likes that things move. Not fast. They're just moving.

Then he arrives at Main Street and transforms into a blank nerve. The quick pace unfolds a painful pressure in his chest. But Christopher needs to walk fast. He tries mimicking the effect of a horse's blinders by looking only at the ground. Never into faces. Crowds are an open sea to him.

The sea does not stare back, but he doesn't know that. When Christopher Ennington is outside, the world simply sees a White man with his dishwater blond head down. At the rare chance one would get a straight look at him, you could see that he is approaching forty. But the lines in his face betray just how young he is. His pastel-colored shirts, including the light blue one from the post office, are too big even for his broad shoulders. He leaps, pulled relentlessly by his train of thoughts. He meticulously keeps it on track, lest a catastrophe arose from the derailment.

Some do think it strange that he only drives his car to places out of town. But that would not be the strangest thing about him, he finds.

Christopher just keeps on walking. Movement is better than stillstand, he thinks. It is far from perfect. He still hurts. But he is moving. Towards one of the four islands outside his home.

Hillsburg's post office is the first island. As his workplace, it is the one he visits the most frequently. It gives him the desired routine and pays the bills. It is a good place.

"Wow! New glasses, Chris?" Richard Shea's enthusiastic greeting hits like a whip. It cements, just maybe, the post office as Christopher's least favorite island.

"Morning," he greets with his smile on autopilot.

"No, seriously. You trying something new?" Richard asks, leaning against the counter. His deep-green eyes are quick with double-edged interest.

"Oh, you mean these? I, uh, lost my regular ones on Saturday. These are the spare pair."

"Huh," Richard says loudly, putting his tongue in his cheek. "I'm hearing rimless glasses are making a comeback."

"Hardly," their coworker Tammy Wilburg coos as she walks into the backroom. "They make you look like a nerd." She looks up from the files in her hands. "Oh. Hi, Chris." She grimaces. "Sorry!"

"Good, 'cause I took that personally," Christopher jokes.

Richard frowns. "You didn't, right?"

Christopher snaps around to face him. "I didn't. Sorry."

"Ha." Richard bares his impossibly straight and white teeth in a grin. They bore into Christopher from the front while Tammy's eyes sting him from behind. "Good," Richard says after a glance at her. "Good to hear you're in a playful mood, Chrissy-Man. You do lean more into the, y'know – IT guy look. I dig it. Great."

He leans in further and lowers his voice so drastically that Christopher needs to step closer. "Hey, um, how long do you plan of being here today?"

Christopher shrugs. "As long as you want me to."

"Oh, great. 'cause I got a *thing* at three and I wondered..."

Another autopilot-smile. "No problem. I can be here all day," Christopher says. He loves days like this. Two birds with one stone: Making himself popular by taking on his colleague's work *and* not going home to be free for any stupid ideas. Win-

win. Not that he gets the *salary* of a clerk for those hours, but hey – can't have everything.

Richard gives him another shark smile and a pat on the shoulder. "Thank you, man. I knew I could count on you," he says, and he completely means it. Richard Shea is a man working almost entirely through his charisma, which many people easily buy into. He would never expect a wallflower like Christopher Ennington to go against any of the social contracts he weaves into his conversations – *especially* not Christopher Ennington, who has nothing better to do than work all day ever since his divorce half a year ago. Right? Not doing sports, not going out on dates. *Especially* not going out on dates. Richard is convinced that him talking to this loner, no matter how condescendingly or exploitatively, means doing the Lord's work. Reaching out to the poor souls that no one cares about. Especially not him. He is the type of person to call someone who knows nothing about computers 'the IT guy'.

Christopher is aware of this, because Richard's shark smile cannot conceal how little he truly cares about his conversational partners. But he doesn't mind it. At least Richard *is* talking to him. He does not want to appear shy. Speaking with other people helps conveying that he is just like them.

Christopher gives Richard another smile and then excuses himself. Throughout conversations like this, his sling bag is like a lifeline to hold onto.

And so starts his Monday. The work at the post office is monotone, but Christopher appreciates its meditative qualities. Sorting parcels and letters, preparing the right stamps, carrying around mail and packages – repetition has made Christopher experienced, and experience allows him to do these tasks smoothly and without stress. Even Richard's work at the counter, too. It's not the job in Christopher's contract, but it's all sanctioned by their manager, ironically. Thankfully.

His heart only sinks when he leaves the island to walk home. He decides to make a detour via his second island.

Grocery stores can be loud and stressful. But Christopher finds them quite relaxing when willingly blocking out everything else. Here too, he moves through the aisles like a horse with blinders. He buys one carton of oat milk and a bell pepper. He tells the teenage cashier the dogs at Helping Paw are fine. He squints. His head hurts from the unfamiliar glasses. When the corner of his eye flashes pink as he leaves the supermarket, it's a sign to go home, he thinks.

Some evenings are spent on Christopher's third island, with his mother. Sometime during his marriage, she moved in with her new partner in Park Street. Tony Morrissey's house has a porch with flower boxes and carpet in the bedroom. Christopher thought it unfitting to join their idyll after his divorce.

He does like to visit, if only to see his mother again.

"Chris, come on in."

"Hi, Tony. Got your pea soup."

"Oh, may you be blessed! Can you believe I forgot to buy it?" Tony asks him with a leery grin.

"I sometimes forget things, too," Christopher comforts him. "Sometimes even when they're on the shopping list."

"Ah," Tony laughs, "I haven't used a shopping list in the last twenty years. Maybe I'll start again in my old age now!"

Tony does smile a lot, but it's not without silent remorse. Growing old is not easy for an energetic man like him. But his generation is not the type to talk about such fears.

Christopher does not push the subject, not even with his mother Mary. He quietly checks for her medicine. The chemotherapy bills.

When not in bed, she is sitting at the kitchen table. An old habit. Tony's dining room with its lace doilies would be cozier. Then again, it has shotguns as wall decoration.

Tonight, Christopher is visiting Mary in the bedroom.

"You got the pea soup?"

"Yes, already delivered."

Mary nods. "Thank God. His Friday dinner would be ruined without it."

"Everyone has their routines," Christopher smiles.

"They do," his mother answers, grabbing his hand. She makes an effort to hold onto it tightly but cannot hide from her son that she has grown weaker. He guards his tongue to not point it out.

"What about you?" she asks innocently. "Food-wise?"

Christopher inhales. This unexpectedly loaded question is not about him deliberately skipping meals. His mother does not know of that. She is asking if he can live without a wife. He cannot answer to that.

She shakes her head when she says, "I can cook for you."

"Mom, no–"

"Yes! I will! In fact we still have some noodle salad, tell Tony to pack that for you."

Christopher averts his eyes and gathers all his strength for the crucial statement: "I'm fine. Really. I'm doing really good."

Mary tilts her head. "Are you sure?" she asks, thankfully in a light-hearted tone.

Christopher nods and gives her a smile. "Yes. Thank you."

She returns the smile and lets go of his hand. But as she directs her gaze into the middle of the room, she sighs. "Such a shame it didn't work out. Are you sure you don't want to… you know, talk it out? For Ally's sake too, you know." She gives him a hopeful look, but this time Christopher cannot bring himself to lie.

"No." He looks down and feels cruel in doing so.

When his ex-wife, a former classmate from high school, had approached him romantically after his thirtieth birthday, his mother had been overjoyed. Finally her son would be safe in a relationship – a marriage even! And then with child!

It has been far from Christopher to rob her of that illusion. It has been for seven agonizing years. And it still is. He won't start now.

"Is that a new pair of glasses?" Mary wants to know on his way out.

Christopher smiles. "Yeah. I'm trying something new."

"Okay. I can buy you another pair, if you want to."

"No, thanks. You don't need to do that." The exhaustion of constantly navigating and evaluating what you can and cannot say weighs heavily. Managing different lies on top of one another can be tricky. Christopher knows it would be far easier to just always say the truth. But his psyche allows that only with those who do not judge him and are never disappointed by him, imagined or real.

The dog shelter is his fourth island. His favorite. If he had more cynicism in him, he'd say it was because it combined the perks of having both a productive distraction and no need for disguise. Nightshift volunteering, though officially not longer than midnight. Spending the time sorting food, towels and toys, keeping an eye on the dogs...

Being there for emergencies...

And then there was also playtime, the dogs' favorite activity. Lucky for Christopher, they are also very much content with lying on the floor and staring at a wall. "Today was exhausting," he whispers.

Shelly looks at him through brown eyes. A large mongrel, already ten years old. Her chances of getting adopted dwindle every day, without any fault of her own. She cannot comprehend the injustice but feels it nonetheless.

"You've had a rough day, too?" Christopher sighs. "Chief still giving you trouble?" Chief is a husky – not dangerous to

Shelly, just annoying. Thrown away, probably after his owners realized just how much energy he could set free. Experience has shown that's often the case with sled dog buyers.

From the kennel next to Shelly, Pebbles sniffs as if to agree. She's a chihuahua down on her luck as well. Having only one eye is apparently reason enough to disqualify for adoption.

Christopher tilts his head on the floor. They're a sad bunch, but at least not of the seventy million stray animals in the US. He loves them to bits.

"I should be setting up the tables for the charity sale tomorrow. You know that?" he asks Shelly.

If she had her way, of course, he'd never do that and just continued tickling her ears for the next eternity or so. She licks his arm. "I know," he smiles. "But the sale's gonna be good for you guys, too. Think of all the donations we'll get. So many *toys*, and *snacks*, and more *towels*." He talks with a child-like emphasis as he ruffles her fur. "And with the money, we can buy *even more* toys, snacks and towels. That sound good?"

She puts a paw onto his arm.

"That's what I thought. So…" He sits up with a groan and looks at her through tired eyes. "I'm afraid I'm gonna get to work now."

In the quiet of the night, he sets up the folding tables from the storage room. Some people already donated knickknacks, books and stuffed animals for the sale during the week. He tries displaying everything in a nice manner.

On the counter still lies the piece of paper where Jeffrey Hobson wrote down his phone number. The dark dust the top left corner looks like dried blood. Christopher looks at it. And decides to leave it there. It is too late to call him now anyway. It now becomes very clear to Christopher that he has spent almost an entire week procrastinating to formulate an answer to the question of 'What became of that dog?'.

It almost overwhelms him, but turning away from the desk is an effective deflection.

When Christopher returns to the parking lot at one, he thinks he saw a bright flash in the corner of his eye. A firework? When he turns around, there's nothing there. No hisses in the starry sky. It is mild tonight, Christopher thinks for a moment. A wave of warmth washes through him –

Overworked brain. Surely.

He is not fazed by not being able to catch up on sleep tonight. He looks forward to Helping Paw's charity event.

Saturday.

The weather is kind to their endeavor. The September sun smiles at the golden leaves swayed by the wind, and the air is light. Families sort their tombola wins and picnic by their cars. Some play peekaboo. Children run through the parking lot with excited squeaks.

"Yeah, that's right," Emely Traeger sing-songs over her microphone, "run to our Helping Paw tombola! We just started! Draw prizes for you and your pets! Here you go, sweetie, that's a bottle of soap bubbles for you. No blank tickets, only wins!"

Christopher is tasked with the sale table outside, for any items submitted today. Most of it is hideous home decoration.

"Thank you for your lovely garden gnome, Mrs. McLaughlin, we really appreciate it."

"Oh, don't mention it! The little beauty has been in the attic for years now."

"I could hardly tell," Christopher smiles. He puts it near the edge of the table.

Behind Wilhelmina McLaughlin, Christopher's coworker Bill Martin has been waiting. "Hiya. Sorry I'm late. Brought ya somethin' for the sale. A candlestick. My wife tells me those are coming back into fashion."

"Sure."

"An Indian wall hanging. Don't know if we're allowed to call it that anymore though."

"Well…"

"And some sheet music."

"Oh." Christopher takes the booklet with a grin. "Piano songs. I might just buy that."

"Please do. I bought it for Sophia, but she doesn't care much for the piano anymore." A surprised smile tugs at his lips. "I didn't know you played."

"Well, I haven't," Christopher says quickly, "for some time now. But my new place actually has an old piano. A bit out of tune, but I might just start again once I'll finally find the time."

"Huh. Good for you," Bill says in that vaguely grandfatherly manner, complete with a grip on Christopher's shoulder that somehow feels like a warning. It works. Part of Christopher thinks that he does not want to buy the piano sheet music of that man's granddaughter.

"And we have another winner! Here you go, little one. A coupon for any XXL pizza you want at Stuart's Pizza Parlor!"

Christopher snorts when the kid starts whining. "But I don't like pizza."

"You don't like pizza? That's unfortunate for you," Emely says without taking the microphone from her mouth. She quickly adds, "Make sure to swap prizes with someone who does!"

Bill Martin shakes his head with a tired smile. "Wow. I'm gonna go inside and check with Stephanie."

"Do that," Christopher says. He watches the girl from the tombola walk away by her father's hand with a pitiful smile.

"We can buy another ticket if you want."

"Don't wanna," she pouts.

"Any chance you wanna trade it for something from this table?" Christopher asks her. She looks at him for a moment.

"The man asked you a question, Keily."

After studying the table for a while, she sways on her feet. "Can I pick?"

"Why of course," Christopher says in the tone of a whimsical businessman. "Anything on this table, in exchange for the coupon at Stuart's."

"I want the dirty gnome," she says instantly, slamming the coupon onto the table with a flat hand.

"Keily!"

Christopher swallows down his laugh. "Okay – perfect, in fact. Here you go. Good deal." Good thing Mrs. McLaughlin brought this after all. Having handed over the lot, he gives the father a less unserious look. "Thank you for coming today."

"Of course. You're doing important work," he replies with a smile, complete with two friendly dimples.

Christopher may just have blushed at the table.

"Bye. Come on, Keily. Where are you gonna put this?"

"My room, obviously!"

Christopher laughs. But it fades away. The image of another father with his child, spending their Saturday together…

He quickly stuffs the pizza coupon into his pocket.

"Hey, Chris," he hears Emely say just then. She comes striding toward him, stroking a blond strand of hair out of her freckled face. "Sold anything yet?"

"A tablecloth," Christopher says with raised eyebrows and subdued amusement, "and an incense stick holder in the form of a frog. One flower vase. *And* I just traded your unwanted pizza coupon for a garden gnome that would have scared more customers away than attract them."

Emely humorlessly shakes her head and groans. "You went out of your way to get those stupid coupons! What kid doesn't like pizza? I'm so glad that tombola is over." She gives him a sympathetic look. "Here, I can relieve you for the time Stephanie needs for her lecture."

"Okay. Thanks." Christopher steps back. "I'm gonna go grab something to eat."

"Okeydokey."

After the excitement in the parking lot, the inside of the shelter is almost too quiet. Christopher breathes in and stretches his shoulders. His hips hurt from standing up. On his way to the office, where his bag is, he passes by the front desk. Jeffrey Hobson's note still lies exactly where he left it last night.

Christopher stops. Maybe right now is the perfect moment to call. He will still have to bring the unpleasant news but could invite him to the charity sale right afterwards. Maybe he'll come and bring his family.

With a determined sigh, Christopher sits down at the table, triple-checks the number, and phones.

After a long while, a quiet voice answers on the other end. "Hello?"

"Hi, this is Christopher Ennington from the Helping Paw dog shelter in Hillsburg. Am I speaking to Mrs. Hobson?"

"Yes."

"Your husband left a note with us," Christopher explains. "He brought in an injured dog last weekend and wanted to know what became of him."

A pause.

"Last weekend?" the voice asks, suddenly shaking.

Christopher frowns. "Yes. Saturday at around 10 p.m."

A sob.

Christopher shifts in his seat, leaning forward. "Ma'am?"

"Jeffrey died that night. In a car crash."

"What?" Christopher composes himself. "Ma'am, I'm so sorry. I didn't know." He swallows. "I'm sorry for your loss."

Another pause. "It's all right." She sniffs. "You might have been the last person to talk to him. 'cause whoever hit him afterwards ran right off. After they… mutilated him…"

Christopher blinks, eyes rapid with confusion.

"I'm sorry," Mrs. Hobson says and hangs up.

The phone beeps bleakly through the lobby.

Mutilated?

Christopher slowly turns the handset in front of him. Around. Around. Probably for too long. He cannot possibly eat right now. He should take out the trash instead.

Yes. Yes, take out the trash, he tells himself. Get up and go outside and collect the trash bags. He does that. Meets Bill on the way back in. Goes in the back to put the bags in the containers. He briefly considers throwing himself in afterwards. The impulse gains strength when he sees the bloody branch from last week next to the bin. *He* was the one who gave Jeffrey Hobson the hint to leave. If he hadn't done that, and just allowed him to stay the night, he wouldn't have died. It's his fault, Christopher thinks. And: take out the trash.

But he'd be too big to fit inside the container, probably.

Barking snaps him out of his miserable trance, a tear falling from his lashes as he blinks at the sound.

On his left, there is a pink flash of light.

Again, he thinks, gone just as quickly. He takes two steps into the direction of the flare before stopping himself. He should get his brain checked out already, he thinks.

He wipes away the wetness on his cheeks before going back inside. Maybe he should eat something after all.

Yes, eating is good, he reminds himself. Denying yourself food is bad. He slumps down in one of the office's chairs and edges his way through the cheese sandwich he packed. He should've packed an apple, too, he thinks. That always goes well with cheese sandwiches.

Mutilated.

Christopher blinks until his eyes hurt. Keeps eating like he wasn't even disciplined enough to consistently punish himself, so he could just as well wolf this down to get it over with. He scrolls through his phone for a while. Considers a visit with Shelly. Anything to keep his mind off –

"Chris?" Emely's blond head of hair peeks through the half-opened door.

"Hey."

"There's someone asking for you at the front desk." She grins wickedly. "Like, a Black King-of-the-North-type looking guy."

Christopher's brain is not yet back on working speed. "What?"

"Just go!" Emely whispers, rousing him with an excited wave of her hands and a toothy grin.

Christopher hurries to the lobby. He has not prepared himself for a conversation with someone asking specifically for him. But Emely noticing he has been crying would have been even more of an ordeal.

So, he's fine.

In the lobby, a longhaired man stands with his back to the front counter, hands inside the pockets of his black bomber jacket. He faces the door. You cannot look outside through the rippled glass, but he doesn't seem to care.

Christopher slowly puts his hands on the desk. "Can I... can I help you?" The man turns around so swiftly his dark brown curls dance around his head in the movement. And he smiles, steps toward him and says his name like he has been looking for him all his life, like he knows him, as though the world has brightened because of their reunion. The crucial light in the darkness.

"Christopher."

For a moment, Christopher is so stumped he cannot speak at all. Brown eyes shine at him from behind a pair of fancy glasses, soft, joyous, just a bit melancholic. With but a look, gratitude and happiness and regret spill from the stranger. All glimmering rapidly over his features.

But the time Christopher needs to process whether this is a real conversation – it very much is – prompts the man to slow down. He stops and thins his lips. His smile stays though. "Hi, um – I just wanted to say thank you," he says slowly, in a British accent. "For taking care of my dog the other night."

Realizing now that this is indeed not a dream, Christopher looks at him with more focus. His lungs resume breathing. "The, uh, big black one?"

"Yes, exactly," the man smiles.

Shit, is the first thought in Christopher's mind. Thankfully his next words come out more eloquently. "I'm really sorry," he says, "but he got away before the vet arrived here."

For only a split-second, the man's expression darkens. Then his thick eyebrows rise, and he says, "He went home. He, uh, came back to me that night." Another smile. "It's all right. He's fine!" he assures Christopher brightly before lowering his voice again. It is deep. Soft and husky. "Recovering, but over the worst."

Oh, Christopher thinks. "That's a relief."

"Yeah." The stranger's smile widens further. "So, again – thank you. You really did a good deed. I don't think he could've made it without your help. And not everyone would've helped him." He looks down before giving Christopher a timid look from below. "I imagine he fought back?"

Since it is asked so softly and through thick dark eyelashes, Christopher needs a moment to overcome the throb on the back of his head and process the question. "Well," he says, possibly blushing, "he was remarkably calm, actually, considering his state. He looked like he'd been to hell and back, so…" He gives the man a careful look. "Do you know what injured him that way, by any chance?"

Now it is the stranger's turn to reply belatedly. His expression sobers. His entire posture changes ever so slightly. "Hunters. Out in the forest."

"Oh." Christopher frowns. "Shit, man."

The man presses his lips together and blinks.

"Maybe don't unleash him in the near future. If he wants to go back to that forest at all."

"Yes. We'll see. But he is getting better. I wanted to let you know that," the man says. He gives Christopher yet another smile as he sways with his hands still inside his pockets.

God, that's a great voice.

This much unbridled charm pulls a smile from Christopher himself, just a bright as the stranger's. "Okay," he says through it, his chest tightening with excitement. "If he needs aftercare or anything, just hit us up," he offers with sincerity. "We're at the limit of our capacity, we always are, to be fair – but if there's any way we can help, we'll try."

The man blushes, but Christopher is too busy with himself to see it. "Thank you for your offer. You're very kind."

"No problem." Christopher waits for a moment, then says, "S-see you."

"Goodbye." The man's look over his shoulder lingers for a bit ere he turns to the door, where Emely smoothly slides to his side.

As though a switch has been flipped, Christopher pretends to be cleaning up the counter. He can hear her giving him her number. She only returns once he's gone outside and joins Christopher behind the desk in looking at the door. "You saw all that crazy hair? Goddamn, he's cute."

Christopher holds his tongue. *Don't slip up now.*

"You know how he asked for you?" Emely whispers. "'The kind man from the nightshift'. I mean, he kind of described you physically when I asked, but those were his first words. And, wow, that accent…" She swoons. "What a cutie."

Timidly, Christopher looks up at the closed door. He feels like a piece of crumpled paper.

'A cutie'. With a reverse dye job, having hazel roots with the rest of his hair remaining natural.

And also a man who did not have his dog chipped. Maybe it's different in the UK, he thinks.

He also thinks: It *is* a dog. A very real dog, with a very real owner.

It is just like his broken brain, Christopher thinks, to make up an eldritch abomination on the exam table rather than accept that he'd let an injured animal flee the shelter.

After the charity event comes Sunday.

And after that, Monday. The work at the post office is monotone, but Christopher appreciates its meditative qualities. Sorting parcels and letters, preparing the right stamps, carrying around mail and packages – repetition has made Christopher experienced, and experience allows him to do these tasks smoothly and without stress. He eats lunch. And Tammy compliments him on a new cologne that he isn't wearing, but he can't bring himself to tell her that.

His heart only sinks when he leaves the island to walk home.

Ever since Saturday, Christopher is acutely aware of what his piece of paper looks like when you would un-crumble and smoothen it. He wants to blame it on the charming stranger at the shelter. He wants him to chip his dog. *And* blame him. But Christopher realizes that'd be senseless. No, *he's* the problem.

Today, he flinched when Richard declared, "Oh, fag, for sure." It's a game he and Tammy play in the office. One would show the other the handwritten address on a letter and ponder whether or not the man who writes in this or that way was gay.

Christopher feels like the rabbit in a cage of tigers. Tigers who have not yet eaten him only because they think of him as a fellow big cat. He prefers to keep it that way, especially when he is but a guest on their island.

At home, his blanket serves as a sufficient rabbit hole. Not the rest of the apartment. Funny thoughts lure everywhere.

Maybe it is also this rabbit panic that makes him see those flashes of light, Christopher thinks as he stares at the dark walls of his bedroom. He woke from a nightmare where Jeffrey Hobson saw such a light and crashed his car.

It's not what he tells the sheriff when he and his team question him by his door. But it's a plausible possibility in his mind.

Maybe it's yet another long-term effect of the pandemic, Christopher thinks. People have all kinds of weird symptoms because of that, he reminds himself. Bodies are weird. Sometimes the back of his head still hurts from his fall in the exam room. Pulsating.

But he is fine, he tells himself. Or at least he will be.

Like on Thursday. His heart sinks when he leaves the island to walk home. But right outside the post office, a voice calls to him over the outside world's waves.

"Hello, Christopher!"

Christopher greets back on autopilot before realizing who has spoken to him. "Hello. Oh, hey, it's you," he says eloquently, struck by a pair of soft, dark-brown eyes behind fancy glasses.

"Yes, I was close by," the man says with a sway around. His hands are in his bomber jacket's pockets and his posture ridiculously straight. He must be an athlete or something. "I just wanted to say hi."

'Hi' from across the waves. Christopher feels weirdly seen.

"How are you feeling, Christopher?"

"Oh, y'know, fine!"

The stranger lights up. "That's good to hear." Those brown eyes are so attentive, his voice so patient and his interest so genuine – Christopher feels bad for having answered with a quick pleasantry. He is not used to so much positive attention or patience; it overruns him like an avalanche. "Yeah," he nods with a helpless smile, adjusting the strap of his sling bag. "And, and you?"

"Me too. I am enjoying the sunlight." That came out weirdly slow, especially on such a gray weather day, but Christopher pays little attention to it. Instead, he wonders what they should talk about now. He had not prepared for another conversation today. "Thank you for coming to the charity event, again," is what he decides on. "I appreciated it. As did the dogs, I'm sure."

The stranger grins. "I'd be happy if they did."

Smiles sparkle between them. There is something about his smile, Christopher thinks absently. It's so soft around the edges.

When a car rushes past them, the man snaps out of it briefly. "I'm – I don't think I've told you my name yet. I am Gyth."

Christopher feels uncultured. "Gyth? Oh, as in 'myth', but with a G?"

"…Yes."

"Okay, got it. Yeah, well – I'm Chris," says Christopher and laughs. "Funny running into you here." He omits other parts – *I'm so happy to see you – I've been thinking about you, actually – and now you're no longer a once-in-a-lifetime encounter.*

"I live around here," the man says. He awkwardly adds, "I can see you going to work. Sometimes."

"Oh. Are you new to town?"

"Yes. Actually, I've only been here for a little time." His next words are even slower. "Still takes a lot of getting used to. Compared to my home."

Chritopher gives him a sympathetic nod. "I can imagine. Not that I've been there myself but, y'know, I read a lot. Things must be very different across the Great Pond."

The man laughs to the ground, then nods. "Yup. Very different." He then gives Christopher another one of those shier smiles, from below his dark eyelashes, before meeting his eyes again in a way that seems less… well, sentimental.

It's a reminder that they're in the middle of the street and not in a staring contest.

Christopher summons his best conversational strength. "Um, hey – would you like to… have a coffee or something? Sometime soon?" he asks, his fingers tight around his shoulder strap. Even in this locked-in position, he's still jittery. "I could show you around town, too, if you would like that. I grew up here, I know this place like the back of my hand."

His offer makes the man light up. "Yes! Yes, I'd love that." But then his face hardens with the realization of what he has just said, and his eyes flicker past Christopher. Through him. "It's just – I am really busy at the moment."

Ah. Christopher sees through the bad lie but accepts it nonetheless. After all, he's the one who suggested it. Richard's words from earlier this week still ring his ears. The fear of being seen as gay is universal no matter the continent. "I understand."

"I'm sorry," the man says.

"I understand. Completely," Christopher repeats, quieter than he wants to. His chest begins to tighten but relaxes at the man's next words: "But maybe we can see each other again, Christopher?" His eyes are full of intent. And hope?

Christopher wonders if his lips are just this impossibly full, or if he was pouting. They're glossy. "Yeah. Sure. Anytime," he says with a nod before focusing to smile. "We can always have chat. It was good seeing you, really."

"It was very good to see you, too," the man says with a soft look. He still smiles as he leaves. Hands always in his pockets. "Goodbye then, Christopher."

Christopher waves and calls, "Say hello to your dog for me."

"I will!" the man calls back. Flashing him another smile as though to give his little paper boat a nudge to make it over the stormy seas.

Gyth. The man who wanted to talk to him, to greet him, and to know his name.

Wouldn't it be nice, Christopher thinks. Nice to... be with someone who owns a dog.

It isn't until much later that evening that he realizes that said dog must have covered quite a distance if he ran from Helping Paw all the way to Main Street, or further, where Gyth said they lived. There were no slime traces on the street when Christopher had driven home that night. Or in the shelter outside of the exam room.

To another person, those would be signals that not all was as it seemed. To Christopher, they are supposed reminders of how unreliable his perception is.

He did not see everything, he reminds himself. That is all. He often overlooks things or is unable to connect dots.

Paradoxically, it is freeing for him to think this way. For the next days, there is a spring in his step when he thinks no one is looking. He laughs when visiting his mother. He sings in the kitchen and the car.

Someone kind and friendly and possibly gay has reached out to him. He finds that worth celebrating. Maybe, he muses, he can unfold and smoothen himself. Maybe he does not have to show his piece of paper to anyone else. Maybe he can fantasize about being with a man and not tell anybody, he thinks. That sounds manageable. Even tigers cannot read minds.

Maybe it's not that weird that he is lying on his bed right now. He has picked up his old guitar first thing after coming home and played a few chords. He looks at the ceiling, framed by the naked posts of his canopy-less canopy bed.

It's not weird to hum a tune and yearn for back row seats at late-night double features and imagine he was singing to someone else. Someone who has reached for him.

A smile crawls onto Christopher's face. It lingers. Stays, even though he hides it in the bedsheet. He should treat himself tonight, he thinks. An XXL pizza from Stuart's would not only feed him today, but tomorrow for lunch at work, too.

That is his merry plan. Usually, Christopher hates when plans, no matter how small, get thwarted. But when the thwarting is a dark figure standing on Main Street, with his hands in his pockets and brown eyes behind a pair of thinly rimmed glasses, he strangely doesn't care at all.

In fact – he kind of prefers it this way.

Gyth seems to be studying one of the maple trees by the grass verge of Main Street. The swaying of its golden leaves against the rose sky is mesmerizing, admittedly.

Christopher's pace quickens on its own. "Hey!"

"Hello, Christopher," Gyth says, his corkscrew curls falling into his face as he turns. He blows them away absentmindedly, giving Christopher another one of his sweet smiles. "What are you up to?" His voice completely lacks the cautious approach one normally uses when speaking to people one hasn't seen in a few days. It's like they had a friendly talk just minutes earlier.

Christopher doesn't notice. He just points to Stuart's right next to them. "About to rob this pizza parlor."

Gyth raises his thick eyebrows but doesn't miss the answer's humor.

"Yeah, I know exactly what I want." Christopher holds up the red snippet from the tombola. "I got a coupon for a twenty-inch pizza, and I intent to get it."

His teasing tone pulls a laugh from Gyth that he tries to contain by lowering his head, though his eyes cannot be rid of their light.

He really is a good-looking man, Christopher thinks. Not just in his memory but in real life, too. In the flesh.

His fingers toy with the snippet, and he takes a far too little breath before saying, "It is quite the task to eat that alone."

Without taking his soft eyes off him, Gyth bites down on his bottom lip in order to hide a smile. Like he pretends to think about it when he has already made up his mind. "I don't have anything else to do right now."

"Okay, great," Christopher grins with a scrunched nose. "I didn't even have to ask."

Gyth laughs. "No, you did not." With another smile, he courteously adds, "I would love to eat with you together."

Christopher stumbles over that slow phrasing. His joy is quick to wave the confusion away though. So instead, he suggests they finally go inside.

Stuart's is a modest but long-established parlor in Hillsburg. The entry leads through a sea of eclectic tables. Some have back-to-back booths in the style of a diner, some are round and petite like in an Italian movie, complete with red and white napkins.

The smell of Mediterranean herbs mixed with fat and roasted vegetables makes him realize just how hungry he is.

Christopher guides Gyth to the tiled counter. Behind it, the parlor's elderly owner chats with a group of teenagers. But he has already seen his new customers and calls to them while still preparing the teens' orders. "Yo, Chris!"

"Hi, Stuart."

"Hello," Gyth says tonelessly.

"Lookin' good," Stuart calls. "Your tombola was a success? Sorry I couldn't be there."

"I was great! And don't worry about it, I know you're a busy man. I still got this one." Christopher slides him the coupon over the counter.

Stuart picks up it up with a grin. "Aah, I see how it be."

"We'd like to share," Christopher says with a look at Gyth. He only now notices how much taller he is. All that hair is deceiving. Gyth must be five inches smaller than him, at least. His jacket is soft around his shoulders, with its peculiar fabric. It's shiny.

Christopher realizes he's staring and quickly looks at Stuart again, whose eyes widen above an excited grin.

It's like an arrow piercing Christopher's chest.

"Stuart, no," he whispers, blushing at the implication. And the way it makes his stomach jump. Or is he just that hungry?

It's not as bad as he had feared, he finds to his surprise. And Gyth hasn't noticed, it seems. Thank God.

Stuart nods and points knowingly at them with a sympathetic smile. "All right, all right. What can I get ya then?"

"I'd say half and half?" Christopher says with another look at Gyth, though his face is considerably more heated this time.

"Yes," Gyth agrees quickly. Not in the nervous manner of someone whose worst nightmare is screwing up a food order but someone who simply does not know what was about to happen next.

Christopher takes it as a hint to go first and proceeds to order his side with his go-to chili, bell peppers and artichokes ere glancing at Gyth yet again. It makes him feel like a kid stealing candy. Stealing glances.

"What about you?"

With a frown, Gyth studies the menu above Stuart from behind his glasses. His hands are perfectly still inside his pockets. "Do you offer… something sweet?"

"Sweet?" Stuart shrugs. "We got pineapple."

"Then I'd like that, please," Gyth says.

A look of faux shock involuntarily spreads across Christopher's face, and it does not go unnoticed by Stuart: "Oh-wee, Chris!"

But, with Gyth seeming completely innocent of his order, Christopher doesn't say anything. His silly mood only makes him speak up when their order arrives at their table by the evening window.

He does not need to rely on suave humor however, much to his surprise. Or any social charades. No, being with Gyth is way easier than that. He talks about how his dog is getting better. How 'overseeable' Hillsburg is. Christopher, again, stumbles over that phrasing but figures he means it in the sense of 'easy to navigate', which he agrees with.

Gyth often uses expressions like that. Things that feel just slightly off to Christopher, though Gyth himself does not seem to find them weird at all.

It's charming.

Christopher turns a straw in his hands. Gyth must be about his age. He is handsome in the most traditional sense of the word, very calm, and yet there is a profound awkwardness about him. Men like Richard Shea have perfected the skill of using of their beauty and charm to their advantage in everyday social interactions. Compared to him, Gyth seems almost… mangy. Despite his amazing style. He does not pout. He does not emote. Most of the time, he is completely still. When he moves at all, it is quite slow.

That is – only when they aren't talking though. When Gyth listens to Christopher, he sways and snorts. His eyebrows rise and fall and furrow. He laughs. His voice is different, so rough and welcoming.

In fact, Christopher observes that even the warm smile that he blesses him with so often almost seems a rarity when talking to other people. It should be rude but isn't. Reserved, rather. His voice is professionally distant and not fast. It gives Christopher the faint impression that Gyth just does not give a damn about socializing with strangers, at all. Deeply, profoundly. It is so admirable it's scary.

It also strengthens the temptation of pointing out the pineapple pizza, now that it is right in-between them.

"I cannot believe I am sharing this pizza with you," Christopher says as he gets their cutlery in order.

His heart skips a beat when instead of answering to the veiled accusation, Gyth just smiles at him dreamily, dark eyes all soft – until he realizes what Christopher meant, with a caught expression. "Ahh – I've wondered about that. Is this such an unusual choice?"

"Oh, it's just the biggest crime against any self-respecting pizza eater ever," Christopher says after a pause. Trying to get that dreamy smile off his mental eye. To diffuse the situation, he much less confrontationally asks, "I thought that was the same in the UK?"

Gyth has taken his hands out of his pockets and stretches his fingers. At this point, Christopher wonders why he has hidden them for so long. He cannot spot any tattoos, rings or nail polish, or anything else Hillsburg might have deemed weird.

"Not putting pineapple on a pizza?" Gyth asks.

"Yeah." Christopher waits and watches him struggle to answer. "No?" he laughs, half in disbelief, half in enchantment.

Gyth shrugs. "I don't know."

"Goddamn," Christopher smiles. "I mean, it is kind of ridiculous, if you think about it…"

"It's a rule," Gyth states in the charmingly clueless tone of someone trying to understand a math problem.

Christopher stares, the napkin soft between fingers. But before he gets lost in brown eyes yet again, he resorts to joking. "Yeah, and it's a simple rule. Don't put pineapple on your freaking pizza."

"Then why do they offer it?"

"For people like you." Mockingly, Christopher adds, "Because ultimately, everyone is free to put *whatever they want* on their pizza. America, Land of the Free."

"Land of the Free," Gyth repeats quietly, eyes squinted. He only lights up when he sees that his effortless humor has made Christopher smile so wide his cheeks hurt.

"Okay. Okay," Christopher says, like he's trying to calm himself. "Enough talking. Dig in."

That is his mindset for the rest of the evening. Getting charmed, calming himself. Taking a breath. Repeat. But it lingers, that damned, beautiful warmth.

There's worse things.

He has to admit it to himself. That he finds Gyth failing to gracefully eat his cheesy pizza slides cute. That his own voice is warmer than usual when he suggests they could eat with their hands instead. That it takes his entire self-control to not say yes when Gyth casually offers him a piece over the table.

Tonight, he will admit to himself that he might have a crush. At the ripe age of thirty-eight. But how could he not, with Gyth delighting over something as mundane as pizza? "Oh, this is so good," he sighs, stroking his nose.

"Right? Best pizza in the area."

"Particularly the pineapple is exquisite," Gyth says with meaningful eyes. And yet again, his soft smile returns when he sees that his deadpan humor has made Christopher laugh.

It's past ten when they part ways.

Gyth is, again, quick to excuse himself with another bad lie. But not without thanking Christopher. "I really need to go now. I have a… duty to attend to. But I really appreciated us eating together, Christopher. I'm grateful for your company, and for the food," he adds with a lopsided smile.

"Of course," Christopher says. "I liked hanging out with you, too. And food was for free anyways, so…"

Yet another pause filled with smiles.

Christopher considers hugging to say goodbye. But hesitates. Normally, these seconds of hesitation are long enough for his moments to pass. But Gyth stays. Looking at him intently. Maybe it's because time seems to flow slower for the guy – Christopher doesn't know. Right now, his lips fall open with a surge of warmth through his body, and before he can do something truly stupid, he throws himself forward to hug Gyth with the grace of a buffalo.

"Bye. Oh, sorry! I didn't mean to…"

Gyth laughs as Christopher awkwardly pulls away. He even puts a hand on his arm. His fingers are long and firm. "I am fine. Goodbye, Christopher."

Christopher smiles, though bittersweetly. "Goodbye."

Gyth fleeing their interactions tears him in two. He wonders if it is a sign of him being too fast and obvious. Stuart has pointed out the air between them at first sight, he remembers with remorse. Maybe he's simply too much for someone who is not… Yeah. A kind stranger running into him *also* being gay is too much of a good thing, he thinks. Who met him at this strange point in his life. Who likes him back.

Christopher would like to believe it was like that though. Maybe his perception was playing a cruel trick on him yet again. But even this doubt cannot stop the joyous wave that carries him so effortlessly through the next days. They are filled with music and with all those novels he has wanted to read for so long. With longing stares through his window, to the bright moon.

With something that for once is entirely his own. With excitement. And easiness. And yearning for those back row seats at some late-night double feature movie night, where no one would pay him any mind, free to escape into the worlds of those cheap science-fiction flicks while intertwining his trembling fingers with those of another man – and he *likes* it.

CLOSER

Is THIRTY-EIGHT YEARS too old? Christopher has been weirdly self-conscious about his age since the divorce, and now the confusion has heightened.

Maybe thirty-eight is the magical age he needed to reach to make his crushes stop scaring him to death. Back in high school, a blush into the vague direction of fellow student Bruce Cain had him panicking about gay rumors. Same as Clarissa DeVasquez making a move on him, only to find out that him wanting to show her his dog postcard collection meant just exactly that.

He feels like he should be old enough to know if someone was flirting with him by now though. Gyth has been at the post office today. Just small talking. Asking how he was. Giggling about stupid things they said before Richard asked him to leave if he did not have any postal business, which Gyth, funnily enough, did indeed not have.

Just days earlier, such a confrontational if relatively diplomatic scene would have instilled the profound wish to sink into the earth in Christopher. But now, he just makes sure to keep his grins to himself. He bites his lips as long as he can, or swallows down smiles. But they are there. In an uncertain, if pleasant, twilight zone.

Gyth and his easy company have really come to Christopher's life at the best time. Mere weeks ago, the news of Jeffrey Hobson dying in a horrible car crash would have sent him into a downward spiral. Coming right after the debacle with the injured dog. And before that, his mother's cancer diagnosis. And the divorce before that. And – the entire gray fog of the seven years that preceded it.

It's this foggy cage that is to blame for Christopher's uncertainty. He feels like he should be old enough to tell when someone was flirting with him. But he lacks the experience.

Knowing Gyth and running into him all throughout town also makes the pink flashes more tolerable. Or 'forgettable', rather. In the empty parking lot by the dog shelter, Christopher's body goes hot and cold whether he sees one. And he sees them often now, in the corner of his eyes, in glass reflections, or shining from dark corners. It makes him wonder if Hillsburg's kids have found some new type of soundless fireworks after all. Surely it must be something like that. Or maybe Christopher's eyes are even more broken than he thought. That would be the more likely explanation. After all, no one answers his calls when he asks, "Is someone there?" into the darkness.

Or maybe it is his brain. Something mentally wrong with him. Or physically? But he feels no pain, at least not more than usually. So he'll be fine. Christopher knows better than to search the Internet for such symptoms.

One would think he'd apply the same logic to the question 'How do I know he's gay?'. Regrettably, he doesn't.

Sitting alone in the lunchroom, Christopher worries at his bottom lip. The fly by the window feels like a spy and the phone in his hands like a bomb.

It's not even the articles themselves that have him in their alarming grip – 'watch for his body language, his lingo, or rainbow-colored accessories' – not even the simple suggestion 'just ask them'. Not even the fact that most of these articles are for women secretly investigating their husbands. No, it's the accompanying photos. All those men are ridiculously handsome, with the whitest smiles and cleanest skin. No rimless glasses to be seen.

Christopher does not think of himself as handsome. He is vaguely proud of his beard every time he trims it properly, simply because of his teenage struggle to grow one at all. But that's about it. He is not particularly athletic. Or half as fashionable as the men in the photos. Those men do not look like they have ED, he thinks. Or too many pounds on their bodies, except in muscle mass.

The only compliment he has even gotten about his body were his 'pretty blue eyes'. He closes them when he remembers who has said it to him.

Gyth, on the other hand, checks every box of 'pretty'. Athletic, too. 'A cutie', Christopher remembers bitterly. Someone who could have literally anyone eating out of the palm of his hand.

It's discouraging.

Maybe Gyth always saying how he wants to see Christopher again were just pleasantries. Him wanting to make a friend in this new town, or simply being polite, Christopher thinks, despite having already correctly observed that Gyth generally gives a flying fuck about polite pleasantries.

Maybe it's a cultural thing?!

Luckily, Christopher's break is over before he can search, 'Do Brits flirt differently than Americans?'. Back at the packing station, he has enough time to think about nicer things. Like how delightful Gyth's smile is.

All these feelings are overwhelming Christopher. It is a good thing he can channel part of them into his hobbies. Yes, he used to have those! When he feels like singing in his bedroom, he now does. He buys an oregano plant for his tiny kitchen because it reminds him of their dinner at Stuart's. And when he is in the mood for a cheesy werewolf romance, he reads it.

"You're positively glowing," his mother has noticed on his last visit.

'Glowing'. He may be delusional, but that does not stop the butterfly chaos in his stomach. He could not shoo it away if he tried.

And he did try, on a Sunday afternoon.

He is at the dog shelter, unassuming, cleaning the kennels as today's form of meditation, until Emely peeks her head inside the corridor. "Chris, the guy from the charity event is here again."

"Who?"

She shifts. "Your new friend. The Black Brit."

"Oh! Yeah, I'm coming." Suddenly, Christopher is acutely aware of how badly he must reek. "Just a second!"

He goes to fetch his bag for some deodorant, and then to the lobby, willing himself to not walk too fast. He doesn't want to look pathetic.

But it is Gyth he sees in the lobby. And he can't help but smile from the other side of the counter. "Hey!"

"Hello, Christopher."

"Is everything all right?"

"Yes," Gyth tells him. His unchanged smile shows how truthfully he said it, though it cannot hide the shadows under his eyes.

Christopher is relieved; he has already feared this visit was about an emergency. Which begs the question…

"Are you here because of your dog…?" Christopher begins, and Gyth's soft face breaks into a helpless smile. He again lowers his head and looks up at Christopher through dark lashes and stray curls of hair. Then he rolls his posture back into its usual straightness. "I was attending to a duty in this area," he says in a lying voice so incredibly bad Christopher has to force back a laugh. But Gyth's next words are soft and genuine: "And I thought… I could come by and see you." He thins his plump lips and inhales as he steps closer to the counter, the only thing separating them now. "I don't have much time. But I wanted to see you," he whispers, in the same relentless calm as always.

Christopher is glad he has an intact chest, because otherwise his heart would have bust out of it, he is sure. "Okay," is all he manages to say at first. "Me too," he adds with a quiet laugh. "I'm always happy to see you."

Face hardening, Gyth shifts on his feet – inhales – and the air between them charges with urgency. He parts his lips. Christopher doesn't break eye contact, to show him he is listening. Although, right now, he would honestly rather do something else than listen, with his face so close…

Gyth blinks and frowns. For a second, something changes in his dark eyes. "Christopher, I – I need to tell you–"

"Chris, could you help me with the inventory?" Emely calls, despite standing right next to Christopher. He cowers. "When you're finished?" she adds in an innocent tone. With a poisonous sideglance, her eyes graze Gyth, who has retreated two steps back as soon as her icy voice had cut through the air between him and Christopher.

His shoulders are smaller now, Christopher thinks with a frown. Briefly, a darkness has darted across his features, carrying with it a thousand curses. Now his face is back to the usual detached emptiness it attires in when he is speaking to strangers. "I have to go." He swallows, his eyes flickering back to Christopher, softening. Then he walks toward the door. Slowly, as thought there was a contact mine beneath every tile.

"Bye," Christopher says nervously.

Before he has time to process what just happened, Emely whispers, "Geez, Chris? Does he feel funny to you at all?"

As though behind a whip, Christopher looks down and re-arranges the documents on the desk. Just to do something. And not gaze at the door. Now it is his turn to lie unconvincingly: "Hm? What do you mean?"

"There's something off about him," Emely tells him with an assertive hand on the desk. "And I'm getting very clear vibes from him. Can't you feel it?"

"Yeah, the guy is weird. He puts pineapple on his pizza."

"Chris."

Christopher continues the streak in the hopes that she would stop bothering him if he was just obnoxious enough. Where was that sudden concern of hers coming from? "Sweet is his favorite flavor. So when he asked for the sweetest option over at Stuart's, they gave him pineapple pizza. And, regrettably, he loved it. Never thought I'd eat with someone like that."

Emely shifts beside him. "Has he asked you – you've had pizza together?"

"Yeah," Christopher says, not half as firmly as he'd like. Is she pointing to…? He swallows. "He's nice."

"That's my point, dummy. Steph said she'd seen you talking by the post office, too. No one knows anything about him. He's being too nice! If you catch my meaning."

So, *that's* why she's so concerned about him, out of the blue. Okay.

Christopher inhales and decides to go for the strategy that has saved in ass throughout high school. "You're not saying this is some sissy thing, are you?" he hisses with a glower. The venom in his voice lends him believability, only it's directed at his self-hatred for resorting to this tactic.

But as always, it works. "Whoah, no, Chris. C'mon, I know you're not like that. And I don't know about him, like, I can't accuse him of anything – it wouldn't surprise me though. I think he actually wears make-up. I think Black guys don't do that unless they're – well."

A knot forms in Christopher's throat at not only such a non-sense notion but also her genuine disgust, a disgust that she is very confident to share openly. It figures. He prepared the poisonous ground for it himself after all. "Okay," he says emptily. "Just so we're on the same page."

But she doesn't stop: "I know about you, but him? Bad vibes all around. When he came in here during the charity event – haven't you noticed how he didn't specify which dog you took care of for him? I didn't, at first. But at home, it hit me. Like, you had to go, 'the big black dog'. And then he talked about it like it was his."

Christopher blinks. "It is his."

"Do you know his name?"

"Gyth."

Emely sighs. "Of the dog, I mean."

Christopher swallows and looks down. The venom is now pooling inside his stomach. "I don't know."

Emely shakes her head. "I'm getting scam-y vibes from him. This ain't normal."

Christopher can see that. Still, his stomach turns at someone attacking the little butterflies inside of it. He blinks away tears that thankfully don't fall. "My whole life has been pretty much abnormal as of late," he manages to say.

Beside him, Emely sighs. "Gee, yeah. I'm sorry. I under-stand you're in a shit position right now. Just don't... be too blue-eyed. Not everyone's a friend."

Indeed. This is the truest thing you have said today, Christopher wants to hiss. Instead, he simply nods with a sad look. Hoping that she'll finally leave him alone.

This time, it works.

He tries to go back to work. But he can overhear Emely talking to Stephanie. And later, to Bill. Always looking at him. Maybe because he's supposed to hear it.

"Yeah, they wait and prey on sad widowers or divorcés. Read about it before. And now it's a gay version. Fucking sickos."

The butterflies inside of him shiver. Retreating but desperately fluttering their tiny wings. This is nothing compared to the stab he felt at Stuart's friendly comment in the pizza parlor. This is a rain of arrows piercing through him continuously, with nowhere to take cover.

Nowhere but the shower back at home, when the floor reddens in thin threads. One, two, maybe three – yeah, he is fine again, Christopher tells himself.

There is a bright side to all of this, he thinks when he stares at the ceiling tonight. If other people point out they were together a lot, maybe Christopher was not imagining things. Gyth saying he wanted to see him again hasn't just been a pleasantry. Christopher has spent more time thinking about this than he would like to admit. After all, Gyth said all kinds of weirdly off-sounding things. And, after all, Christopher has a skew perspective due to his… history. That is all.

He shifts beneath the blanket. His thigh burns.

In essence, Emely has been right. Christopher does not know anything about Gyth's life beside his dog and that he moved here from the UK. That he has a vague 'duty' he always refers to. That's it. Then again, he does not seem like the kind of person to go around telling people his life story. He's a private guy. Hell, maybe he has had a difficult history himself.

Christopher does not want to risk hurting him or getting him into trouble. He likes him too much for that already.

Gyth is simply mysterious, Christopher thinks and chuckles into his pillow. 'Dark and mysterious'. He already thinks like the swooning main character from his werewolf novels.

That's how easily Gyth can pull him out of these holes.

And he likes it. He does not care. Tomorrow is Monday. And still, thinking of Gyth is a better balm for his soul than he could have ever imaged.

When he now thinks back to the situation this afternoon, a certain heat forms in his stomach – anger. He lets it sit. Allows himself to indulge in it instead of shoving it back down.

Maybe, he thinks as he falls asleep, Emely is so hostile toward Gyth because he has not texted her. Because he's not into her, because *he's gay*. That's a vindicating image.

Christopher does not see Gyth on Monday.

It's not that he misses him, he tells himself half-heartedly. But if he had met him, they could've developed a strategy of how to keep this lowkey.

Because Christopher very much wants to keep it.

But the look on Gyth's face, no, his entire body has been so disturbed when Emely had cut through their conversation. It *would* be nice to have his number, Christopher thinks as he stares through the window. Just to check if he was all right after such a confrontation. Not doing stupid things, cutting his thighs in the shower, for instance, like an idiot would.

Although – if he told Gyth about his worries – 'People are talking about seeing us together...' – Gyth would surely say something like, 'Let them talk, right?' with the softest smile. Tinted with a good bit of his mischievous humor. 'People talk when they have nothing better to do. Unless you want to give them something to talk about?'

"Ayo, sunshine, what're you smiling about?"

Absentmindedly, Christopher looks sideways to find Richard Shea's green eyes boring into him. They are stale as ever in his grinning face.

"Lunch," Christopher lies just a bit too dreamily for it to be convincing.

Richard doesn't notice. "Yeah, me too, man. Listen, um, we can switch today, too, right?"

'Switch'. More like 'share the work unevenly', as sanctioned by their boss. "Of course. No problem."

"Aw, thanks, Chris. You're my savior. By the way, you're keeping the new glasses?"

"Um, yeah."

"Great. Plus the new cologne, great, great. I dig it. Good talking to you."

Christopher hums as he leaves, watching his perfect but uninteresting back as he rushes to their manager Eleanor.

And he plays with the pen in his hand. He should continue imagining talks with Gyth. His husky voice...

He doesn't smoke, at least he doesn't smell like it. But sometimes, when he speaks a bit louder, his rough voice is almost scratchy. It's a rockstar kind of voice. Maybe he is a musician, with his dark looks and a little bit of a growl. He could be in a British band. He certainly has the style. And the ultimate head-bang hair.

And the voice! Christopher really adores it. So much so that he wonders if you could crush on a voice alone.

Gyth probably calls his dog with that voice, too. Someday, he'll explain what kind of ancient British hound that dog is while they walk it in the hills. Instead of his thin bomber jacket, he'd wear a thick coat. With the collar up, probably. Fashionable and mysterious. They'd both be packed away in warm scarves and gloves. Their breaths would crystallize as white fog between them when they'd laugh. And then the first snow-flakes would fall onto Christopher's face.

The pink flashes are still giving him trouble though. When Christopher goes to his pickup in the shelter's parking lot on Saturday night, the light hits him out of nowhere. Electricity crackles, birds flee from the trees, the streetlamps flicker – and go back to normal.

Pressed against the car door, Christopher's eyes dart to the shelter. There's a faint rumble. The dogs bark.

His hands won't move from the window – oh, he's frozen.

But something is back there.

The dogs' howling is what finally pries his fingers from the car. Grasping his keys tight, Christopher makes his way back to the door as fast as his stupid lungs allow.

The sky is crystal clear tonight. It's weirdly unnerving. With the clouds gone, there is no privacy shield from above.

Is someone there?

Christopher wonders if, on this short way from his car back to the door, he was being watched. The notion creeps into his bones and refuses to waver.

The keys tinkle appropriately in his shivering hands, but he manages to open the door, switch on the lights, and put one foot in front of the other, in the direction of the dogs' corridor.

It's quiet behind the heavy steel door. Luckily, just when Christopher wants to open his mouth to call and signal to the dogs it was him, he notices the doorhandle and stays quiet.

It is curved upwards. And twisted around itself, like one of those fashionable candles from the '90s. The indentations aren't deep. But they're there. The black plate is warped. Curved. Like a frozen funhouse mirror.

Christopher stares at it for longer than he'd like. Has it always looked this way?

A quiet whimper snaps him out of his thoughts. He fumbles for the keys and is glad the right one still fits.

When he enters the corridor, no dog jumps against the bars. No barks. The first kennel on the left belongs to Shelly. Christopher finds her cowering in the far corner, curled up and eyes round with fear. The other dogs look the same. Wanting to fuse with the back wall.

And suddenly, function returns to Christopher's body. His eyes focus as though he woke from a nightmare. "Jesus. Hey. Hey, it's all right. Shh…"

He uses the clinking keys to enter Shelly's kennel and caress her. She's stiff with fear. "It's all right. Good girl," Christopher whispers as she curls herself into the curve of his body. "You're safe. Nothing's here." He swallows and closes his eyes. "You've seen it too. Right? A pink light? Fucking fireworks."

As though on a cursed cue, a violent rumble shakes the building. The dogs whimper, cry out. Trying to get distance between them and the bars. An earthquake again?

Another rumble. Christopher gasps. He uses the momentum from his crash against the wall to heave himself up. Hurries into the corridor, to look through the small hopper window at the very end.

The rumble, the commotion, came from outside. The floor vibrates, like ripples through water. Are the tiles screaming? Or are those echoes from outside?

The ripples pick up speed. They roll toward Chief's kennel. The big husky is a shell of his former self, snarling helplessly at the ground before him. He jumps from corner to corner when it starts shooting tendrils at him. White and shiny like the tiles they sprung from. Sharp, supposedly.

"No – no, no, no, stay back!" As if on autopilot, Christopher jumps to the bars in front of Chief, holding onto them as he

68

kicks down the tendrils. They are hard against the soft sole of his sports shoes but shatter on impact – with a screech.

Christopher pants. Goes flying to the moving floor when the metal door to his left crashes shut. Heat burns white behind his closed eyes.

His voice gets caught in his throat – *who is there?*

As all the lights flicker with a roar – can neon lights catch on fire? – red darkens the hopper window. Through the color cuts a pink light, flashing, brightening, shimmering, melting down the window into curves as the rumble grows so loud in settles in Christopher's knees, crawling inside his brain, every crack, piercing, drilling –

And then, it's all over.

Christopher inhales so much air it almost makes him lose balance. With a hand ghosting over the cold bars to his left, he sinks to the floor. And his hand is fine. Somehow he had thought pressing his hands so firmly on his ears would have bloodied them.

But he is fine.

Panting, he reminds himself to breathe steadily. Count to ten. Maybe glance at the window.

It is a window. The funhouse shapes melt back slowly, in synchrony with his senses coming back.

No pink light. And no screams.

Christopher knows nothing better than to crawl into Shelley's kennel, where she whimpers in the same corner as before. "I'm here," he wants to say. But his voice is shaking so hard he isn't sure if an actual sound has left his mouth.

His hands do not obey him. They don't caress. Just shudder.

"I'm here," he repeats. "I'll stay."

He does. Over time, the fear oozes out of his body, onto the files, hopefully into the drain. Exhaustion takes over. It weighs down his bones. And eyelids.

But he cannot sleep. Not with that creeping feeling that makes his skin crawl every time he dares to think about it.

They were not alone. When this building shook and the light appeared by the window – there was someone there. That shit doesn't just happen in nature. Someone caused it to happen. Christopher is sure of it.

And then later, when he returns to his car at four in the morning, after cleaning all sixteen kennels, limps hurting from lying on the cold tiles next to Shelly, he is not so sure anymore.

The black doorhandle looked perfectly fine on his way out. Rounded plate and straight handle, made of matt plastic. Like you could buy in any hardware store.

And tiles can't move. And they certainly cannot scream.

And so, Christopher spends this dreadful Sunday wondering what was real anymore. He needs to ask other people about the flashes, he thinks. Maybe casually point them out. Ask. If they saw them, too. Maybe they were just as scared. Maybe they had seen who was responsible for them. Maybe he could even help someone by pointing out the danger.

Then again, the danger was probably just inside his head.

It would be weird, Christopher decides when he rolls onto his back, staring at the ceiling. It's weird to harass people with his strange imagination. His sick brain, making up fantasies and scaring the dogs.

That's how it has been. Right?

"Chris, the dogs are acting kind of weird. Did something happen last night? That might have scared them?"

The phone shakes in Christopher's hand. "I thought I saw something," he presses out. "And I freaked out. I probably scared them to death, 'cause they're so sensitive to human moods, and, and–"

"Oh my God, Chris!"

"I'm sorry…"

70

Stephanie groans, remembering that this particular, badly needed volunteer needs 'special care'. "Nevermind, it's fine. It's fine. Don't worry. There aren't any visits planned for today anyway. So they have plenty of time to calm down."

Christopher nods. When he realizes Stephanie can't see him, he whispers, "Okay."

"And we'll see each other on Friday, right?"

Friday was so, *so* far away.

Christopher nods. "Yes. Okay. It won't happen again. Thank you, Stephanie."

Dogs read and adapt your own mood. They smelled that he has been electrified by his own fears, Christopher thinks. Someone this crazy should never even be near dogs, he thinks. And then: it is probably time for a shower.

His blood swirls into the drain. Threading. And when Christopher looks at his hand now, he thinks – Gyth is real, is he not? With a real dog. A real owner of a real dog.

Gyth is out there, in this world.

Would he think it's weird? Gyth seems like the kind of person who'd answer, 'What's normal anyway?' if you asked them, probably. Or is that wishful thinking?

He could just as well be like, 'What a fucking weirdo. I don't want him near my dog ever again.' And then Christopher would have diminished the few chances he has had with him in the first place, and if Gyth was gone, then –

Crawl back.

Yes. Yes, he thinks when he retreats below his blanket. Being careful is in order. Simply stay in your shell, he tells himself. You can make it. It's almost Monday.

The island is almost in sight.

It comes with the alarm from his phone. Social pressure keeps him together, like a vase about to burst.

Lunch, he reminds himself. And breakfast.

The kitchen is white with light through the window. Instead of staleness, the oregano's friendly smell welcomes him. Christopher turns left to where the table is. Table, him, kitchen counter. There is not more room in here. But he appreciates it. The smaller the rooms, the more they felt like cozy little caves.

Christopher's hand ghosts over the oregano's leaves. He likes the texture.

It is so strange, he thinks when he sorts yet another package of letters just an hour later, that he feels better out here. He is far from safety here, amidst all those people more powerful than him. But at least all that pressure around him reliably keeps him from killing himself.

Richard's shark smile passes by as always. And Christopher reminds himself – be a predator like them. But after his eyes met Tammy's from across the room, he wonders – do they smell fear?

They surely know how to intimidate. They do it on Tuesday, too. Wednesday. Thursday.

On Friday, when they are in the middle of closing up shop, their intimidation has kept a dark figure outside the office. Its pretty face is notched by a furrow above dark-brown eyes. Timid.

Unable to stop himself from smiling, Christopher raises a careful hand.

Gyth's eyes focus through the window. He smiles back. And, belatedly, pulls a hand out of his pocket to wave back. Mellowing joy overtakes his entire posture, almost like he was relieved to see Christopher; he knows better than to come inside now though.

Christopher knows what it's like. But he's feeling lucky now. "I'm clocking off, guys!" he calls. He's not so brave that he averts his eyes, no, he still politely says goodbye, only to have silent stings pierce through him as he does. A half-hearted "have a nice weekend" leaves his lips as he slips outside, where the air is fresh.

"Hello, Christopher," Gyth smiles – it is that same smile, Christopher notices, that has shone from his face during their first meeting at the shelter. Or at least, it makes his tired heart flutter in that same way.

"Hi. Good to see you," he says, truthfully. 'Good to be washed up on your shore.'

"You too," Gyth smiles, his brown eyes all soft. "I have missed you."

Oh? Who greets someone they barely know like this? But Christopher has to admit, "Yeah, holy hell, I've missed you too." Clinging to his bag's shoulder strap with the stupidest grin.

His reply softens Gyth's features with mirth.

Before the moment can take an unexpected turn – they were still in front of the post office's windows – Christopher adds, "I'm on my way to the shelter, actually. If you don't mind, we can go this way. To my place, so I can get changed quickly."

"Yes, of course. I'm on the hop myself, actually."

"Okay."

It will take Christopher several days to realize this is the first time he has been comfortable enough to have someone accompany him home. To know where he lives. With Gyth, he does not give it a second thought. Instead, they merrily cross Main Street, over the greenery, to walk to West Street.

"Walking is, like – second nature to you Europeans, right?" Christopher asks. "I think I once read you walk way more than us. Shorter distances, healthier lifestyles…"

"I really enjoy walking!" Gyth says with oddly more excitement than the statement warrants.

"'Enjoy' would be too strong of a word for me personally. I mean, my workplace isn't too far from home. But I still get weird comments, from my mother and her partner. A neighbor once asked me if I could get rid of the car in front of the house then. Make some room. And with all the gas prices, and cardiovascular problems…" Christopher shrugs to shake off his embarrassment. "Now with you, I don't have to feel all that weird."

"Weird as in 'bad'?" Gyth asks, skipping over the statement's first part entirely.

"I don't know. I mean, yeah."

"Weird can be good," Gyth suggests, sure enough.

Christopher looks at him. And after rolling their previous greeting around in his head for a few silent moments, he suggests, "Should we get in touch via, y'know, phone? To text when we wanna get together again?"

"Ohh, yes," Gyth says in an apologetic tone. "Your shelter colleague asked me about my phone, too." And then nothing more.

Christopher frowns, adjusting his bag. "It's totally cool if you're not comfortable sharing your number. Y'know, boundaries and such."

"Oh, no, Christopher, you weren't overstepping any. It's just…" Gyth glances at a tree above them before giving him a shy look. "I do not have a phone."

Christopher registers it with an equally slow "oh, okay".

"Sorry. I realise it would be more convenient."

"No, it's all right. Admirable, actually." Christopher laughs. "It's okay, honestly." With another adjustment of his shoulder strap, he tries putting on a low voice but drops it halfway through the sentence: "Maybe I could just send you good old-fashioned letters from the post office then."

Gyth smiles beautifully at him. "Yes, why not?"

"Hey, dear Gyth," Christopher announces in a funny voice, "are you free to have pizza tonight? H.M.U.!"

Again, Gyth smiles, but this time with a shadow of confusion on his face.

Christopher sobers. "It's, uh, 'hit me up'. 'Get in touch with me'."

"Ah." A bemused smile shakes through Gyth as he adds, "All right", quietly. And disappointedly? Does he actually want to get pizza tonight?

But Christopher just grins. Maybe it's because of the afternoon sun that makes Gyth squint so adorably, or the pale shadow of the moon in the light blue sky. Or maybe it is the way they're walking side by side.

They must look... normal, right? Two normal people, walking down a normal street, in a world that is pretty ordinary.

Gyth, too, is lost in his thoughts for a moment. Then he says, slowly as always, "You really could just call my name. I'd come flying."

His eyes are so intent, his husky voice so firm, that the words sink into Christopher like a diamond into the ocean. "Maybe I will," he says blissfully. "I'll take your word for it."

"Anytime," Gyth assures him. And as they smile at each other, with such relentless kindness, warmly, mutually reaching out for the other, Christopher realizes it is time to stop walking. So now, they're standing at the shadowy crossroads, where it is colder but also protected.

"Hey, how about Saturday?" he asks. "Tomorrow, that is. I can take the evening off if I switch with another volunteer at the shelter. Then we could go for a drink over at Brian's." He points over his shoulder. "Brian's Bar, with the neon signs. You can't miss it."

Although the suggestion has left his lips so easily, his heart still jumps at Gyth's smile-laced answer: "Yes, I'd love to."

"Tomorrow then?" Christopher asks, wanting to make sure he heard correctly. "I can be there at eight."

"Yes, me too. That sounds lovely."

Joy bubbles up inside of Christopher. It's vibrating with an almost juvenile buzz. "Great. Honestly." He inhales, nods and adds, a little less uncompromisingly, "I'm looking forward to it, man."

"Me too." Gyth pauses for a moment. His face is soft despite the wind that harbingered the end of September. "You are very pleasant to be around, Christopher," he says. "I wish we could have seen each other sooner. But I am grateful we did right now. I deeply appreciate our togetherness."

Once again, Christopher's ears stumble over the phrasing, but his heart is too busy racing to question it. "Y-yeah. Same for me."

Their smiles are shakier than before. Christopher knows it would be wise to act quickly now. "Cool. Should we hug?" he asks, his arms already open wide. Anything to stop him from just leaning in for a kiss.

"Yes, please," is all he hears before Gyth is right in front of him, in his personal space. It is great. Much better than that aborted thing in front of Stuart's Pizza Parlor.

Only Gyth doesn't hug him like he's supposed to now. He slings his arms around Christopher's waist, up to his back where they rest warmly – with his face buried in the crook of Christopher's neck. And relaxes into the touch, like nobody's watching.

It's *wrong* – but perfect at the same time. Christopher's eyes flutter shut.

Gyth is warm beneath his hands. And soft, he will think later that evening, even though the muscles under that shiny fabric of his jacket were angular and hard. His body was not pliant. He steadied him in his embrace. Strong in all the right ways. In the forbidden ways.

Despite all this chaos in his head – their hug is warm. Here, he was secure, Christopher would think later.

But right now, he is quick to pull away again, with the tangy and sweet notes of Gyth's perfume settling deeper and deeper into him. "Okay. Okay, see you then."

"Yes, until then."

But strands of Gyth's long curls are caught in his jacket's zipper. They both reach out to untangle themselves, hands brushing against each other and their bearded chins.

"Oh my God, sorry," Christopher mumbles – his face heats up so hard he wants to explode. They're too fucking close, he can't even open his eyes.

Oh, this is – pathetic –

Gyth's voice is warm and low as always. "No need to worry. I got it."

With his eyes closed, Christopher cannot see that the hair basically detangled on its own. He only starts breathing again when Gyth steps away, out of his personal space. And the world returns to normal.

"S-see you then," Christopher repeats.

"Goodbye," Gyth says slowly. His smile is gone. Instead, his eyelids are heavy with darkness, and his face hardens. "Christopher, there is something…" His eyes flutter under the weight of his thoughts, weak with hope. He hesitates – maybe taking a breath would help – and so, his lips part, ready to overflow with everything that has been weighing him down.

But it does not come to that. A car passing them by reminds him of their environment. His gaze dulls before it falls to the ground. "I'm sorry, I have to go," he utters, ready to be rejected. "I'm sorry."

But Christopher is adamant in his understanding. "It's okay. Take care." Those are the words that he gives him to take along. If only Gyth could believe them, he thinks bitterly as they separate. If only…

Gyth is not the only one lost in thoughts tonight. Him fleeing yet another interaction, just when he was about say something, like a fucking confession, instills danger in Christopher's mind. Gyth's fear is contagious. He's scared.

He is able to contain that impression when he asks Bill to switch with him. Despite the effort it takes him.

"I'm sure my wife won't mind," Bill has said. His old eyes have been wary. Even if he did suspect Christopher going on a gay date, his generation would never talk about it. A strange rescue from intrusive questions. But a rescue nonetheless.

The whole process is agonizing, making it seem like a stupid idea in the first place. Christopher wonders how Richard does it.

Now that everyone is gone, he caresses Shelly to distract himself. She always calms him down. But one terrible thought stays in his brain like a leech and now starts crawling around. What if Gyth has overheard his homophobic comments to Emely? What if he had fled the scene because he did not want her to see anything, only to linger by the door, sorting his thoughts, as he distantly heard Christopher raise his voice at her?

'You're not saying this is some sissy thing, are you?' – Who says shit like that?!

He'd be rightfully angry at Christopher. Hell, he probably already was. And scared if he was like those jocks back in high school who made a sport of beating him up. Just some guy wanting a manly evening together, who panics when Gyth signals him it's something *else* in his mind.

Maybe Christopher has sounded like such people to him. "I can't even blame him," he whispers to Shelly. "He'd be right. Even though I didn't mean it."

He is despicable for talking like that, he thinks. A bad person. A good person wouldn't have had to retort to bigotry to save their own ass.

He's a bad person, now poisoning Shelly with his nonsense.

He forgets that he has just secured a date with the man. His mind gets twisted like that.

And the longer the evening goes on, the more another notion joins the dark swirl of his thoughts. White hot. Screaming in multiple little dots that start growing inside his mind.

He comes to the realization that no, he has not seen the big black dog since the incident a few weeks ago. He *has* seen Gyth being out of touch and cryptic – heard him say that he'll 'come flying' when Christopher calls his name. Emely's words of caution painfully echo inside of him. And women are more perceptive when it comes to dangerous people, he thinks.

Dangerous. Maybe that is what Gyth is after all.

He chuckles when he parks his pickup in silent West Street at one in the morning. The idea has its appeal. Maybe Gyth is a werewolf of sorts after all. A monster that has lured him into a false sense of security. Only to be crushed by him first because that is what he does – breaking whatever he touches. Possibly, that's been Gyth's entire purpose from the start. To be sent to this world to finally make Christopher crumble with his destruction.

That is his punishment, he thinks. And his exit from this world. When he destroys the last thing that that has kept him here, he would be free to finally leave.

And now *that* – that truly calms Christopher. A heavy serenity settles inside of him. The stars tonight look friendly to him instead of hostile. Won't be much longer, he tells them before going inside.

When he dreams of being devoured by the wolves tonight, he is strangely at peace with it. 'You killed one of our own,' they snarl with desperation. 'Why? What has he done to you? You monster!'

They wouldn't rip out his throat first. They'd save that for the very last round. Rather, Christopher would need to stay awake to witness his own dismantling. So, they'd start with his limps. Maybe scratch open his torso until his insides began to drop and spill. They'd look all dark in the moonlight. Or shining red?

Christopher wishes it would be red. Bright and raw.

He'd twitch as they take him apart. Maybe it would hurt. If it did, he does not feel the pain anymore. He'd lighten, with so much being taken out of him. And from him. He'd feel free without his legs. The thighs. And without his stomach. All torn away and chewed up and swallowed down.

Maybe he'd turn his bloodied head to look sideways. There, above all the noise, he would find Gyth. Emptied brown eyes staring at him, frozen in the horrific moment of his death. Is the blood across his face his or Christopher's?

It would not make a difference, he thinks. He still reaches out to take his hand. Maybe the wolves would leave their hands, he thinks as they take apart his chest. His heart gone, his head gone, but their intertwined fingers remaining.

Christopher's dream burns holes inside his head. They allow this serenity to settle. To him, it is not faulty. Just calming.

He would not have to depart tonight, he reminds himself in a grotesque wave of selfcare. He could take his time, he tells himself, now that he knows what the small future has in store for him. No need to rush.

And so, Christopher finds himself in a surprisingly good mood in front of Brian's Bar, where the music is fast and loud. Five minutes to eight. He has crossed his arms in front of him. It is colder outside than he has expected. He looks around.

Couples and friend groups flutter through the night with laughter. But Gyth is nowhere to be seen.

Christopher sniffs. Should he wait inside? He has no idea how this sort of thing usually works. Ten past eight. He wonders if people were looking at him strangely by now. A grown man, freezing outside a bar.

A bar that he had frequented very often when he was younger. Now it feels like the backdrop of a bad sitcom set.

He wills himself to stay a bit longer. Maybe Gyth forgot the time or has trouble finding the place. Or maybe he changed his mind. The thought does not trouble Christopher as much as it should, he thinks. Is this his cue already? To go home?

A pink flash snaps him out of his suicidal thoughts like a whip. He shifts on his feet. Someone exiting the bar bumps into his shoulder. Apologizes for not seeing him there.

Christopher can't reply, at least not in time. He shivers. He gets out his phone to pretend being busy for the nth time. But with nightfall already turning navy-blue, this open sea is close to overtaking him. If only he could call him…

Almost eight thirty.

An amusing thought enters the whirlwind carousel in Christopher's mind. He steals a glance to the right. To the left. To be sure no one was there. Then he whispers, "Gyth? Can you come to me?"

The sad smile on his face turns into a grimace when quick steps approach him from the left. A dark figure emerges from the shadows around the bar's corner. "Christopher."

Christopher well-nigh drops his phone. "F-fuck." He swallows – is this a dream? "Hey. Hey, Gyth." Goddamn.

"Hello," Gyth smiles. Stepping into the neon lights tints him in beautiful colors. Greens and reds and pinks. Like a buoy in the sea. Christopher stares for a while.

Gyth does not seem to be cold, despite wearing only his bomber jacket. As always. Christopher can't help but smile, warmth blossoming in his chest.

Suddenly, his world is back to normal – just like that. Real enough for him.

"Should we go inside?" he asks.

"Sure!" Gyth follows Christopher, who leads the way.

"Did you have trouble finding the place?" Christopher asks without the weight this question has had in his mind only minutes ago.

"Um…"

Christopher smiles as they step into the stuffy bar. "Simply forgot the time? That happens to me so often!"

"Yes," Gyth says immediately. "I forgot the time," he repeats in a way that should tell Christopher he barely has a grasp on the concept. It doesn't.

They cut their way through the crowd to the bar. There are no vacant tables, but Christopher stays unfazed. Maybe they could find a quiet corner to stand in then.

While Brian's Bar is decorated with bright neon signs on the outside, the inside is remarkably rustic. Red brickwork and wooden pillars give it a distinct New England charm, complete with Irish signs and Hispanic posters on the walls. It still smells of beer and fries, Christopher notes with a twinge of nostalgia. He hasn't been here for… yeah, seven years, he realizes. It's like yet another piece of his former life's puzzle softly clicks back into place.

Four or five bartenders are busy keeping the Saturday night crowd happy. Christopher and Gyth get in line. "I wonder what you'll have," Christopher chirps.

"Me too," Gyth retorts drily. Christopher snorts and notices again how Gyth wills his smile away until their eyes meet. He wants to make him laugh, apparently. And he keeps succeeding.

The bartender cuts through their stares with a cheery voice above the pop music: "Hi, welcome to Brian's! Your orders, please?"

"Hey! I'll have a beer, please," Christopher tells her, adjusting his posture to look more serious.

She types it into the card reader. "And for you?"

Gyth shifts on his feet, looking like he needs to take a metaphorical run-up. "A hot chocolate, please."

Christopher blinks as though it would help understand whether he heard that correctly.

"I'm afraid we don't serve hot chocolate. I could make you a coffee though."

"Um... What else do you have?" Gyth asks, his voice as slow as ever.

Supporting himself with one hand on the counter, Christopher smiles to himself – there is something oddly comforting about being in the company of a man his age who struggles to order at a bar.

"We got all kinds of soda. And alcohol. Beer, whiskey, rum, vodka, cocktails... Pick your poison." The bartender slides Gyth a laminated piece of paper. "Here's our menu. I can also mix you drinks that aren't on here. Just ask!"

Gyth raises his eyebrows, thanks her quietly, and looks at the menu.

And keeps looking.

Christopher licks his lips, trying not to meet the eyes of the women behind them. He counts to three in his head, sweating. But Gyth is like a statue. An admirably undaunted statue. It does not bother him that there are almost a dozen people waiting behind them, on an overcrowded Saturday evening. He even has the guts – something that Christopher would never dare – to bite back.

"Oh my God, what is taking you so long, my guy?"

"I haven't decided on my drink yet," Gyth tells the woman behind him with a glance over his shoulder. Not rude but firm.

"Please decide faster," she says as her grin fades.

"I didn't know I was support to rush."

"Oh my God…"

From deep inside of him, the need to tell her off arises in Christopher. But he does neither have the balls nor the determination. And Gyth seems to be pretty much to handle such a comment, unlike himself.

Shier this time, he glances past the brown curls falling into Gyth's face. He watches his dark eyes wandering away from the menu. On the counter, they spot a fruit basket and light up. With his voice ever so neutral, he finally asks, "Could you make me something with pineapple?"

"Sure, absolutely," the bartender says. "A piña colada, with rum?" She helpfully points to the menu. Christopher finds her surprisingly friendly – he would have thought she'd be annoyed by now and serve someone else.

"Yup. Sounds good."

"Okay. So, a piña colada…"

Just in time, Christopher decides, "Actually, make that two, please. Delete the beer."

"Very well. That'll be 10.90 each then, please. Are you paying together or separately?"

Christopher holds up his credit card, but Gyth beats him to it: "I will pay for us together."

"Okay."

"Thanks," Christopher says.

"My pleasure," Gyth smiles.

It takes his stylish black credit card a few tries to get accepted, but his stoic calmness stays throughout. The bartender gives him a friendly smile. "So… Yes, perfect. Thank you! Your drinks will be ready in a second."

"Thank you for quenching our thirst."

With his fingernails digging into the counter, Christopher stifles a painful snort. Gyth frowns at him but softens when he sees his smile. "I'm sorry if that was inappropriate," he tells the bartender, not minding the women derailing behind him.

Thankfully, the bartender just laughs, too. "It's my job!"

They turn away from the counter to give the people behind them more space. They shove and try to make Gyth smaller. It would be easier if he didn't have his hands in his pockets all the time, Christopher thinks with a smile.

"I really wanted to try a hot chocolate," Gyth says ruefully. "Last time I wanted to order one, I did not have my card with me yet. That was in a different place though. Not here."

Christopher wonders what Gyth's life has been like before moving here. Inviting him to a hot chocolate is tempting. While he ponders if he should simply ask, he notices a couple getting up from their table by the wall.

Yes, a couple. She throws an arm around him as they leave. Maybe he and Gyth could pretend they were buddies waiting for their friends. "Hey, um – why don't you sit down over there? Save us that table? I'll bring the cocktails when they're ready."

"Yes, all right," Gyth smiles. He maneuvers surprisingly smoothly through the crowd. But because he stared after him for a little while too long, Christopher is not fast enough to tell their bartender she does not need to put the mandatory glitter flags into their glasses.

So much for not looking gay. Terrific.

Christopher almost laughs when he realizes how little it affects him. He now just makes sure to not bump into anyone on his way to Gyth. Their table has two diner seats, with Christopher facing the stage in the very back of the bar. They have tables on there now instead of instruments. It figures; space is precious in here after all.

"Here you go."

"Thank you." Gyth accepts his drink with a beaming smile. It fades when he sniffs it. "It *is* poisoned."

Christopher laughs. "The best kind. I know what you mean though, they are not shy with the rum here. Never have been." He smiles. "Cheers."

Instead of struggling, Gyth relaxes when he shoves his glass over the table to chink. Then his full lips close around the straw. "Oh, it's good! Pineapple after all," he says with his entire face lighting up. Christopher laughs to hide how attractive he finds him right now. Maybe it's the low lights in here.

"Piña colada. There's a reason it's one of the best."

Gyth squints his eyes. "Then pineapple is desirable in a drink, but not on a pizza." He hums. "All those rules – I shall start a list." Once again, Christopher's laugh after his dry joke is what brings out his smile. "I've never had one of these. I'm glad the pineapple is stronger than the... bitterness," Gyth says, taking another sip.

Christopher smiles in disbelief. "This is your first ever piña colada?" he asks.

Gyth does not answer – because he is busy drinking the entire glass through his straw. Christopher blushes when his cheeks hollow, throat bulging – God, you're staring like a sixteen-year-old, he scolds himself. Get a grip!

Just like that, Christopher becomes painfully aware that this is a date. He has developed a crush on a man, asked him out, and is now on an honest-to-God date with him. He panics, regretting that he hasn't picked out a nicer shirt. A black one, preferably, because Gyth likes black. He presumably doesn't like scars on thighs. Or fucked-up heads. Is this a date to him, too? Probably, right?

Christopher is sweating. The alcohol isn't helping either.

And he has also successfully instilled self-consciousness in Gyth, who stops drinking when he notices Christopher's look.

"I used to play on that stage," Christopher says a bit too loudly, even over the booming pop music. The coconut creme is sweet on his tongue.

Gyth needs a moment to understand but then looks over his shoulder.

"I was in a band, in high school," Christopher continues, finding that he could just as well use his diversion for genuine conversation. "Guitar. Sometimes piano, and background vocals." He mockingly rolls his eyes and singsongs, "Yeah, now the cat's out of the bag – I was a theater kid."

Gyth laughs, an adorably subdued little sound. Like his voice, it is rough around the edges.

"It didn't hold for long," Christopher recounts. "I was into musicals, the others not so much – I think they all went to Boston after graduating. Or someplace else, maybe. Don't know if they still make music." He smiles into his glass. "I recently picked it up again, as a hobby. Singing cabaret and '80s glam metal in the kitchen. And in the car." And on the bed, thinking of you wrapping your warm arms around me, he adds in his mind, taking another gulp.

Gyth smiles at him through dreamy eyes. "You have a wonderful singing voice, I bet."

"Did my mom tell you to say that?"

The joke pulls another laugh from Gyth – Christopher loves the sound. It's nice to repay Gyth for all the laughs he has given Christopher already. It's so easy to talk to him.

So easy, in fact, that a wave of vulnerability now washes over Christopher. For but a second, he wants to spill it all out. 'I wish I could say that music has always been there for me, but that is not the case – I fall into impossibly dark holes at times and nothing brings me joy anymore – I am not okay – after the separation from my daughter, I was one hundred per-cent sure of killing myself until I met you – I'm still thinking it is all part of the plan, to take me up high and make the impact of my fall all the worse – but right now I want to live – I want both of us to be okay.'

But in the time it takes him to breathe, the wave recedes.

"No," he says, "in all honesty, I can't sing much anymore. I guess the pandemic has permanently screwed up my health, my lungs are killing me – if I cross the street a little too fast, I'm puffing and panting. Especially now that it's getting colder. Plus the concentration problems – but my brain has never been my strong suit anyway, so…"

Gyth looks at him sympathetically. The wave across Chris-topher's body wasn't lost on him. His voice is thus rather heavy when he replies, "I'm sorry, Christopher."

But Christopher raises his chin with a smile. "Don't be. I've made it hard enough on myself already." He thrums on the wooden table, full of scratches and memories of strangers. He looks at it thoughtfully. "What else is there to say? I'm Chris-topher Ennington – my mother's name, my father was Sulli-van, died real early – I'm thirty-eight years of age, Gemini – and talking too much." He laughs.

Gyth doesn't. "You're not," he says in the sincerest voice.

Half-heartedly hiding his smile behind a hand, Christopher studies him. The smudged darkness around his eyes is really make-up, huh? "What about you?" he asks.

Gyth questioningly raises his eyebrows. They twitch in un-certainty.

"I mean, we talked a lot already, but I don't know much about you," Christopher explains casually.

The glittery flag chinks quietly against the glass when Gyth touches it. Not jittery, just absentminded. "I have been trying to be… elusive."

"Ahh," Christopher goes, only half-sarcastically.

Gyth gives him an apologetic smile.

"Well, I can't guess your zodiac sign, but…" Christopher squints, not breaking eye contact. "You don't care what people think. You like the color black. Walking. And sweet things."

A boyish smile sneaks onto Gyth's face. Gradually. But he still keeps his mouth shut.

After another pause, Christopher nods. "Let me think of a question then." He leans back – and then throws a playful grin across the table. "What's the name of your dog?"

Gyth slowly says, "My dog? My dog is named… Gyth."

Sure enough, Christopher snorts, and Gyth smiles with him like it's infectious.

"Okay. Wait, seriously?"

A funny grimace dances over Gyth's face. But his eyes fail to hide his uneasiness. He *is* a bad liar, Christopher thinks. Instead of pointing it out, he decides to comfort him by continuing their irony game: "You named your dog after yourself? Fine. Okay. Fits the 'elusive' part."

Gyth defends himself mockingly. "Now, I did not say that." His eyebrows rise even higher when he says, "Perhaps I named myself after the dog." He makes a wiggly gesture with his fingers before they reattach to his glass. "I might steal your name next. I quite like it. The sound of it. But perhaps that's a given because it belongs to you."

Christopher can't help but return his soft smile. He's right, he does say his name a lot. In his lovely, husky, British dream of a voice.

While Christopher still swoons, Gyth sobers. He looks into his glass. Toys with the flag. Then swallows. "Sorry. I'm aware this is not fair toward you." He pauses. "There is quite a lot I want to tell you, Christopher. I just…" – he presses his lips together – "I don't know if I can do that already."

Christopher nods. "Hey, that's okay. Look, I'm the last person to squeeze something out of you that you don't wanna share. Honestly." He leans forward and gives him an engaging smile. "I'm sorry if I sounded like I wanted to pressure you. You've got all the time you need."

'All the time he needs' – yes, Christopher, too. If Gyth still has time on this Earth, so does he, he decides. Just like that.

Sadness sinks into Gyth's smile. His eyes blink slowly, head tilting. A few of his curls fall into his face – before his eyes dart to the door. And afterwards, there is a loud thud.

Christopher looks over his shoulder. Frowning. Other heads turn, too, but no one seems to be able to locate the noise.

"Do you – do you mind if we…?" Gyth's voice is unsteady. He's already halfway out of his seat when Christopher finally replies, "Yeah, no. Okay. We can leave, no problem."

Before he knows it, they're through the sea of people and outside, in the black night. It's drizzling. And their drinks aren't even finished.

Christopher would lie if he said he was not a little bit downhearted that the evening took such a quick turn – but what exactly has he expected? That they sit in there for the next few hours? How do first dates usually go? Christopher is unsure. He shivers.

At least *he* didn't fuck up the situation and cut things short. That's oddly comforting. In front of him, Gyth's dark figure is building up. He broadens his shoulders as he looks around, scanning the street for anything that could have been the source of that noise. His arms are tense now that they're not resting in his pockets anymore.

He whirls around when the neon lights above them flicker. Eyes alert. Instead of a buoy, he now looks like a warning siren. "I'm sorry. I thought there was... something here," he says, still looking around.

Christopher simply nods, packing himself further away into his jacket. Just when he thought he has understood the kind of person Gyth was, this happens, he thinks bitterly. Gyth has clearly looked to the door before the noise. Christopher is sure of that.

What exactly is Gyth looking for now? He is taking a few steps back, to the street.

Christopher rummages for his phone. Not even half past nine.

Gyth's body stills. "I think it's gone."

"What's gone?" Christopher asks. As the words leave his mouth, images of last week's incident by the shelter bubble to the surface of his mind. He forces them back down, wishing he hadn't even asked in the first place.

Or... could it be possibly that Gyth saw things, too?

Gyth falters. "The noise I thought I heard," he answers slowly. When he turns around now, his apologetic expression makes him look like a wet puppy. "I am really sorry, Christopher. I enjoyed us talking – now it's cold outside and–"

"Yeah, it is," Christopher says with a faux grimace. Nothing can destroy his good mood when he's with this guy.

Gyth returns his smile, but it's sad around the edges.

"I mean, now that we're outside – we could go for a walk, if you like, and continue talking," Christopher suggests. Walking is their thing, after all. Or it could be. "Honestly, I don't mind the rain."

Gyth looks up as though he wanted to trace the drops back to their respective clouds. "Me neither. Let's go walk then."

"Okay." Christopher catches up with him and pats his back. "Don't worry about it, okay? That's my job."

Gyth's hard face breaks into a laugh to the ground. He still apologizes, but Christopher is having none of it. He is in a surprisingly silly mood. He can't understand why he has ordered this fruity, expensive cocktail, or why he is sweating instead of freezing. And why does he laugh so much?

New things can be confusing when you have no memory or frame of reference for it. Right now, Christopher is content to just walk with Gyth. Side by side, through the night.

They don't make it far though. The drizzle turns into a proper downpour. Christopher opens his jacket to put it over their heads, but it's no use. The raindrops are like stones.

Unbelievable – caught in the rain on his first date since whenever! Where he's had a piña colada! Only the song didn't mention your socks getting wet.

"Next thing we know we'll find ourselves on Cape Cod!"

"Does it rain there?" Gyth calls back.

"Bet on it! That's New England for you," Christopher jokes. Laughing through it all, they take cover by an abandoned autoshop, away from Main Street. Now they're safely under a rusty canopy.

Christopher exhales through a grin, touching Gyth's arm in a half-hug. Gyth just smiles at him softly, damp curls sticking to his forehead. The raindrops on his glasses shine with the golden light of a faraway streetlamp. His beard glistens. As do his luscious lips.

Suddenly terribly aware of how close they're crammed in here, Christopher sobers. Even their knees are touching. There is no room to step back. Not without getting wet anyway.

His inexperience hits him like a whip.

The rain really is loud.

He takes off his own sprinkled glasses to clean them, in an attempt to defuse this heated air in the space between them. But it stays, warm and soft, when he looks at Gyth again.

Christopher licks his lips. Right now, the night rain feels like a shield around them. Protecting him from the cruel world just a step away. He feels safe enough to touch Gyth's arm again – blinking in disbelief when he breathes hot against his lips – are they really standing this close?

Do you kiss on the first date?

"I'm sorry," he utters, hands still wandering across Gyth's wet jacket. And the hard muscles beneath it. He can't help himself. "Sorry, this is – I'm making it awkward, aren't I? Is this too fast?"

Gyth does not retreat. Christopher dares to look him in the eyes, to search for consent. His gorgeous smile flickers with something more. "No, it's nice." Brown eyes wandering just like Christopher's hands, before stilling dreamily. "I want to kiss you, too."

Shit.

Neither his heart, though pounding so restlessly against his chest, nor Gyth's words can pull him forward. Instead, Christopher makes the conscious decision to lean in. He gulps. "I've never done this before," he confesses, resting his nose against Gyth's cheek.

"Me neither," Gyth says through a smile. A smile that Christopher can now feel against his own lips.

Shielded by the rain, they kiss amid the darkness. The unexpected tenderness chases away all fears and doubts, blossoming between them ever so delicately.

Their first try is just that – a try. Careful and soft. Though Christopher relishes the feeling, he is unsure when to pull away. Or whether to pull away at all.

Gyth just… lingers. He has never felt anything like this. When Christopher's lips first touched his, his stomach had jumped. Now a profound warmth surges through him, through his entire body. He leans in, needing to dive deeper into this feeling, to get engulfed by it. By *him*.

He inhales and takes another dive. Takes in the feeling of Christopher beneath his fingertips – he is helpless under this spell. It should be strange that Christopher's magic is both antidote and amplifier to it. Strange and beautiful.

Gyth tilting his head deepens their touch. Christopher sighs against his lips – that hand on his neck is perfect to lean into, warm and rough. They touch by their foreheads and noses. Their glasses clank quietly, but that only makes him smile into their kisses. Nothing can disrupt their unyielding tenderness. Not the glasses, not the wet clothes, not the beards – no, the beard makes it better. It's surprisingly soft against Christopher's own. Just the right amount of friction.

Their lips find each other once more. And again. It takes them a few attempts to overcome the unfamiliarity of it all, but they always come back for more. And every time, a sigh falls from Gyth's parted lips. Just as plump and soft as they look.

In the back of Christopher's mind, he wonders if he's doing this right. If everything was just so smooth because of the rain on their faces.

The rain has nothing to do with them both parting their lips now though. Gyth stills, his breathing shallow like he needed to process this new kind of touch before he could move again. When he does, Christopher is met with a kiss so deep his hands grasp the thin bomber jacket like a lifeline. And yet, he wants to be pulled deeper yet, closer still –

Gyth works his jaw like he has never done anything else in his life, slow and steady. His hands are gentle on Christopher's neck and waist, his feet steady in spite of their awkward position. Even his tongue is tender despite its curiosity, not brash, not forceful. Tasting faintly of rum and sugar.

Christopher would think it was a dream, if he were with anyone else but Gyth. But this is real.

Heat rushes through his ears when he cannot stop himself from moaning into their kiss.

But there is no need for shame, because Gyth feels the same. He groans, breaks away, taking a shaky breath of air before leaning in again. Upwards.

He is like a wave, Christopher thinks blissfully. An ocean surging against his rocky shore, again and again. Relentless as the tides. Cradling him in his gentle embrace.

Just perfect.

The descend from his high is anything but peaceful. With his mind in this haze, it takes Christopher painfully long to realize Gyth's next moans have not sprung from pleasure but pain. He holds onto Christopher tighter, fingers clawing into the thick fabric of his jacket – grunting.

His voice is but a rasp when he speaks. "We can't – we can't... *ha*..." He stifles a moan, squirming.

Christopher blinks, laying a hopefully comforting hand on his arching back. "Hey..."

While his right arm is supported by Christopher, Gyth slams his left one against the door beside them. In the faint light, it looks like his skin was pulsating.

"I'm fine. Just – my body is–" From below his wet curls, Gyth laughs through the pain. "As I said, I've never done this before..."

When he manages to raise his head, Christopher sees his pupils multiplying. Black dots parting, further and further.

"Your eyes..."

Gyth hisses and shakes his head. His left hand claws into the door, splitting the rotten wood with bare fingers. Without spilling any blood. And his right one – is now throbbing in Christopher's. It's terrifying to see his tower of strength so broken. What should he do? Should he call an ambulance? What should he tell them? That the door beside them has started twirling and circling and curving like a vine? That all of this felt eerily real? Has he grown so pathetic that this is what half a cocktail makes him see?

As Christopher still tries to sort out his thoughts to understand what was happening – *it must be real if Gyth is here, because Gyth is real* – the hand in his own grows steady with determination.

"I want you to know the truth, Christopher," Gyth presses out. "I should've told you much sooner. So much sooner. But I was afraid." He moans. "You deserve to know… that I am not human."

As strange as the statement is, it grounds Christopher like a stone sinking to the bottom of his mind. All he can do is not. 'Not human' – yes, that is what he has suspected. Finally, he says, "Okay."

Strengthened by this calm reaction, Gyth exhales and straightens up. Wills away the pain as best as he can. His hands are back to normal, as are his dark eyes. But he is still breathing hard. "I'm not human," he repeats weakly, shaking his twitching head for emphasis.

Christopher swallows. "Okay."

"Okay?" Gyth's kiss-swollen lips break into the happiest smile. Hope heaves his chest. "You're not scared of me?"

For the first time in forever, Christopher fails to smile back.

Gyth nods, his smile fading. "You deserve to know the truth. The whole truth," he says. Trying to catch his breath. Whatever just happened has clearly left him exhausted, Christopher notes. His own senses are alert now. Yet all he can do is stare, overwhelmed. Waiting.

Just what has the universe sent him as his ultimate punishment? A werewolf? A demon? An alien, maybe, choosing him to toy with, having its way with him, until the inevitable destruction?

Suddenly, the rain is earsplittingly loud. And so cold…

Before him, Gyth straightens his posture anew. The deep sigh before he starts speaking again is like a gut punch. "I hail from a dimension far beyond your own. I am a guardian. I protect the innocent and helpless from the whims of ancient hunters from beyond your world."

Despite his efforts not to show it, Christopher is so taken aback he lets go of Gyth's hand. He blinks. "A guardian?"

"Yes."

"Uh-huh. In, um – in a long line of guardians?"

Blinking slowly, Gyth realizes he has lost Christopher. He is slipping away from him. "Beside me, there are only a few others that I know of," he tries to explain.

"Okay. Then it's not some… I don't know, sacred mission or something?" Christopher sniffs. His voice is empty. "Are you guys, like, a chosen guild or…?"

"I chose to do this. I wanted to fight the injustice I kept seeing." Gyth smiles to engage him, to catch his eyes again. "Much like it happened with you. Nobody told you to work at the dog shelter, right?"

"I don't know if that's the same."

Christopher's blue eyes are wide and dull with disappointment. And fear. Gyth's shoulders sink. "I did scare you."

It will take him a few moments longer to realize that Christopher's shift is not directed against him, or the truth he just learned, but primarily himself. The sole disappointment is that Gyth is not the punishment that he wished he would be.

"No," Christopher says finally, throwing himself into his train of thought. "It's just… a lot to think about. Protecting the innocent – what if someone isn't innocent? What if your ancient hunters kill bad people? Do you save those, too?"

Gyth shifts. Christopher's empty voice makes it clear he does not believe him. Retreating into hostility. Gyth looks away, trying to chase his sorrow away with blinks. "Hunters do not have a moral compass. They don't kill to exercise justice or to feed. It is pure sadistic pleasure that they derive from hurting those who do not stand a chance against them. Where I come from, I protect those who cannot not survive without a protector. Anyone." He shifts, trying anew to make eye contact. "And your protection has become very special to me."

Christopher does meet his gaze now. Chin raised. "Yeah? How so?"

"You saved me," Gyth utters. His Adam's apple bops with a forceful swallow. "You've only gotten in harm's way because of me. You showed me kindness and enabled me to go home to heal. That put a target on your back. I returned as fast as I could, but even then, innocent beings have been hurt. My scent attracts some really messed-up guys. They know very well their victims are never too far from a guardian's blood." He blinks at the raindrops crashing into the puddles on the ground. "Normally they'd pass right through this dimension on their journeys for new hunting grounds. There would be nothing of interest for them in your world. But I've led them here now." Gyth's voice turns bitter in his mouth. "Now they're running wild, trying to get you. So far, I've been able to stop them." He looks at Christopher and frowns when he notices his shallow breathing. Oh, none of this is how he wanted it to be! He needs to be strong for the both of them now and show Christopher that he is safe.

"Please, do not be afraid."

But Christopher cannot see the hope glimmering in Gyth's eyes. He looks to the ground with a hard face while realization dawns on him in dark colors. It tells him that everything has been crystal clear ever since that fateful Saturday. A gorgeous man lying to him. Sweet-talking him. Pretending they met by chance, even though he's probably been stalking him the entire time. He just didn't see it.

"It sounds unbelievable," he says tonelessly.

His distress is more than obvious to Gyth. He's trying to comfort him. "I know it must be unsettling to you, knowing that such forces are passing through your world, every day."

Christopher avoids his empathic eyes, however painful. He shakes his head. "No, not… that part. I mean, yeah, but…"

Gyth shifts so that they're even closer. He tilts head. And with that, he sees right through him. "You think you deserve to be hunted?"

"Exactly. Yes," Christopher says, louder now. His voice is a rocket. "Because I'm a prick! That's the whole thing about me, that I fuck up everything I touch! I don't *deserve* protecting!" He stumbles sideways, back into the rain. A bitter laugh bursts from his mouth. "You must admit, it's kind of out there. 'Protecting' me from the monsters lurking under the bed!" He scoffs, extending a frustrated hand. "Let's roll with that, shall we? If I was gone, or hunted and, and eaten or tortured, no one would care. They wouldn't even notice I was gone!"

"That is not true."

"They'd be better off without me!"

Gyth swallows. "I would have died if it wasn't for you, Christopher. You saved me."

"Yeah?" Christopher calls, loud and bitter. "And now you think you know everything about my life?" He looks away, closes his eyes. Feels the water run down his face. And he half-hopes a pink flash would knock him out right about now.

That does not happen. Instead, Gyth steps into the rain. But not Christopher's personal space. His voice is full of intent when he says, "I do see you, Christopher. And I would not let anything happen to you."

Christopher laugh-cries, putting his arms around himself as he screws his eyes shut. This is too wild, his brain starts whispering to him. It cannot be real. Look, even the door is back to normal, too. Nothing of this is real. Just the rain dripping from your face. Soaking your jacket, your shoes and socks. That's real.

"This is good," Christopher sniffs. "This is good. Good one. First kiss with someone I actually care about, and I get *this*. Do you tell that to every guy? Or just the especially delusional ones?" He stumbles away, like a hurt animal. "You're an asshole, talking shit like that – mocking people who have it hard enough already, you know that?"

Gyth's eyes are full of pain. "I've told you nothing but the truth, Christopher."

"Bullshit! That's–" Christopher stumbles closer again, pointing a weak finger. He has become a caricature of himself. "If you really are as otherworldly as you say, why don't you show me? Don't just tell me some shit and do a party-trick when you don't want to make out anymore, and, and want the other guy to just g-get lost. Show me that whole monster shtick of yours is true!" He gestures nervously, eyelashes heavy with rain. "Show me a bit of your eldritch horror routine. The end of the universe."

"I can't."

Sharply, Christopher hisses, "But I want you to prove it's all real." Because if it is, he adds in his mind, letting myself get swallowed by whatever is lurking out there is just as possible.

Gyth shifts, his face soft and sad with regret. "One glimpse into my mind would drive you to insanity."

"Of course!" Christopher calls without any edge left in his powerless body. The rain on his face mixes with tears. "Maybe

I *want* to go crazy, all the way! Just for once." He sobs. Slumps down into himself and wants to shut out this entire godforsaken world. He's had enough. He can't do this anymore. He is weak. Always has been. So, he cries, "Can't you just hug me? Can't we just fucking – be?"

His voice shakes. But he does not pull away when two warm hands close around his. Rough and dry and warm.

Sobbing, he leans into their touch. Is grateful for it even. *Weakling*, his brain whispers.

"Christopher," Gyth's husky voice says. It's a veil around them. "Go home. Go to your bed. Your mind is playing tricks on you. It distorts your self-image." Faintly, he adds, "I've never kissed anyone before. I did not know what would happen. I am sorry things turned out the way they did." He strokes hair out of Christopher's wet face, slow and deliberate, before his hands still. "But know that I see you. And no matter what you may think right now – you deserve to live."

Christopher gives in. His sobs are hot against Gyth's wet jacket. He clasps it with shuddering hands. Gyth's hands rest on his shaking back. With this motion, this helplessness, everything comes back to him. He thinks of his daughter – of when he wasn't sick and exhausted from those endless mood swings – of when he didn't feel guilty about liking men – of when he wasn't haunted by pink lights. None of this awful stuff.

He simply wants *this*. To be seen. Not for what he lacks, but for what he is. Or what he could be. Plain and simple.

But he cannot have that fairytale. *Never*, his mind whispers. Then what?

"I just wish… things would go back to normal."

He practically melts into Gyth when he hugs him then. Holding him, stroking his wet hair. Breathing deeply. He answers, "I can give you that. At least in approximation. I can offer you to part ways. I will always be with you, hidden from your eyes, looking out for you to keep you safe." He pulls away. But only to sadly smile at Christopher. This will be the first time he can only protect someone via distance instead of proximity. Mirroring Christopher's words from before, he says, "From the monsters under the bed. Do you wish that?"

With the pressure behind his eyes so impossibly sharp, all Christopher can do is nod, before they shut again.

What gruesome and cruel magic – something inside of Gyth breaks apart and floods him. His voice shakes when he says, "Then so it shall be." Beyond his sadness, he wants their good-bye to be like their time together. He gives Christopher a last smile. "Go to bed now," he says, stroking his forearm.

More than anything, he longs to remember this touch. He does not want to forget.

"Go to sleep, Christopher."

The words echo in his mind. Like ripples through water.

SLEEPWALKER

THE SUNLIGHT IS filtered through gray clouds. It softens the shadows. Renders edges less crass. But no matter how you turned it, it was still filtered. A cloudy day.

A popcorn ceiling can look like upside-down mountains, but it doesn't without the contrast between tiny shadows and dots of light. Maybe this is what the surface of the sea looks like from below when it rains, Christopher muses. Each drop a crash.

That's pretty romantic. But maybe this is just what human skin looks like up close. Infected skin. Rough and irritated. Maybe it does not look like anything. It's a ceiling. Sprayed on top of the 1930s wood, painted over, done. That's probably it, Christopher thinks.

He shifts on his pillow. He has already tried counting the pimples, time and again. During his previous episodes. At least the ones right above him. The ones that are nicely framed by his canopy-less canopy bed, like a modern painting in an old oak wood frame.

He has often tried counting them but never succeeded. He has always stopped before he counted every single one. Maybe today was the day! It was possible he could succeed today.

"One, two, three – four, five – six, seven... No, one, two three..."

It is difficult to keep track with the shadows so soft. The pimples are more distinct in harsher lights. Maybe he should change his strategy. Instead of counting every single one, he could just concentrate on the ones above the bedframe. One horizontal line, then one vertical line. Then multiply. Like in grade school. That sounds manageable. Doable.

"Okay. One, two, three, four, five, six, seven – eight, nine... ten..."

The problem remains. They're too hard to distinguish. Christopher squints his eyes harder. "One, two, three."

Once again, he gets sidetracked. This time, the distraction is the missing canopy. He has thought before, time and again, that a canopy bed with just a naked wood frame looks odd. Like his new bed has been a huge wooden box in its former life. Then someone got inside and kicked out the walls, leaving only the frame. And turned it into a bed.

It would be easy to make it less naked. If Christopher had curtains of, like, twenty feet – he could simply throw them over one crossbar. Then the other. Adjust the lengths on both sides, and *voilà*. Romantic canopy bed. Make that *white* curtains. Several, layered on top of one another. Slightly transparent, to let through the light.

There is no light today, he remembers. He wants to research how expensive that would be. Just a bunch of white fabric that he could cut into the desired shapes. Couldn't be too costly. No curtain rings or anything of that sort needed. Just, say, two hundred square feet of a white-ish fabric. Linen, maybe. Linen has a nice texture.

Christopher wants to research that. But if he took his phone now, he'd see the time. And he does not want to know what time it is.

It's a cloudy Sunday afternoon. He is lying safely in his bed. That is all he needs to know. All he wants to know. He also wants to know if his mother was doing okay right now. But if he asked, she'd ask him back. He'd have to lie in order not to burden her with his bullshit, and he's not strong enough now. So he doesn't.

He rolls to his side because now, the sight of the ceiling makes him sick. He rests his head on his hands.

His piano is collecting dust. He wonders if he could still get it tuned in this life.

This life.

Swept away in the realization that he will survive, Christopher's mind wanders. Over the waves, through the sea foam. To Gyth.

What is he doing right now?

Living, probably, too. Just like Christopher. He is real. The fact that Christopher is still wearing his rain-soaked clothes from last night is proof of that.

"I did scare you."

He'd looked so broken when he said that.

Gyth is a good guy, Christopher thinks as his eyes close. An innocent guy. He doesn't know just how easily Christopher scares. He's scared every time he enters his own car, because he is afraid someone was hiding in the back. He's afraid in the dark. He's an absolute wimp.

A horny wimp, lusting after this poor stranger, he thinks.

It's good they drew a line. It's better if they don't see each other again. Better for Gyth. He should not have to deal with someone this disgusting. No one should, with someone as fucked-up in the head as him, Christopher thinks.

And he himself – he'll get by. Somehow. If he was being honest with himself, he does not have the guts to kill himself. That won't happen in the near future. He's too sentimental. Plans of decorating his canopy bed are enough to keep his mind off of it. Or the thought of seeing the shelter dogs again. Hell, he hasn't moved away from Hillsburg because of those dogs. And Ally.

Besides, who's to say his suffering would end after dying?

His life is a limbo, he thinks. There has been no cesura, no turning point after that perilous divorce, like he had hoped. A hiccup, maybe. But his life just continues with the same misery. The same little joys. Repeating circles of mood swings. Around and around.

Around and around…

He sways around literally when he finally leaves the bed. He's dizzy, and his knees are weaker than usual. Circulation problems like that arise when you haven't eaten anything for over a day.

He calls in sick. He hasn't done that in years. Except during the pandemic. He is not sure if he really is sick today, but he cannot stand up straight. That seems reason enough.

In the kitchen, he makes himself a bowl of cereal. He should eat it more often, he thinks. It is so easy to make.

Depression food, he thinks with a chuckle ghosting over his lips. The tiny kitchen window lets in a bit of sunlight. It warms his back. But it is too much for the little oregano plant. Maybe it could be cockered up again. Maybe not. The leaves are yellowing. They smell of sadness.

He decides it's not worth racking his brains about. He throws it into the trash. Takes the trash out the house. Notices the leaves outside have darkened their golden colors to reds and browns. He returns to his apartment. To his bed. Wishing he could sleep forever.

And just like that, the world has turned October.

It is colder now. Not nice but helpful. With so many people getting the flu and generally being wearier, his depression does not show as much when Christopher is outside.

He is wary of the pink flashes. Always prepared. When he walks past the places where they had hit the corner of his eye before, he half-expects one to reappear. It never happens. But he stays on his toes. That eerie light lingers in the back of his mind. It does not vanish. Much like Gyth's words. About 'the monsters his scent attracts'.

Going back to work, Christopher really wishes he had not heard that part. Tammy once again commenting some new cologne that he was allegedly wearing – combined with her icy gaze and Richard's shark smile – that shit makes his skin crawl. Tigers seem friendly to what they look like now.

Christopher makes a sport of not being alone in the same room with either of them. He almost finds it ridiculous, getting nightmares of them sniffing him. But he cannot help but shudder. Every day, he thinks Tammy's nostrils are flaring wider and Richard's eyes are getting staler. Two green rocks sitting inside of an empty skull. Always watchful.

Christopher starts taking his car to work. It is just a seven-minute drive, full of red lights. But seven minutes with armor around him are better than walking the open seas with 'a target on his back'.

Gyth should not have said that. He really shouldn't have.

As the days grow darker, Christopher starts driving everywhere. Even Tony's house. His car looks wrong, parked in front of the wooden porch. The flower boxes with chrysanthemums are not quite as idyllic behind a rusty heavy-duty pickup truck from 1986, with too many dents to count.

However, it is Tony's home itself that has lost its idyll. "Your mother isn't doing great this week. She barely eats. She is very weak." Christopher hears the information and nods and says, "Okay."

"She didn't want you to worry, so we didn't call, but… it's not looking great."

"It's not your fault," Christopher says tonelessly. "I should've checked on her sooner."

Tony looks away. "What would that have changed, kid? Nothin'. No, she's… she's not doing great at all this week. Not at all. That's life."

Christopher stares at the roses on the kitchen table. Yellow, his mom's favorite. They had often bought them in the supermarket when he went with her as a kid.

How can health deteriorate inside a thriving home? How can you die when you're doing everything the right way?

He is convinced that it is his fault. He has been busy with himself these past weeks. Hell, months, if you count his time with Gyth. The grand cosmic plan is quite transparent.

It hurts to enter Mary's bedroom and not have his greeting returned. She is fast asleep. The flowery blanket heaves with her breaths. Christopher raises his walls to not cry in front of Tony. And then hates himself for succeeding – if you can hold back your tears so easily, you don't really care for your dying mother, his brain tells him. You're incapable of loving even your mother, you psycho.

The cosmic plan is quite transparent.

Gyth really should not have said all those things, Christopher thinks. To anyone else, he could have.

But not someone whose mind is already as fragile as his. It heard all that cosmic nonsense and, despite hoping that it could not possibly be true, runs wild with it.

The naked night sky might have been frightening before. But now it is unbearable. Cold and full of horrors staring back at him. No clouds, no leaves on trees to shield him. Just galaxies veering at impossible speeds, ready to spit him out at any time.

Block it out, he orders himself. Fear is a feeling, and you're incapable of those. So, shut it out.

But now it dawns on him: fear seems the last emotion left inside of him. Christopher wonders if that means he should hold onto it. Sometimes. Other times, he wishes he could just cut out his entire heart.

Richard's nervous food taps are like a drill when he asks him about 'that dude with the crazy hair that was following you all the time'. That he hasn't seen his 'made-up face for a while'. He asks if he finally realized Christopher 'ain't a fellow queer'.

Christopher's evasive maneuvers are useless against Richard's hooks.

"Man, I know he's gay for sure." Richard crosses his arms. "And he was spending so much time here. And outside. He smiled at me a couple times too often, and I didn't even talk to him that much. He must've, y'know, hinted at something. To you. He was talking to you the most."

"We didn't talk about that sorta stuff."

"I don't know, man. But it's over now anyway, right? If he ever makes a move on you again, you need to clearly tell him you ain't interested. 'cause I think he's *very* interested." Which, in Richard's mind, is the most ridiculous thing about all of this. "You were being way too nice to him," he continues, just vaguely accusatory. "You're too nice. Now, he wouldn't let go easily. But, man, those people need to know their place. He would've overstepped my boundaries, like, long ago. He just made me so uncomfortable! Now, you know I ain't a homophobe or anything, Chris, you know that. They can do whatever they please in their own spaces. And hell knows they got plenty of those these days. Which is good! They just shouldn't be bothering normal guys like us. 'cause he ain't normal. Nothing bad. Just not the norm, y'know, and he needs to accept that."

The stream of words passes through Christopher like a poisonous river. Richard has never talked to him like this before.

'Normal guys like us.'

What is 'normal'? Christopher feels far from that. He lowers the files in his hands. Still avoiding Richard's emerald eyes, he says, "A lot of crazy shit has gone down in my life over the past few weeks. The past few months." He swallows as he stares at the gray rain hitting the windows. What is he supposed to feel? "I feel like... the world is going insane."

"Amen to that, brother. Good talking to you," Richard says. He leaves to make coffee without Christopher. But it is no matter. He still looks like a fellow tiger to him, right? Not smelling of fear? Not smelling of midnight rain kisses?

What if it's not the smell? What if someone saw them?

'Normal'. It's not important to understand it. Just *be* it.

Christopher can be normal, he realizes, if none of this happened. None of this mattered. If they never kissed, no one could've seen them. Richard would invite him for a coffee another time.

Another time.

Time flows weirdly these days, he finds. Maybe that's simply because he doesn't keep his weekly planner on the fridge anymore. Days just melts into one another as he lays in bed. Another time.

October must be over soon, he thinks. The world goes to sleep. It takes his fear with it.

The stones in his stomach, butterflies from once upon a time, grow and make it hard for him to move. His train of thought can no longer pull him forward. The autopilot he only needed for a few moments a day is now his default. If he does not think about anything, it won't affect him. If he doesn't talk to Tony about his mother, she cannot get any worse than she already is in his memory. If he does not expect the pink flashes, their absence can't unnerve him. If he doesn't look Shelly in her eyes, he won't see her old soul and get emotional.

If he pretends hard enough, nothing about this is real.

The possibility has always been there. His pain was never real, and neither was his imagined acceptance by the outside world. Why should anything else be? It is freeing to no longer agonize about what he made up and what not.

He'd rejoice at the efficiency of this new technique, if he had not turned into a stone already.

He isn't even tired of this tremendous swing of his mood pendulum, or of his guard constantly being up. Tiredness would be something he could feel. Now it's all gone.

He is invincible, he learns, when he goes to Stuart's to pick up a pizza. Four teenagers are sitting by the door. They are giggling and whispering about bets. When Stuart places Christopher's pizza box in front of him, they realize he will leave soon and take their chance. In a caricature of a British accent, one of them calls, "Yo, dweeb, where's your boyfriend?" They laugh. "Hey! Hey, four-eyes, I'm talking to you! You're being a rude old fag!"

Christopher's usual body would have shut down. A single shallow breath before his lungs would've refused to carry on. Now, he's fine.

"Ey. Ey, get up!" Stuart's eyes are wide in anger when he steps around the counter. "Get yo' asses outta here! You go eat that somewhere else! Go!"

The kids laugh. "Oh my God!"

"Go!"

It is Christopher's first instinct to apologize for the scene. He is too slow to speak though.

"Chris. You all right? Fuckin' rats."

"I'm fine. They're just kids," Christopher says.

"'cause anyway, I thought it be an extra-cheese-kinda day," Stuart rants. "I put some extra cheese on there, Chris."

"Thank you."

Stuart fixates him. His face wrinkles with worry. In front of him is a man in need of help. The provident words he decides on are, "It's hard times. I know. Just – you gotta know, Chris, you can come here anytime. This is my place, and I decide who's welcomed here and who ain't."

Chris looks up at him, blue eyes all red. And empty! God, they look so old – the boy isn't even forty and looks like he was about to fall to pieces. Stuart has known him since he was seven and never seen him like this. Gone is the joy he radiated when that Brit was with him. Lord knows where that guy has gone. No one has seen him lately. Something must've happened, Stuart can feel it in his bones. He can see it in Chris' face. He knows it too well to ignore it. He wants to say, 'If I gotta paste a damn rainbow sticker to that door – Lord help me, I will.'

But he doesn't – he is not a hundred percent sure if Chris is like that after all. Like Darleen. He doesn't want no trouble, so he doesn't ask. But Lord, he reminds him so much of his daughter Darleen. Before her coming-out, the days before, where she was nothing but miserable. And that happiness all over her, when she eventually introduced them to her girl-friend – that was the same, too. The same relief, like she didn't have a care in the world.

But Stuart can only speculate. He won't ask Christopher about any of this. Just hears him whisper "thank you" and watches him take his pizza. If he knew about Christopher's mental island system, he would be the first in line to become a new island for him.

112

But for now, Christopher is gone. That an elderly Black man had to stand up for him weighs him down heavily. Stuart has it hard enough already. And now he lost a bunch of customers and caused a scene because of him.

Just a few days ago, that would have sent him spiraling. Now he's fine, he thinks.

He genuinely forgets that he has not had hard stool or restful sleep in weeks. He believes to finally be in a stable state. Not good, not bad. Stable. Away from lights and shadows.

Christopher goes on to live like this. He does not know just how thin his stone hull really is, or how badly the lights and shadows have ravaged Hillsburg beyond his gaze, until his sleepwalking ends in a fateful night by the dog shelter.

It's two past midnight when he unlocks his car. The keys clink when a scream startles him: "Help! Oh my God, please, help!" Three girls come running to the parking lot. They're supporting one another, make-up smudgy with tears. Their clothes are far too cold for a night like this, Christopher finds, shivering himself. They reveal the arm of the girl in the middle, twisted around itself. Like a fashionable candlestick.

Christopher blinks it away. "What happened?"

"Something attacked us! Something's in the forest!"

"We were camping, and… and…"

They're in panic. "Stay here in the parking lot, okay?" Christopher says. "There are lights here. And good reception. Call someone to come pick you up." He blinks at the arm, anew. It's too short. It's missing a hand, he thinks. It *looks* like she's missing a hand. But it's not real. "Does your arm hurt?"

Against Christopher's expectation, the girl nods, tears streaming down her distorted face. "It's just like that one guy's leg, that was all over my feed lately – oh God…"

He steps back. "Talk to your parents about seeing a doctor, okay? Yeah?"

"And the things…?"

"I'll go have a look."

"There's three! Sir, there's three of them!" one of the girls calls after him, her extended hand frantic with fear. "First it was, it was – a tree or something, I thought it was a tree. And then there was a second thing. And a third! It was" – she sobs loud and rough – "*something!* I can't describe it. It was – all the wrong things in all the wrong places – eyes and hairs and bones and… It was so horrible…"

"Did you see it, too?" Christopher hears himself asking the other two. *What are you doing?!* You're making it real, his brain scolds him.

"Yes! Yes, we saw it, we saw them all!"

"Are you sure?"

"Yes! God, you have to believe us!"

Please, why don't you believe me?! Why don't you–

Christopher blinks. The night air shivers against his skin. The moon is bright in the sky, when it's not covered by the clouds, carried by the cold wind announcing November. Rolling the dead leaves like toys over the ground.

Ghosting over that poor girl's arm.

Once more, Christopher blinks. "You go call your parents, or a teacher, anyone, you understand? You got your phones?"

"Yes, sir."

"Okay." He nods. "You'll be fine, okay? I'll go have a look. Don't worry." He says that, and then turns to the dark forest beyond the road. The sea of its trees gapes before him like a castle whose borders even the streetlamps' light cannot penetrate.

Maybe *he* should worry.

Christopher's steps are as firm as his body's condition allows. He'll just go in there, he tells himself. Look around a bit. Find nothing. Return home and go to bed. Sounds like a plan.

One step more. Now the leaf-covert ground rustles under his shoes and the fangs of the trees swallow him into their bony stomach.

The girls must've come from uphill. It's steep but manageable, even over the wet leaves and moss. Christopher uses the naked bushes and trees to hold onto.

His focus lies solely on climbing uphill, so that he does not see the twisted markings on the bark.

Thanks to so many trees having lost their leaves already, Christopher doesn't even need to use his phone's flashlight. The full moon brightens the entire night sky. Its pale light drops down here, too.

That's how people in the olden days navigated the night, Christopher thinks in an afterimage of daydreaming. But it's fallacious. Another gust of wind, and clouds darken the forest.

He stops to look around. The trees and branches draw all kinds of strange shapes. Silhouettes, faces. Eyes.

Like a light switch, the moon returns. The stars gape coldly down onto the forest. Christopher shivers. Just when he starts doubting that the naked branches above would shield him from the eyes of whatever was out there, he remembers – none of this is real.

Walk on. Then go home.

He staggers forward. Behind another rise, a plastic tent sticks out from the forest ground. A camping lantern, and a skull mask.

Christopher sighs. "Bravo for your Halloween shenanigans." They must have played a prank on him after all. Nothing real. One second more, and someone will jump from that tent with a phone camera directed at him.

But that does not happen.

The wind's howl makes Christopher falter. He crosses his arms; it's getting colder. His gaze wanders further uphill.

Uphill means closer to the stars. A shiver runs down his spine, his legs, into his toes. Why are those trees cracked like matches? And their branches twisted and torn?

Taking a deep breath, Christopher bends down to pick up a large branch, holding it up like a baseball bat.

You idiot, his brain scolds him. *You're making it real.*

His fingers curl tighter around the wood, eyes on the slope before him. "Come on," he whispers, mostly to make certain he still has a voice. "Come on, let's go."

Step by step, he makes it uphill. Deeper into the forest and closer to the stars. The trees above him now curve like giants, pale in the moonlight. It switches off, and Christopher stops.

Was that a growl?

Just wait until the light returns.

There. Now go on.

His heart is beating out of his chest, and he thinks it because of his bad stamina. The branch in his hands grows heavier. A path of crushed leaves broadens before him, circling the hill upwards. Christopher takes it. It drops after just a minute of walking. Behind the slope is a wide valley of darkness, shadowed by the hills so that not even the moonlight reaches it.

From there, a bear stares at him through glowing eyes.

It must be a bear. It is a bear, Christopher tells himself, holding onto the branch in his hands that now feels featherlight.

The bear charges. Or rather, it crawls forward in an unnaturally smooth motion, as though it travelled over the shadows on the ground, raising dead leaves in its storm.

Christopher adjusts his posture, makes himself bigger, and swings the branch with a scream.

The bear sucks it into its body.

Gasping at the loss of balance, Christopher stumbles downhill, twigs and leaves scratching his ankles. Above him, the bear hurls away a wooden spiral.

Is that the branch?

The bear's growls mix with clicking noises. Its eyes glow fiery red before they burst out of its skull, ripping it open like a blood-soaked flower with wet, wrinkly petals.

It is sick, Christopher thinks, just like the dog. Some sort of infection. Or an illness, maybe, that makes its split face move like a kaleidoscope, to pump forward a limp.

As the blood-covered arm hits Christopher, screams echo inside his mind. He pants, reorientating himself on the ground. Orange nail polish – that's the girl's arm. Severed.

No – that can't be real.

Christopher gasps, her coppery blood bitter on his tongue as the bear grows bigger above him, its face now lit by the moon. Or rather, what was left of it. With earth-shattering growls, it grows higher and higher, the trees around them curving, groaning, like they're trying to escape.

It can't be real, can it?

Whimpering, Christopher stays glued to the ground. It vibrates below him, ominous and strange, before turning into what feels like quicksand beneath his hands. The mossy forest now smells of sulphur. And to his right, a pink flash lights up the trees beyond the hill.

This is the end then. Just wait for it. You simply gotta wait for it.

Christopher closes his eyes.

With the boom of an explosion, a shadowy gust of wind hurls the bear downhill, crashing into a tree. It's taken countless leaves with it, rustling, and Christopher, too. He rolls to his back, gasps at the suddenness of it all. His back screams in pain. Not literally. The forest has fallen silent, too, like forests usually are at night. And he's in one piece, isn't he? Here are his hands. Two. Covered in blood and dirt. But two.

About one hundred feet away from him, the bear's fleshy body heaves painfully against the spikes of the broken tree it fell onto. It moves upwards, crunches, like bones jumping back into place – and from that impaled, shadowy mass, a dark figure emerges – screaming, curls wild around his blood-covered head as he tears his body from the gaping wound.

"Christopher! Christopher!"

Even through his hyperventilating, Christopher manages to gasp his name: "Gyth." The word makes him taste copper.

Gyth comes running toward him. Kneels by his side, eyes searching. "There was another one downhill. I'm sorry I couldn't come to you earlier," Christopher hears his husky voice say. *That voice* – it is like balm on his soul.

Though the night colors it ink-black, blood covers Gyth's skin. Like a grotesque painting.

Relentlessly, Gyth's familiar dark eyes take in Christopher's state, his trembling limbs. "No need to worry. You'll be all right," he says, placing a warm hand on Christopher's chest as though to ease his painful breathing.

Christopher believes him. God, he does. A thousand words lie at the tip of his tongue, but he could not speak if he tried.

Behind Gyth, the bear growls, deeper than before. Gyth raises his eyes to the sky. The clouds rush away even faster, as though to take cover. They reveal the full moon in all its brightness, but its steadfast light cannot reach the bent ground they're cowering on.

Gyth's brown eyes meet Christopher's again. "I know we ought not to talk again. I'm sorry I could not keep that part of our promise." His pained expression, even through all that splattered blood, softens with a comforting smile. "But I stand by what I said to you that night, Christopher. I am a guardian. I will protect you."

With that, he stands up to face the bear. Or monster, rather.

Menacingly, it continues to peel itself from the broken tree trunk, shreds of flesh tearing it across the ground. Moving forward. Its roar shakes through the ground and then Christopher's entire body. But Gyth stands before him like a shield. The wind around them picks up when he says, "Run as far as you wish, but always stay behind me."

Christopher has no idea about what would happen next. Why should he run? Could he even do that, in his breathless state?

He counts two legs. Which is something he cannot say of Gyth any longer.

His arms, clothed in that precious bomber jacket, shoot down into the ground. Once they have a hold on it, his torso starts curling forward, darkness tinting the red flesh. Brown eyes slither from the juice, giving way to a plethora of pink irises as big as footballs, before they're swallowed back into ink-black flesh. Bones crack and click as Gyth's body reassembles itself like a nightmarish toy, growing larger and larger.

The same thing is happening to the torn bear. It rolls up to them with ominous sounds of splashing blood, so much blood.

But Gyth is unimpressed. "I am here," he tells Christopher, or rather, the resounding, demonic growl that once was his husky voice does.

His body shows no signs of stopping. On the contrary, it's changing faster and faster, rushing brown flesh like water.

For a split second, the giant shape resembles a thirty-feet-version of the black dog from the shelter. Then it jumps forward, rendering any attempt of recognition futile as it clashes with the equally dark mass of his enemy, creating a crater of trees that bend to get away from the fight.

And Christopher figures – right, this would be an excellent moment to get lost.

"Fuck!"

Good thing his senses have finally returned. Following Gyth's advice, he tries making his way in the opposite direction and crawls over the leaves. Is he an asshole for running away? He didn't ask Gyth to protect him, right? Is this how you handle exes?

They are hardly exes, are they?!

Luckily, a flash of red light makes Christopher postpone these questions and get his ass going. Hurrying on the ground, he looks over his shoulder.

The moon illuminates the fight in all its chaos. The ink-black mass, now reaching as high as the trees, drips with shreds and vines of flesh and roars dangerously through fangs as large as a man, against its red-eyed opponent who tries to tear through its brown-veined throat. The bear.

It's not a goddamn bear, Christopher reminds himself, stilling. And that other eldritch thing – that's Gyth.

He is full of fire, determined to keep Christopher safe. It is a glorious task, one that he takes on more than happily. But it would be easier if dear Christopher had made his move already.

The cold air in his lungs makes Christopher gasp. By a twisted tree, he manages to pull himself to his feet. It unwinds around his hand, scared to death. "Sorry!" he calls. He has no idea if the hill seems less steep because he is standing now, or because the cosmic fight behind him has actively altered it.

Whatever the reason, he still can't go as fast as he wants to. Fuck those weak lungs and buckling knees. And dirty glasses.

"Come on… c'mon, Ennington…!"

The crest comes closer. Once he's there, he can just slide down the other side. Almost there! Almost –

A hot flash to his back sends Christopher against a thick tree. It screeches in terror, much as he when he turns around and sees the unidentifiable mass of monster bodies charge toward him from over the crest. It reeks of decay and sulphur and shit and really, every unpleasant thing Christopher has ever smelled. But that should be the least of his concerns. Out of the everchanging mass, full of eyes and fluids and bones, two powerful muscles shoot into the trees, left and right of Christopher's head. The bark curves against his back, much like he himself tries to get distance between him and the dripping flesh in front of his face.

Then it twitches – shrieks – falls silent – shimmers pink – and the two tendrils pop into a pair of arms. Human arms, attached to a human torso. With a very familiar human head of hair on top, a pair of soft brown eyes included. With multiplying pupils, but, y'know, still soft.

"I'm holding him off," Gyth tells him from inside the transmuting mass. His smile is so brilliant it makes Christopher's heart skip a beat. He tilts his head as a gesture for Christopher's escape route under the left arm. "Go there and get away from this hill. Yes, excellent. Can you stand? Very good." Another smile. "I'll take care of the bastard."

Christopher can't speak. He just stares. If Gyth's last expression was meant to be a comforting wink, well, he has failed. It rather looked like his face got sucked back into the glowing meatball through his eye sockets. The earsplitting roars return, and Christopher stumbles backwards. Away from this madness. Downhill, with all those leaves and branches that would like to accompany him on his escape.

This is a goddamned hell of a day.

Christopher curses his lungs. They can't provide him with the air he needs right now. And not this sulfuric hell – just normal, nightly forest air, please, that'll do.

His adrenaline helps him to a rock by the foot of the hill. He holds onto it with trembling fingers when the monster mass rises anew on the hilltop, bending the trees around it, at least those it wasn't cracking like matches. It's always in motion, one bodypart overtaking another, ripping it apart, tearing the

121

flesh in blacks, grays, browns, reds, and pinks, as though those were the real colors underneath. Many creatures have these colors on the inside, right? The color of organs?

Christopher recoils – a gust of wind explodes from the monsters. Tendrils grow high, pink eyes opening auspiciously, staring down. It grows fangs all around, like a demonic halo.

And then, a pink shimmer from inside the flesh reaches the outside. It is the same fuchsia tone Christopher has been seeing all those weeks. Bright and vibrant. Glittering, as though refracted by a crystal, if said crystal was constantly changing its form. It grows brighter as it makes its way down the wrinkly flesh, fringing at the ends like flames, descending, further, further, unfazed by the helpless cries that keep singing higher, drilling inside Christopher's head through his ears. But it goes on and on, scaring away the trees further and further, twisting even the night sky above it in its image.

It's feeding, Christopher realizes. That pink light. It's feeding on whatever it was eating right now.

"F-fuck…" He disappears behind the rock he has held onto, now trembling under his hands.

It's feeding on it.

Just when the shimmer and the creature it sprung from reach the ground, with the other monster completely engulfed by it, a bright pink flash ends the spectacle. The black and brown mass now folds back into a smaller shape, cracking bones and spilling blood, squeezing giant eyes into more human-sized forms. Stifled screams make clear how painful the transformation must be.

The shape it turns into is Gyth, without a doubt. Only him. No bear, no other crazy stuff. It's all there, the black bomber jacket. The dreamy curls. Even the fucking glasses. Yet Christopher can't catch his breath. No relief unwinds his shoulders, no laugh of respite leaves his mouth. He just stares.

That is Gyth. Luring the trees back into their original position as his body shrinks and transforms. Although his mouth contorts in pain as he folds back into this unnatural human shape, his name still tears from it rough and deep and raw: "Christopher!"

Christopher wants to reply, but as soon as his mouth opens, he simply draws much-needed breath.

Gyth slides down the leaf-covered hill, the forest entirely back to normal. Even an owl sends out a cautious call, now that the eldritch creatures are gone. Leaves rustle faintly in the night wind. The bear monster is gone like it has never even been here.

A forest like it's supposed to fucking be.

Gyth huddles down beside him. "Are you all right?"

Christopher shudders. That is Gyth, the same face, the same worried crease of his thick eyebrows. He reaches out, and Gyth takes his shivering hand in his. But despite the longed-for contact, Christropher rolls away. Looks away.

"He is gone," Gyth tells him. His voice is rougher than usual. From exhaustion, no doubt. His hand is still strong. "There are no hunters left here. They're all gone, for now." He withdraws, remembering that his proximity can be dangerous to Christopher. "I will leave if you want me to."

"No! No, please…" Christopher croaks, extending another shivering hand. "Stay with me, please. Please."

A sigh of relief falls from Gyth's lips. He takes both his hands in his. "I will, Christopher." He pulls him close and strokes his hair.

His body must weigh nothing to him.

The mossy scent of the forest now mixes with copper. The moonlight is not calming. It's cold and observing, and yet Christopher sweats. For a while, he shakes so hard his breaths come out as sobs.

Somewhen Gyth asks him if he can stand up. They make their way back to the dog shelter together. Gyth supports him with strong arms and kind hands.

Christopher wants to apologize to him. He needs to. He needs to talk about what the hell just happened and what he really saw. But he can't. Talking about it would make it real, realer than it already is. It's over for now. And he'd like to keep it this way.

He is trembling from the whiplash of having his previously empty body filled with thrill, a renewed crush, and now fear, all in the past hour.

He keeps his mouth shut even when Gyth accompanies him to his car and holds the door for him like it's some horse-drawn carriage. Christopher's hands close slowly around the wheel, holding onto it like a lifeline with bloodied fingers.

Gyth accompanies him home.

Christopher stares straight ahead. He barely drives twenty miles an hour. "That – out there," he says tonelessly. "Is that what killed Jeffrey Hobson?"

"Yes. Not them specifically. But other hunters like them." Christopher sniffs, fixating the road like it might split open at any moment. "Okay," he utters. But no apology, although he wants to. It's on the tip of his tongue – which he still has, right? He pushes it against his teeth. Yes. It's inside his mouth.

He hisses. The traffic lights at the intersection to Hillsburg have him on edge. Glowing red just like those eyes.

He somehow wishes they were pink instead.

By the time they reach 27 West Street, he doesn't even have to ask Gyth to accompany him inside. One look is enough for both of them to know that Christopher would not be able to make it up the stairs in his state, let alone find the keys to his apartment. Once he's outside the safety of his pickup, the night is too terrible to face alone. Cold and loud and unforgiving.

Gyth is the opposite of that. His rough hands are warm. And he doesn't need to say anything to convey his kindness. While he can make the blood on his own body disappear – God knows where it goes – Christopher has to take a shower. And he has to do that while convincing himself that nothing will jump from the sprinkler to claim his body and tear it apart. To feed on it and make him disappear.

He gets over with it quickly. Maybe it is the frightened pressure of time, or his heightened heartrate, or the fact that there is no warm water left – either way, the only blood washing down the drain tonight is someone else's.

When he returns to the corridor, he tells Gyth that he'll sit down on the couch in the bedroom now, but that he is welcomed to stay. He could simply say, 'I don't want you to leave.' Just like he could say, 'I'm sorry I yelled at you. I'm sorry for the ugly things I said. I'm sorry I didn't believe you.' He does neither.

The couch's fleece blanket is not nearly warm enough around his shivering body, but at least it is soft. It is like a shield to melt into. To shiver against. His fingers clasp it. Caress it. It's the familiar texture, even fluffier than he remembered it.

He has purposefully left the door to the corridor and its lights open. But they are like intruders in his darkness. Isn't light supposed to be comforting?

The howling wind surely isn't. It storms through the tubes, rattles at the windows. Could it carry the stars inside?

Although he is tired as hell, with eyelids as heavy as stones, Christopher can only endure the loneliness for so long. He makes his way to the kitchen. There, he stares at Gyth's motionless back. He's facing the tiny window, even though you could not see anything through it.

Well, human eyes couldn't.

"The three adolescents from the forest are now with their families," Gyth says absentmindedly.

Christopher nods. Hisses, raking his trembling fingers through damp hair. He should drink something. But when the water bottle from the fridge shakes so hard in his hands that he can't even raise it to his mouth, Gyth turns around. He whispers words of comfort as he guides him to the table, to sit down. Desperate for contact, Christopher grasps his hands.

The realization now sinks in. Not heavy, not painful. But it steeps him nonetheless. "It's all real."

Gyth sits down on the other chair, studying him. Usually, Christopher is blinded by his anxiety, conditioned not to trust his own senses. The confrontation with something unbelievable pains him beyond compare.

"That… in the exam room…" All this time, a distant part of Christopher has thought that his brain had made up images of a sick dog. A reasonable reaction that, ironically, ought to keep him sane.

His hands tremble on the table. Gyth closes his own over them. "It's all right, Christopher. I will keep you safe from the madness."

Wouldn't that be nice? Christopher nods and exhales. Closes his eyes and pulls away his hands. Not avoidant, just to wipe away his tears. And breathe in. "I had no idea…"

"You could not have known."

"You fucking told me. But I didn't believe that out there was even possible. Or you, for that matter." He sniffs and looks down. "Sorry. I'm sorry, I just don't get how you can be real. Even though you've been the one thing that always kept me grounded. It's been a shit few months." He grunts, deciding to be honest, both with himself and with Gyth, just to say it out loud for once. "A shit few years, more like." His voice is all quiet when he confesses, "You were right. It is horrifying. That whole cosmic shit. God, I was so stupid…"

"Don't say that." Gyth pauses. His next words are soft and thoughtful: "It's because you have a flawed impression of the world. It is not solid or divided into 'real' and 'not real'. It is fluid. It is everchanging. This here is an unusually solid dimension. All things have a place. And there are places certain things should not be. You people have so many sets of rules and regulations…"

Rules, yes. Christopher laughs. Rules for everything, ranging from food to who you're allowed to fall in love with. "Pineapple," he says eloquently.

The tired word strikes a genuine nerve with Gyth. "Yes! That is hard to grasp. Pineapple is delicious but undesirable on a pizza, even though you can still get it if you want to. But it's okay to put it in a drink."

"That we shouldn't have ordered, because we're men." It was meant as another joke, but Christopher is too tired to successfully hide his bitterness. Gyth isn't a man. Right?

Christopher rubs his face. "So, yeah. Many rules and regulations." With a twinge of sadness, Gyth smiles at him. Empathetically. "I believe that is what makes you so vulnerable to consumption. And naturally afraid of change."

Christopher laughs silently. "Or maybe it's the other way around. Or both."

"Perhaps."

Christopher raises his eyes. Before him sits a perfect replica of a human. Not only 'perfect' in that you wouldn't think that his body was basically a costume, or rather, a corset for Gyth's true form – also perfect as in 'beautiful'. Perfectly, uncompromisingly masculine. Perfect eyes, now round and soft with thought. A perfect voice, adorned with a wonderful accent.

Spilling from perfect, glossy, plump lips. Even the glasses Gyth formed for himself suit him perfectly.

They give him just the right amount of peculiarity. Not weirdness. The weirdness comes from other places.

Would it be wise to ask him about his home? It must be pure chaos, Christopher thinks. No rules at all. In the end, his fear about the answer is too big for him to ask. So instead, he just nods and rolls the implications around in his head.

A vast universe, with humans as insignificant and unappealing as a speck of dust. Just a bunch of insects busy with the destruction of their planet and each other, Christopher thinks.

Does it have to be like that? "As an otherworldly being…" he asks, his voice all rough, "do you think we have the potential to surpass ourselves? One day?"

"Everyone has."

Christopher smiles weakly. "Even this puny human?"

The self-deprecation conjures another sad smile onto Gyth's gorgeous face. He strokes Christopher's cheek with a flat hand. "You're a giant to me." Then a spark lights up his eyes, even though his humor stays dry. "And not just because you're an entire head taller than me right now."

A laugh shakes through Christopher's tired body. And sure enough, Gyth smiles back at him. A bit unsurely, actually. Or is it disbelief? Either way, his thumb is drawing soothing patterns on Christopher's cheek, over his beard.

He looks down with a blush. "You calm me. Fuck, you really soothe me. I even talk slower, like, my entire system is calmer. I don't know what the hell I'd be doing without you now. Or, hell, I know. Nothing good. I know myself." He smiles and allows himself to lean into Gyth's touch. Lays his own hand over his. He could stay this way. It could all stay this way, if it was up to him.

"I'm glad you're here."

Gyth's eyebrows rise, full of hope. Words bubble from him like water. "Me too. Me too, Christopher, truthfully. I am overjoyed to hear you say that." He wills himself back and looks down. Looking for words, too. "I saw you hurt and just – somewhere along the line, I found myself wanting to spend more time with you. Beyond my wish to protect you. I wanted to talk to you. And to be around you. And then, to touch you, and be touched by you, in every corner of my body, because I was so attracted to you…"

The words hit Christopher like bombs. Gyth's thumb is devastatingly gentle on his cheek before he stills his hand entirely. His voice is but a whisper when he confesses, "I still feel this way. If, after everything you saw and learned, you would still have me…"

"Yes. Yes!" Christopher is astonished to have enough breath to say this. A dam breaks inside of him, floods him with possibility. With promise.

His eyes search for Gyth's, watch him stand up from the table, kicking down the chair in the process, and rush to him – and then they close. The kiss is clumsy and desperate but strong enough to chase away the horrors of the night.

Their lips break away. Find each other again.

It's been stupid to part ways in the first place, Christopher thinks as his hands crawl up Gyth's back, the curve of his body pliant against his every touch. Gyth holds his head like it was a holy treasure, and he tilts it and gifts it with kisses, deep, deeper still –

Christopher has no breath left to say, 'I fucking missed you.' With his lips lingering, savoring, he hopes his kisses would convey the feeling wordlessly.

It's been stupid to part ways in the first place.

LOVER

IT IS NO EXAGGERATION to say that Christopher has never been kissed breathless in his life before. He feels obscene, letting his hands slide down Gyth's lean back to stroke his ass. Breaking their kiss just so he could bury his nose in the crook of his neck instead, inhaling his scent.

Gyth smells tangy and sweet. Not of death.

It's ridiculous, sitting on the tiny kitchen chair when his body is so eager, everything happening too fast and too slow at the same time.

So he stands up, gets a hold of Gyth's jaw to keep him in place for another kiss. Breaks it only to gasp for air.

Then he guides them to the doorway. His destination is the bed, simply because it'd be more comfortable – not because he has thought this trough.

But all the possible paths from here wash ashore to his mind like glittering jetsam when Gyth moans into their kisses. He pushes Christopher against the doorframe with just the right amount of pressure. His jacket looks so lewd when it's slipped down to his arms... A perfect tool to keep him in place as

Christopher pulls him closer, legs sliding wondrously against his own. "Christopher…"

Gyth's desperate voice, laced with joy, has him spiraling. The guy genuinely *wants* this.

Christopher swallows, tentatively picking up one of the crystals from his mental coast. "Do you wanna continue this?"

Even though Gyth's hands just caress Christopher's face, they are trembling with hunger. "*Yes*, I do."

Christopher takes this as a 'I'm fine'. Gyth's pupils are not multiplying. They're just… blown wide. He closes his eyes when he leans upwards for another kiss, soft and quick. Although it's a transitory caress, questioning, it lingers.

Christopher nods. "Okay. Then we'll…" He shifts his body and puts his hands on Gyth's waist to guide him a room further. "Just tell me if we should stop, okay?"

"Understood." Gyth smiles, steals another kiss. "You, too."

"Yes. Okay. Okay." Christopher collects himself. His heart is pounding in his ears, heating up his face like a volcano. "So, then… this…"

He curses himself for being so inarticulate. But tugging at Gyth's jacket has the desired effect, too. They drift away from each other. Christopher turns around to pull his sweatshirt over his head – ridiculous, right? They're going to see each other naked anyway. Still, a veil of shame lingers around him.

Around Gyth, not so much. While the debate about whether or not to leave his socks on still rages inside Christopher's head, Gyth hugs one of the bedposts that rise to the dark ceiling. His clothes have quietly disappeared into his skin. His face has eaten the glasses. Christopher has taken his off, too, making him look like an entirely different person. The change, however quickly he adjusts to it, twists Gyth's insides in tight excitement. He only half-patiently waits for Christopher to turn around, to supply him with more of this sizzling energy.

It is already straining his body. But he manages to keep himself together.

Christopher, though not a transdimensional being, fights a similar struggle. Seeing Gyth like this takes his breath away – a Greek fucking God, brows furrowed in pleasure, his erection rock-hard against the bedpost he's leaning on. There is other-worldliness in the way his muscles shift, now that Christopher knows what they are, and he can't see a ball sack. But who cares at this point?

Gyth goes adrift when Christopher takes a step toward him, and once more, their hands are all over each other. They caress and explore simultaneously, hugging and stroking, wandering and lingering.

Gyth is warm all over. Hot even, as though the core of his body was boiling. He smells incredible. Like rosewood or something. Not blood.

And his body, despite all their differences, is a body like Christopher's. When his beard rasps against his, he is once again acutely aware that he is *kissing a man*. Leaning down, he gasps, lips parting against Gyth's neck. He can feel his veins against his lips. His Adam's apple. So human, so inhuman at the same time. Both of them sigh when Christopher caresses his ass. It all comes so naturally to them...

They could've stayed like this forever, in their own little world. Christopher marvels at their quiet sighs filling the room, tender and intimate. A hiss mixes into their melody when Gyth's lips return to his body. They shower him in kisses, drinking eagerly from every touch.

But you can only reach so many places on your feet.

Sighing against Christopher's chest, Gyth descends onto his knees, tracing the dips of Christopher's hips. His mouth ghosts over his belly. He cups it with both hands. Tenderly, he nuzzles the soft trail of dark blond hair leading him further downward. Over large thighs and weak knees, and back upwards, dragging his tongue all over him. Oh, he adores those long legs!

Although he wants to, Christopher does not have it in him to support himself on Gyth's muscular shoulders. In the heat of the moment, he forgets that he is not too heavy for him. Instead, he leans against the bedpost for support. He closes his eyes, but the tension still crawls from his shoulders into every inch of his flushed body.

His brain makes him see this situation from the outside, and man, he looks ridiculous in comparison to Gyth and his trail of kisses. He suddenly finds himself so undesirable that somehow, he just wants to get this over with as quickly as possible.

He falsely believes that he knows Gyth by now and how he would react to a lover not getting it up, even during a blowjob. He'd maybe say something innocent yet hurtful. Then he'd give him a silent pitiful stroke before suggesting they do something different. Disturbed by the scars and scratches across his thighs. At least then he won't suck him off.

Gyth does nothing of the sort. It never even crosses his mind, delirious and flushing as it may be right now. But Christopher does not know that. His insecurities and fear have twisted the trust in his perception. He cannot see Gyth's admiration for him. Unlike Gyth, he cannot hear the joy of his laughing voice, or see how his blue eyes twinkle when the sunlight falls into them, once it's gotten past his delicately curved eyelashes. He has never connected his brown beauty marks into constellations, not on his neck, not on his arms. He has never seen the way his long legs bend under tables. He cannot feel the brimming excitement in his smile or the warmth of his kindness.

But Gyth intends to show him. Bathe him in adoration, as best as he can. This wondrous energy Christopher fills him, sparkling, straining, invigorating, is in stark contrast to the traces of fear all over his skin. It trembles beneath tongue and eyes alike.

Why?

He is vulnerable, Gyth understands. Wounded, in body and mind and everything in-between. A forceful alteration from before – yes, he realizes – from before Gyth himself has crashed into his world. All this time, he has thought that it has been primordial madness clouding Christopher's mind, poisoning it. It was not. These are older wounds. At the surface, they are physical cuts. Battle-scarred from fights over this body's hegemony. Deeper even, from beneath his skin, they scream for help, and more than anything, Gyth wants to become that for Christopher: help. Something, or someone, to show him that he deserves to be safe.

But he falters. This is new to him. An unknown enemy who he cannot fight anymore. Yes, someone from the past. Someone who has once hurt Christopher and estranged him from the body he inhabits in every moment of his life. Made him a *stranger* in his very own body. Who would do such a thing?

Right now, he is different. Gyth realizes it is easy to hurt humans in this sensual state. Connecting with them in this heat, then using it for violence and betraying their trust. If there has ever been any to begin with.

Violence and betrayals do not suit human creatures at all, Gyth finds. Especially not now – Christopher's body is pulsating beneath his human hands and kisses, a deep sigh emerging from his chest, touching, running a grateful hand through Gyth's hair, tangling his fingers.

A moan falls from his lips. Christopher's lips.

Gyth likes these sounds beyond the power surge they pump into his human-shaped body, pulsating and throbbing.

They're lovely. Like a song. He distantly wonders if those who hurt Christopher thought so, too.

Another kiss. Another odyssey across the shy curve of Christopher's bent shoulders. Gyth takes his time, takes him in. But he wonders just how much this human shape could take. Drinking more power, *oh*, he was about to break apart! It pulls them closer, dolorously close to bursting at his seams –

Oh, but he must be careful with dear Christopher, careful...

They sink onto the bed, always touching. Their legs entangle as they embrace, grinding against each other. Slowly at first, featherlight. Christopher wants to make sure he does nothing wrong. He wants to keep his composure and hides his face, boiling with shame, in the blanket below Gyth.

He *wants* this – desperately. He is hornier than ever. But his dick is not even half-hard.

Nonetheless, when it slides against Gyth's erection, they both tremble in pleasure. And Christopher does find Gyth moaning his name like that comforting.

His hands wander to Gyth's shoulders, to hold onto him as they try to find a rhythm.

Gyth's fingers dance through his hair, over his neck, the curve of his back, his ass, as he whispers and moans in-between kisses, sucking in desperate breaths when the tips of their cocks slide against each other. He rolls his hips upwards for more friction – wave after wave.

This could've been it, if it was up to Christopher. But in his mind, this only counted as foreplay. Surely Gyth was expecting the whole thing.

With his own dick flaccid like this, there was only one way they could continue, he thinks. Gyth is apparently not interested in oral. So instead, he could take him with that gorgeous cock of his, all the way from purple tip to thick base. An all-new experience. He'll be fine, Christopher reminds himself, he just showered.

He raises his head, heavy with lust, to meet Gyth's eyes. They're closed, framed by his beautiful, long curls, bobbing softly in the rhythm that rocks them back and forth.

Christopher's mouth is dry and his voice rough when he confesses, "I haven't – bought any condoms yet. I don't know if you wanna…"

His words trail off when Gyth's brows furrow, his lips parting, and Christopher gives in to the impulse of wanting to hold both their dicks in his hand. He reaches down, kissing Gyth's collarbone on the way, to curl his fingers around their cocks – thankfully his hand isn't cold, having wandered over Gyth's hot skin for so long now – and just holds them.

He can't help but compare. Gyth's erection is smaller than his, if he had one. He cringes at how soft he is. And at the unfamiliarity. He hasn't touched himself for a while now. Ever since last year, he thought it wouldn't make much sense.

But now…

An ecstatic moan bubbles out of Gyth. He practically melts into Christopher's touch, presses up against his body as though his own had lost control. He thrusts into Christopher's hand, again and again, back arched, holding onto his shoulders as their rhythm intensifies. His head rolls back onto the blanket, Adam's apple bopping hard against Christopher's nose before he lets out a rough laugh. His voice is but hot breath against Christopher's skin.

"S-shit… Oh, Christopher…! Keep your hand around us, keep it there. Hold us close." Slow toes curl against Christopher's legs.

So much for 'just foreplay'. "Okay. Okay, I can do that." Christopher laughs against Gyth's neck and blissfully kisses the thumb stroking over his lips. Pleasure builds up tight in him, pooling in his middle. Wave after wave after wave. He is shocked by how well they work together. Maybe, he distantly thinks, it's all Gyth, and he's just along for the ride.

Gyth carries him through it all. No demands, no conditions. Just enjoying each other. Although Christopher is careful not to crush him, they lie so comfortable, all warm and close. Gyth's leaking precum makes every movement slick and easy. He moans through it all with his heavenly voice, writhing and grinding so in synch with Christopher that, for a blissful moment, he's sure they're going to come together.

But just when the edge of his orgasm builds up, Christopher feels a vibration shake through Gyth – accompanied by a grunt so distorted it hurts his ears.

Christopher needs all of his strength to pull his cuddly body away. "What's wrong? Hey? Hey."

Below him, Gyth tries to steady his breathing through another painfully rumbling vibration – even in the dark, Christopher can see it travel through his body. And when he opens his eyes now, his pupils are separating, multiplying. "Shit. S-shit. I'm sorry. I'm sorry." His rough sentences are clipped by moans and gasps. "This state I'm in… makes it hard for me to keep this form."

Right – a corset. If a kiss has had Gyth tearing through a door, what pain must he be in right now? A pink glow travels under his pulsating skin like the shadow of a shark in the ocean. He pants, his hands trembling on Christopher's arms, his heat turned cold.

This is a no-brainer for Christopher: "You wanna change forms?" He nods to give his words emphasis. "Do it. Change."

An otherworldly grunt emerges from Gyth as he rolls to the side, away from Christopher. "No."

"You're hurting. That's not how this is supposed to be." Alert with worry, Christopher places his clean hand on Gyth's back. Cold flashes cut through its heat, shivering – and feeling eerily smooth. "This is supposed to be pleasing," he professes.

A pained gasp makes him pull away his hand. "I just need a moment to control it – this energy," Gyth grunts, his back muscles shifting under their glow as they yearn to melt. "It's leaking from me. *Everything* is."

"Then give in to it," Christopher says, as if he had any idea about how this worked. "Do you wanna give in to it?"

Gyth's back heaves up and down, and he shakes his head – white fangs grow erratically inside his mouth. But Christopher can only make out so much in the dark, illuminated solely by that dim pink light. "I can't. You're so vulnerable right now – I'd terrify you." Gyth groans, convinced that he cannot allow to let himself go. He cannot let Christopher lay eyes on the everchanging kaleidoscope of his body anew, not when they're having sex. His body is the mad thorn in every sanctum of this rule-loving world. He remembers: "'All the wrong things in all the wrong places'."

Christopher mentally kicks himself for not getting it earlier. "Jesus. You don't – you're not…" He gives up on trying to use his words and instead reaches out for Gyth's face, now covered in blood blisters.

With a gentle hand, he guides him back to the bed's center. "Here. Come here…"

Their eye contact is fragile, with Gyth's face looking like it was about to burst from the inside, desperate, sweaty. Fear spreads in his eyes. But Christopher will have none of this, not in his new home. Not when he himself has had to go through it for seven years straight.

Above his welcoming chest, Gyth gives in. He breaks down with a helpless sound from the back of his throat. His hands wander, trying to remember their movements from just moments earlier, twitching.

Determined to keep him comfortable, Christopher cups his cheek. He caresses his pulsating neck, stays calm even when Gyth grows erratic on his chest. "It's your body. Nothing to it," he says. "Do it. Let it all out."

With a guttural grunt, Gyth props himself up on shaking arms, looking down at Christopher through – six, seven, nine eyes, plopping through the blisters. His glowing back bursts open and unwinds him from the inside. "Christopher...!"

Calmly, and with a stunning amount of trust, considering that a bulk of deep-red organs is currently attaching to his shaking ceiling, Christopher says, "Go, change for me."

And so he does.

With a grunt, echoing and resonating inside the room, all of Gyth's eyes close. Following the flesh from his back, tendrils and tentacles sprout from his arms, his head and legs. The last thing that changes is the skin that touches Christopher. The slick mass swallows what was left of Gyth's human body, flowing in the air as though moving through water. Muscles shoot to the corners of the room, like a net. The bed cracks dangerously, and maybe even the ceiling – but before Christopher can worry about any of that, the world around them brightens.

After blinking a few times, he finds himself surrounded by the color pink. And nothing else. The same fuchsia tone that has shimmered from Gyth's body before.

Where is he?

Christopher's heart jumps when his naked body is guided upwards. Yeah, he is touching something supple and warm – it embraces him. Is he underwater?

Illuminated by the pink light, black tentacles travel up his torso. They're soft and moist, complete with a lighter underside and two rows of suckers each. Some are billowy, others smoother. In their coating, they shimmer with other colors. Dark tones of blue and green, and then pink again.

They don't quite attach to Christopher and yet still make him shiver. After a tender squeeze, they fuse with flesh growing behind him, then separate again, splitting into more and more parts or merging with others.

They're slow and strong but don't hold him in place. Christopher can move as he pleases; he spreads his legs just to test it. The warm flesh follows him, twirling around him, as though he weighed nothing. And just when he thinks it will overtake him – it retreats, almost playfully.

Engulfed in this net, Christopher raises his head. A giant creature towers above him. Easily the size of a mansion. Its dark body, dusted with pink buds, blacks veins, red wrinkles and silvery shadows, thickens the higher it grows, sprouting tendrils and shreds of flesh wheeling around it. A few pink eyes look down at him before dripping away. The body is in motion, erratically. Here it forms a spider leg, here a row of snow-white bones that break apart to give way to something new. Some places look like static, flickering in black tones, as though Christopher's human eyes were unable to comprehend the underlying forms.

The creature travels closer, leans down. An eye the size of a car grows from its body. Although the quick motion of the emergence unsettles him, Christopher would call its look 'fond'. It's gone just as suddenly though, swallowed by its thick lid. Soft trilling sounds echo in Christopher's ears.

He swallows, eyes wandering to take in the spectacle. With the unmatched eloquence of a lovebird, he says, "Hi."

His greeting is breathy and distorted in this otherworld but heard nonetheless. Gyth's answer echoes it in a dreamlike melody, with trills and growls. Like whale song.

Christopher laughs quietly. This is very different from the fight in the forest, and yet the same. This is *all* Gyth – he wonders how many of these movements are conscious or unconscious. How much can he move without hurting him? How sensitive is that body? Right now, Christopher doesn't even dare leaning into the touch on his cheek.

Shreds of red and brown muscles drop down from the mass above. They form a somewhat human-looking torso. Arms with eerily long fingers caress Christopher's. He marvels at the texture against his palm, changing from soft and supple to rough and coarse, full of friction.

Tendrils from the fingers reassemble into a head, or at least the shadow of one, complete with playful curls and large eyes all over. Every single one, pulsating with colorful irises, is fixating Christopher over a toothed mouth. The fangs are as long as the fingers.

Christopher does find the attention flattering, but he shivers nonetheless – he's seen what those fangs, or previous versions of them, are capable of. And his body is significantly more fragile than that of the bear monster.

From in-between those fangs, a worm-like tongue grows toward him, pink and sheening with saliva. The longer it grows, the fatter it gets, now as thick as a thigh. Its countless bumps and buds betray how soft its motion is around Christopher's neck and jaw.

He snickers. "Tickles."

But his blush goes deeper than that. All of this is Gyth trying to get him accustomed to that new body of his. And while his attempts may be clumsy, they leave Christopher absolutely charmed.

He presses a kiss to the dripping tongue. A sigh falls from his lips when the higher tendrils gently squeeze his hand. They melt away now, taking the eyes and mouth with them. For a few moments, Gyth flows around Christopher, slowly taking on different forms. Changing like the ocean's tides. From the flesh twirling around his lower half, a set of tentacles grows upward. Like being upheld by a kraken, Christopher muses, leaning down to press a kiss to the one in the front. Its coating is warm beneath his lips, and it's responsive. The muscles twitch ever so slightly.

Gyth moves it delicately but still grazes Christopher's dick, making him moan at the sensation – aflame with the possibilities of *what else this thing could touch*.

"Ohh, fuck, that was loud." His eyes flutter shut in shame before he glances upward once more. The largest part of Gyth's slithering body is mere inches from him.

"Sorry," Christopher mumbles, feeling terribly obscene. He still has his fucking socks on. He shifts his left leg, but the accidental touch against Gyth's tentacle makes him thrust forward. When he leans backward to lessen the friction, he meets the touch of two other tentacles, curving along his ass.

"Sorry. Sorry…!"

They're all still. Even the big one in the front is unmoving. It hovers over his dick. Questioningly?

Christopher is unsure how this is supposed to work. *If* it was supposed to work at all. But the one thing he knows is: he *needs* it to work.

Throwing back his head, eyes closed, he uses his left hand to guide Gyth to his dick. Gyth lets him. At first, it feels wrong. Then again, Christopher thinks absentmindedly, people say gay sex is wrong. So, he could just as well be with an eldritch monster in the first place.

His voice is but a breathy hiss when the tentacle slides against his sensitive skin. He gasps when Gyth lifts him up higher, slow and careful, to have better access to his lower half. He curls his tentacle around the base of Christopher's dick – slick and slow, it twirls around it, to the tip.

Christopher bends his back, fighting the urge to thrust forward. The sensation of Gyth's hot tentacle is incredible – it gently rubs against the slit on his glans – and then pulls him forward by his cock with just the right amount of force.

Following the motion, back and forth once more, Christopher stifles a moan. His ass is steadied by the powerful bouquet of tentacles behind him, caressing his buttcheeks, twirling around his trembling legs. And arms. He won't fall down, he's safe and sound in place.

They quickly find their rhythm. Christopher now gives in to the temptation of looking at Gyth's giant body in front of him – below him, too. Everchanging shreds of floating flesh, stroking him here and there. The whale song returns, cradling Christopher beautifully in this warm embrace.

Gyth wraps gentle tendrils around his wrists, where he must undoubtedly feel Christopher's pulse going crazy. When his eyes flutter close again, more tentacles travel up his body. Not to overtake him but to stroke his chest. Gyth attaches suckers to his torso, over his nipples, and starts sucking gently in all those places, sending sparks of pleasure through Christopher's pliant body.

A loud moan tears from his mouth, followed by labored breaths, and he desperately leans into the touch – God, he feels dirty right now –

Rhythmically, Gyth squeezes his dick. He is beautifully curled around it. He attaches the tiny suckers by the tentacle's tip to Christopher's glans to mirror the sucking on his nipples, wet and hot and soft.

He's so big, but his touches so focused, so controlled…

It *is* unbelievable, Christopher will think later, to be had by an eldritch abomination that he knows could tear him limb from limb but feeling safe under its touch. Not being creeped out. Not caring where up and down is anymore.

But in this moment, all he does is relish the bliss of Gyth rocking his body like this, soft smacks echoing through their dreamlike world. It is *all* Gyth – every deliberate movement, every bodypart.

Christopher pants. "God – I'm sorry, I'm so loud…" He laughs breathlessly then, realizing that he is talking to a giant, shapeless monster. "Silly. You can't understand me anymore, can you?"

He can't even tell if Gyth's voice – is there a mouth somewhere? – is inside his ears or his mind when he answers, "I do, Christopher. I hear you, whether you're loud or hushed. I enjoy your every sound. Along with the blood throbbing through your body in mine…"

In *that* case –

The spooky intimacy of those words tears another moan from Christopher. He tenses in Gyth's grip but lets himself fall anew right afterwards. Thrusts his hips in a way that makes his balls brush against his tentacle. Gyth gets the idea and sprouts more tendrils to curl around his scrotum, wet and slick. He takes good care of his balls, caresses and tugs at them in unison with the tentacle pumping Christopher's cock.

"Oh, fuck…"

Christopher's climax is edging closer with each movement. At least he thinks it's a climax. Maybe it's this sugary air he pumps into his lungs, or it's some sort of cosmic radiation or something worse – but either way, he feels like his orgasm will be accompanied by an explosion, and he's just fine with it.

He raises his arms from Gyth's embrace to stroke the tentacles across his chest. Gives them some love in return, caresses them when they cup his cheek and cover it with their slimy coating. He lifts them, testing their weight, heavier than expected. With even a touch as little as this, he can feel their immense power under his fingers – dynamic muscles, vigorous – and yet all gentle for him.

It's all real. Or rather, everything right now is happening, and Christopher knows that it is happening, however unbelievably his lust was raging right now. Real or not real, it doesn't matter. It is happening. He opens his eyes to take in the moving masses of Gyth's everchanging body, so pretty with its elaborate veins, brown shadows, red wrinkles and countless things to see in blink-and-you'll-miss-it moments. Tendrils curl from it happily. Some of their movements flutter, like the atmosphere was too much for Christopher's brains.

He wishes he could see behind those occasional static flickers, to comprehend their true form. But everything's a blur now anyways. A roar, like his head was about to overload. But if he goes out now, he'll be happy it's because of this sight of Gyth and the touch of his kind heat.

How many ever get to witness his spectacle and affection like this? And for *him* to ever feel like this…? It overcomes him, tears in his eyes: "Come closer… closer – *kiss me*."

He cannot tell if Gyth pulled him forward or moved toward him or both. It's not important. He drags his mouth over his hot, wet flesh, flowing against his lips and tongue, slithering inside. It faintly tastes of sugar. Or rather, the memory of it. Savoring the sensation, Christopher moans against Gyth's mass. In turn, it swallows his sobs and vibrates wondrously against the insides of his mouth and his neck, craned for Gyth as far as Christopher can manage, safely cradled by his countless transmutations, leaning back into them with sinful moans.

And, well, Gyth cannot help but delight. Now that he has assumed his natural shapes, the sexual energy surging through him does not tear him apart. It broadens him. Everything he has gathered in his human form now blossoms beautifully inside of him, and he has no intention of stopping it, however unorthodox it may be.

Christopher feels the same – all that energy makes his heart race, pounding against Gyth's touch. Gyth anticipates this same boost building up inside of Christopher, too, with all his senses. He wants to prepare for his release, to be there for him when it happens – but he himself is getting swept away by this gorgeous display in his embrace. Christopher is unwavering, so very human. Even in this carnal state, he is considerate enough to keep touching him back. He is stroking every part of him he can reach with his small body, seeking contact further and further – it feels good on a physical level, but deeper, too. Or higher? Gyth does not know anymore. His body sprouts more shapes than it can swallow. He is brimming with Christopher's magic energy. Letting it guide him.

Taking care of each other like this binds them together. But not enough. He wishes their heightened nervous systems would interweave and fuse. And feel what the other was feeling. He wishes Christopher would become his tether, an anchor for him in this vast universe. Bound together. And in turn, he'd make Christopher experience the universe and his adoration firsthand. Firstheart, first-everything.

Bathing in this bliss, human fingers form and intertwine with Christopher's. They keep transforming, changing, ever-changing, when pink sigils glow around them in the floating circle of connection.

Be one with me…!

But, just in time, Gyth remembers, pulled back by the energy release of his body. As it grows, the spell fades – oh, thankfully!

Tiny Christopher tenses in his embrace before unravelling, too. Helpless and candid, so very human. His erratic movements, his shallow breaths and arching body enchant Gyth in all their glory. He comes onto his tentacle in short and hot spurts. Hot threads of a present for Gyth, just for him.

He wraps more twitching tendrils around Christopher's body. Searches for as much closeness as two separate parts could share. He sucks and licks and strokes him in perfect unison with his orgasm, on and on and on, as they rise to the surface –

Side by side, they land on the bed. It squeaks under the impact. Both lie on their backs, utterly messed up. They make for a debauched display: colorful fluids leaking from their bodies and gasping for air as the ceiling above them returns to its solid state. It's grousing but glad to be back. As are they. Truly.

"Fuck."

"Christopher?" Panting hard, Christopher glances at Gyth's worried eyes above him. Brown and very human eyes.

"I'm fine. I'm fine. Just… catching my breath." He groans. "Oh, fuck. That was insane – and I wasn't even hard. Fuck me."

Softening, Gyth falls back onto the bed and exhales through a grin. Their voices are back to normal, too. "It was" – he grinds his jaw sideways – "very fun. Wasn't it?" He flashes Christopher the most brilliant smile, his hair all tousled from sex. Even though it technically hasn't even been there. Or has it?

Christopher rolls sideways into his body and closes his eyes. "Yeah," he smiles. "Hell yeah. It was out of this world."

Gyth snorts. "Ha. That's funny." His hand, rough and warm, is playful against Christopher's. He gently strokes his knuckles to ease his orgasm's afterglow. They're both so sweaty and wasted…

As though by magnetism, their bodies draw nearer.

"Thank you for coming so beautifully," Gyth growls, eyes closed.

Christopher's brain is too fucked to think – and too content with the effect of his ironic remark from before. "Wha… You're welcome? I mean, that's your work, buddy," he mumbles into his chest. "You turned me into this mess."

"I think it was you," Gyth murmurs blissfully. "You and your body."

"Yeah, my body. Chemicals or hormones, I guess, technically." Christopher shifts, wanting to forget the tears he has shed. He needs to get something else off his chest now that he is snuggling against a human Gyth again. "But you – um, seriously, that thing before, when you suppressed yourself like that, and it hurt you," he mumbles, "that was way scarier than your true form could ever be. I couldn't stop looking. It's so fucking fascinating."

They exchange a smile and more caresses.

"Seriously. All the right things in all the right places," Christopher emphasizes. His eyes wander when his legs entangle with a moist warmth. Gyth's lower half is still a mess of black and brown tendrils, so massive they're spilling off the bed. But they're calm now. Christopher lovingly strokes one of them before putting a cuddly arm around Gyth. He can even hear a heartbeat, in synchrony with his own. He doesn't care if that makes it artificial. He's a giant sap. He adores this.

In fact, it's all he ever wanted.

Gyth wondrously smiles down at him through messy curls. "What do we do now?"

"Now comes the best part," Christopher announces in a mumble against his chest. He drags tired kisses over it.

"Yes?"

"Yeah." Christopher tugs a large, moist tentacle around them. Though the juicy sound of its impact is funny, the warmth is comforting like a blanket. Safe as a fortress. Smaller tentacles follow it. They collect the sweat from his skin before covering them both in a snuggly hug. Then stilling entirely.

"What do I do now?" Gyth wants to know, his whisper laced with curiosity.

But Christopher is already falling asleep in his arms. He snores, his body relaxing against Gyth – at peace.

"Oh. All right. I'll just – wait here then."

A veil of bliss flows around them. A lovely moment in time.

Far away from it, beyond the stars, lurks the chaotic vortex of time. Cold and ruthless. Always and never. Krysuldom makes his way through it relentlessly. Having earned his name, his old body and conscience are heavy with experience. And grudges. He has been tracking this pesky guardian for a while now. A particularly dogged specimen, that one. A hunter as accomplished as Krysuldom, ancient and potent, needs not resort to the crude methods of those who have tried consuming that little pest before. Dilettantes, many of them not even bothering to blend with the strange dimension he has stumbled into. That would be the proper technique. One needs to lure prey before chasing it.

However, Krysuldom has no need for such methods either. Indeed, he has cast his gaze to the annihilation of this particular guardian. Too long has he thwarted the hunters' plans, disturbed their work, and gotten away with it unpunished.

Pesky fucking little guardians, the lot of them. This one especially.

Krysuldom thus plots a gruesome end for him. Sophisticated and appropriately painful. He will get to him and put an end to his oh-so-righteous campaign and to whatever has helped him disappear from Krysuldom's grid just moments ago. Gone. As though snapped away from the universe. Or hidden? Laughable. What could hide a guardian and the unbearable stench of the dirt he calls his blood from the reach of Krysuldom the Dark?

Just when the guardian's absence has begun to sow confusion, he has reappeared. Clearly. Indeed, Krysuldom thinks, meandering through the galaxies – he cannot hide from the ancient hunters, able to witness all, at any time.

Moving on, Krysuldom pays the disappearance no further mind. He *smells* the pesky little scourge, *sees* him roving about that tiny planet and masquerading as one of its bugs. He already *tastes* his death cries in his very core. A guardian torn to shreds. A warning example to his cursed little lot. The first of many to perish.

Indeed, Krysuldom prophesies, nothing will shield the guardian from the wrathful fate the ancient cosmos is preparing for him. Nothing can.

The night groans under the weight of his curse.

WATER

CHRISTOPHER WAKES UP to warmth and darkness. The shapes of his bedroom watch over his morning. When he turns his head on the pillow, his nose grazes curly hair. Dark eyes open to look at him. They're framed by coal and impossibly long lashes, and they're warmer than any blanket could ever be.

Sighing, Christopher closes his eyes and snuggles up closer to Gyth. Truly, he could stay here forever. In this dreamy haze where nothing is expected from him. He stretches his legs and delights in the softness around them, be it his bed or Gyth's tentacles. He loves it here.

But eventually, the sun pushes him out of paradise. Together with a funny smell. Christopher squints against the rays falling through the windows. Yeah, he didn't lower the blinds last night.

Last night, when he has been busy running away from monsters and then fucking one.

With the elegance of a stranded whale, Christopher shoves his arm around the bed. Gyth should be here. But it's just the blanket. Christopher props himself up. His chest heaves with labored breaths. It was a dream, he thinks. Or worse, Gyth left him. Or – Sharp clangs snap him back to reality, metal on metal. That smell – yeah, something's burning back there.

Slipping only into his briefs and sweatpants, Christopher hurries to the kitchen. He rubs his eyes under the glasses at the brightness in here. The clangs come from the pan dancing over the cooktop, led by a tentacle curled around the handle. Another tentacle pours disquietingly runny dough into it, causing more and more smoke to cloud the room. Yet another tendril shoots upwards to open the tiny window in the back, and another grabs a bottle of water to quench the heat of the cooktop, hissing painfully. Slime traces a route of misery to a soaked egg carton on the counter. A particularly thin tendril is busy trying to reassemble the tragic shards into a whole egg.

"Hello, Christopher," Gyth says in a shaky voice. He is wearing, or rather, *has grown*, nothing but his pair of black jeans. With his eyes cast down, he elongates his neck to give Christopher a kiss.

Christopher hums into it, surprised – and amused. "Good morning. Are you okay?"

"Yes, I am doing amazing," Gyth tells him. With the whip of a fleshy cirrus, he brushes stray curls out of his eyes. "It's just" – he returns his fluttering attention to the burned food – "I may have misjudged the difficulty of making breakfast. I thought you would like to be fed. It was meant as a surprise, but I am making a real cock-up."

Christopher snorts. "Well, nobody's perfect. Here, let me give you a hand." As he makes his way to the cooktop, all tendrils stop, one after the other. He's sure Gyth is staring at him right now, but he doesn't mind. Despite being half-naked. In fact, Christopher laughs. The thought of Gyth wanting to feed him is beyond cute. He turns off the stove and puts the pan in the sink. Dish soap won't do anything for this poor thing; this is a job for the tinfoil.

"How do you even know what breakfast is?" he laughs.

"I've observed humans for a bit now. A certain number of meals per day, scheduled for regularity…"

How it should be, Christopher thinks. Having three meals is difficult for him when he's in the trenches of his of own thoughts. Gyth makes it sound charmingly easy.

"…and many like to have this meal as the first one after waking up. Like pizzas. Only tinier, sweeter, and less crisp." Christopher raises the pan dramatically. "Well, this one is so crispy it could pass for a stone." He looks over his shoulder to find Gyth glancing at the burned remains of his pancake, always at a safe distance. "Sorry."

He may not be a werewolf, but he has the puppy dog eyes down to a T.

"It's nothing. Honestly, no problem. We'll make new ones, as soon as I've cleaned up." Christopher decides to grimace rather than make his even more sentimental than it already is – because usually Gyth doesn't care about what others think, right? He's so adorably nervous all of a sudden.

"Do you even need to eat?"

"No."

Christopher laughs so hard he coughs on the smoke, supporting himself on the counter. He closes his eyes with an unbelieving shake of his head – Gyth wanted to *feed* him! So, on top of being kind and quirky and an amazing kisser, he's also caring? What a dreamboat.

Christopher can't stop smiling. "You really made all of this just for me?"

Gyth shifts. "Well, I did want some, too. I always like eating with you."

A blissful laugh tears from Christopher as he turns around. He kisses away a splash of maple sirup from Gyth's beard. Yeah, he'd be happy doing nothing but eating pancakes together all day. "I know you do. Me too," he says. "It's… fucking perfect."

Gyth gives him a lopsided smile – God, he's the best.

"However," Christopher adds with a sideways glance, "I suggest we breakfast something else. Then we can clean up and have pancakes for lunch. Or dinner, hell, fine with me."

"All right," Gyth smiles when they're already halfway making out again, with his hands cupping Christopher's naked belly and two tendrils curling around his ankles.

"Urgh, I must have morning breath!"

"You taste luscious as always," Gyth tells him in that stunning accent.

Yeah. Perfect after all, Christopher thinks, smiling into their kisses.

Gyth later apologizes for the twisted handle on the pan and warps it back into its normal shape. It's more complicated to control his body when parts of it are still tingling from the afterimages of Christopher's touch.

Although he feels obnoxious for it, Christopher likes when Gyth acts a bit flustered. Almost a bit like he was when they first met. But he much prefers him unapologetic, like right now, when they're playing footsie over their cereal breakfast.

"Can I ask you something potentially crass?"

"Anything." Gyth grins as he tickles Christopher's ankle with warm claws, formed by wrinkly flesh.

Christopher hides his smile. "Did you, um… You *did* come? Right? Last night?" He'd be concerned if those meaty explosions and song had been something else.

"Ohh, yes," Gyth laughs, rough and deep. "I really enjoyed it. I have never experienced a sexual climax before."

Christopher's suspicion, fueled by insecurity, thickens. "Then are you, um… Before last night, have you done something like that before?"

Gyth grimaces. "Considering I've never been human before… I would say, not exactly like that."

"Well, not necessarily in human form. Just… y'know, doing something sexual."

"This is the first time my body has been able to produce sexual energy. It's fascinating what human shapes make possible. All those chemicals, hormones and energies are so new to me."

"So… no?"

"No." Christopher's eyes go wide. "Nothing like that?"

"No? But *something* like that. I think," Gyth shrugs.

That's good enough for Christopher. "Ahh, I figured," he says, relieved.

"Why?"

"'cause you were really freaking good," he grins. "Like, really good. Insanely good." So good and considerate and kind that it made me cry, he adds in his mind, not as remorsefully as he expected.

"So were you," Gyth says from below his dark eyelashes, almost boyishly so.

"Wow." Christopher chuckles to the table. "And you really stayed."

Gyth's eyes light up with their signature spark. "Of course. I will stay with you for as long as you'll have me."

Christopher's turns the spoon in his hands. It clings softly against his bowl. "Okay. Okay, yeah. I'll have you any day of the week."

Gyth's reply is a bright smile.

"But do you…" Christopher weighs his words. "Y'know, you'll leave. Right? When you sense danger?"

"I will. But I'll always let you know."

"Okay. Just… y'know, I don't wanna keep you from doing your job. Duty, I mean."

"Thank you for being so understanding," Gyth smiles. "If necessary, I will leave. But always return. As long as you want me to." His bare foot, with only four toes for simplicity's sake, presses playfully against Christopher's calf. It makes him blush. "Okay. Okay. Yes, please do return," he chuckles. His brain tells him how *gay* it is that he wants to move in with Gyth after having sex one time. But he doesn't mind. He likes him sitting cross-legged on that tiny kitchen chair. He likes making him tea the proper English way, as well as promising he'll buy cocoa powder to one day serve him hot chocolate.

His enthusiasm is not lost on Gyth. He ponders it when Christopher leaves to shower, get dressed and brush his teeth, over the swirl of the milk in his black tea.

Throughout their time together, Christopher's sad eyes have so patiently waited to be freed from… that uncertainty. And fear. Gyth desperately wants to pull him out of it. More than anything. That wish is vibrating in every fiber of his body. To hold him where the fear would never reach him again, in safety. Pull him from those unbearable depths that keep dragging him down whenever he tries to move against them. More than anything, Gyth wants to end that terror and help him regain his wings. But he finally admits to himself that this task scares him. A shame for a guardian. If he wants to be with him, he needs to be careful. If *he* drowns Christopher and buries him in the depths of his mind, there'd be no saying if he'd ever make it back. A guardian, leading an innocent creature into the very same madness he swore to save it from?

A shudder shakes through his human-shaped body.

No, he needs to be *careful* with dear Christopher, he thinks. And Christopher deserves to know the dangers of being with him. Unagitated.

But Gyth fails already in simply concealing his sorrow. Christopher can see it drawing circles on his back, even though it is now clothed in the black bomber jacket.

He should've gotten serious a lot sooner, he thinks. Gyth has been very different this morning. "Hey," he says, sitting down opposite of him, "what's wrong?"

Gyth just cups his teacup with a practiced smile.

For the first time today, Christopher's face tenses. His eyebrows furrow. "Talk to me."

A pause.

"I am thinking about last night," is what Gyth settles on.

For a terrible second, Christopher thinks he was having second thoughts. "Okay?"

Gyth laughs softly. "I wouldn't have changed anything about it. It was wonderful. Honestly. I'm still overjoyed that we trusted each other and ourselves like that."

They exchange a smile. "But, um…" Gyth swallows as his smile fades. "I don't quite know how to say this but – I feel the deep need to tell you that I… almost joined with you. I stopped myself in time."

Christopher tries to wrap his head around it – not literally. "Join? Is that what you… do to the bad guys?"

"No, no," Gyth is quick to say. "It's not consumption. Joining is… the purest form of connection. Sharing. Merging, blurring. It's about being absolute equals and becoming one, mentally and physically. Even if just for a few moments. It's… the most wonderful feeling."

"And you want to have that? With me?"

Gyth nods with furrowed eyebrows. Quietly, he says, "Yes. Last night showed me just how strongly I yearn for it."

A playful grin grows across Christopher's face, only partly for Gyth's comfort. "You don't need to hold back with me. I can get freaky."

But Gyth shakes head, looking at the table. Christopher cannot understand the implications. How they could heal but just as well destroy. "To join is… complicated. It's a delicate balancing act. If the spell is performed in the wrong way, the results are devastating. And so many other things factor into it. If the fractions are not equal, they cannot connect."

"Like oil and water."

Gyth strokes his mug. "One part could get rejected. And find a gruesome death. To join can be a terrible weapon."

Christopher attempts a sobering conclusion: "So, we're not equal."

"I didn't say that." Gyth lightens up as though to comfort him. "Equality is not a state."

Christopher is unconvinced. Picturing his tiny human self next to a giant eldritch horror monster makes him laugh quietly. "I don't know."

"There's no saying until we try," Gyth smiles. Sincerely, he adds, "But I'm not willing to risk a life just to find out."

I will find another way to help you, he adds for himself.

Christopher can't believe his luck. "You're so honest." Kind, quirky, amazing kisser, caring *and* upfront about his feelings?

His face breaks into another smile. "Jesus. Thank you for telling me that. I don't know if that's what you wanted to express with it but – I do feel safe around you. And that says a lot, 'cause I get freaked out by everything."

With a smile, Gyth reaches out to hold his hand.

Christopher takes it blissfully, rubbing his thumb over the rough knuckles. He then looks up, intrigued. "So. There's a spell? You gotta at least tell me the spell."

Taken aback by Christopher's enthusiasm, Gyth clears his throat. "Translated, it would be something like… *You and me, from me and you, taken and given and found. A part from me, now no more parted.*"

Wow. "That's beautiful." Christopher raises their inter-twined hands in the hopes they'll cover his blush.

Gyth smiles at the enchanting touch. His gaze falls to his tea. It has perfectly mixed with the milk, creating a fluid in one consistent color. Somehow, that serenity gives him hope.

When he looks up again, his fingers, still held in Christopher's hands, have melted into tentacles. "Oh, sorry!"

But Christopher just smiles and kisses them. "No, they're cute." His laughter is glowing with adoration. And that is pretty much what the rest of their Sunday does, too: glow.

They kiss and cuddle. Cuddling can truly be incredible when it's without expectations or conditions, Christopher finds. They procrastinate tidying the kitchen but eventually do it together, to the musical backdrop of Christopher singing princess cleaning songs from Broadway. He also teaches Gyth how to properly make pancakes. They eat them together, over afternoon TV.

When Gyth does eventually leave to fight a monster, Christopher looks out the sunset window like a damsel waiting for her knight to return. He eventually strikes a few chords on his guitar to pass the time.

Gyth hears them when he returns. Though he is eager to see Christopher singing, he realizes it would be more appropriate to enter his home through the door rather than materializing in front of it. So, he melts backwards through the wood to knock.

But Christopher has already seen his filamentous shapes floating in the corridor. "Who's there?" he grins.

"It's me! I'm back."

Christopher mockingly lowers his voice. "Password?"

"Um…"

He opens the door. "The correct answer is, 'Honey, I'm home'," he tells Gyth, but his voice trails off when he sees that he is entirely soaked in deep-red blood. "Jesus fucking Christ, come in – you okay?"

Confused, Gyth asks back, "Yes? Oh, this isn't mine." A quick pink shimmer eats the blood away. Stepping inside prim and proper like nothing happened, he brightly asks, "Would you like me to call you honey?"

Christopher stares. He exhales through a laugh as he fumbles to shut the door. "You can call me whatever you like." He quickly leans for a kiss to swallow down any pet names he'd call Gyth – babe – sweetheart – or *big guy*...!

"All right," Gyth says in-between kisses. "Christopher."

Pulling away, Christopher bursts out laughing. But there's no denying that his name sounds very fancy in Gyth's accent. As does 'Monday Station'. Christopher declares it the next morning when they roll out of bed together and Gyth mimics his words like the dork he is.

Picking out clothes, packing food, leaving the house – everything is more fun together. They wave goodbye when Gyth drops Christopher off by the post office. "Four o'clock-ish here again?" Christopher asks.

Gyth shifts his feet in embarrassment. "You will call me, right?"

"Yes," Christopher laughs, "I'll just call you. See you then!"

"Goodbye, Christopher," Gyth smiles. He then sharpens his senses to scan the area around the post office. Over the street, further away – *there*. Another hotspur.

None of the supermarket employees notice the veiny shadow crawling through the warehouse. Scurrying through the shelf canyon, it takes on Gyth's human form, just to be sure in case there were humans here after all. At the end of the corridor, between the Monday special offers and vegetables, a small woman puts her hand on the doorhandle that separates her from a supermarket full of clueless people.

The cracking of Gyth's transformation makes her head snap. Her eyes widen beneath a receding hairline. "Are you lost, sir?"

Gyth doesn't consider her worth answering. To complete her disguise, she even went through the trouble of copying a name tag, not unlike Christopher's.

"Sir? You're not authorized to be here."

In contrast to her innocent tone, a tendril crashes into the shelf right next to Gyth's head. Having anticipated the movement, he turned in time, using the momentum to kick the huntress off her human-shaped feet.

He attaches to her shoulders, holding her in place as she squirms, kicking her feet against the door. Gyth hurls her in the other direction. Veins pop on his human arms as they tighten around her head. "I said, your hairy asshole has no fucking *jurisdiction* here!" she screams in distorted tones, eyeballs inflating.

"That's a nifty word for such a vile little bitch."

With that, Gyth unceremoniously splits his head open to make room for a tongue dragon to devour her. She tries melting through his grip but only entangles further with his body in the process. He sticks his tongue, now the size of a human itself, meticulously down her body. It creates flowing bulges in her torso before tearing it open to reveal purple shreds of flesh shuddering in fear. Blood splatters across the Monday offer onions ere melting into the depths of the cosmos to rot.

Of course, Gyth's pink light prevails. Though important – the humans in the supermarket should be safe now – this is quick and easy work. A guardian's 'bread and butter'.

Not unlike Christopher, who has a duty, too. Sorting letters and packages, outgoing and incoming, processing mail all day.

Today, there is a spring in his step and a hum on his lips. If Christopher has been annoying on Mondays before, that does not even begin to compare to his rose-colored glasses now. They're heart-shaped and glittering and about as obnoxious as metaphorical eyewear can get.

A large chunk of what contributed to those rose-colored glasses is the freedom – yes, *freedom*, Christopher finds – of not wasting his entire time with Gyth together fucking. They've shared other forms of intimacy, too.

He has only spent one day with him after the forest fiasco. In that time, they have eaten together, cleaned, sung and danced, cuddled, made up stupid jokes, and watched reruns of '90s FBI shows that Gyth has been so charmingly enamored with. And before that, they've gone on dates. Hell, Christopher has taught Gyth the basics of baking, and how to break open an egg without soaking the entire kitchen. It is nice, he finds, to do actual activities with a partner. He is not used to that.

At the same time, an ugly speck covers his impeccable rose-colored glasses. While he's glad Gyth doesn't ask anything of him, Christopher likes remembering their roll in the other-worldly hay. Images of Gyth's powerful tentacles flash by his mental eye at the printer, the back office, even the front counter when Tammy asks him there for help.

He sees a stamp and thinks, *Gyth could use any part of his body to wet it*. And for that, Christopher feels dirty. He feels filthy at the memory of how readily he would have accepted having Gyth up his ass, when all he had ever even close his butthole was his own finger back when he was a teenager feeling rebellious.

He thinks it contradictory, hypocritical even, that he's glad to not be a living sex toy anymore while simultaneously yearning for Gyth's flowing flesh throbbing against his mouth.

But before he can spiral down this fallacy, another idea burns brightly into his mind. The pet names. Gyth would definitely be a 'big guy'. Or a 'sweetheart'. 'Darling'.

Christopher rolls the word around in his head and before he knows it, it has transformed into an avalanche. Images of that pink colored world crash into him like a fucking tsunami. Gyth would hold him up in that muggy brightness, every part of him exposed and cherished – he'd fuck him so hard his eyes would turn back inside his head – but with tentacles stuffed both inside his ass and his mouth, he wouldn't be able to call Gyth any pet names, would he? He'd pull out to hear him say it. And then respond, while continuing to fuck him senseless. 'Oh, you are my darling, too! My darling Christopher...'

"Chris? Hey."

With a bright red head, Christopher blinks at Richard leaning over the table. Thank God he has ED, or else his coworker would have gotten a very pictorial glimpse inside his mind. He's been thinking about Gyth all day. In a cold shudder, he wonders if this was eldritch obsession already.

It isn't, of course. He's simply infatuated. But that too, like so many other things, needs to be learned first. "Y-yes?"

"Hey, buddy. How long do you plan on being here today?" Richard chirps.

Christopher checks the wall clock. "I'm scheduled 'til four."

Richard nods with a tongue in his cheek. "You got an appointment?"

"No," Christopher says, putting down his pen. "Nothing in particular." It's a lie of only three words, but he smiles when its meaning sinks into his mind: He can do whatever he wants.

"Ahh, okay, good. 'cause got this *thing* at three, and I will need to leave early."

Christopher decides to let him dangle. "Did you speak with Eleanor?"

Richard flashes him a purposeful smile. "No, um – Chris! I thought you could help me out with that, y'know? Since you're working anyway."

"Sorry, Richard, not today," Christopher smiles.

"Really?"

"Yeah."

Richard's tongue is frantic inside his cheek as his patience leaves him. "It would be really helpful if you did, man."

"No, sorry."

It should be strange that, of all emotions, it is disbelieve that brings liveliness back into Richard's dead eyes. "Okay. No hard feelings. It's just…" He nods frantically. "There was a time when it wasn't a problem. That's why I asked."

"Okay."

"Okay." Richard clears his throat and leaves. And although Christopher enjoys his little victory, a sting of shame stays with him. Can Richard know that he just wants to see Gyth again? The 'not normal' guy?

It was stupid to let him drop Christopher off at work. The rose-colored glasses shatter on icy ground. You're in the wilderness, dammit, Christopher's brain tells him. You gotta stay on your toes. Enough with the daydreaming.

Another glance at the clock – three hours until he needs to maneuver around his colleagues seeing Gyth.

Gyth spends that time looking for other hunters, or at least the smell of their traces. The next one that his nose – that's the organ he can taste with, too – leads him to has switched from humans to even more vulnerable victims.

Gyth makes quick work of his nasty ass.

He doesn't realize that his blood-soaked body might be counterproductive in approaching the survivor though, a large isopod – oh, it is no isopod! Gyth has rescued a small monster, just as otherworldly as him. The legs of their disguise have grown all the way up to their back, fangs eating away at the hairless skin from where the hunter has grabbed them to savor the protein-rich flesh.

Gyth curses himself for not getting here earlier. Carefully extending some tendrils, he crawls closer. Relief warms him as he touches the traces of connection all over the alleyway, proof that their pack members have been able to flee in time.

The small monster squeaks, though still strong enough to change shapes. They do not communicate verbally with Gyth but instead show their distress in body language. Bubbles of fear come and go on their skin. Still, they stay feisty, snapping at Gyth's extended tendrils. They're fine then.

This world is dangerous now that it has become a new hunting ground. It would only be a matter of time before this little one met their untimely end. This is worrisome. Gyth only wanted to stay here for as long as the hunters found their way here. Now the hunted are stumbling into this dimension, too.

And Christopher is here as well.

The small monster sniffs Gyth's tendrils, then trills when he caresses them. Should he take them with him – like a rescue dog? Gyth discards the idea immediately. Too dangerous. But Christopher would surely *talk* to them, like he had done to instill that profound calm inside of Gyth during their first meeting, so Gyth decides to do just that: "It's all right, little one. I am friendly. I can get you home if you… stopped fuckin' squirming, bloody hell."

Okay, Christopher's wouldn't say it like this.

After his clumsy speech, Gyth opens a rift to the cosmos' feral dimensions, making this world fall it into its well.

The monster gives him a look through pitch-black eyes.

To his own surprise, Gyth instinctively smiles and gestures for them to leave. "Go!"

As though they understood him after all, the little one trills as they scuttle through the rift. Gyth closes it behind their little antennae. Helping helpless creatures like this one always leaves him with happiness. He wonders if Christopher had felt the same when he had helped him back at the shelter. He must feel like this with every rescued dog, surely.

Gyth eagerly awaits his call.

So eagerly, in fact, that he accidentally melts through the ground once the sonar of Christopher's voice reaches him. A woman stops dead in her tracks. The shopping bag she drops onto him makes him remember he should probably enter this dimension someplace else.

"Hey," Christopher greets him. "Wow, this really works."

"Of course," Gyth grins, stepping around the corner with a hand on his head – perhaps groceries include brick stones, who knows?

Christopher wiggles out of his hug rather quickly. Without getting into it, he suggests walking down the street to go home. Gyth has no objections. But he does take note of the way Christopher's hands clench around the shoulder strap of his bag. The image brings back unpleasant memories.

Christopher asks him about his day. Sure enough, he delights in the story of the little one flying back home. Still his voice and eyes are restraint. Even when they pass by a place Christopher describes with the words, "Aw, man, I've always wanted to go here."

Gyth stops walking to take a look. It's a brick building like all the others, with a white marquee and frills. "Then why don't we go inside?"

Christopher bites his tongue – he should've seen that coming. Of course Gyth would've wanted him to go buy donuts. He can't know that his ex-wife has been forbidding him to go there for the past two years, shortly after the place opened.

"We can buy food here, can't we?" Gyth's gaze is warm.

"Yeah," Christopher goes, courting apathy. "Donuts." He softens when he remembers Gyth's favorite flavor. "They're sweet, you'll like 'em. Let's get some."

"You, too," Gyth reminds him as they step inside. The entire shop is filled with flowers and frilly vintage furniture – maybe his ex hasn't been afraid of him getting fatter but gayer, Christopher muses with a sad exhale. "I don't know," he tells Gyth with a sting in his stomach. "I'm not hungry yet." No assistant either.

"I'll go buy you one for when it's feeding time," Gyth says, and his matter-of-fact tone pulls a laugh from Christopher's tired face. He knows it's better this way, so why should he fight it? "Yeah. Yeah, all right." He glances at donuts in the glass display. "I think I'll take one with applesauce. You?"

Gyth studies the letters with the same intent gaze as the menu back at Brian's. Just when Christopher thinks he might not be able to actually read English, he says, "They all smell delicious." He presses his lips together. "How could I make a choice that I won't regret?"

"I mean, we can just come here again," Christopher suggests before he can stop himself. Gyth flashes him a grin before sinking back into thought. He reminds Christopher of when he was a kid, so indecisive. That makes him wonder: "How old are you anyway?"

Without thinking about it, Gyth says, "Old."

Christopher raises his eyebrows. "As in… not as old as 'ancient'?"

"I have never given it much thought. There are no time units or age datings where I come from. Just… age, I guess. I do roughly understand how time works," Gyth tells him.

'Roughly'. Okay… "I mean, I can understand your confusion, so… It gets dark, a day ends. A new day, with new breakfast and such, starts when the sun comes up again." Clumsily, Christopher adds, "Or, from your cosmic perspective, I guess, when the Earth circles around it in a way where sunlight hits the planet's parts we're standing on."

"Yeah, for that rule to work, you'd have to be on a plane of existence where you can notice the sun," Gyth says, still without looking at him.

Christopher nods to hide his astonishment. "I guess it *is* difficult, if you put it that way."

Finally picking up on the awkwardness, Gyth straightens his posture to look at Christopher instead of the donuts. "I mean, for you it's natural. It is your everyday plane of existence," he acknowledges.

"Yeah. It *is* hard to… not 'notice' the sun." Christopher frowns but can't let it drop. "Let's say you would've been born in this dimension – plane of existence, I mean."

"How old would I be if I was from here? I don't know." Gyth stares into the middle distance through his self-made glasses and sighs in concentration, using the Earth's core as well as nearby celestial bodies and their atmospheres as references. "A few hundred millennia? Give or take?"

"'Give or take'?" Christopher laughs. Yes, he actually laughs over this difference. Maybe in the future he'll worry about them finding it hard to relate to one another, he thinks in the back of his mind. That's how these things go, right? But right now, he's simply charmed.

Gyth is, too. He smiles at him softly and eventually, after the assistant noticed them, orders a donut so sugary it's giving Christopher second-hand diabetes just by looking at it. But Gyth loves it. So much so that they indeed come here the next day, too, when he orders five of that same donut.

"These four on display are the last ones we still have, I'm afraid," the assistant tells him.

"Can I have those four?"

"Of course! Right away."

"Thanks." Gyth studies her hands, with colorful nail polish and rhinestones. "Your nails are very beautiful."

"Thank you!"

The comment makes Christopher nostalgic on their way home. "Y'know, I thought you wore nail polish before. I was kinda surprised you didn't, in fact. It'd suit your style."

Gyth lowers his first donut to look at his nails. They grow and darken, while mimicking the colorful rhinestones of the girl – fashionable. But now Gyth can't hold his donut without destroying it. He grimaces at the mess in his hands. "Wow, that is – very impractical."

Christopher snorts. He could've known Gyth would want to try it out, but he's still surprised.

Gyth pauses anew, concentrating on his nails. "Just let me…" They shrink. With a meaty sound, the rhinestones sink back into the blackness. "There. Better." He grins happily at Christopher, his brown eyes full of excitement. It's a gorgeous spark amidst the dark on his features. Aided by the contrast of his eyeliner.

Coquetting, Christopher whispers, "Hello, handsome."

"I bet they would look handsome on you, too. Ah, but you'd need to get paint for yours first, wouldn't you?"

Him? In a shiver of internalized fears, Christopher clenches his shoulder strap. He glances around Main Street to check if someone was staring. If they did, he looked away too quickly to actually notice. "I'm not… I don't think I'm the type of person to pull this off," he mumbles. "I'm too old. And old-fashioned. But for you – You're looking good. You honestly do." He is proud of himself for saying this instead of telling Gyth it's another unwritten rule that only women can wear nail polish. That would be cruel. Gyth looks at ease and, indeed, kind of hot with nail polish.

Gyth theatrically raises his chin. "Thank you, young man."

"Okay, *old man* – now eat your donut, will you?"

"I bloody will."

But even without long nails, Gyth struggles to take a bite. The sugar coating and syrup filling escape his hands and mouth.

"There's only so much food you can actually eat gracefully," Christopher says, trying to console him, before Gyth elongates his tongue to catch the sugar that keeps falling off. It's not exactly discreet. Christopher looks away but still laughs. "Okay, I stand corrected."

And he laughs again when Gyth downs the entire donut in one go.

As much as Christopher enjoys walking with him, the outside world is still the open sea to him. He only truly relaxes when the apartment door closes behind him.

Right now, the most wonderful island to stay on is his bed. It is not strange for him to share a bed with Gyth, who leaves for his nightly monster battles without waking Christopher once. He adores sleeping together. Christopher surprises himself in that regard. When he had slept on his own for the first time in years, he had thought about how he would surely resent ever sharing a bed again. Having someone so close, always watching, always ready to touch him. To Christopher, a bed is only now a bed again, and not a serving plate anymore.

With Gyth, desire grows naturally. They cuddle tonight, as they have done before. Lying on their sides in their underwear, facing each other. Exchanging caresses as though their hands were their blankets.

The unfamiliarity of the black nail polish catches Christopher off-guard again and again. Curiously, he raises Gyth's hand and turns it in his. He presses a kiss to it.

Gyth's first reaction is a giggle. But soon, his voice starts to shake. Christopher's lips travel over his rough knuckles to his fingers and fingertips. His kisses are most pleasant on the tips, where human nerve endings bundle so extravagantly.

Cosmic energy pulsates against Christopher's lips. It reaches out – tiny suckers connect to his lips from the fingers' skin. He drags his tongue over them for more contact. Just when he wants to take them into his mouth entirely, Gyth sucks in a shaky breath. "Christopher, I…"

That husky voice makes it hard to reply. "Me too."

"*I want you*," Gyth utters. He props himself up, hovering over Christopher with his long curls like a curtain around their heads. Holding back.

That restraint still staggers Christopher. "K-kiss me," he stammers, so quietly he can hardly hear himself. Gyth nuzzles his nose, cups his face, then his lips crash down. With them, he rolls his body against Christopher's. His everlasting waves…

But then he shifts to lie on top. Straddles his hips, too quickly, too easily.

Christopher's smile dies in his kisses. They're now stale instead of sweet. His brain screams at him: This is the same as –

"Stop," he breathes. His legs are numb. The paralysis suffocates him.

"Christopher?"

There, he can move. Or at least transform his shudders into movement. Like a fish on land, Christopher rolls to his side, to get out of this *position*. Pressing his legs close. He half expects a shadow looming in the doorway, staring him down. But the door is closed and made of wood. It's only the two of them.

Then it is not the same – not the same as back then.

Gyth's warm voice, though tinted with worry, is balm for his psyche. "Have I hurt you?"

Christopher takes a deep breath, sucking in the air like he wasn't sure when his next chance would come.

It might have felt the same. But it wasn't.

"I'm fine," he says. "I'm fine, I just – I had something like a flashback or somethin'." He meets Gyth's puppy dog eyes.

They ground him. As do the inhuman, pink eyes that now retreat back into his shoulders, and the labyrinth of tentacles pooling around them.

Gyth is with him, she is not.

"It's – when you climbed on top of me," Christopher explains. Heat settles in his cheeks. "Maybe don't – sorry, but I think it'd be better if you w-wouldn't do that again."

"Don't apologise, please," Gyth says, softer now that Christopher has regained some color. But the shock lingers in those bones – he has seen glimpses of what Christopher has seen, sharp like a knife. He is glad Christopher has been able to pull it out of his head on his own.

"It's not that I want to tell you what to do or anything..."

"It's all right," Gyth assures him, stroking his temple. "Top or bottom are not important to me anyway. Your body is loveable all around. I'll have you any way you desire."

If anybody else had said that to Christopher, he would've called it a night. But with Gyth, he knows it's true. He's experienced it firsthand – eldritch sex knows no such dimensions – and Gyth is the kindest guy he's ever met.

He laughs, and Gyth joins him, relieved. "Do you want us to stop? And do something else?" he smiles.

Oh, damn it, *how* can he be so considerate? "No," Christopher goes as he sits up on his knees. "Actually, I've..." He swallows and rubs his face to gain time to think. How do you talk about this stuff? "I've sort of prepared. For something I thought that we could maybe... y'know, try out."

"Yes?"

"Can you..." Christopher closes his eyes at the return of his filthy imagination. He's washed himself in the shower and used a hand mirror to look at his ass. It's still a dirty place to him. His brain is still trying to tell him it's depraved. Looking at his asshole alone has made him feel vulnerable. But he also remembers his daydreams about Gyth. And he's seeing him in front of him now, sitting on the bed amidst his dark tentacles, with their red wrinkles and blue-ish shimmer before mixing into his brown skin, and he's looking at him all soft. Patiently.

Christopher exhales. "Okay. I'd like you inside of me. Please."

Curiosity widens Gyth's eyes ever so slightly. And they darken. His lips fall open in a smile but don't say anything.

Christopher gives him a pleading look.

Gyth blinks and reaches out to caress his face. "All right."

With a sigh, Christopher leans into his touch. "I've never... y'know, I've never actually communicated about this sort of stuff. It's hard. Goddamn." He smiles shily. "I feel like a bumbling teenager."

"It's all right. If you cannot talk about it, perhaps... show me what exactly it is you would like."

Christopher exhales. "Okay? Like... here." He raises a tentacle from the bedsheet to his mouth.

Once again, pure lust swirls through Gyth's eyes, intensifying his gaze – Inside of Christopher's mouth? That tiny little space? The thought alone sends sparks of desire through his body.

Christopher blushes as he guides another tentacle to his ass. "And, um... here." Gyth just nods with a soft smile and caresses his face, pupils blown wide, all sex-drunk – his gaze is so intense it could make knees buckle.

"All right. If it's what you want, Christopher," he verbalizes, "I'll go ahead and make love to your wonderful mouth and your pretty bum."

Christopher laughs quietly and looks down. "Okay. Yeah, exactly. All right. We have that out the way then."

Gyth's hands still. His eyebrows furrow when he asks, "Can I kiss you again?"

"Yeah, of cour–" Christopher's answer is muffled by Gyth supple mouth. Both his subsequent apology and Christopher assuring him it's fine are lost in-between their kisses. Every time Gyth's tongue changes its texture, shape or length inside Christopher's mouth, their intertwined fingers squeeze. But even kneeling like this, Gyth won't be robbed of the pleasure that comes from exploring Christopher's torso in this upright position.

Christopher's eyes are closed. But the faint cracking, accentuated by soft gasps, announces another body change. Sooner than he knows it, a new pair of hands is caressing his belly. Gyth adores touching it for some reason. At first, his hands only rest on it. Then his palms draw circles, fingers dancing tenderly over the soft fat. But with all the sexual energy rushing through him, his hands soon travel further.

Gyth leans back onto the bed and takes Christopher with him to lie on top. He moves his hands around him – his arms must be unnaturally long by now – to slide under the waistband of his briefs. Again, his hands rest there at first, taking in the sensation of each bodypart they're touching. He caresses the supple flesh before he sinks his fingers into it.

Christopher stifles a moan in the croak of Gyth's neck – he has thrust against his rock-hard cock, now pressing firmly against his own.

Gyth is on Cloud Nine already. The friction of their clothing is a whole new sensation, and he likes it. But not as much as naked skin on skin, slick and hot. With but a thought, his own shorts submerge within his lap. He pulls down Christopher's waistband just far enough to make the tips of their cocks touch, ever so brief – it sends another vigorous wave through him.

Christopher pecks his face before a sigh falls from his lips. "Please, Gyth…"

As if Gyth would forget his wish!

The hands below Christopher's briefs shift. While one keeps kneading his ass, the other transforms with a wet sound, brushing against him gently. "I will gladly enter you, Christopher," Gyth whispers. He closes his eyes – he has learned by now that taking away one human sense heightens the others.

Already, the first touch makes him greedy for what's to come. Christopher's asshole has a rim of muscles and nerves around it. Its tension shows Gyth it is a sensitive bodypart in more ways than one: both pleasurable and vulnerable. Another entry into Christopher's body, deep into it.

It tenses so beautifully against his tendrils...

But before that, Gyth travels further down. The perineum below the hole is soft. Through the curly hair, he touches Christopher's balls and marvels at how heavy they are against his thin tendrils. He wets them gently, sliding against the creak where they meet his cock, then lifts and lowers them with his tendrils and rolls them around in them.

But despite Christopher's hums, this is not the part Gyth will pleasure right now. Patience is a virtue, as humans say.

With his breathing heavy from desire, Gyth pulls Christopher closer. Christopher writhes when the freshly formed tentacle slides into the crack of his ass, pulling him toward Gyth in a rocking motion. It then melts past the sensitive muscles of his rim, inside of him – faster and thicker than he'd like.

He hisses, tensing upwards to try and ease the pain. "Ahh, fuck!"

Instantly, Gyth shrinks inside of him, slithering backwards. And that alone pulls a moan from Christopher. Gyth kisses his sweaty forehead. "I'm sorry. Forgive me, I was too brash. I will not go that deep again unless you want me to." He smacks his lips. "Is it better now?"

Unfamiliar, still. But definitely better. "Hm-m." Filling him up, just sitting inside of him, wet and warm for him and his every wish – "Yes, perfect." Christopher resumes breathing and no longer clenches Gyth's shoulders. His entire weight rests on him now.

He could swear the tentacle twitched ever so slightly when Gyth whispers, rough and warm, "How long do you want me to stay still, Christopher?"

Christopher presses a kiss to his collarbone. It's like jelly under his lips – God, that's kind of cute. "I think I'm ready now."

With a quiet gasp, Gyth starts moving. Christopher's inside is hot and full of new walls to flow against, full of nerve endings. He slowly makes his way further down before retreating again. Thickening and thinning, curling and pressing against those walls, unable to grow further – except deeper inside, past that curving…

Christopher feels heavenly, being worked open like this. He heaves his head up to look at Gyth. He has closed his eyes with his head thrown back in pleasure. Below them, sliding against Christopher's thighs and calves, his bottom half continues melting into countless tendrils and tentacles, big and small, soaking the entire bed with their erratic movements.

Christopher smiles. "You like that?"

Demonic undertones vibrate through Gyth's hum. "Your legs… And the inside of your body, it's so tiny and tight and hot – the loveliest confinement – you lovely human, Christopher, you feel *so fucking good*…"

On his last word, Gyth grabs his ass tight, then caresses it as though to soothe him. He repeats the motion softer, to contribute to their slow rhythm.

Blissful as he is right now, Christopher can't help but blush at the weird dirty talk. He likes all the things that Gyth calls him. Even more so in that voice!

"Good. 'cause you do, too. To me," he pants, leaning into his touch. He can't think of the last time he moved his ass this much. It feels like he's being fucked from behind. Except this is Gyth, and he's below him, and 'anatomically correct' is a hilariously inapplicable concept to this situation anyway.

All slow, Gyth moans as his curling tentacles travel up their bodies, soaking wet. Christopher kisses one. "Change. Whenever you want to."

Gyth smiles through a silent moan. "Not yet. Not yet." He catches Christopher's lips in a kiss. "First I need… to garner more of this *sublime energy*." His husky voice trails off in a moan when their cocks rub against one another. Christopher's heart skips a beat as Gyth tears his briefs like a piece of paper. That mindless show of strength has him gasping in his arms – yet again he wonders how Gyth can be so gentle with him, with all that cosmic power pulsating through his body.

Now that Christopher's briefs are gone, Gyth can move his tentacle freely. He slowly twirls it into Christopher, giving him a kiss before pulling out even slower.

"Oh, that's – that's perfect…"

Gyth's reply is but a gasp.

He growls lovingly in Christopher's ear, a gentle hand on his neck, when Christopher reaches between them to get a hold of their cocks in the way Gyth liked so much during their first time. He strokes his thumb over the leaking tips, rubbing his palm over their bases, his hand sinking into the hair around them as he moves.

Gyth replies by pushing himself deeper into him, then out, then inside again. Each thrust fills him with more heat, more pressure behind his eyes and in his cock.

It is a lovely cock, Christopher thinks absentmindedly. It's so heavy in his hand, so masculine –

Why is it in his hand?

The wish to be fuller overcomes him like an avalanche. "Can you – I want more. Please." He expects the tentacle in his ass to thicken, like Gyth had done before – instead a second one eases into him. It's less smooth than the first one, with its suckers creating marvelous friction all round his closing muscle as Gyth moves it – sometimes in unison with the first one, sometimes alternating. Always so slow – God, this is the pace of paradise.

That fucker must've done this a thousand times already, Christopher thinks, that's how good he is at it. But the new tightness even has Gyth on edge: "Yes, confine me, constrain me…"

Christopher honors his not-so-strange request by clenching his muscles and squeezing their cocks in his hand at the same time. Gyth's reaction is a demonic growl so powerful it vibrates in Christopher's brain, pulsating just like his tentacles.

"*Oh…*"

"Fuck…" He joins the rhythm Gyth heaves into his ass. And when a bouquet of tendrils rises next to his head, he catches them between his lips and sucks. It's a lot to take so suddenly, but damn, if he doesn't find this hot…

And he's not alone. Gyth squirms beneath him, moaning like sin incarnate. "Don't stop…"

Christopher relishes the way he throbs inside his mouth, against his teeth and tongue. The tendrils are as warm as when he has kissed them before. Only now, when he actually gets to taste them, he can take in their clear coating. It's thick and warm and *sweet* – like syrup.

That tentacle slime is like honey.

Christopher raises his head in a slick motion. "Oh my God."

"You don't like it," Gyth fears, eyes closed as he keeps fucking him. "That's all right. It's all right if you don't like it."

Christopher laughs. "I don't like it – I *love* it. C'mon, c'mon, give me your sugar…" And they slither back inside of him, accompanied by a sigh of relief from Gyth that travels through his body, all the way up to the fingertips on Christopher's back.

It is a good thing Christopher has his mouth full right now, because he is surprised by himself for such dirty talk. He catches another tentacle to suck on it, humming in relish while others stroke his head. They cover him in Gyth's warm honey, running down his temples – slick and oily instead of sticky.

It must be lubricant, because the tentacles in his ass move quicker and quicker, making soft noises as they slide against each other.

The movement, so in synch with the one pumping into his mouth, makes Christopher see stars – *God*, this feels good, so good – so much better even than his daydreams...

He arches his back just a little bit, for more friction.

Gyth's next thrust is deep. With it, the bedroom's lower half begins to glow in a bright fuchsia light. His moan echoes through it, travelling with the light as it overflows into the room. Weirdly self-conscious about how wet and sweaty he himself is, Christopher takes in Gyth's sheening face. Below it, wet abs split open to reveal more tentacles, white bones, deep-red organs –

Gyth lifts him up. Flows around him in this quasi-human form to embrace him from behind, unfolding more and more shapes to make up for the loss of touch against their cocks as he heaves his flesh into him. The *sounds* of it all would make a porn star blush, Christopher is sure.

A single thick tentacle reaches over his chest. Suckers attach to only his nipples, working them in their wonderful rhythm, taking in his heartbeat.

Although Gyth's mouth is empty, he can't close it either. With parted lips, he fucks into Christopher's gorgeous body – so welcoming in its marvelous connection to him. The density of the bodyparts he put inside of Christopher rises, craving more touch. He fights back the urge to go deeper, deeper still where there's no walls, in fear of tearing dear Christopher apart, of breaking his bones. No, he must be gentle –

But it is *hard*.

His restraint does not go unnoticed. 'Go ahead, go faster,' he hears Christopher suggest, although he cannot speak verbally with his mouth so stuffed, so overflowing. He caresses a helix of bones beside his head before it disappears. 'Can you... can you understand me?' he tries again. Gyth is always slow, when he talks, or moves, or kisses. He could try a little acceleration for a change.

"I do." Gyth groans when his coating drips from Christopher's red lips, onto the sensitive, naked flesh of the tentacles on his chest, shivering beneath the fluid that Christopher so generously milks from him in this haze. Faster, yes, a good idea. If he cannot go deeper, he'll go faster. Brilliant idea, so brilliant, oh, *yes* –

Gyth runs wild with it. He can't help but moan Christopher's name, so light in his voice yet heavy with adoration. He holds him closer. Presses his still-human chest against his back and strong, broad shoulders as he holds him up, tentacles descending into his mouth that hums so wonderfully around them before they pull out again, spilling so excessively, just like the ones below. Gyth fights the mental image of thrusting so hard they could meet in the middle of Christopher's body.

Dearest human Christopher...

Gyth wonders if his name could transform into a magic spell if he just uttered it often enough.

Perhaps it already has?

Christopher takes him in wonderfully. And, oh, yes, he has the best ideas. Like fruit from a tree, he plucks another tentacle to stroke in his big hands before guiding it over his thick shoulder. 'Here, babe.'

And while Christopher himself dwindles into embarrass-ment over that pet name, Gyth soaks right it up. That, and the tentacle, too.

Closing his eyes, he runs a tongue along himself – and be-fore he knows it, it's inside his mouth. He'd recognize these protein components in his sleep. Memories blossom inside of him. He's tasting sweet on this human tongue.

Christopher's voice is breathless despite its non-verbal na-ture. 'Thought you'd like it,' he snickers.

Wrong – I love it, Gyth wants to say, to mirror his words from before. But he can't. After a brief moment of pressing against the constraints of his own body, feeling the walls against his own skin, leaving him with the sheer *need for more*, he lets himself get swept away by his pleasure. He streams into himself, now without restraint or fear of breaking something, deeper, down, down, up again – his eyes turn back inside his skull before dripping away in the flood of his flesh.

This is too much – being pleasured on so many ends simul-taneously –

His body melts into its free forms. It streams into Christo-pher's tiny form and out again, over and over, pounding, throbbing.

Christopher gladly takes it all. His jaw hurts just a bit, but all pain is forgotten when Gyth's whale song emerges from the depths of the light, too fucked-silly to consume his entire bed-room.

Gyth is so hot and quick inside his mouth he could very well melts his brains, Christopher thinks, and he'd be entirely fine with it. It's amazing to feel all this change around him *and* in-side of him. The tentacles twitch and shiver when a shadow of eyes grows above Christopher, gazing at him from that man-sion of a body – yeah, that does it for him. He loves his de-bauchery. But he'll be quite happy to come now.

Lucky for him, Gyth has made a discovery during his streaming around and throughout Christopher. Just behind the walls he was drilling against in Christopher's ass, there is an organ, about the size of a human's eyeball.

In his mindless curiosity, Gyth brushes against it – and Christopher moans so loudly around him that he fears suffocating the poor human. He pulls out of his mouth to caress his wet face instead, as well as he can with these bounces.

"Good, Christopher, breathe..."

"Fuck!" Christopher finds his voice is a joke, so hoarse from the blowjob. He whines.

Gyth's next thrusts against his prostate are so hard they finally push him over the edge and into the stars. And he keeps hitting it, picking up speed, fucking *vibrating* –

"Fuck – Gyth...!"

Clenching around his lover, Christopher holds onto the tentacles on his chest, presses them harder for more friction. But with him being fucked so fast, and his hands so slippery, it's hard to get a grip.

Though he originally mourned the loss of stuffing in his mouth, he is now grateful to be able to fucking breathe. His eyes are closed, and yet he sees blurs, colors, streams of light.

Gyth gently spreads his legs to help him deepen their touch, now pouring the largest part of his density into him, slow and hard, once, twice to make him scream –

It hurts, but in just the right way. Christopher is surprised he doesn't mind having it rough. After all, this explosion of an orgasm is accompanied by a shower of forehead kisses and the eager encouragement of Gyth's husky voice.

"Yes, yes, beautiful, Christopher... Beautiful." He gasps. "So beautiful and tight around me..."

With a yearning sigh, Christopher's head rolls against his flesh, leaning into the loving touch. Gyth milks him all the way through, stumbling into his own symphony of an orgasm in the process. He savors every last drop of pleasure. Even when they sink back onto the bed, he uses his forming human hands to fondle Christopher's balls and nipples.

And he kisses him. Slides back into a human form, so much easier than after a fight. He marvels at the change. He kisses Christopher, warm and soft, rubbing their beards, nuzzling his cheek as he holds him from behind. Safe and sound.

Christopher is utterly boneless. Like sandbags, they collapse side by side, still hugging. He snuggles closer into the embrace to make up for the loss of weight inside of him. And that heavenly vibration against his sweet spot.

They change positions to face each other. Both still breathe hard, and Gyth's hair is tousled to the four winds, but his hands are steady on Christopher's back. His gaze through those dark eyelashes is, too.

Christopher pants against his neck. "Just... amazing."

"Agreed," Gyth smiles. He rolls his hips against him, like a tender aftershock. "Being partially inside your body is wonderful. Especially inside your mouth." He draws circles on Christopher's wet arm. "I would love to return the favour to you."

It only now sinks in: He really finds him desirable. Every corner of his body, just like he had said. Just for the hell of it. But the bliss is overshadowed by the proposal's baggage. Christopher pauses to think. Even when he speaks, it is slow: "I don't have good memories of oral. When I'm receiving it. So I'd rather... I'd rather you don't. For now. Or maybe longer. I don't know."

He curses himself. What guy doesn't enjoy a blowjob? He tries a smile. And swallows down an apology just in time – Gyth is right, this is nothing to be sorry about. It's his personal boundary. End of story.

Although Gyth replies softly, his voice is full of understanding. "All right. Of course."

He doesn't ask any questions. Christopher needs no interrogation. But still part of Gyth wonders who instilled those bad memories in him, scurrying over his sweaty skin, leaving scars. Who hurt him this way? He cannot trace those memories. He doesn't want to, either, lest he'd hurt Christopher in doing so.

That gloomy cloud doesn't stay for long though. Somewhen, Christopher announces he's in dire need of a shower and gets out of bed. Gyth hears him laugh from the bathroom.

"My beard is one wet mess!"

His amused call makes a hearty laugh erupt from Gyth. But he has to admit, the state of the bed isn't much better. He keeps lying on his back, using tendrils and a few spells to clean and dry the sheets around him.

"You tidied up?" Christopher snickers when he hurries beneath the blanket after his shower.

"To better keep you warm," Gyth says and kisses him. He considers himself lucky, being able to still smell Christopher's lovely scent under all that soap.

"Hm, nice… Smells like freshly laundered. Thank you."

"Don't mention it."

"Goodnight then."

"Goodnight, Christopher." Gyth gazes at his half-lidded blue eyes. "I will watch over you. You go dive into starlit dreams."

Christopher just sighs in his arms. He could use some dreams. Truly. To escape this madness. He much prefers *Gyth's* madness, so kind and hot. His life is a bit brighter now that he knows it exists. Still, one question continues to wheel inside his mind. "That pink place, the light… What is that?"

"That's my world. My very own," Gyth smiles. "A pocket dimension I once created. I can raise it anytime."

Christopher fears he's already dreaming. "Your world? And you're letting me in? Just like that?"

Gyth nods, caressing his cheek. "Yes."

"Wow. That's... Thank you." Something flourishes in Christopher's tired body. "It's really beautiful. Your world."

"It is most beautiful with you in it."

Christopher grins into his chest. "Oh my God." That's sappy. Some tacky, cheap *telenovela* shit – he loves it. Somewhen his thumb stops drawing circles on Gyth's shoulder. His sleep is heavy and sound.

He sleeps better ever since he's with Gyth.

But walking is hard work the next day. And his neck can't crack enough. Nonetheless, Christopher is pretty sure Gyth has straightened his back out with that tour de force. And his beard and skin are softer, probably thanks to that slime. The ways in which Gyth leaves his marks on him are colorful, sometimes literally.

In the morning, Christopher laughs at the red circles around his nipples.

"Have I hurt you?" Gyth asks.

"No. Quite the opposite." Christopher grins – he's never looked at his own chest for so long. "I like them. Tentacle hickeys." He turns his back to the mirror to give Gyth a kiss.

He likes himself better now, he realizes. Moments of doubt still creep up upon him – *Am I good enough for him? Am I passionate enough? Should I wear more black?* – but after a few more days of living together, he gets the impression that Gyth is actively trying to fight them.

Like on Friday, when Christopher is singing rock songs to him in the bedroom. They're both half naked. Originally, Christopher only wanted to get changed. But somehow, he has now ended up dancing toward his wardrobe to get the blue feather boa, one musical tune after the other on his lips. It's fun to be this campy, he finds. To sway and sing without fearing ridicule.

It doesn't hurt that Gyth is having a blast, too. "Amazing," he beams, clapping his hands. He is sitting cross-legged on the bedroom floor, just in his jeans, like Christopher.

Christopher dips into a theatrical bow as deep as his back allows. "Thank you, thank you. Give it up for the Distasteful Divorcé!"

Gyth still applauds, but his smile melts into confusion. "The what?"

Christopher plays with the boa to try and hide how awkward he just made this. Gyth just continues clapping. "Stop calling yourself unkind things. You were wonderful."

"Yeah, well – I was feeling it," Christopher says, courting nonchalance. "But what everybody else sees is a lonely troll, rapidly approaching forty. In a gay-ass outfit."

"Who said that to you?"

"The popular kids from my school. Twenty years ago. Well, they didn't say exactly that. They can't see me now. But they did then, and they never missed a chance to let me know."

Gyth stops clapping. He studies Christopher for a while. Then he shifts his bare, four-toed feet, and gives him an earnest look. "I suppose my transdimensional eyes see differently than a human's then. I thought you were radiant."

"Radiant." Christopher hums in amusement as he plays with the boa. Irony could stifle this awkwardness. "Tell me more."

Gyth's answer is dry and determined but without real anger. "I bloody will. You're absolutely gorgeous when your eyes light up with fun. They twitch a little before that, or blink, which I like to watch, because it announces your beautiful smile, and I get to look forward to it – and to us bathing in your joy together." In one smooth motion, he stands up and touches the feather boa, then Christopher's shoulders and torso. His accent is thicker when he says, "And this looks bloody amazin' on you. It's so light and fluffy, and it moved gorgeously with you, flowin'–" With gravitas, he adds, "It changed your entire silhouette, going here, and there, without a care…" A lewd smile tugs at his lips.

It makes Christopher blush, as does the costume-drama-esque shower of compliments. It melts away any irony and gives way to shy curiosity, without any disbelief, surprisingly. "You like me when I dance?"

As though waking from a trance, Gyth exhales and looks up to give him a smile. "You looked superbly fluid. Your voice had so many colours – I adored you. And this, like a vivid extension of your body, your shoulders…" His fingers dreamily glide through the plastic feathers.

Not sure what else to do, Christopher puts the monstrosity around Gyth's neck. "You're pretty in it, too." He snorts at his simpleton tone.

Gyth giggles, still touching him. His hands are like butterflies on Christopher's hips.

"Just one of my old theater props," Christopher explains. "Or, accessories, I should say." He has an idea. "Y'know what else I got?" He turns to the wardrobe to rummage through the bottom shelf. Shortly afterwards, he presents his pair of shiny, black, high heel plateau shoes. "Boom. Size twelve."

"Oh. Is that… rare?"

"It's a woman's shoe. But made for men." Suppressing a sigh, Christopher follows through with it. "Who are not supposed to wear it but do, under certain circumstances."

"Like a pineapple pizza you're not supposed to order."

Christopher clicks his tongue. "You got it."

Gyth huddles down to study the shoes with investigating eyes. "Can I try them on then?"

Christopher is glad Gyth suggested it himself, so that he doesn't have to ask. He himself isn't in the mood to wear them anyway. He hasn't for years and he won't start again now. "Be my guest."

"I will be, thank you."

With a splashy sound, Gyth melts his feet to fit inside the shoes. While Christopher still worries about the dust they've collected over the years, Gyth straightens his posture. Now they're the same height. He wobbles around the room, trying to keep his balance with his limps extending and growing unnaturally to help him not fall over or break something – Christopher covers his mouth at the cute display of otherworldliness.

"It *is* possible to walk in them, I suppose."

"Yeah, go for it," Christopher encourages him.

Gyth frowns in concentration, but he does get the hang of it. He proudly raises his chin when he struts a few steps, meeting Christopher's eyes as he puts down his feet. The feather boa seems to come alive around his naked shoulders.

"Wow!" Christopher applauds the crazy catwalk. With the make-up around his eyes, Gyth looks quite campy himself. Only he is unapologetic about it. "You're killing it!" Christopher beams. "Crushing it! Positively!" he laughs.

Gyth attempts to put a leg on the sofa to strike a pose but falters. A second pair of arms helps him regain balance. "I don't know how *you* would do it though, without flexible insides to pull you into the right direction."

Mockingly defensive, Christopher says, "Y'know, there's people dancing in these, okay? We're not doing half bad, we humans."

"Dancing would be quite the task, indeed," Gyth mumbles in his charming accent. He concentrates but still falls over when he puts his foot back down. Christopher steps forward to catch him. But they both lose balance and fall to the floor, onto fluffy feathers and soft flesh.

Blue fluffs of plastic fall from Gyth's curls when he raises his head to check for Christopher. "Oh, bugger. Are you all right?"

"Yeah. I had a soft landing." Christopher raises a tentacle from the fleshy mess that Gyth has extended to catch his fall. He kisses it. The red veins on it glitter in the afternoon sun. Or were they a dark pink? There probably are a thousand poems to describe this sight...

He sighs. "I'm not really good with words. So I'll just show you how amazing you are, in the ways I can," he says and presses another kiss to it. Amazing, in spite of being monstrous and against the rules – or because of it? Beauty truly lies in the transdimensional eyes of the beholder, huh?

Cheeky bastard.

Gyth sighs blissfully.

Christopher turns his head on his fleshy cushion. He wants to teach him dancing – slow dance, maybe. He also wants to kiss those plump lips and touch all those muscles Gyth has crafted as his body. He pauses when Gyth opens his mouth, looking for words. "Is it not... *time* to get changed?"

"Oh, shit," Christopher laughs.

He arrives late at the shelter, but no one cares. Behind the desk, he wonders if he could ever bring Gyth here again. After everything Emely has said, he doesn't *want* to bring him. He wants to have him all for himself. Not those who won't appreciate them. It is comforting to know that, even if he cannot entrust his coworkers with that thing he shares with Gyth, there are others who will gladly listen to him.

"I've met the best guy in the world," Christopher tells Shelly later that night. She looks at him and rests her head on his thigh.

"I'll introduce you someday. Yes, you too, Chief," he laughs when the husky comes stepping along to get some ear tickling himself.

Christopher looks at the two for a while. "I'm really happy at the moment," he says, though this time more to himself.

He is happy. He hasn't racked his brains about stupid nullities for some time now. And he feels masculine. A side of himself that he hasn't really explored so far. He thinks it's ironic, that he should feel this way now that he is in a gay relationship.

Is it a relationship?

It certainly is a connection. Or a process. A learning.

Gyth would agree with that assessment. He certainly learns a lot of new things with Christopher. About humans and their strange and wondrous dimension. But also himself. Christopher keeps surprising him with new things to unlock within himself.

One night, Gyth could persuade him to go back to Brian's Bar and get two piña coladas. Christopher said it's better to order six. That way Gyth would have more to drink, and they could circumnavigate the rule they have broken on their first feeding here by pretending they were only couriers for a bigger party and not two men ordering these forbidden drinks. "Two birds with one stone," Christopher has said, a phrasing that Gyth finds most peculiar. He's happy to see the kind bartender again, too.

Christopher informs him it is late already when they leave the bar with a paper carton of pineapple drinks. But Gyth is not quite ready to go home. What has caught his attention when they were still inside the bar is now even more visible to him.

In the parking lot behind the building, three men buzz around a woman 'waiting for her boyfriend'. She is intoxicated and unable to get away from them. One of them turns around, and his cheeky grin dies. "What're you looking at, fags?"

"Come on," Christopher whispers, already leaving for Main Street with their drinks.

Gyth walks in the opposite direction.

"Don't," Christopher hisses. "They're looking for trouble!"

"Exactly."

"It's none of our business!"

In a spark of disappointment, Gyth turns around to face him. "She is unsafe. That makes it my business. You don't have to come with me," he offers. Being a guardian comes with few principles. But they're generally not hard to follow, in contrast to all the rules humans have.

There *must* be a rule against standing so close to people who don't want you close, Gyth thinks when he approaches the scene. "C'mon, puppet, you don't have to lie to us. We're nice guys. You shouldn't be out here alone."

"Good thing she isn't," Gyth says. He waves to the woman, then points over his shoulder to where Christopher was standing. "Hello, how are you? Why don't we go over there?"

His intervention is not appreciated. "Oh my God." One of the men, carrying a glass bottle, mirrors the woman's shaky steps. They're far gone from the life of the night in this parking lot, without even a streetlamp to spare some light. Gyth's plan is to keep those men here: "Do not follow us."

"Huh?" The man with the bottle turns away to talk to his companions. "Guys, did you hear somethin'?"

"Nah, man," is the humorless reply. "I don't speak faggot."

Behind Gyth, Christopher grows anxious.

"Are you all right?" Gyth asks the woman. Sure enough, she shakes her head. When she staggers into Christopher's direction, he uses his free hand to support her.

"Can you walk?" Gyth asks her.

"Yeah. Have you seen my friends? Three? They left early…"

He exchanges a look with Christopher – whose blue eyes are wide. His heart is racing. Gyth understands that he is afraid. His reaction is only natural. Despite being among fellow humans, Christopher himself could be unsafe in this environment. Still, he gathers his courage. "We can go back to the bar if you want to," he suggests to the woman in a low voice. "Should we do that? Can you phone someone to come pick you up?"

"Yeah."

"Go." Gyth guides them away. The shadows are filling up with strange forces. Reason enough for him to want vulnerable creatures gone.

His heart may have broadened a bit at Christopher helping the woman out of here despite being afraid himself. "I will make sure you won't be followed," he calls after them.

"Oh, yeah?"

Gyth turns around with a smile – instead of a grimace for that rude interruption. "Yup."

"Great. What a great catch you are," the guy with the bottle says. One of his companies points at Gyth with a weak finger. "Can you believe this guy? Now they're taking away our girls. I thought you didn't wanna fuck them, huh?"

Gyth's smile melts into a confused frown. "No?"

The guy with the bottle steps closer. "You wanna pick a fight then, huh? You wanna play with the big boys?"

"If you are the big boys? No, I most certainly don't."

The third man imitates his accent: "Ouh, he most certainly does not, indeed!" After that, his tone gets rougher. "You think you're really it, shorty – huh?"

"New fag in town, willying your schlong all over the place like it's yours. With children around! You sick-ass psycho!"

Gyth tilts head at the tirade, trying to follow.

192

"Yeah, damn right. We've seen you and your big friend, at the bar. And at Stuart's. We see you! You're in the Army, the movies, *God*, a man can't go five steps without getting some gay dick in his face, whether he likes it or not!"

"Yeah! Just for that shit near the children you should get shot down! For real, if it was up to me, you'd get fucked, man. But if I say that in the wrong place, I'm some 'straight cis homophobe bigot'!"

"Yeah! Woke shit."

"For real. What about your big friend, aye? He wants that BBC? You give it to him?"

"Dude, I think you can watch that online, actually."

"That's not what I meant!"

Gyth desperately tries to understand anything he hears. The men's accusations derail increasingly, calling him words that they cannot seem to agree about themselves.

Eventually, the guy in front of him raises his bottle to drink, but not before hissing, "Fucking pie face."

All right – Gyth closes his eyes. It seems they aren't even trying to communicate with him.

"Now get out the way before I punch some sense into your woke ass." The guy tries to strut past him, but Gyth holds him in place with a well-positioned hand on his chest – now *this* is his element. In a bitter-tasting spark of panic, the guy jerks away his hand. "Get that off me!" His companions rally up behind him. "Take a hint and get lost, disgusting piece of shit!"

So, they *have* been trying to tell him something? Gyth looks at his hand. A human hand, five digits, black nails. A hand that has held Christopher's before – he gets an idea of what this could be about. "Is it because of a rule violation?"

The answer to his genuine question consists of glares and screams. "Oh my God! If you don't get lost, I'mma violate your ugly-ass cock-sucker face!"

The man pushes him backwards. Gyth regains his posture, sighs. Indeed, Christopher has been right. Those guys are just looking for trouble; they are not the type to reinforce any rules, he thinks. If so, what would that say about the rules? Nothing good, he muses.

Still – interesting reaction to his touch. Christopher is afraid of them, and yet deep-seated fears reign those people themselves. Gyth muses he could use that to buy Christopher and the woman more time.

Although their exact fears are unknown to him, a universal twinge of primordial madness should serve the purpose just fine. "You really don't like my face, do you?" Against his instincts, Gyth's mouth contorts into a grin. It is only a harbinger of what's to come next. "Lucky for you pus-filled maggot arses, I have many more."

With that, he puffs himself up. It's only a short moment before he steps up to his opponents. But their screams tell him they very well saw the bloated, white eyes and shadowy veins popping up on his head.

The men stumble backwards; the one with the hat lands on his butt. "Fuck me!"

"Oh, I'm afraid no one ever will, you nasty little arse-worm," Gyth lets him know, making sure the words really wriggle into his tiny head.

Glass splits on Gyth's skull – they have thrown a bottle at him. Though a bit belatedly, he decides to let the blood spill out in a fountain.

"Fuck! Fucking hell!"

Content with that reaction, Gyth falls to his knees, in front of the man on the ground. "What have you done?" he utters in his best haunting voice. He uses a shaking hand to pod the wound on his temple. Blood and flesh stick in his hair.

The man in front of him whimpers.

In a flash of horror, Gyth fixates him. "What have you done?!" He twists his fingers deeper through the hot wound. It's a lot of work to get past the blood and cerebrospinal fluids, but eventually he meets a squishy mass.

It's so soft to his touch that his next move is more than obvious. A no-brainer, as Christopher would say.

With a pained howl, Gyth scratches away bits and pieces through the wound. "What have you done?" he yells – with primordial undertones for more flavor, in case the brain tearing wasn't enough.

The organ waste lands before the men's feet with a splash. One of them throws up his dinner. "Oh my God!"

"It hurts so much," Gyth cries, taking out a bigger chunk. In fact, he could just pull out the whole thing, he muses, like a noodle, and take some pieces of his skull and strands of hair, too, while he's at it, all the while fixating the terrified eyes of the man in front of him, now lying in a pool of body juices. None of them half as pleasant as Christopher's, in Gyth's opinion.

"Shit, shit!" the guy cries. "Holy shit, holy shit, holy–"

Bam! Gyth has seen the kick of his friend coming and decides to play along. His unmoving eyes stare at the wall from the ground up, and for a moment, the scene falls silent.

"Shit! *Shit*, man! What the fuck!"

"What the fuck, man? Did you just kill him?"

"I don't fucking know! I don't know, okay, he pulled his fucking brains out himself – dude, puke somewhere else, will you?! Goddammit…"

"I don't know, man. I really don't know. He looks fucking dead to me. You knocked out his entire fucking – like, all his teeth, man."

"Don't – don't fucking touch him!"

"I wanted to check if he was dead!"

"Shh!"

"I *said*, I wanted to check – Jesus, Dylan, you fucking killed a guy! We gotta get lost!"

"I did not. I did not. He pulled his fucking brains out."

"You threw a goddamn glass bottle at his face!"

"In self-defense! Yeah? Okay? Okay?"

"Oh, you wanna plead self-defense?"

"I don't know, man, *I never fucking did something like this before.*"

"Can we run now? Can we please just run?"

"And then what? Then what?"

"O-or at least hide? Until someone comes here? He was screaming like hell, somebody must've heard him."

"Makes more sense to hide *him*."

"Hide? As in, hide a body?"

"Oh my God…"

"Can we *please* not discuss this here?!"

"So, you wanna let him lie here?"

"I don't know! How can he be dead, man? How can you know for sure?"

"Like this!"

That next kick against his body goes wrong as well. Gyth lets the foot stick in his liver.

"What the fuck?!"

How about legs sprouting from all those teeth scattered across the ground? Yes, eight each, with nice and hard exoskeletons. They prop themselves up and chase the men around the place with terrified screams.

Gyth uses that time to heave his body up, freeing the foreign foot in the process. "Off me…" he growls, earning himself another outcry.

The only escape, except for crowded Main Street, is an alleyway in the back. The men desperately try to reach it. Gyth sprouts some spider legs for himself to block their way. Oh, what a fun way to move!

"Hurry! Fuck, hurry up!"

"Fucking get those teeth off of me! Ah! Ahh!"

"Where is he? Fucking God, where is that thing?"

"Peek-a-boo," tears from Gyth's gullet when he reveals himself from the walls he scuttled along. The last human features of his face melt away in a horrific squeal, echoing through the alleyway and in the men's ears as he towers above them. They run in the opposite direction before the blood shower reaches them, like the scared little rugrats they are, chased by the teeth that have now sprouted some insect wings.

Never before has Gyth tried to purposefully scare someone. But his joy is immeasurable. Not only is this a fun way to try out new shapes and movements – somehow, this is also very gratifying. What a pity he won't be able to scare off any hunters like this, he thinks as he lowers his body from the walls of the alleyway. The men are gone, carrying their screams and wet pants with them onto a car, from where they manage to climb over a wall and into the depths of the town.

Grunting, Gyth folds himself back into a human shape amidst the languorous warmth of satisfaction. He catches his fly-teeth to put them back inside his mouth. There, happy end!

All that was left to do was absorbing the blood. And walking around the corner, one foot before the other. Like a human. One, two – there you go.

Gyth cannot help but grin when he lays eyes on Christopher in those colorful lights of the bar. He's so *happy* – truly, there can be no rule against this, he thinks. Human rules are strange and their enforcement hilariously inconsistent, but this – this is the most natural thing in the cosmos, he thinks. If his joy spills from him now, he doesn't care.

"Christopher! Are you two all right?"

"Yeah," the woman says over the booming music. "My sister will come pick me up." Weakly, she adds, "Thank you for that, just now."

Christopher exchanges a smile with Gyth as though to check if he was all right, too. Gyth nods. Christopher then turns to the woman. "No problem."

A no-brainer, Gyth thinks with a giggle.

"Do you want us to wait with you?" Christopher asks. She reddens. "Only if you want us to," he clarifies.

"If it's no trouble to you…"

"Absolutely not," Gyth beams, giving her and then Christopher a smile. He can hardly wait to drink all those piña coladas. And tell Christopher what he helped him learn.

One learning Gyth could have done without though.

He has known for a while now that Christopher's mother is very sick and that the illness she is battling is terminal. He also knows that Christopher feels bad for not having visited her for a long time. "I have to catch up on this now," he tells him after a phone call. He agrees to Gyth accompanying him. Their drive to the house in question is quiet, but Gyth likes looking out the window. And at Christopher, if only to exchange a comforting smile.

"Yellow are her favorites," Christopher tells him as they pull up by Tony's house. The roses are packed in plastic, crackling softly in Gyth's lap.

"You're anxious," he notices.

Christopher just nods. His eyes are burning already. "Listen, um – could you do me a huge favor?"

"Anything," Gyth says and breaks Christopher's heart, because he knows it's true. "Could you maybe not come in with me?" He swallows. "Like, not through the door?"

"Not like a human," Gyth clarifies.

Christopher pulls out the keys. "Just appear next to me when I call you," he says. Shame rips his stomach open from the inside. "I feel terrible asking this of you."

"Don't," Gyth says. But Christopher is already out, flowers shivering in his hands. Cold November air hits his face. His tunnel vision is back.

How can the chrysanthemums still be in bloom? Why don't they die, but his mother does?

Tony opens the door for him with a weary smile and a hug. "Chris. Come in, come in."

Christopher doesn't turn around to check for Gyth.

His stomach burns when he enters Mary's bedroom, with its flowery blankets and wooden crucifix. "I'll leave you two alone," Tony says. Christopher doesn't move when the door clicks shut. He just stares.

That sleeping body on the bed is his mother. The body that birthed him. That brought him through childhood. Went to the supermarket with him, where he could choose one item for her to buy him, in exchange for helping with the groceries.

How, he wonders, can you have a happy childhood and then fuck up the relationship to your mother as an adult?

He steps closer to lay the flowers on her bed. Her gray hair is tousled and the wrinkles around her eyes as deep as gorges. She breathes weakly through her nose.

Christopher was sure he'd cry when he'd see her alive for what could very well be the last time. But he doesn't. He does not feel anything. How can that be? He has been fine these past days. No stonification. No clouding his heart in frozen walls, like the last time he saw her. He has been fighting tears back then. So why doesn't he cry now? There are no confessions to make, no soft words to speak.

The implication makes him shudder. His breath shakes. "Gyth? Why don't I feel anything?"

Behind him, a dark figure emerges from the evening shadows. Gyth's hands are back in his black bomber jacket's pockets and his slow steps unnaturally silent on the carpet. His eyes take in Christopher instead of the room.

"What should you feel?" he asks.

"I'm supposed to cry," Christopher whispers. But even saying it out loud lets no tears fall. "Men don't cry, except when a loved one dies." When he pries his eyes loose from the bed, he can see Gyth biting his tongue. "Why do you think that is?"

"I do not know," Gyth shrugs, stepping closer to the bed. It's another badly disguised lie.

Christopher straightens his back. "Tell me."

Gyth glances at him through the dark veil of his curls. "I do not know of the intricacies of your relationship. I simply think maybe she is not a loved one to you."

"She's my mother."

"I can see that," Gyth says, eyes returning to her body. He sees her insides, looks deeper to glance at her genetic makeup. He also sees her illness. But it is overshadowed by the loud vortex building up in Christopher.

Gyth turns to face him. "You're not unkind for not having exclusively positive feelings for her," he says simply.

Christopher's blue eyes snap back to reality like raindrops. Should he tell Gyth this was breaking the simplest rule a child had to follow? "She is sick."

"You cannot force feelings." Gyth leaves it at that. He resumes his studying of the illness. Slowly steps around the bed. Tilts his head to hear them better, those multiplying cells. Invaders, all over her body. "What is it called?"

Christopher's answer is belated and quiet. "Cancer." He sniffs and steps to Gyth's side.

"Who infected her with those cells?"

"She herself, if you can call it that." Christopher shifts. "Those are her own. Just in the wrong place. Just rude little cells. Like her body didn't know any better."

Gyth steps back, still looking. A very human illness, he finds.

Christopher shudders. He still cannot quite believe it, that his mother should die of that dreaded cancer shit. Normally, it's always other people. He remembers his nightmares after she had told him about the diagnosis. Cells spreading, growing into tumors, eating away her organs irreversibly…

A fatal spark flies through Christopher's brain then. "You do eat your enemies, don't you?"

Gyth gives him a look. "Consumption is not exactly eating." He squints his eyes, smelling the idea growing in Christopher's mind.

He doesn't like the smell.

Christopher shifts as his heartrate quickens. "Can't you… can't you consume the cancer cells? You can see them, right?"

"Yes."

"Can you… consume them?" Christopher's blue eyes are round with hope. With a plea. Gyth can see that he promises himself this would be an act of kindness. Of saving his mother. Gyth needs to be careful with his refusal: "I could try. But, Christopher, I do not know the ramifications of consuming parts of a human being. I have never done this before."

"Well – there's a first time for everything," Christopher says. His smile is meant as encouragement. But it is shaky.

Gyth realizes how much it means to him. And to himself, too, doesn't it? As a guardian? He could protect her from her illness. He turns around to view Christopher's mother anew. Her body is a dying shell. Carving out the dangerous pieces will not be easy, because a human's body is not as separated from their mind and everything else as they think. If he even so much as *scratches* her mind –

"I'll take the responsibility," Christopher says. "If anything happens."

Will he? Gyth thinks about it. What kind of responsibility could Christopher take in this? But his sheer determination is enough to push Gyth over the threshold of doubt.

He positions himself by her head.

Christopher's eyes are glued to Gyth's hands as he takes them out of his pockets and places them on Mary's face. He expects them so change their appearance and shape themselves into something new. They don't.

Instead, Gyth's back arches. His skin glows with tension, veins popping as he reaches out. He is walking a tightrope. One slip and he'll break her.

Mary's eyes twitch before they fly open. Just like her gaping mouth, they glow with Gyth's pink shimmer – so brightly that Christopher cannot make out her eyes anymore.

Her hands twitch and slap the blanket they've been resting on. Too weak to scream, she gasps instead. Trying to breathe.

Christopher's eyes are restless. "Gyth?" He doesn't dare looking behind the curtain of his curls.

"No," Mary gasps. Inhales in a rasp. Then screams out.
"Gyth!"

"I am not touching her mind." Gyth's voice is but a demonic growl. His fingers tremble between the columns of light.

"No!" The shimmer brightens, arching Mary's weak body.

"Chris?" Tony calls from below.

"Stop it," Christopher pleads. Pain crushes through him. What has he made Gyth do?

Gyth's hands leave Mary's face, and with them, the shimmer vanishes, too. Christopher hurries to her side. Her eyes are not burned out but wide awake. They stare at him.

"Mom?"

Her mouth twitches so hard even her teeth shake. Christopher is too busy cradling her to see that she was not staring at him but the thing behind him, the mass that melts the room in a pink light, into the cosmos that lies beyond, that just won't stop, bright and terrible – dark and twisted – everchanging, everlasting.

She cries out.

"Wait in the car," Christopher tells Gyth.

And Gyth obeys. He watches Tony enter the room. Two humans hovering over the one he touched. Her screams echo inside of him, even when the shrill ambulance drives her away, out of Hillsburg. The doctors will say that her cancer cells have disappeared. That her organs remain damaged. That her mind is damaged. They'll say, "She's gone mad." And convince her family, Tony and his children, that she'll live.

Gyth knows better. That sort of madness – *his* – will kill her. Maybe years from now, maybe right this moment. At least she won't be alone.

Christopher hugs him tight that night. "She was gonna die anyway," he whispers. They both know that does not make it better. And although he doesn't verbalize it, Christopher's self-loaded guilt screams, even without a mouth. Gyth is wary of it. Of that, and of the thing he learned tonight: No matter how careful he acts, he could always hurt humans. No matter how hard he tries – one day, perhaps even in an act of protection, he could break Christopher.

Careful, he tells himself. He binds himself under this spell. *Be wary of yourself*. He should not let anyone cloud his judgement anymore, including Christopher. He has been wrong about the men by the bar, and now his mother. Gyth cannot trust his judgement pertaining something he is naturally incapable of understanding. Gyth's laxity has hurt them both.

He wonders, how could he ever have taken joy in scaring humans? A true guardian never would have done that. Shame overwhelms him.

"I will watch over you," he whispers in his ear when Christopher expresses his wish to fall sleep.

Christopher squeezes his hand. "Thank you."

Humans need sleep in order not to die, Gyth reminds himself. He is anxious to even move.

Nightmares need sleep, too, Krysuldom laughs from the depths of the universe. They thrive in sleep, when the mind is naked and dreaming. He could not have chosen a better sowing time. He will plant them so that they'll grow, stronger, stronger, stronger, until one night they'll be powerful enough to break through their host and his weak human skin. And then forth, into the guardian. That guardian that continues to escape his reach, hiding in whatever it is that shields him. He will find his end soon.

Pesky, incorrigible, wretched, lonely, little guardian.

DRIFTER

NOVEMBERS ARE COLD and gray. They are the season of twilight. Without the colors of Octobers, or the lights of Decembers.

Gyth is like a candle by a blue window. He brings light and warmth, especially if you got close to him.

Christopher is grateful for him being there. He is always there for him. He himself is jittery these days. Fragile. Afterimages of his mother's stare haunt him. Though probably not as gruesomely as they should, given the situation's horror.

As best as he can, Christopher avoids thinking about the implications. And, amazingly, that is very easy these days. With Gyth around, there is always something pleasant to experience as distraction. Like his pride over finally nailing the walk in the black high heels, or his never-ending joy over pineapple pizza. Or the way he watches the sky and its wandering clouds. Or crosses his beautiful eyes behind fogged glasses.

Gyth soaks up trivialities like a sponge, and just as eagerly, Christopher absorbs him. It's like Gyth reminds him that snow will be falling soon. Lakes will freeze over. They'll watch fern frost grow on the windows from the inside, from under a warm blanket, with that damned hot chocolate.

"This is the traditional variant," Christopher explains to him over the kitchen table, sleeves rolled up. "Blocks of chocolate, not cocoa powder – melted in hot milk. This is oat milk, which is decidedly not the traditional way–"

"It smells delicious," Gyth says with sparkling eyes. Like, literally, sporting multicolored glitter in his brown irises.

Christopher could stare at him forever. He makes him six different mugs of hot chocolate, and he would've made more, if he had more mugs. Cinnamon, marshmallows, clove – Gyth should have it all. He deserves it.

Still, when Christopher kisses away the last mug's whipped cream from his beard, melancholy spreads in his chest. All this joy is their secret. No one must know.

"Do you want to talk about it?" Gyth whispers. As always, he sees right through him.

Christopher gives him a smile. "Not right now."

"As you wish." Gyth kisses his forehead. "Then we can attend to the important questions: In which of these hot chocolate variants would you put pineapple?"

Christopher closes his eyes in adoring disbelief. "You fucking sicko." He melts into Gyth's embrace when he hears him laugh. Rough and warm.

When they are this close, Gyth can feel Christopher ripping in two. The consumption of his mother's illness leaves him terrified but also relieved. And Christopher wants to cut off the latter part. Gyth must make sure it will not come to that. Just like a body grows, so must emotions.

Christopher is precious to him. So dear to him in ways he has never known and doesn't quite comprehend himself yet. He *needs* to let him know. He can't feel what Gyth is feeling – they may be connected but have not joined. To mimic the effect at least a little bit, Gyth reminds himself to let Christopher know every bit of himself.

It may be helping but it often circles back to his body. Gyth admires it, both because of and in spite of its solid nature. Its changes are subtle but its wonders broad. Sometimes Christopher needs help to see them. Especially when he's standing in front of a mirror, in blue jeans and a pastel-colored shirt in his hands. Pensive.

"You said you found me attractive."

"I did." Gyth grins as he looks him from behind, as an image in the mirror. "I do."

"Like… metaphysically or something, right? Or metaphorically?"

"Metacorporally?" Gyth suggests cluelessly.

"Like – not *this* body. Right?"

Gyth keeps sitting on the ground because he knows it would be useless to stand up and slide his hands over Christopher's belly right now. Christopher's skin would be nothing but tense under his touch. Instead, he asks, "Why not all of those things? I fancy you in every way you can imagine. And those you can't."

Christopher laughs quietly. "That's actually insane." Before Gyth can intervene, he adds, "I mean, in contrast to you – you take off your glasses and you look like you're from a porn magazine or something."

"I do not know what that means," Gyth says truthfully.

"It means you're handsome and I'm not. Or – well, you're meeting a certain beauty standard and I'm not," he clarifies mechanically.

"Is that important?"

"Normally it is for getting laid. Like, this here ain't exactly cotton candy. But, hey" – Christopher smiles – "what do I know?"

"I do know that your body is doing a great job in carrying you through this world. It's doing so many things simultaneously." Gyth rests his head in his hands. "It is connected to your mind and this world in a way I could never know. It's your home."

"It's treacherous," Christopher says with a weak smile. "My lungs are a mess. My knees, too. My stupid dick. I care about that." He turns to meet Gyth warm eyes outside the mirror.

"That's okay," Gyth tells him. "It isn't trivial."

Christopher nods. He looks back at his reflection. Them. "But I guess I care a little less when I'm with you. I think a little less."

"And that's good?"

"I think so, actually. It sounds so overdramatic when I say it out loud, but I'm able to let down my guard around you and just… be me. In my body. Like, usually when I'm hyper-aware of it, it's because I'm disgusted or scared. But not when I'm with you. It's all different now. Like, sometimes, I even…" He looks down, smiles in disbelief. "I feel *desirable*. In my body."

A brilliant smile creeps onto Gyth's face. "I bloody desire you and your body. I'll gladly conjure a few more hickeys onto it, if you want."

"Those were fun, not gonna lie." Christopher lowers the shirt in his hands. Gyth loves his hands. They are shaped to hold and create. To strum a guitar, flick paper pages in books, and cook food. But Gyth adores many parts of Christopher's body beside his hands. His beauty marks that form silent constellations on his cheeks and neck. His eyelashes, which are so incongruously curved and make his eyes even prettier behind his angular glasses. His belly, soft and supple beneath Gyth's fingertips, and his long, hairy legs. His strong thighs and ass.

His insides, throbbing red and tight.

And every day, there's something new to discover. When they're naked and lying side by side in bed, facing each other, Gyth admires the make-up of Christopher's pectoral muscles, so round and warm before his ribcage. His nipples stand out gorgeously from his chest hair. Their glands lead deeper inside his body. Their areolae share the pink color of his lips – just as soft beneath Gyth's touch.

The only thing more fascinating than Christopher's chest is his reaction to having it touched. His sexual energy always spikes when Gyth attaches tentacles to it. But this makes his blue eyes flutter close, when Gyth drags kisses over it. He leans into the warmth of Gyth's mouth when he closes his lips around a nipple, to feel this tiny part of Christopher inside of him, against his tongue. And teeth. Their texture is so different in an otherwise soft human mouth. They graze the soft flesh, nibble at it. And its counterpart, when Christopher shifts his torso for Gyth to reach it. Oh, truly, this one has been neglected. It is cooler in Gyth's mouth. But also bigger. He flicks his tongue against it, tugging at the other with his fingers to try and lure it out in the same way.

Christopher's quiet moans are as beautiful as the song at the edge of the cosmos. Gyth would not be able to choose between those and the loud screams. Both sounds enchant him. Maybe he could conjure forth a less restraint moan?

As Gyth keeps experimenting, Christopher slides his long legs below the blanket – which Gyth finds endlessly alluring. He looks forward to the moments when Christopher shifts from shyness and self-constraint to indulgence.

However, he thinks it cruel to only pleasure one nipple at a time. He splits his tongue in the middle, to grow across Christopher's chest and flick against that sensitive flesh anew. He licks it, curls around it to tug gently, before closing his mouth around them again, one after the other, sucking and holding Christopher throughout his care.

It feels peculiar, to always be aware of the cosmos around him and still zero in on just this one body, in one moment, and forget everything else.

And indeed, Christopher's sounds become louder. He caresses Gyth's side with one hand. He uses the other to stroke his cock under the blanket, his head pressing into the pillow as saliva runs down his chest. "Fuck…"

Gyth's voice is warm and low in-between his ministrations. "You're so wonderful, Christopher. You come apart very beautifully. There are so many pleasures to unlock all over your body. So many sounds you can make…" He plants another lazy kiss on his left nipple – teasing him with a weak suck that makes him hum in need and smack his lips. "I fancy your chest. And the fascinating things it can do."

Christopher swallows. He's too horny to speak coherent sentences. "Yours can't? Do this?"

To his misery, that question makes Gyth halt and think. Christopher bites back a whine at the loss of touch and instead watches Gyth transform himself. He makes a mouth emerge from the palm of his hand, lips and all, and lays it over his left nipple – and gasps when he sucks on himself. His eyes go wide with surprise.

To feel himself inside his own body, just like when Christopher sucks it off –

His gratitude for Christopher's thought-provoking impulse is swallowed by the desire eating away his body. He forms a second mouth for his right nipple on the other hand and closes around it, hot and wet and full of friction. He rolls onto his back, unable to close his mouth – oh, his lower half is unwinding already. Excited tentacles splash around him as the newfound pleasure fills him up. One wraps around his cock to stroke its throbbing length in unison to the sucking on his hard nipples. His human skin is soft over his cock's stiffness, adorned with veins and cavernous bodies, full of blood. It's beyond him how even his human bodyparts can change so quickly.

Far is it from him to complain.

The same goes for Christopher: Wantonly, he stares down at the display that sometimes disappears behind pitch-black static. His dick pulsates in his hand when a long moan emerges from Gyth. It makes him press his chest up against his own hands, back arching beautifully. He's excited, all right – his handsy mouths leave his nipples with soft pops so that he can slide them in-between his fingers, then rub them. His cock strains at the tension, fat veins glistening with sweat and pre-cum and, according to the sweet smell, the honey of his tentacles squeezing it. They pool around him not unlike his hair on the pillow.

In everyday life, Gyth is such a sloth – which usually translates to fantastic slow sex – but now? He can't touch himself enough. Christopher could've come from the sheer image alone. "You wanna keep doing that all by yourself?" he rasps.

Gyth apologetically meets his gaze with furrowed brows and a slack mouth. Goddamn, those puppy dog eyes will be the death of him.

"Not that I mind," Christopher smiles, licking his lips. "I'm just sayin' – I could give you a hand. Or two."

Gyth's entire body lights up. "Yes, please," he breathes. "Give me all your hands."

"Afraid I only got the two," Christopher admits, putting his glasses somewhere on the crammed nightstand.

"More than enough," Gyth smiles. He welcomes Christopher with open arms and tendrils, pulling him close, into his warmth.

The room is cold, but Gyth is always running hot. Christopher dives in, curves his body against his, sighing. Gyth strokes his head with tentacles, and his shoulders and back with pulsating hands. That can kiss him, too! On his ass, they fan out to knead it, stroke it. Gyth curls his tentacles around Christopher's thighs when their cocks rub against each other to broaden their touch.

"Come on," Christopher whispers. He gently guides him upwards to the headboard. He pulls a pillow behind his shoulders to rest against. "This is *Casa* Ennington, make yourself comfortable, please."

With that out of the way, Christopher straddles his naked hips so that their cocks are squished tight. He guides away Gyth's arms to have better access to his chest, so ripped – Goddamn, even his nipples look designer.

Christopher tilts his head and flicks his thumbs over them. Slower, quicker, alternating. Pausing often enough for it to tease.

Gyth bites his lip. With a smile, he presses his crotch up against Christopher's. Tentacles leak around his legs, curling upwards slowly. They're unbelievably slick already.

"You like that, hm?" Christopher whispers.

Gyth's hum steams with satisfaction. His muscular arms spread from the pillow across the bed. Their bones crack, growing longer until the reach the bedframe to hold onto. He arches his chest against Christopher's hands when he strokes his pecs and cups them gently. They melt into his touch – so simple yet so powerful.

"I love your hands. Christopher, I adore them. Please don't take them off me…"

"Oh, I won't. I promise. 'cause I love your entire body," Christopher smiles, blissfully taking in the beautiful bouquets of tentacles and threads where Gyth's legs used to be. "Whatever shape it takes on."

Gyth sighs, eyes closed in pleasure. Christopher slides his hands over his taut nipples to roll them between his fingers.

He could swear they grew into his touch.

Dizzy with desire, Christopher sinks down to catch them between his lips, one after the other. Sweet little buds in his mouth. He sucks, and Gyth hisses and writhes beneath him, a slick tendril coming up to caress his back sack.

"Oh – oh, I want that, too."

"Can't you make some?" Christopher suggests. Wet noises from below show that Gyth wastes no time. His tendril reaches from Christopher's balls to his own brand-new ones, curling and squeezing when Christopher sucks on him in the same rhythm as they do.

"Oh, no… they're so tight already. S-shit, Christopher…"

Wow – it really doesn't matter if Gyth is on the giving or receiving end. This stuff does a number on him. Not that Christopher judges, having pretty sensitive nipples himself – he appreciates being with someone who shares that. He rubs Gyth's left nipple with two fingers. Giving it a tug. "You could take the other," he suggests before giving it a lick, teasing a bit, then closing his mouth over it again.

Gyth agrees more than eagerly. Instead of prying his mouth-hands loose from the edge of the bed, a fat tentacle from below comes flying to his chest and lands on it with a juicy sound.

Christopher gives it an appreciative stroke, humming around him – and then the tentacle attaches to Gyth's other nipple, sucking *hard*. Its muscles billow in the motions.

"You wanna suck your brains out of there or somethin'?" Christopher chuckles.

Instead of 'brilliant idea', Gyth's reply is enwrapping his head with hungry tentacles and hands alike, moaning through sparks of energy pulsating under his thin human skin.

Christopher takes it as encouragement. He hollows his cheeks, works his jaw like he's sucking on something way bigger. But goddamn, if his isn't hot – Gyth is coming apart just from that. The tentacle around their balls shivers. And *vibrates* when Christopher starts nibbling. Aha. The excited splashes around them tell him he's onto something!

Gyth arches his chest so hard he must be breaking bones. Indeed, when Christopher caresses his side, his ribs ripple below his sweaty skin. His new pair of hands is tight around Christopher's neck. "Keep – using your teeth, *Christopher!*"

"Can I bite down?" Christopher asks, maybe naively so: His working partner – meaning the huge tentacle on Gyth's right nipple – splits open on all sides. Snow-white fangs with serrated edges move up and down as the tentacle keeps pumping him mercilessly with its smacking sounds. It detaches to reveal a lamprey mouth of teeth, dripping with his clear juice, before crashing down again, biting and tugging like a beast.

And all that mere inches from his face. Christopher's cock twitches.

"Christopher?" Gyth's voice is a high-pitched whine, as if to check whether he's still there.

"Y-yes," Christopher says belatedly, before resuming his ministrations. Oh, fuck, he's going to come from this too, isn't he… He bites down broad into Gyth's pec to still have room for his tongue to flick his nipple from in-between his teeth.

"Closer, please…!"

"Okay, okay," Christopher breathes. It goes against his grain to willfully hurt Gyth. Much to Gyth's despair, it takes him another moment to bite the bullet – or, well, the nipple.

After a quick inhale, Christopher's teeth come down hard. He tugs – tears? – at Gyth's flesh, holding him down by his impeccable abs.

He is rewarded with a whale song that accompanies Gyth's helpless moans. Thank God, he really does like this, huh?

Christopher licks the nipple to give it time to soften before repeating his bites. Gyth's skin pulsates in a manic heartbeat beneath his hands. It must restrain him painfully hard by now.

"You can change," Christopher breathes before biting down again. It's like coming up for air, Jesus Christ.

Gyth writhes. "It'll grow bigger," he warns him. "I will be tight inside your hot, little mouth – I'll tear you apart…"

"Go big for me then," Christopher suggests almost nonchalantly, because by God, he needs to keep this casual if he wants to last any longer. Gyth makes good of his promise with a happy trill. The nipple between Christopher's teeth bubbles, fattening –

It actually grows. Christopher tries to keep up, biting down even harder onto the soft flesh. He resorts to sucking when it has the size of a thumb, afraid of accidentally severing it.

But Gyth keeps whining about his teeth.

"Jesus," Christopher sighs. By now, Gyth's nipples – yes, the other one, too – have the size of dicks. And they keep going. Gyth squeezing his balls tight is a good sign that Christopher is on the right path when he starts stroking his nipple at the base, biting down on the tip. He doesn't hold back anymore. Poor Gyth must be sore as hell by now. Christopher's strokes help them find a rhythm. He now uses both hands – that thing just keeps going – and it even throbs like a cock against his palms.

Gyth's sigh echoes in his ears like a song. "I want to fuck your mouth, Christopher… Will you let me fuck your mouth?"

"How could I say no to that?" Christopher smiles. He pecks the nipple in front of him and caresses Gyth's chin to show him it's all right.

He won't even need to be careful with the teeth this time.

The nipple he's still holding twitches when Christopher puts his mouth over the tip. Gyth finds the rest of the way on his own. He slithers down his throat and up again, flowing, elongating – and yes, grazing against his hard teeth!

Saccharine scent fills the pink air.

Christopher hums around the unusual texture on his tongue, hard yet wrinkly. He keeps stroking the base. In the corner of his eye, he can see Gyth's tentacle twirling around the other nipple. They're the same size by now, one a luscious, dark brown, the other ink-black with blue undertones in its veins. And sharp-ass teeth.

To join in on the fun, Christopher curves his right hand, indeed his entire arm, around them.

Gyth sighs beneath him. With a splash, the toothed tentacle retreats, leaving only him and that serpentine nipple.

Christopher's heart skips a beat. Is he supposed to satisfy that thing alone? Surely a lamprey tentacle would be better at that.

Timidly, he pulls a large stroke around it down to Gyth's chest. It makes his hair come alive with excited tendrils.

Okay, Christopher thinks.

With new courage, he sits up straight on top of Gyth, slick shreds of flesh travelling up his back to support him. He holds Gyth's nipples in his hands like he usually holds the tentacles, long and curling. The left one keeps fucking into his mouth, while the right one thrashes around in unbridled pleasure.

By now, Gyth's arms are melting away, too. He heaves them around Christopher's hips with a splash, gently holding him in place. He ruffles his hair with brown tentacles, soaked heavy. "So good… You're doing me so good…"

Christopher hums around him. With a moan and his head rolling to the side, Gyth's presses his other nipple against his hollowed cheek.

Christopher needs no second invitation. He unclenches his jaw and takes the other in as well. They thrust into him in unison, grazing his teeth, pulling his posture up and down with their movement. They throb violently in his hands, too – so full in both his hands and mouth…

Gyth is practically singing by now. He is *very* effusive. "You make me feel so good, Christopher – your inside is the most wonderful place to be. Keep taking me in, please, *please*, confine me…" Each of his thousand movements speeds up, red and brown and pink.

'You don't need to say all that if you can barely breathe,' Christopher offers mentally. 'I mean, I love your voice! But it's hard though, isn't it? Just relax.'

"I need… to let you know though…"

'I'm aware you're havin' fun, believe me.'

The obvious amusement lacing Christopher's voice soothes Gyth. But still – "You need to know something else – I want to go faster," he presses out.

Christopher briefly interrupts his tentacles jobs to give him a double thumps-up.

With a grunt, Gyth's hair swallows away his head. They splash into his pink world as though the shining bed has simply been a diving platform. Christopher even sees the colorful reflections of water bubbles dance around them for a moment – just made of light instead of water – or were they? He can't tell, and quite frankly, there are more important things to focus on right now.

Though he feels decidedly lighter in this dimension, with its weird gravity, he's aching with the weight in and around his body. He wants to come.

Gyth's state is no better. He has reverted to his natural shapes, but they're running wild. The tentacles on Christopher's back slide around him, his ass, his chest and legs so slick and fast that he fears falling down.

But Gyth holds him close, no matter how wide his body spreads. It's easier with two tentacles attaching to Christopher's wet chest. They suck hard, searching – and find his lovely nipples.

Christopher cries around the tentacles in his mouth.

Gyth wills himself away. "Forgive me…"

'No – just right. I like it when you're rough', he assures Gyth. A happy trill is his answer, but it's lost in the sinful chaos around them.

Christopher jerks forward into the suction of Gyth's tentacles, held back only by his tight grip all around him.

Gyth rises, his tentacles growing higher. Christopher throws his head back so that they can pour straight down into him. A waterfall of flesh and muscles.

Isn't this when his gag reflex is supposed to kick in? Not that he minds. He just *needs more*. And he needs it now.

It's hard to keep up the pace of his strokes. And breathe through his nose. Burning passion is a fabulous pain killer. Still, his arms hurt like hell.

Just when it's about to become too much, Gyth curls around them. Or rather, snaps around them – he's moving and changing so fast Christopher can barely make out his individual shapes anymore. It's all one glorious, mad blur.

"You're so good…" Gyth's voice husky and warm as ever. But sex-ridden. "Just come for me now, Christopher. I yearn to see you come undone."

Christopher moans obscenely loud as Gyth slides out of his hands. He finally lets himself fall. Gyth detaches from his chest to tug his damp nipples outward and flick rapid tentacles against them, and he does the same to his balls.

It tips Christopher over the edge beautifully – finally, he's out of his debauched hell, this wonderful, lush paradise – he screams around the tentacles in his mouth, not caring how loud he is, held tight in the grip of his technicolor orgasm. Gyth comes to his aid again. He milks his by now hypersensitive cock with long strokes. Thankfully he also puts his heavy suckers back on his nipples, and he *sucks*, all right –

Christopher faintly wonders if Gyth was *drinking* something straight from him, that's how eager he is.

The impression not entirely wrong. Each suck, each powerful stroke and rub fills Gyth with more and more energy, expanding him so agonizingly yet sweetly. Christopher blossoms in his embrace, sucking him off sedulously despite softening in the descend from his high… If only they could have even more…! He yearns to be greedy.

While Christopher still marvels at the sweetness returning to the tendrils in his mouth – they're transforming into tentacles, suckers and slime and all – Gyth uses his remaining energy to restrain and still himself. Despite wanting to *explode*, he forces one part of his body to form a solid shape. He presses his two tentacles into the very corners of Christopher's stuffed mouth to make room in the middle.

Christopher's tired eyes light up when he sees what Gyth has put in front of him. It is, in all its throbbing glory, his human cock. It curves upwards, bouncing in the slick movement of a stray tentacle noshing on it. Leaking with his precum from its beautiful, purple tip.

His voice is but a helpless echo. "Christopher…"

'Bring it on.'

Gyth sighs as he slides into the wet heat that is Christopher's mouth. One slick motion. Confined, constrained, by his teeth and tongue – and Gyth's own body, still fucking in and out of Christopher's walls. Warm liquid mixed with his saliva drops down Christopher's throat, bulging so beautifully as he takes Gyth in, keeps taking him in despite his hurting jaw and reddened lips.

But Christopher is glad to do all that. He is dizzy with devotion. He could fit Gyth anywhere. He sinks his hands into Gyth's soft flesh, kneads it, feels it flow between his fingers – and shudder against his wrists.

It doesn't take long for Gyth to come down his throat. Fresh and hot, and all for him. Christopher does his best to swallow both the load of his cock and the sugary liquid of his tentacles. Well, *if* his cock has ejaculated, the salty semen is now lost in the flood of honey. It goes on and on.

Christopher's Adam's apple bops forcefully, tears streaming down his face, but it's just too much to take. He spills over with Gyth's love. It floats out of his mouth, drips onto his chest. Streams down onto his dick. And it's in his hair now, too, with Gyth caressing him in the last waves of his orgasm. Like molten sugar, it keeps leaking out of him.

His overflowing honey is accompanied by his voice echoing in Christopher's mind. It is laced with awe and adoration, soft as though not to be heard, intimate. Like a prayer that solely consists of one word – his name.

Terms of endearment do seem kind of ridiculous in comparison, Christopher thinks.

He swallows as much of the load as he can. Even when Gyth slowly pulls out of his mouth, he keeps sucking on his cock like a lollipop. And he bites down once more, making Gyth whine in pleasure. He wants the very last drop. He keeps stroking it as it softens. And somewhen, his bed is back under his knees.

Above him, Gyth's human body reassembles itself out of fleshy currents. Like smoke falling closer into a gravity well to form a star. His human skin sheens with sweat. And other stuff, too, presumably. Breathlessly, he reaches for Christopher's head. He shivers when he pulls him close, to the pillow. "I'm sorry," he sighs, eyes closed. "That was a lot. I did not know I could get so wet…"

Christopher grins with bliss. "Don't you worry. I love that sweet stuff of yours." Gyth's helpless sighs make him lick his exhausted lips. "Like dessert after the main course. Here…" He collects saliva on his tongue and heaves himself up to let it drop into Gyth's mouth. He takes it in with a moan, then hums when Christopher kisses him, to really let him taste himself. He shivers in the afterglow of his orgasm when their tongues slide against each other, slow and warm. Grazing Christopher's teeth makes him pull his legs closer. He glows with peace as they share his sugar and shudders with adoration.

There is a joke somewhere here, Christopher thinks. 'You must give me that recipe.' Fucked-silly and exhausted as he is, he imagines Gyth as the charming chef of a cooking show. In a professional-looking black apron. Well, maybe not that professional. It'd say 'kiss the cock' or something.

He snickers into their kiss and lays down to nuzzle Gyth's face. A relieved sigh travels through Gyth as he caresses Christopher's torso. Slick and hot.

"Got a nice chest of your own, by the way."

Gyth laughs, warm and rough. "Thank you, I made it myself!" He snuggles up closer and sighs, "Christopher, I'm so happy."

Christopher smiles back at him.

"I'm so happy when I'm with you. And this... all this..." Gyth closes eyes in post-orgasmic bliss. "It's bloody fantastic."

Unsurely, Christopher shifts his head on the pillow. "What do you mean? Like – nipple play...?" He should order a few toys then, he thinks. Would be a sensible investment, seeing how they both liked it. A lot.

Gyth's smile doesn't fade as he looks at Christopher to think for a while. His voice is low when he replies, "They are two things. Though they conjoin very often. One is a profound and unabashed joy whenever I'm with you. And listen to you sing. Cook. Laugh. I marvel at the wonders you show me." He smiles and gives him a kiss. "And the other is... this energy. Streaming through our bodies. When we're here – entangling – and touching – and, yes, 'nipple playing'." They laugh. "I am overflowing with all of it. With this fun. You give me so much pleasure. I am so glad we have found each other like this."

Christopher caresses his face and sighs. "Me too. Genuinely. I've been feeling the same way." He pauses. "I am very glad you're with me."

Gyth hears the worry swinging through his voice.

Christopher sighs and shuffles closer, holding onto him as though he might slip away any second now. "I honestly did not know I could feel like this again. Like, ever, really."

Gyth caresses him, listening.

The knot in Christopher's throat is strong, but he manages to swallow it down. Closing his tired eyes for the things he is about to say. Not even Mary has taken him seriously.

But she is gone now. It is a strange and terrible encouragement to try anew: "I did not know I could ever... trust someone again. Let alone have sex. Sex was part of what almost erased me. So that nothing of me was left. Looking back – I was a living dildo for seven years straight. And when my depression got so bad she couldn't even make me hard anymore, she

222

finally divorced me." Christopher tries swallowing another knot but fails. "And told me it was only natural that I couldn't get it up anymore. 'cause I'm unable to love. Or whatever."

'She'. The pain in that word is more than obvious to Gyth. The cluster in his mind is growing; he has suspected Christopher's mother as one thorn already. Now another one grows into the light. Its new visibility comes at the cost of blood flowing from the heart, where it has been cultivated for so long, without any gardener to take care of it.

"Oh, Christopher. That's not true."

Christopher smiles at him. "I know. Like, deep down, really deep down, I hoped it wasn't. But then sometimes, it felt like the only logical explanation." In a whisper, he adds, "I feel like you help me remember it isn't true."

Gyth pulls him closer. "I'm so sorry for what happened to you." He kisses his eyelids. They tremble over hot tears. "And I'm sorry we talked about something so hurtful just now."

"No. No, it's – it's the exact opposite." Christopher frowns. "It feels good to talk about it. It's freeing. That hasn't been the case in the past. So don't apologize. You're a great listener."

Gyth caresses his hair. The only regret greater than having been unable to shield Christopher from that pain of the past is that he is unable to lift it from him now, although it is very much in his power to pull those cursed thorns from his heart.

He could lift that pain from Christopher so they could share it, if only they were one –

He chastises himself for the cursed thought in silence. Joining could kill, he reminds himself.

Is he at least allowed to dream about what it would be like?

Meanwhile, Christopher snuggles against his chest where he finally lets his tears flow. There must be rules, Gyth thinks, against such hurtful and devastating relationships. Not theirs, like he has suspected. They are both happy. Christopher, back then, was anything but. So much so that those shadows still haunt him in the present.

To Gyth's relief, his smile is back when he heaves his head upwards now. "I'm so full… but I still need to take a shower. And, like, open a window."

"Very well." Gyth smiles into their kiss. It is slicker than unusual… "Oh, um – actually, let me clean up first."

"What?" Christopher looks around. The entire room, its ceiling, its furniture, its windows, is covered in monster goo. It drips from his canopy-less canopy bed in thick threads. And covers the floor in glistening puddles. Christopher snorts. With his sex-ridden body, he probably wouldn't have made it to the bathroom without slipping and breaking some bones.

This is out there, he thinks. All of this is. In the past, he has hated when the room smelled of sex. But for the first time, he doesn't mind. He doesn't feel dirty. Instead, he welcomes the sweet scent and the butterflies back in his stomach.

He yawns. "Okay. While you do that… I'd cheer you on. But I think I'll take a nap in the meantime."

"That's all right," Gyth assures him. His human body lies still in their cuddle while his tentacles go collect their liquid honey in a playful spell. Like those cleaning songs.

Christopher's sleep tonight is tight. And yet he is uneasy when he wakes up in the morning. He does not remember any nightmares. Or dreams, for that matter. The sky feels like his inner state this morning. It is empty but its blue tones gray and subdued. Those must be clouds. But he cannot see them.

Not much time to think about this though. Duty calls – Gyth into the darkest corners of this world, Christopher into the post office. The train of everyday life doesn't stop.

It pulls him so meticulously that he does not notice the change in his coworkers at first. He sorts the mail, outgoing and incoming, then sorts some stamps, then gives the floor a wipe.

Today's absence of the drills that are Richard's and Tammy's eyes goes unnoticed until lunchtime. He keeps looking for them. No clerk is at the counter. Although it is not his job, Christopher accepts five online shopping return deliveries and then sells a bunch of Christmas cartons. His hands are sweaty on the cash register. Fortune does favor fools – he knows how everything works thanks to all his 'switching' with Richard.

Where is everybody?

Christopher lacks the courage to stave off the remaining customers. When all is processed – and that is a lot, in Christmas time – he hurries to write a "we will be right back" note and disappears in the backrooms. His heart is beating out of his chest.

"Eleanor?"

His manager doesn't answer. He goes knocking at her door. It is open, just a crack.

The hunters couldn't have come here. Right?

With his heart pounding so hard he can hear it in his ears, he pushes the door open. Eleanor's office chair is empty. When Christopher turns around, the corridor is long and empty in front of him. He takes off his glasses, rubs his eyes – the floor is not dissolving, those are your eyes.

With short breaths, Christopher strides forward. The common area is now lit up. This time without knocking, he rushes through the door.

Inside, he meets the green poison that are Richard Shea's eyes. "Speak of the devil," he greets him coldly. "We already finished lunch," Tammy informs him. Eleanor is by her side, silent. No lunch boxes are on the table they stand around. And nobody has answered to his calls.

It takes Christopher a few moments to take in the situation. He frowns. "Yeah. Yeah, cool. I've been at the counter for the past thirty minutes," he lets them know.

"And we've had lunch," Richard says.

Christopher shrugs in a flicker of new-found courage. "Okay. You could've said something." Anger pools in his stomach. Has this been sanctioned by Eleanor, too?

Tammy gives him a terrible smile. "We didn't invite you in case you wanted to eat out with your boyfriend. I bet it's not good to keep him waiting. You don't wanna make him angry."

Okay – Christopher's shoulders rearrange themselves vindictively. A glimmer in his brain suggests where this is going, but he blows it out immediately. They wouldn't *dare* –

"Oh, no, don't give us that look," Richard complains. "It's not like you never ate with him. And never took over the service counter. We're not the bad guys here, Chris, and you know it. We've always been honest with you."

Christopher looks to his manager for help – but Eleanor is just side-eying him. He huffs. Don't say anything, his brain cautions him. If you say something, you make it real.

They know. They know, but he is not terrified, to his own surprise. He's disgusted. Maybe he has been too generous in comparing his colleagues to noble tigers in the past. They're just a bunch of assholes.

"Yeah, whatever – just don't leave all at once the next time, maybe?" he suggests in as friendly a voice he can manage. He's already halfway through the corridor when Eleanor calls after him: "Chris! I'm sorry it escalated this way."

Oh, he won't have this conversation. Not now. Christopher still turns around. "Yeah, thanks. I'm not getting paid to do the clerks' work – that's all I was saying," he fumes. He sure as hell will not 'switch' with anyone ever again, only to get paid less. A billion other things press against his pinched lips – *keep Gyth the fuck out of this, whatever was going on back there* – but he bites his tongue.

"Your situation right now is hard," Eleanor says in her sympathetic corporate voice. "And it affects the entire team. Everyone here has been worried for you for months."

"Eleanor, look–"

"I think you should take a time-out, Chris."

Every fiber in Christopher's body freezes.

"I think it'd be better that way. For you and the team. Don't you think?" Eleanor tilts her head at him – she really believes what she's saying.

Christopher glares. He swallows hard before whispering, "You know I need this job."

She sighs. "I know. And I know it's been hard for you. It is hard for a man to go through all what you've been through. But do you really think the way you're living your life right now is leading you onto a better path?"

Yes – Christopher wants to scream at her! Yes – how dare she? Ever since Gyth has stumbled into his life, he is a changed man. He sleeps better, eats better, he talks instead of bottling up – he hasn't fantasized about killing himself *for weeks*.

For his boss to diminish all that *and Gyth* –

"We do not always recognize sin," Eleanor tells him, her face a parody of kindness by now. "The devil comes with countless faces, many of them friendly. I wish you all the best. I genuinely hope you'll find a way to see beauty in the natural way of life again. May God bless you." She turns to leave.

And with that single motion, Christopher falls apart like a toy block castle. He *wants* to tear his stupid name tag off and crush it into her hand, giving her a real piece of his mind – how he doesn't want to work here anyway and that they're all a rotten bunch of snakes. That she can kindly shove 'recognizing sin' up her ass. That'd be the manly thing to do.

What he actually does is walk after her with his head ducked. "Please, Eleanor, I need—"

"I already called John. You can take the rest of the day off." With that, she shuts the door in his face.

There goes his island.

Christopher stares at the door as though Eleaner had put hooks into his eyes before closing it. When he finally snaps out of it, he goes to grab his bag. He makes sure he leaves nothing here and hurries past the customers waiting in the entrance, head down, shoulders tense, desperately trying to block out their irritated questions in this crazy Christmas time.

They cannot fire him because of his sexual orientation, or some religious offense – can they? But *is* he fired? Will he get a termination letter mailed to his home?

Breathing hard, Christopher rummages through his bag. He wouldn't put it past them to sneak it in there when he wasn't looking.

He wants to yell at them. For exploiting him all those years. For treating him like this – and pulling Gyth into their bullshit. He wants them to pay for all that, be it in court or in a meat grinder. But what he actually ends up doing is breaking down. He sobs against his door as it finally closes behind him.

Good thing Gyth isn't home. He must make a pathetic display, with sweat stains on his uniform despite the winter temperatures. And his face all red. And hands shivering from fear.

He rakes his fingers through his hair. What about rent? He'll have to terminate the rescue dog donations, too. Won't even be able to help them financially anymore. And what about child support? What about a Christmas present?

Shit – he hasn't bought anything for Ally yet. Will he be able to gift something to her at all?

'Sorry, baby, daddy's been fired.'

Has he been fired? His brain paces in this twilight zone.

If he were to call the office now, Eleanor would tell him, "I knew you'd play that card. I didn't fire you, and you're not discriminated against. Stop making everything about yourself." And she'd hang up, and there was nothing he could do.

Christopher's lungs go crazy. His heart is beating so hard it must punch against them. He sobs into his hands.

Retake control, his brain whispers. You know how.

Christopher sobs. He doesn't *want* to.

You don't have the luxury of choice right now, his brain reminds him. *Do what is necessary.*

That's right. The old action plan gives Christopher tranquility. He heaves himself up. Stops sobbing. Takes off his jacket, hangs it up orderly on the coatrack. Adjust the sleeve, add your bag – there you go.

He steps down the corridor. The bathroom is at the very end. Before it come the kitchen and bedroom. The doors are open. Christopher looks inside. His Helping Paw uniform is already on the bed, ready to be put on. He folded and placed it there this morning. The shelter, an island that still stands, despite the recent rise of water levels. He can go to the shelter. Clear his mind. Take care of the dogs. He wanted to go today anyway. He could just as well come early. His fingernails dig into the doorframe. "Yes," he says out loud. It is better to go to the shelter.

After that mental statement, it's almost laughably easy to step into the bedroom and get dressed.

Christopher is focused during the drive. Twilight is approaching fast now that they're back to standard time. Despite announcing the arrival of darkness, Christopher finds the pastel colors nice to look at. They're gone far too soon.

The shelter is restless. Pebbles has had visitors whose children treated her poorly. "She didn't bite," Stephanie informs him in the corridor.

Christopher swallows. Biting a kid would've meant a string of complications for Pebbles' future adoption. "I thought these would be the ones," Stephanie says, rubbing her eyes in exhaustion. "Fucking kids."

I would adopt her, Christopher wants to say. That tiny, one-eyed chihuahua. In a heartbeat. But now he doesn't even have a job to pay for his own food, let alone a dog's.

He takes Pebbles with him into Shelly's kennel tonight. "You were so close, hm?" he whispers, holding Pebbles close while he tickles Shelly's ears on the ground.

Pebbles closes her eye.

"Yeah," Christopher says. He kisses her tiny head. He wants to sleep, too. Preferably for an indefinite amount of time.

"C'mon, get down."

Pebbles hops from his lap and next to Shelly, where she rolls herself up. Christopher pats her, at peace. "At least you have each other, hm?"

When he goes home, he will be alone. Maybe Gyth has not yet returned from his watch over this world. And Christopher calling his name would be distracting. Maybe he'd get hurt because of him.

Maybe he could just wait for his return. Or go to sleep.

Actually, why not? Christopher's back straightens at that realization: In the past few weeks, he's never woken up alone.

"I'll leave you now," he announces.

Shelly gives him a soft look as if to say, 'Get lost already.'

Christopher pats her. "You'll look out for the little one? Yeah? Good girl."

He drives home tired, keeping his eyes open via earsplitting rock music booming from the radio. He can't possibly know where Gyth is – or hell, if something has happened to him during his crazy stunts.

His *duty*, Christopher corrects himself.

But somehow, he knows. He can feel it in his bones. That they're going to be all right, as long as they're together.

He hopes they'll be together. Still, he feels pathetic whispering, "Please be home."

The keys click softly in the door. And inside, the TV is zapping from channel to channel.

Gyth is sitting on the sofa with his knees pulled close and only a T-shirt, despite the cold temperatures. His eyes are firmly on the TV, glimmering through the dark room just like the screen. This explains the strange order of the channels. Gyth is changing them with his mind. "Hello, Christopher," he says without looking up.

Although it's a grimace, Christopher can't help but smile at him. "Hey."

Gyth is still as a statue. "I am looking for the two FBI agents. I cannot find them."

Christopher may be tired, but that doesn't stop his ironic mood. "There can be only one explanation – alien abduction."

Now Gyth looks at him. Although his eyes are no longer glimmering, his face is strangely empty. Christopher remembers this look from the way Gyth has dealt with strangers in the past. Don't look into it too deeply, he reminds himself. Gyth has maybe had a shit day as well.

With an important face, Christopher grabs the TV guide. "Let's see… My research suggests they will be back by 1:55." He quirks an eyebrow at Gyth. "Just gotta wait a bit longer."

"I see." Finally, Gyth's face softens, and his limbs along with it. Back to his old self. "How are you?"

Christopher puts the guide back onto TV stand with a weak smile. "Tired."

Gyth's eyes, now clearer than before, scan him. He knows there is more to Christopher's answer. But he doesn't push the topic. He can't.

They just hover around each other.

Christopher ignores his 'deer in the headlights' stare and steps over to the wardrobe. "I'll get changed and join you."

Gyth swallows at his choice of words, however carelessly spoken. "Yeah. All right." He curses himself for the slight delay of his reply – it makes Christopher turn around.

"Hey, what's wrong?" Without taking his eyes off Gyth, he goes to switch on the lights. The TV flickers, hisses.

Gyth finds it hard to avert the attention. "I have had an encounter," he presses out. "I've just returned."

Christopher nods. "A nasty hunter?"

Gyth presses his lips together – and for a few terrible seconds, his eyes are stale with anger. 'Nasty' doesn't even come close it to. After what feels like eternity, he says, "I'll have to tell you sometime." When he looks at Christopher now, he softens anew. "But not tonight. I still need... time to think about it. I'll tell you once my confusion has dispersed."

"Whenever you're ready," Christopher says. He comes over to the sofa and caresses Gyth's face. Lifts him up to his knees by his chin. But he's too weak to kiss him. Or tell him that he's been fired because apparently this stupid world and its 'natural way of life' don't want them to be together – his deepest fear – the core of his ugly little heart that can't even speak.

Standing by the armrest with his head down, Christopher sobs. "You're always so honest."

Gyth shifts beneath him.

"You open up to me all the time... about who you are and that pink world of yours..." He inhales, trying to compose himself. "I feel like I cannot give myself up to you. In the way you deserve. You deserve *the world*."

Gyth pulls him in with tender hands on his waist. "You've told me yourself, there is no need to rush. Share with me whatever you want whenever you want."

His hug is like spikes into Christopher's body. "What if we do need to rush? What if we don't have time?"

"That is a philosophical question for someone who doesn't know how time works."

Christopher barks out an ugly laugh. Then stifles another sob.

Gyth's gentle hand stroking his back is agonizing. His voice is softer when he says, "Let it out. That's another thing you have told me."

Yeah – let out your eldritch body. Not some pitifully concealed anxiety attack, Christopher thinks. "Men don't cry," he presses out. "I should be *angry*. After everything that happened today, and in the past seven years… I should be furious. And I am!" He gasps. "But all I can do is cry."

"Then cry. Stop trying to do what others want you to. Do what *you want*." Gyth's voice is unusually hard. But his hands are still tender. "You don't need to share anything you don't want. What is yours stays yours, Christopher. You are your own person."

He then runs the pad of his thumb over Christopher's cheek to catch a stray tear. It's all Christopher needs to finally let go.

He sobs without trying to think of the neighbors. Without trying to think of his mother if she could see him right now, shedding tears into the black T-shirt of a man.

A man who is also a monster.

His monster, he thinks, burying his face in the crook of Gyth's neck, pulsating with the exact same heartbeat as his. His darling monster…

His fingers twist in the artificial jacket that is Gyth's skin. "Damn all the others," he croaks.

Gyth's eyes are dark with cosmic ravines. "Yes."

They lie close on the sofa tonight. By now, cuddling is Christopher's favorite kind of physical contact. He enjoys Gyth's tender fingers stroking his hair. He loves the weight of his body against his. And the comfortable silence.

Somewhen, Gyth breaks it. "Your shoulders are tense," he whispers as they watch some late-night news. Sports section. American football.

"I probably have knots all over," Christopher shrugs. He kneads his nape and grunts softly. His eyes hurt from crying and now from watching TV in the dark.

Gyth's eyes are no longer on the TV. "I can do that for you."

"Yes, please." Christopher sighs when two hands close around his nape and shoulder. They clutch, but significantly softer than he did. He snorts. "I'm not made of glass. Give me a good squeeze, c'mon."

Gyth tries it out, making Christopher exhale.

"Oh, that's good."

A smirk tugs at Gyth's lips. This is not sexual. It's like sleeping. Regeneration for Christopher's body.

His fingers melt deeper to stretch Christopher's tired muscles. He relaxes into the touch like a pillow. It hurts just a little bit, far less than Christopher would've thought. He can't think of the time he'd last gotten a massage.

He thinks his enjoyment is quite obvious. But he remembers Gyth's tendency to voice his thoughts and compliments him, "You're very good."

Much to his contentment, he can hear the smile in Gyth's answer: "Thank you." Though both his hands are busy on Christopher's shoulders, another one grows from his cracking body and reaches out to intertwine their fingers on the armrest.

In the past, Christopher has been so wary when it came to cuddling. Though he enjoyed it very much, it has usually served as some sort of twisted foreplay. As though by consenting to touch at all, anything was fair game.

All that baggage comes back, now that Christopher has Gyth all over him again. His groin tightens when Gyth grows further to work his lower back. He exhales through his nose, shifting on the worn-out sofa.

It's not the same. It might feel similar, but it's not. Those tentacle-like fingers can't belong to anyone but Gyth.

A sigh leaves Christopher's lips at that thought. He shifts closer to Gyth, who is still busy working his tense back. Christopher rolls his head to the side, exposing his neck.

Gyth doesn't shame him for it. Instead, his whisper is warm against Christopher's skin: "Can I kiss you here?"

Christopher hums appreciatively.

When Gyth lowers his lips, he tastes Christopher's arousal and mirrors his hum as soon as he is on his skin – long and vibrating through him, making Christopher shiver. Gyth stills himself to not change the touch on his back and hand. But his mouth still drinks his strange energy, the one that both satisfies and intensifies his hunger.

Christopher gasps quietly from below. Blood is rushing through his body. And being stopped.

Gyth looks up curiously, unprepared. Christopher is swelling below his clothing.

Now Gyth's movements stop for good. "You are changing," he says, only faintly aware of how his voice must be dripping with enchantment.

Without opening his eyes, Christopher says, "And it's entirely your fault. Your fault." He squeezes Gyth's hand. Why it's coming back now, he doesn't know. But somehow, he fears that looking might reverse his growing erection. However, he has the feeling that, with Gyth getting so excited about it, at least his arousal will stay. He chuckles. "You wanna touch it?"

"Yes."

"I was hopin' you'd say that. C'mon, do your thing," Christopher drawls, relaxing even further into his otherworldly touch after muting the TV.

And Gyth does do his thing. He grows a sleek tendril, careful to move slowly, to reach across Christopher's thigh. His cock is a bulge below his clothes. Gyth strokes it, surprised by the change in texture. It is harder – not as much as Gyth has observed in his own human body, but still so different from usual that he cannot help but stare.

Christopher sighs at the clothed touch, squeezing their hands again.

"Does that feel good?" Gyth wants to know.

"Yeah. Would feel even better without the sweatpants."

Gyth hisses above him, shifting to tug at the two waistbands. He slowly pulls them down to expose the half-hard cock, nestling in curly hair. His hands leave Christopher's back, one resting on his shoulder, the other lying down on his chest. His heart pounds against it.

And the third hand still holds Christopher's.

Instead of cold fingers, a warm, moist tentacle caresses his dick. He sighs. Gyth swallows above him, curling his tentacle around him to erect his dick higher.

Like one of those twisted candles, Christopher thinks with a chuckle. God, he's tired. But he does open his eyes now.

What he sees *is* smaller than he thought, because he feels gigantic right now. Having Gyth curled around him like this, being able to feel every pulse of his cosmic body on his dick, is another layer of heavenly. "It looks so beautiful," he smiles.

Gyth chuckles, rough and warm.

"I'm serious," Christopher drawls with a smile, not caring how dopey he might look. "'m serious. You're so gorgeous."

Gyth bites his lip. His caress across Christopher's chest is adorably shy.

Christopher tilts his head to lean it against his pecs. "It's really changing colors, huh?" The shades of Gyth's tentacle fade from turquoise to pink and green, and blue back again. Or is it the backdrop of the TV? The weather forecast?

"Would you prefer a permanent colour?"

Christopher snorts at the salesman-like sound of that question. "No. I like you just the way you are." He looks up as the emotion sinks in. Gyth's eyes meet his in a sweet gaze.

"I mean that so, so honestly."

"The feeling is very mutual," Gyth whispers against his lips before they kiss. It's soft and chaste. Who knew a tentacle job could be *chaste*, Christopher wonders.

Gyth works him tenderly, with just the right amount of pressure. He squeezes him to move up and down, as one would with a slow hand. Only this one has two rows of suckers that rub wonderfully across his sensitive skin. And attach to the tip of his cock. Gyth suckles a bit, then detaches to lazily slide the thin tip of his tentacle against the slit.

Christopher sighs into their kiss. Their tongues crawl against each other lovingly. By now they know what the other likes. The glasses don't get in the way either. Christopher lowers his head to suck on Gyth's clothed nipple. Gyth gasps at the wet warmth around it, at the tension of the fabric.

But when Christopher bites down through the T-shirt, Gyth denies his own sounds. He exhales and relaxes as he guides Christopher's head away with a gentle hand. Even his tentacle comes to a halt.

Afraid of having hurt him, Christopher's eyes dart upwards. But Gyth's expression is soft. With half-lidded eyes, he asks, "Would you like to practice 'giving yourself up to me'?"

Christopher needs a moment to understand.

Gyth caresses the beard across his chin, wishing for his undivided attention. "I just want you to relax, Christopher. You don't have to give me anything in return right now. This is for you. You can let me take care of you."

Christopher shifts. "I don't mind 'giving you something in return'."

"I know." Something in Gyth's smile changes. "But it's not about that, is it?" His brows furrow ever so slightly. "I know it is harder for you to give up control than it is for others."

Christopher sucks in a breath, breaking their eye contact. Gyth can truly see right through him, he thinks. "It does scare me, I guess," he whispers.

"I know," Gyth says. There is more emotion in his voice than warranted – he can't possibly *know*, Christopher thinks. He can't know what he has been through in the past. Maybe he just gets the gist of it and that's enough to skyrocket his empathy.

Christopher licks his lips. He remembers how he once wanted Gyth to be his punishment, by having his monstrous way with him, no questions asked.

But things turned out different, didn't they? Very different.

He meets Gyth's eyes again. "I think I'd like to try… to give up control." He feels ridiculous, having to verbalize such a basic thought. But he's still learning after all.

A smile softens Gyth's features. "All right," he says, caressing Christopher's face. "I promise to take good care of you. Tell me if I should stop." He gives him a kiss, adding, "You've had a long day."

Christopher can't help but smile – that's a cute expression for an out-of-time creature to use. "Okay," he says, squeezing their still intertwined hands on the armrest.

Gyth rubs his thumb across Christopher's when he kisses him again. Christopher sighs into his mouth. He lets Gyth take off his glasses so that he can shift their angle, to deepen their hot touch.

Christopher gasps at the strength of his tongue. Gyth taking the uncontested lead in their kisses is a departure from how they usually do it. But Christopher would lie if he said he didn't enjoy it. He feels featherlight. All slow, Gyth licks across his bottom lip, straightens – and resumes his rubs on Christopher's dick.

Christopher tenses with pleasure, before resting his forehead against Gyth's strong neck.

"That's it," Gyth whispers. "Breathe."

He's right, the air does Christopher good. It surrounds him, fills him. He resists the urge to use his free hand to stroke Gyth's body. Instead, he cups his cheek to hold him in place. God, that beard is soft. He'd ask Gyth what sort of oil he uses in it. But that'd be useless, he thinks with a smile.

Shit – he's already too turned on to speak.

"Very good," Gyth finds. Christopher swallows – that husky voice still does a number on him. What was that thought he once had, about falling in love with a voice…?

He moans when two suckers attach to the base of his cock to keep it in place. Gyth uses the upper half of his tentacle to work him heftier. Christopher's mouth falls open, his hips and legs tense.

"Don't hold back," Gyth whispers. He's smiling himself, from the sound of it.

It's all the encouragement Christopher needs. His hips buck upwards to meet Gyth's touch. It's slick and makes a sound so obscene it sends a shiver down his spine. "Oh, fuck…"

"That was very good, Christopher," Gyth encourages him. "Try again?"

He does, and Gyth squeezes him tight as he thrusts upwards, into another wet and soft sound. Christopher grows desperate. He wants to reach down and jerk himself off. He is not in the mood to stay on this plateau much longer. But both his hands are firmly connected to Gyth. Although he has his entire weight against Christopher, he is pliant and soft against his own body. Steady. Not disgusted by jerking off a half-hard dick. He's fucking good at it, too, the way he uses his suckers. Just not vigorous enough.

The words on Christopher's tongue overcome his barrier in a moan: "I need more... Please, Gyth." With a snap, a second tentacle twirls around his cock, snuggling against all the places not covered by the first one. Gyth squeezes him tight, still moving up and down so wonderfully, and Christopher is cradled, covered from all sides – and that's all he needs.

Thrusting upwards, he comes over both tentacles. They work him in unison, firm and slick, while Gyth's hand reaches across Christopher's chest to tug on his clothed nipples. The hardest touch is the squeezing of their hands, and it's somehow so goddamned intimate Christopher wants to cry.

"So beautiful," he hears Gyth's voice – it makes him gasp for air even louder, desperate against Gyth's neck.

This orgasm is much more intense than their lazy position warrants.

It drags on relentlessly when Gyth shoves his tongue into Christopher's mouth once more, making him tilt back his head to lick him out nice and clean. Nice and kind.

When the waves of pleasure ebb away, he gets floppy in Gyth's embrace. The sound of the tentacles separating from his dick sends aftershocks through him. They let go of him simultaneously, like a modern art sculpture, threading his white cum between them as they still in their erect positions, curved at the tips like they were exhausted from fucking.

Christopher cannot bear the image – it's too sexy. "Oh, God..." He reaches down to his hip bone and caresses it for a last squeeze of pleasure.

Gyth joins him by thumbing at his nipples, lighting up sparks in his mental eye. "That was so good, Christopher," he murmurs.

Christopher moans – Gyth's own voice is heavy with desire.

"I'm so proud of you. That was bloody good."

Any possible reply gets caught in Christopher's throat. This is ridiculous, he thinks – he has been fucked high in the air, with tentacles both up his ass and deep down his throat – but *this* is what drives him nuts?

Is this what trusting your partner can do to you? Or is this cosmic madness? Whatever it was – holy hell.

He lowers his head to rest it in the crook of Gyth's neck. Shielded by his long curls around them. "Oh my God…"

"Take your time," Gyth whispers, again with the foreign expression. He strokes Christopher's craned neck with tender fingers. It's warm and safe, and Christopher could've fallen asleep in here.

But his dry mouth waters when Gyth's sticky tentacles crawl back to his own body. From the sounds of it, they're making quick work of Gyth's jeans and briefs.

Christopher sighs as he reaches down to join them. Gyth pulls him closer with a moan. Another one falls from his lips when Christopher cups the twisted moving and sucking sculpture around his cock. No ball sack to tickle today, so he instead strokes Gyth's exposed hip bones. They're vibrating.

Gyth is straining with that "sexual energy", as he calls it. Something only a human body can generate within him.

Christopher wants to pay him back. He shuffles away from Gyth's neck. "Here, let me…" He bends his head down to catch Gyth's clothed nipple between his lips. He mouths at it to wet the shirt, creating the loveliest friction. Gyth forms another tentacle solely to rest it on the back of his head. He moans when

Christopher lifts the fabric with his tongue, to bite into it without the nipple underneath.

"Oh, Christopher…"

It really is just another layer of Gyth's skin, Christopher thinks. That realization intensifies his shiver when the shirt tears to reveal Gyth's naked chest. He continues sucking on his nipple in the same rhythm of Gyth working his own cock, running hot.

Gyth's eight naked toes curl in the air. His head falls against Christopher's. Although he wants to sing his praises, strokes over Christopher's shirt convey his feelings just the same, he thinks when Christopher hums around his nipple. He cannot use his other hand to play with the second one, because it is still intertwined with Gyth's hand on the armrest. So, Gyth twists his torso to offer the second nipple to his mouth.

The deliverance is sweet on his lips. And teeth…

Gyth is utterly spellbound. Christopher is smelling of sex and very lavish with his energy. His blood is so close to Gyth's own, reddening his lips… Oh, yes, his inside is the most wonderful place – so different from the outside, so disorganized –

More than anything, Gyth wishes to see inside of him.

Christopher hums when the nipple between his teeth twitches. And grows. He gives it a lick, and Gyth moans helplessly above him. The tentacle on the back of his head claws into him. He pulls away to look at what transformed in front of him – a human eyeball, white, with a fuchsia iris around a dark pupil. It floats in front of Christopher's face, connected to Gyth's chest by thin, red muscles and veins. The materialization of his wish.

Christopher chuckles blissfully. "Aw, hell yeah."

With that, his lips are right back on it.

Gyth moans, tightening his tentacles around himself in a surge of pleasure.

The eye is moist with the same sweet liquid that covers his tentacles. Christopher licks across it. It is not perfectly round. The iris and pupil bulk out slightly, just like on a real human's eye. He tries closing his lips just around that hump and sucks.

Gyth rewards him with yet another hand in his hair and a moan so lovely Christopher can feel it travel his lean body. He takes him in entirely then, humming around the eyeball pressing against his tongue.

Gyth's touch around his cock grows erratic. Instead of slow and gentle, it is entirely helpless by now. And the best thing are all those rough tones in his moans, Christopher finds. He licks the eyeball like a live lollipop. It's not that much of a stretch, with that sweet liquid covering it. He uses his hand to hold it still by the muscles, to suck harder. Though delicate against his touch, it is strong enough to withstand a little roughness, delights in it, even.

He takes it out of his mouth with a soft pop, before sucking and engulfing it again. He repeats that a few times, softly smiling. "God, you're really something else. An honest-to-God eye candy."

Gyth does laugh at that, but it's a short, helpless sound. He is at an end. With this eye, he can see how red and white Christopher's mouth is, how it would glitter with his load inside, before he'd swallow and take him into the deepest parts of his body. His body of wonders and imperfections. A human treasure box. Now he twirls his fingers through the sensitive muscles growing from Gyth's chest, through the optic nerves that are now so close to his fingertips, where nerves flow together so excessively, so indulgingly.

So wonderfully close – but still separated. Not one.

Against the agony, Gyth wills himself to pull away his head. To look at Christopher through starry eyes, the cosmos' ever-changing colors shining onto the human beneath him through the bright holes in his irises. Christopher's skin does not scream for help. It welcomes the foreign touch, drinks from it to fuel Gyth's impending release. He welcomes the debauchery – welcomes Gyth – and would welcome him further. He said so himself.

There is only that one way to experience what Christopher was feeling, and to let him experience Gyth in return, before neither could make out which sensation has been whose to begin with. To truly be one. Gyth wants to share it with him. He wants to share everything with him. He wants to *free* him, to finally leave the horrors behind. They would be so happy together…

Gyth's eyes flutter when he draws in a breath. Like distant thunder, the joining spell forms on his lips. *"You and me…"*

With his eye at the back of Christopher's throat, where his muscles work so hard to keep Gyth in place, a helpless cry of pleasure escapes him, cutting off the spell.

He spills all over himself.

Then cool air hits his eye. Christopher's quiet gasps against his chest bring him back to the bedroom. Confusion overcomes him.

"Here," Christopher rasps, extending a hand to grab his cock and both tentacles around it. Oh, yes, Gyth remembers, he's supposed to keep moving during a human climax. Christopher's large hand works its magic on him with its usual ease and talented wrist movements. Wetted by his juices, it brings Gyth back onto the wave and helps him ride it until the end. Licking over his eye as he does. And he also catches it in his mouth again, to bite down once more. Just when Gyth thinks it is over, Christopher heaves him onto another wave of pleasure. Rubbing his nipple, sucking on his eyeball, stroking his cock so masterfully –

"Thank you," Gyth croaks, unwinding under the touch of his dear Christopher. But shame rages through his body, urging him to end soon. And clean up the mess.

His tentacles and additional arms fold themselves back into his human form, cracking in the rushed transformation. What has gotten into him?!

When their foreheads touch, Gyth whispers an apology. Unable to look at Christopher. "I'm so sorry. After everything I said, I still – oh, Christopher, I'm sorry."

But Christopher has no trouble looking. "I'm not mad at you." He opens his eyes to take in the pink one in his hand. Still a puppy dog look. But the color is more intense now because the TV's light has changed to pink as well.

With his last ounce of strength, he leans in to kiss the eyeball and draw it closer.

And with all those shooting stars having moved on, the night is quiet again.

Christopher remains gentle with him no matter what. Gyth tenderly nudges his head. Curls fall into his face. When he looks at Christopher now, he smiles. Humor bubbles up inside of him, tired but yearning for connection. "You have caught my eye, Christopher Ennington."

Christopher laughs heartily, more than such a pun warranted. Gyth loves to play on words. Christopher decides to ignore the joining stuff he has tried. The poor guy can't help himself, cut off from home in this world that must be so different from his own, Christopher thinks. He doesn't know what Gyth knows. He just wants to ease his mind. Like he eased his.

And it works: His laugh widens Gyth's smile. Even the eyeball in his hand twitches fondly, bright with infatuation.

Christopher shifts tiredly. He sits up straighter, letting go of Gyth's hand that he's been holding this entire time. It's still pulsating. Gyth hasn't changed his human body as much as he has in the past when they got hot and heavy.

"You good?"

"Yes," Gyth whispers. "What about you? I didn't want to hurt you."

"I assure you, you didn't," Christopher smiles. He plays with his curls. "Y'know, you could just... I mean, when we're around the house, you don't need to masquerade as a human. Or something solid at all. You can change all you want."

Gyth smiles softly. The brown of his eyes looks golden. "Thank you. I know how much it means to you to be with a human. Particularly this manly shape."

"It does but – it also means a lot to be with *you*. More, actually, than the other thing." Christopher doesn't sound as casual as he wants to.

'Human Gyth' running around as a man is both comforting and disquieting. People oppose them being together because they're two men, but Christopher wouldn't want Gyth to present as a woman. They've never really talked about it. Partly because in the end, Christopher figures, it wouldn't matter anyway. The point is that any solid form is a corset for Gyth to suppress his real self.

If Christopher is being honest with himself, people's view of them would only be marginally better if Gyth was pretending to be a woman instead of pretending to be a man. That's just the way this works. If Christopher had connected with *that* Gyth the way he has with *his* Gyth, somehow – even then, 'female Gyth' would still be a sloth, be out of touch and not know how to talk, act or dress. In the eyes of Hillsburg, 'male Gyth' is too feminine. Surely 'female Gyth' would be too masculine.

In the end, they would maybe dodge the big gay bullet but instead hit a dozen others, because they would both still be queer, just suppressing it even more.

All that shit… all not worth it.

Christopher is sick and tired of how highly he values that outsider perspective. He learned in preschool that it is not important what others might think of him. And yet, he is dependent on them. He needs them to like him, or at least not outright oppose him. But there isn't much he can do anymore. He's at his wits' end. All he knows is – there are no others with them right now.

They're on the sofa. Waiting for the cosmically shocked TV to restart.

Gyth wordlessly caresses his chest. Christopher cannot fool him into not seeing all that thought chaos. He lowers his voice and gives him an earnest look. "Be yourself, y'know. This here is my home. There's no need for all that pain here."

All that *unnecessary* pain for some invisible audience – yes, Christopher is sick and tired of all that play and pretend.

Before his eyes, Gyth inhales and shifts. His skin and hair twirl into the familiar black and brown and red and pink mess. Like smoke in meaty water. Christopher cuddles against it as Gyth changes around him. He cradles him warmly and safely on the sofa, with his soft clicks, trills and growls. Christopher nuzzles him playfully and watches him glide all the way around the canopy-less canopy bed. He laughs when Gyth hits the ceiling with a thud.

"There, there," he goes, caressing the flowing flesh above him. It's not 'the sky is the limit' with them, is it? The ceiling of Christopher's stuffy third floor apartment is the limit.

Before melancholy can overtake him, Christopher cups both his hands to hold the pink eyeball that has stayed with him throughout Gyth's transformations. Except it has grown to the size of an orange. Christopher nudges it gently as he leans sideways into the flesh that has become his backrest. Warm and soft, sometimes moist, always flowing.

He dozes through the majority of the FBI show. Gyth hungrily takes in the television waves. But he flinches when Christopher's fingers absentmindedly glide through his optic nerves again.

"Sorry," he mumbles in half-sleep.

Gyth blinks through the credits. "It's all right."

Christopher shifts. Gyth really wants them to fuse. Christopher wonders how that would work – *if* it worked, and that, even Gyth doesn't know for sure. His tiredness makes it impossible to stop his mouth: "Have you joined with someone before?"

Gyth's answer is a soft whisper, close and yet distant. Like summer rain. "Yes. It was wonderful." Remorse laces his voice.

"How did you know it would work?"

The question makes Gyth curl away like a snail into its shell. His eye melts through Christopher's fingers. He thinks of his fellow guardians – what were they doing now? Were they safe? Or were they in the currents of dimensions as strange as this one?

"Those were no humans..."

Christopher swallows. "I see." With that, he drifts off into uneasy sleep. It is deep like the ocean.

It will take him time and power to return to the surface.

He is lost in a sunken temple. Ancient columns block his way. They're overgrown and glow with a green shimmer. Christopher doesn't recognize the occult sigils inscribed in the stone. He does recognize a gray head of hair. His mother floats in front of him, facing one of the stones.

"Mom?" Fighting the pressure against his body, Christopher steps toward her. He reaches out.

Her head whips around, bright with her glare. "Chris."

Christopher flinches.

Mary grimaces. "Look at you," she spits through gritted teeth. "And what you've become!"

Christopher raises his hands. They tremble – but they look the same as always. "What do you mean?" he asks, eyes wide.

His mother is distorted with disgust and sadness. "What kind of thing have you turned into? What son would do this to his mother? You sicced a monster on me!"

"I was trying to save you…!"

"You condemned me to death!" Her echoes mix with another voice. Christopher turns around. Shreds of flesh wrap around his hands, pulling him toward another column, right through the painful pressure shredding his skin.

Christopher lets out a scream, his bones too heavy to move.

"Yeah! What citizen would do this? What have you done? You're a disgrace to all Americans." Those bleeding remains belong to Jeffrey Hobson. "What have you done? Why did you leave me to die? Will you devour me now or leave me to rot? What has gotten into you?!"

Christopher pries himself lose from the demonic touch. "I'm sorry," he utters.

"Are you?" Bodies crawl over the stone ground, over ruins, like spiders through the dark. Tammy Wilburg's eyes bulge out in weird distortions as she inhales his scent. Her head bubbles as though to contain her boiling brain. "What sort of a colleague are you? You sick pig…"

When she snaps her head, Christopher gasps, allowing water to flow into his lungs. *Is* he underwater? The emerald stones of Richard Shea scratch across his own eyes. "That's just like you – scared, even though we did nothing to hurt you. What sort of a man are you?"

"What sort of a human are you?"

"What sort of a son are you? People will talk! You sully your mother's reputation with everything you do, even though she is sick! What a monster you've become!" Mary accuses him, tears in her angry eyes. In a wave of pity, they blink. "And that body isn't yours either, is it now?" She gives him a sad smile. "Why did you steal it, Chris? Why would you do that?"

Christopher shakes his head.

"Why did you do that? Do you not know that stealing is bad? I have asked you a question, Chris Birk!"

That name – that is not what his mother used to call him. Her voice twirls and changes into another, one that Christopher has dreaded to ever hear again, that voice that cuts into him like cold razors. That pins him in place. He can't even move his eyes. Even his thoughts are coming to a halt.

Where is she?

"That body isn't yours! Give it back! Give it *back!*" Every scream is like a thunderclap. "Back! Chris! What sort of a husband are you?!"

Fuck wherever she is – he needs to run. He stumbles over the ruins, he needs to get away – get away –

The voice melts into distorted yells and shrieks, "It's not yours! Give it back!" Other voices join the choir. "Pay it back," Jeffrey Hobson rasps.

"Give it back, Chris!" Mary orders him. Christopher doesn't turn around. His lungs burn up. Something snaps around his ankle, icy and sharp. Nails dig into his calf and tear through his skin to create more entrances. His hands land flat on the ground as he falls, trembling, cracking under the water pressure. Still he pulls himself further, he *needs* to, just away, away, in spite of his body ripping apart –

"Give it back! You'll break it! It's not yours to break! Chris!"

FOSTER

THE NIGHTMARE HOLDS Christopher captive in its claws. When he's had bad dreams in the past, he has usually woken up from moments of shock. He doesn't this time. The horrors continue to creep into him, to crawl across his body to trap him in his sleep.

Sleep – he is sleeping – or is he? If he is asleep, he can wake up.

With a scream, Christopher thrashes around until he hits the headboard with his wrist. The pain unscrews his eyes – that's his ceiling – and stretched across it, a fleshy monster. Its edges resemble a man's face. But incomplete. Dripping. Meat and hairs peeling away, eyes rolling out of what once must've been a skull poking out of this body-wide open wound.

Holding onto his wrist, Christopher shuffles away. Any scream he has left gets caught in his dry throat. He whimpers when he slides off the bed. His foot is still up on the edge. His foot – the razor must still be inside – if that monster shoves it deeper into him now –

"Christopher?"

That name pulls a short cry from him. He thrashes his foot, kicks it across the edge.

It's still inside of him. It must be. It's in his calf. It must leak from his stomach. They've ripped his stomach in two.

With trembling hands, Christopher pushes away the blanket across his torso. Bit by bit, as though touching a hot cooktop. There is no blood. There's not even a wound.

It's just his body. Old and hairy and full of sleeping lines.

And this is his bedroom.

His grounding is broken by the sound of cracking bones. And splashing flesh. "Christopher..."

Christopher takes a shaky breath. "Gyth?" As his senses return, his face contorts. "Oh, fuck..."

"Christopher..." With a gasp, Gyth heaves himself around the bed. "I did not mean to frighten you," he groans, dragging a half-formed leg across the floor. He's taken on his human form for Christopher's comfort.

He could've kicked himself. "I'm not – you're not..." He sighs, covering his face with his hands. You didn't frighten me, he wants to say. But he can't bring himself to lie. This time, in the aftermath of that horror, he was truly scared.

"Are you all right?" Gyth hovers on the floor by his side.

Christopher sobs against his hands. "No."

"You're going to be. I am here." Gyth's voice is like honey. Like the morning sun, golden and warm. Christopher melts into his strong arms when they straighten him up. This is no cold ocean. This is his home.

But even when he lowers his hands, he cannot bring himself to look at his legs. His face is boiling with shame. "Gyth?" he whispers. "Can you – take a look at my foot?"

Gyth cranes his neck. Not unnaturally so, just like a human would.

"Is there... something sticking out?"

"No."

"Not a wound or, or anything?"

"Nothing," Gyth tells him, before meeting his eyes again.

"It was all just… a dream," Christopher realizes. He exhales, burying his face in Gyth's naked chest. "I had a nightmare." He nods, as if to reassure himself. "I've had a bad dream."

"Wherever it has taken you, you are here now. You are safe."

"Yeah." Christopher collects himself. 'Safe' – that just now was *pathetic*, that's what it was. He can't even remember shit. "I was… on the sofa."

"I moved you into bed. I thought that would be more comfortable. I'm sorry, I won't do it again."

Christopher frowns. He even tucked him in…

"No. No, thank you, don't apologize," he whispers, but it's barely audible to himself.

Gyth hears him anyway, though his senses are otherwise occupied. Despite Christopher's leg looking normal, there is something strange about it. Something… changed. A foreign smell that lingers in Gyth's nose.

Anger bubbles inside of him, ruffling him. It's that 'she'. Her. Reeking from yet another wound. Even after everything that has happened last night, that Gyth had not yet told Christopher about, she has somehow made her way to him in his sleep – *his sleep*, that which is so important to humans!

May she rot, Gyth curses, against his better judgement. May she *rot* in the trenches of the universe. But although his outrage, boiling hot, is directed both at her and at himself for his violent thoughts, there one thing burning even whiter inside of him. He reproaches himself for not having stopped Christopher's nightmare. In the fashion of a blinded guardian, he thinks he could have spared him the pain.

And just like that, Gyth is led down the garden path laid out by his persecutor.

Unaware of the cosmic pitfall, Gyth dutifully helps Christopher through his morning. He watches the shower for him while he is inside, feeds on cereal with him and helps him pick something to wear.

"Not the uniform?"

Christopher replies belatedly. "No, I'm not going to work."

He is not going to work. He is not singing and not dancing. Just lying by Gyth's side, though not quite sleeping. He is trying to recharge in a way that would spare him any more bad dreams. But humans need sleep, Gyth remembers as he strokes his hair.

At least by midday, Christopher is spirited enough to feed again. Although he does not want to stay alone, he agrees to Gyth picking up pizza by himself.

His fear of being seen together is still mightier than his fear of loneliness. It shouldn't be that way, he thinks. He broods.

Meanwhile, Gyth's task is simple and quickly fulfilled. Twenty minutes after Christopher's phone call, he materializes near Stuart's pizza parlor.

The old man is happy to see him again. "Here you go, son. One with artichokes an' one with pineapple."

Gyth thanks him. "Christopher gave me this." He extends his hand to drop the paper money into Stuart's little tray.

Though he takes it gratefully, there is a shadow spreading in his wrinkles. "Is he doin' okay? I mean, you two – are you doing okay?"

Gyth gives him a look. "I think so, yes. We have both been… bathing deeply in our thoughts lately."

"I see, I see." Stuart shifts on his feet. "I mean, I hear the folks talking." He scratches his head. "Or, well, sometimes I ask. And what they're telling me is bullshit. I mean, I've known him since he was a child, I've seen him when he's down" – he gives Gyth a serious look from beneath his gray eyebrows – "but when he's with you, the boy lights up."

Gyth smiles at the memory of Christopher's emotions tinting the air around him. "I know what you mean."

Patting the pizza boxes, Stuart nods. "Yeah, yeah. So, you're happy together, right?"

"Very much so," Gyth finds.

"That's what counts, son. Don't let anybody tell you otherwise. You're good for each other, I can see that."

"Thank you." Gyth takes the pizzas but tilts his head when doubt crosses his mind. "You don't think us being together is wrong?"

Unfortunately, Stuart's reply is very slow. His face hardens when his gaze wanders into the middle distance, to places Gyth cannot see. "Me personally, I don't think so. I mean, this is America. Ain't nobody gonna get yo' ass for being, *y'know* – they can't. Normally. But reality is different. The people in this town, certain people – some will never understand." Stuart meets his eyes in a sympathetic smile. But it's soft with sadness. And memories. "It's difficult. I know it is."

Gyth nods. He has had that impression with Christopher, too. And those cursed rules. 'Difficult'. He misunderstands that word for 'complicated'.

It is complicated to him. That those 'certain people' can get away with so much hurt, while innocent ones get punished.

Gyth returns to Christopher with knots in his heart. "Was I gone too long?" he wants to know.

Christopher shakes his head. Gives him a weak smile, with his hand around his chin. He only does that when he's uneasy, Gyth has noticed.

He does relax genuinely when they eat their pizzas though. His face is soft when he looks out the small kitchen window.

The sky mirrors the blue of his eyes. "It's a nice day." He shifts and gives Gyth a smile. "It's not good to stay inside all day. I know that. Sunlight and fresh air are good against thinking too much. Just like you."

"You mean to say I'm only good for dumb conversation?" Gyth asks him drily.

He rejoices at making Christopher laugh: "Yeah, you're a real simpleton. I *wish* I could talk about existentialism and the grand cosmos with you!"

"Yes, a pity."

"A pity," Christopher smiles and leans in to kiss him. Gyth kisses him back. But the melancholy is bittersweet, even through the pizza scent. He studies Christopher when he pulls away. "I would love to go outside and bathe in the sunlight with you."

"Okay. Cool." A shadow scurries over Christopher's face. "I thought about driving out of town. To the hills."

It is true, he has thought about that. He'd like it. Taking a sunny afternoon stroll through the woods outside of Hillsburg, away from unfriendly eyes and mouths. Away from the red-blooded small-town. Just the two of them, walking side by side, laughing, listening to birds. Alone. Leaning against a tree to kiss and sigh in that oasis, where the sky behind the tall branches was blue and wide. He'd be at peace out there.

But gas is precious now, and Christopher can't waste any. If there was an emergency of some sort where he had to take the car and was out of gas and gas money alike, just because of one self-indulgent forest frolic, he'd never forgive himself. So, what he settles on is: "But I'd rather walk."

Gyth nods. "Whereto?"

"I kind of wanna go to the park," Christopher says truthfully. "I haven't been there in ages. You know, just walking. That's our thing, isn't it?" He sniffs, looking away. "I couldn't go on walking dates in the past, or any dates, really, so... I'd really appreciate that."

Gyth knows it now. He strokes Christopher's arm for comfort. "It's a good idea, Christopher. Let's go then."

Truly, for someone who could not share any activity with their previous partner, be it buying donuts, taking a walk, or simply cuddling – Gyth wonders if all that is as new and exciting to Christopher as it is for him.

It is sad, he finds as they take their stroll through the park, considering that Christopher has spent his entire life in this dimension. It is his home. Yet he is just as much a stranger.

Not only a stranger, as Gyth is reminded of today. The estrangement grows much deeper. He realizes this when they walk down the path of pebbles, beneath the sun lighting up Christopher's eyes. He tells Gyth how much he likes this season. Indeed, Gyth has noticed this world has changed since his arrival. Now the trees are black and naked, to let through even more light. Over this season and the next, they will go to sleep, much like humans. Their leaves form a rug of oranges and grays on the ground. Gyth likes to watch them when the wind picks up and lifts them off the grass and paths.

Humans are also dressed differently. Now many go with scarves around their neck to shield them from the cold. Gyth has formed one, too, after he saw how fluffy the one on Christopher looked. It's just as blue as his eyes. Light.

When he laughs, a cloud of crystalized air forms and disappears in front of him. He is still under pressure but easing in this cool air, below the soft sunlight from that closest of stars in the sky.

Gyth is glowing with hope. But just when he thinks this world could offer something *more*, it shoves him back.

He watches a couple of humans walking, just like them, but with their hands connected. "Do you want to do that, too?"

As though under a whip, Christopher's smile dies. He looks down, tensing as he understands. "No, let's not." He clears throat, quietly adding, "Rather not."

Gyth's confusion must show on his face, because Christopher is quick to clarify: "Not because I don't want to. I do. But... y'know, maybe not here."

Gyth understands, grimacing at the fear spreading between them. "All right. Another rule," he says – too sorely.

Christopher stares at him, then looks around. "I mean it, it's nothing personal."

"I understand." Gyth meets his eyes, now pale against the starkness of the sky. "I understand your devotion to the rules. And I know they're complicated. I'm just... seriously starting to question their validity."

Christopher stops walking. "Are we doing this?"

"Are we?" Gyth asks bitterly. It's always the same – always!

Christopher blocks his way with a shivering hand, hissing his name. "Gyth! This is not about some goddamned pizza," he whispers. "This is serious. I don't wanna push our luck, simple as that. What's the matter with you?"

"I am fed up with your rules," Gyth says truthfully.

Christopher chews around that childish word. "There is a reason they exist. I had to learn them the hard way."

Gyth shifts on his feet, his eyes narrow as he sees through Christopher. "But do you actually believe in them?" They don't seem to matter to him when they're alone. This conditionality is irritating him.

Christopher stares at him wide-eyed before anger overtakes him. "What – it doesn't matter what I believe, Gyth! That's the whole point! My life depends on that shit. They're for survival! Is that so hard to understand?"

Gyth does find that hard to believe. "It is. Tell me what happens if you don't follow the 'serious' rules."

"You get beaten up!" Christopher seethes, still whispering. "In an alleyway, or a parking lot! You get kicked out of your family, onto the streets, even if you're only a teenager! You get assaulted and ostracized and fired from your job, or quasi-fired so that you've nothing on them – and I'm not sure you understand that." Even his pause is filled with anger. "I've been laid off. And if you don't know what that means – it means I can't go to the post office anymore, and I won't get money to buy the stuff I need – food, gas, the roof above my head, *everything* a human needs!"

Gyth blinks, softening in a brief flutter as he realizes what happened. "I'm sorry, Christopher."

But now the damage is done: "Yeah. Don't 'Christopher' me now."

His words pierce Gyth with the violence of that branch that once tore through him.

"I would've gotten beaten up in that parking lot, too, or worse, like it has happened to a thousand other guys already. And according to 'the rules', those bullies would be right."

Gyth looks away, sorting his thunderstorm of thoughts. His human nostrils flare at that implication and Christopher's firm belief in it. "Do you not see how that doesn't make any sense?" he growls. "To punish that supposed rule violation with assault? What harm is there in holding my hand?" The echo of Stuart's words from earlier cut open his skin. Pressure builds up in his human eyes: "When we both want it?"

He cannot understand why Christopher would treasure his hand in the dark but fear it in the light.

Christopher's eyes burn, too, and his heart races so helplessly Gyth wants to reach inside of him to hold it still.

"I am not discussing this out here with you. This is childish," he says with finality. He breaks their eye contact, but not without telling Gyth, "And don't you dare disappear into the earth right now. If you wanna leave, walk the other way, like a normal human being."

With that, he is on his way. Whereto, Gyth does not know. But it is leading away from him. He feels terribly light without this anchor. He is abandoned. And Christopher is leaving a trace of blood flowing from his heart. It is screaming, deafening loud to Gyth – but Gyth alone. For Christopher, it is a technique to go undetected.

Like prey.

He puts on his blinders. Lets himself get pulled forward by that relentless train of thought. Fighting in public, with the man that others perceive to be his gay partner, is the last thing he needed today. The very last. Oh, this has been a stupid idea, stupid, stupid, stupid!

If he wasn't so busy keeping his breathing on track, he would have laughed at himself. He imagined a fucking *future* with Gyth. He could never relate to Christopher's struggles, or he to whatever cosmic principles Gyth was following. They could never truly understand the other, he thinks bitterly – hell, eventually they'd be separated by death anyway. There isn't any future they could share.

For the first time in months, Christopher thinks back to his real punishment. The grand cosmic plan. The shiver shakes him up.

Don't let anybody see you. Just get home, go home, nobody will hurt you if they don't see you –

But once again, he is seen. From across the meadow, like a lighthouse through a storm, a voice calls out to him. Christopher has to look up to make sure he has heard correctly.

"Daddy!"

A seven-year-old girl comes running toward him from the playground. Her hair is neatly braided and her smile as wide as ever.

There is no time to ready himself for a reunion with Ally, no matter how long he has yearned for it. Christopher simply rubs his eyes, then squats to stop her charge toward him in a hug. "Whoah!"

Ally giggles as she wraps her small arms around his jacket.

"Hey. Hey, baby! How are you?"

"Good, and you?" Ally studies him through keen eyes. "Are you feelin' better?"

Christopher can't stop his smile. To downplay it, he nods. "Yeah, I am better."

"Good," Ally finds. "Then you cried of joy?"

Christopher bites his lip. He prepares to lie to his daughter. "Yes," he says through the pain. "Yeah, you got me there. It's just such a nice, sunny day."

Ally just giggles. Her happiness over seeing her father again is blinding her usually sharp attention. Before she can ask more questions, Christopher quickly goes, "How about your friends? And school? Everything okay?" It feels illegal. His voice is fast and low.

"A-o-kay," Ally replies in their familiar singsong. It is accompanied by a rhythmic shake of her head. Christopher has missed it, goddamned. He holds onto her arm like she might get carried away by the currents at any moment now. "Awesome," he says, using the other hand for a high-five.

Ally points over her head. "I'm staying with Carla and her family right now. Mommy's at the hospital, but she'll get out soon."

Because the faces by the playground are familiar, Christopher lets go of her. "Oh. Okay." He tries another smile. Some fatherly talk. "Be nice to Carla. Don't pick fights."

Ally enthusiastically shakes her head.

Seeing her again is like a course correction. Christopher's head is light all of a sudden. His daughter and her happiness, that's what's really important. Not the would-have-beens surrounding his mother and his workplace. This present is what's truly important to him.

And… Gyth is in that picture, too.

Christopher mentally kicks himself. He clings onto the hope that, when he looks over his shoulder now, his eyes would meet that warm gaze he had once fallen in love with in the first place, back at the dog shelter.

Gyth is still there. All alone. Hurting and lonely in his all-black outfit, with that sad scarf – but still there. Looking at him with the same regret of their first encounter wheeling around him.

It's as though he has known all along that being together would be difficult.

But their eyes do meet. Their nonverbal communication doesn't work outside of Gyth's pocket dimension, and yet he does walk toward them when Christopher wishes for exactly that.

He sighs in relief and clears his throat, turning back to Ally. He takes a deep breath. "Okay. Hey, um… Baby, I'd like you to meet someone."

The November wind blows dark curls in Gyth's face.

"That is Gyth. Gyth, this is Allison. My kid."

Gyth steps closer, albeit awkwardly. He has never talked to a human child before. "Hello."

Ally gives him an overplayed wave. "Hiya. You've got cool hair!"

Her enthusiasm conjures a smile onto Gyth's face. "Thanks, I made it myself." He squats next to Christopher, warm and familiar. But the look they exchange is still distant.

They're all distant, all three of them. Normally Christopher would've picked Ally up into his arms to talk. But he does not dare doing that. So, they're just talking on the ground.

Ally doesn't mind. "I wanna do my own hair, too!"

Gyth shifts, puckering his lips in a frown. "I'm sure you can... when the time comes."

"I don't wanna wait until I'm a *grown-up*." Ally groans around that detested word.

Unsurely, Gyth replies, "Well, you will grow. I'm sure. Until you're... a human size."

Ally giggles at his accent. "You sound funny."

"That's just his voice," Christopher chimes in mockingly, swept away by the peculiarity of their conversation. Ally then scrunches her nose in a grin. "Is he your boyfriend, daddy?"

At that whip of a word, Christopher's smile dies. He has become too comfortable. His instincts tell him to look at Gyth for support, but he does not dare it. Panic twists his throat with loneliness.

Beside him, Gyth gets on read on his reaction by remembering the rules – and the ramifications of him and Christopher being together. His mind reels but finds its footing eventually. Allison is different from the other park visitors. It is no wonder, he supposes, because she was raised by Christopher.

The wind is soft in his hair. "I am a friend of your father, Allison," he says. "I moved here not too long ago. When hunters hurt my dog, your father helped him recover. That's how we got to know each other."

Allison's eyes are wide. "Is your dog fine now?"

Gyth smiles as he thinks about the question. Sweeping himself. "Yes. He is doing well. I thought he was going to die alone, in this strange new world, with all of his friends so far gone. But your father helped him pull through. Even though he himself was scared to death."

Allison's mouth is agape.

Christropher just softens. He smiles weakly at the memory of Gyth on that table. A giant dog, leaning into his touch.

Strictly speaking, *that* has been their first encounter. Fucked-up and blood-soaked.

He meets his daughter's round eyes. "Your old man is still good for surprises, hm?"

Ally visibly puts on her role; she tilts her head in an overly cool way. "It's not a surprise, exactly," she finds. "It sounds like somethin' you could do. Dogs are your favorite animals. And they're my second favorites, after fire salamanders." She smiles unsurely at Gyth. "Sorry, what's your name again?"

"Gyth."

"Gyth, where's your dog now?" Ally asks slowly to sound polite.

"At home."

It's just two little words, but they have Christopher biting back tears. He wishes they had something to call their home, he and Gyth. A place to be who they are. With Ally. With a dog and not a care in the world, except for what sort of ice cream they wanted to have for dessert. With no one giving them trouble. Even if it's not forever, or only now – no matter when – he wants *that*.

He looks down, nods and sobers. "Okay." He sees people at the playground talking. Carla and her mom. But, as a matter of fact, Ally's mother is not there. "It was good meeting you, baby." He stands up, terribly aware of his hurting knees. Beside him, Gyth rises much more gracefully.

Ally is very childlike again, slipping out of her cool role. "Can we play again soon, daddy?"

Christopher smiles sadly at her dark blue winter coat. This will be their first Christmas apart. "I don't know," he says, quieter than he wants to. "I can't say for sure right now. I wish I could, baby."

"It's okay. I understand," his daughter assures him, so unaware of what she was actually saying.

Close to tears once more, Christopher nods. He only shortly meets her eyes when he whispers, "Okay. Okay, thank you, Ally. Bye."

"Bye-bye!" She waves as she walks away. She picks up speed once she turns around to her friends. And their mothers, staring and talking like they weren't even trying to be sneaky.

Christopher pries his eyes loose from them. Gyth is much better to look at. He always comes back to this guy, doesn't he? His kindness keeps drawing him in.

Goddamn, he wants him. Him and his stupid, easy happiness.

Only slightly, Christopher opens his arms. Gyth understands in an instant and hugs him. He buries his head in the crook of his neck, past the scarf around it. Christopher's scent is faint under his sadness. But it is there, and Gyth will wrap it in his warmth. Christopher is shaking. Even his heart trembles. And while Gyth wants it to stop, he understands now that he cannot blame him.

He raises his eyes to glare. Looks, both cowardly and shameless, bore into them. People walking past a hug as though it was a crime. Speculating about who they are – "I've seen that one before." – "He works at the dog shelter out of town." – "What's their deal, so close to a playground?"

Why *are* they in this good, old, honest American smalltown?

Every look, every comment, is a sting to Christopher. He holds tighter onto Gyth, screwing his eyes shut, as though merging with his monster was his only escape out of this loud world.

Truly, Gyth thinks bitterly, positive feelings light them up like a beacon, while suffering serves as a cloak. All his life, Christopher has lived through this distortion of empathy. Gyth realizes it has been foolish to question that. Foolish but righteous.

All those humans are eerily similar to hunters surfacing to target their victims. Far outside of any food chain because there is no such thing as human prey or human predators.

Their vitriol is directed against Christopher and Gyth alike. He remembers the men in the parking lot, who were scared of both his human and inhuman shape. He and his body, as it is now, are part of the problem. Hunters, sanctioned by the rules.

This is just the way this merciless system functions, Gyth knows that now. It is working exactly as intended. According to this treacherous system of rules, Christopher's pain is not an anomaly. His happiness, no, his sheer existence as anything other than silent prey, *is*. It is an unacceptable anomaly. And what is acceptable is dictated by the rules.

Just like an inhuman body: the mad thorn in every sanctum of this world. That is what the rules say about dear Christopher.

The notion disturbs Gyth. To assign those categories of predator and prey, visible and invisible – *to humans*. So arbitrary and random. Once a human was locked into one of these rigid categories – which happens quickly, as it did with Gyth himself – there was no escaping it. Not in this world which valued solidity and stagnation. The rules and their enforcers were mighty.

But all powerless compared to him.

He could snap all those humans out of existence. Swallowed by holes that led so deep into the cosmos that they would fall and could never, ever be found again. So quickly, so distorted, that they wouldn't even comprehend what was happening to them. They'd die in cold fear. Alone.

'Damn all the others,' Christopher had said. Gyth, despite his nature, despite his better judgement, despite a guardian's duty, is on the verge of doing just that. The wind picks up.

A guardian…!

He stayed here to protect these humans, and now he wants to condemn them. How did this happen?

Confusion shakes through him, but listening to the heartbeat in his ears is calming. Christopher's heart beats the same way. Gyth holds him when he slides out of their hug and nods. "Let's go. I need a shower."

His Christopher...

Christopher's eyes are cloudy for the rest of the day. He feels sick and immobile. Like he's been pulled out of a freezer and not quite thawed yet. It matches the cold weather. Evening rain softly hits against the windows of his apartment. He watches it drip down, gray and lonely.

Gyth looks in the same direction but far beyond the raindrops. Christopher thinks he has put a distance between them. He doesn't know that Gyth's dissociation lies elsewhere. They are both floating, not daring to touch the other.

Christopher's hands are weak when he rummages the dresser in the corridor. Eventually, he finds what was looking for. A photo of him and Ally on the back of his pickup truck, trying to out-grin each other. Though the memory of who took the picture makes a shiver run down his spine, he looks at it fondly. And ruefully.

He leans against the bedroom doorframe for support. "She was a real brat that day," he says into the space. "But that made for great smiles. On both of us."

Gyth looks at him now instead of the window. "Your daughter is very kind."

Christopher breaks into a smile. "Right? She's just the best."

"Very small. But friendly." Gyth's soft expression melts into a frown. This is the first real conversation they have since their fight in the park.

Christopher smiles bittersweetly. He *wants* to talk. And he knows he can trust Gyth with his past. "You know, when her mother finally had that positive pregnancy test, I was relieved at first. 'cause it meant it was finally over. That whole… ordeal. That's what it felt like to me."

Gyth steps closer to him, listening. His warmth reaches out carefully.

"But then I got devastated. I watched her belly grow and grow… and I was certain that a spawn of hell would come out of it. I was so prepared to despise and fear what she would birth. Like, a demon. But when Ally was there, it was… the complete opposite." Christopher's brows warp painfully. "She was so precious. She was funny, she was worth all the work, all the hardship, like – it all vanished when I held her in my arms and sang her to sleep. After two months with her, I remember thinking – that I couldn't bear if something would happen to her."

Gyth understands. "You wanted to protect her."

Christopher hides his sad smile. "And I couldn't." He swallows. "Something deep inside of me wished that her mother was right every single time she said 'you're imagining all of this'. 'I'm not hurting you, you're hurting *me* with all your nonsense'. Like, I… in dark hours, I really wished that that was all true. Even it meant that my own pain was not real – it also meant Ally would be in safety with her."

Words boil up inside of Gyth. Christopher's hurt dulls the air around them in dreadful colors, looming. Gyth observes them and simply holds his tongue.

"I don't know," Christopher whispers. "When she said her mother was hospitalized, I did not know how to feel about it. Believe me, I've fantasized about her death. There were days when I wanted to rip her into pieces." He frowns. If some-thing happens to her mother, he will need to care for Ally. "I still don't know how to feel about it now. But I guess we'll see as soon as she gets out."

With these words, Gyth's composure crumbles. He turns away. "She will not get out."

Christopher raises his eyes to look at him, but Gyth stares straight ahead, through the window. "I should've told you sooner, Christopher. It is the reason I was so on edge and… different to you lately."

"Actually, I'm–" Christopher nods rapidly, now that the elephant in the room is addressed. "I'm sorry. What I said to you today was not okay. I was a dick."

Gyth's voice is sharp. "No, you – you lived the way you needed to survive. I was out of line to question that." Even the black T-shirt hanging from his back is shaking. "Watching you leave me was hard, but I understand why you did it. I should have respected your view more. Any apology that is due is mine. I was very ignorant." I was a hopeful fool, he specifies silently. And now I'm a cynic.

Christopher nods. "It's okay."

His belief in those words is apparent, but Gyth still hesitates. Thoughts he had trapped successfully now threaten to escape. "It's just…"

"Tell me what you wanted to say," Christopher offers. It is too gentle to resist. Gyth aches at his magic pulling him in. He realizes this is the right way. His breath steadies. "When I was out looking for hunters some days ago, I was unable to save Allison's mother from consumption," he says, slow and pained.

Christopher doesn't reply.

"I tracked down a hunter as they were about to attack her," Gyth recounts. "I stepped in but – when I touched her, fierce flashes of violence hit me. I saw you, I *felt you* – and the erasure you spoke about, and your pain, all flowing through her, *from* her – like a tributary. Of all those rivers flowing into you. Finally I found the cursed root of that thorn." He blinks. "And then I faltered. Such visions of connectivity are not rare after previous contact with the creatures in question, and a guardian never judges by what they see," he says, mostly to himself. "But that was *different*. When I felt all that pain, part of me struggled to find a reason to save her." His face contorts into a confused grimace, that's how foul these words sound on a guardian's tongue. "I did not know what had gotten into me. But the time it took me to come to my senses and finish that hunter was enough for their consumption to damage her irreversibly. She will very much not get better. One day, her body will inevitably succumb to the pain she is experiencing right now, every waking moment, her mind ripping apart…"

He remembers the wound on Christopher's leg, reeking with the same pain, and finally turns around to face him. "I am sorry. I was not sure how you would react to this. So I did not tell you at all." He cannot stand Christopher's blue eyes for long and looks away in shame – he also did not tell him because of the disgrace in his duty. Not *wanting* to save a hunted, wanting to condemn her even… This world's twisted rules want him to think she is but a predator, hunting out of natural instincts. But there is no human prey and there are no human predators. Gyth is *sure* she is a huntress. But that is him alone. What would Christopher think of him if he knew Gyth could not even follow his own principles?

Being a guardian comes with few principles, such few principles…!

As though to support himself against the dresser, Christopher leans back slowly. He nods as he processes what he learned. He arrives at the same conclusion as before: He does not know what to feel. After a while, he says, "Thank you for telling me now."

Gyth gives him a sad look through round eyes.

"You did what you could." Christopher means it but it sounds oddly shallow.

Gyth notices. He shifts away, upset. "I now comprehend this world better. I understand that it designed this to happen, and that pain makes invisible. But I *still* don't understand how no one has stepped in when she tortured you."

Ah, yes. Christopher swallows. "Yeah, well – all I could do was tell them. What they would do with that information was their thing."

"'Their thing'?" Gyth's indignation is red in his eyes. "She hurt you so much – she violated your body, your mind, your heart – perhaps you understand my confusion now! Your world has so many stupid rules, and not a single one of them forbad her what she did! All these rules do is *twist!*"

Christopher has tears in his eyes. "I don't know."

Gyth scoffs.

Now Christopher's tears flow. But just from talking. He's not crying, he has already shed all the tears of a lifetime when it came to this topic. "You wanna know some of the rules sur-rounding that whole thing? What other people said? 'That's what you get in an interracial marriage.' Or, 'You're a man, you should enjoy it. You did enjoy it, didn't you? Who wouldn't enjoy a wife like that?'" He pauses when he thinks of his mother, the only human he ever talked to about this. "'With such an accusation, you would not only destroy her life, but your own, too. Don't make a mountain out of a dust speck.'" He exhales. "It's always the same, be it man or woman. My special rule was, if she did something I didn't like, I should've fought back, 'cause that's what a man would do. And I didn't. Even though I didn't enjoy it. And in the end, I didn't even get hard when she tried jerking me off. The one who broke all the rules was me."

"To *hell* with those rules!" Eldritch shadows spring from Gyth and darken the rainy windows. Christopher's knees shake in the demonic rumble across the building.

Gyth's eyes strain with wrath and confusion. "I've *had it* with this arbitrary-arse system! There was injustice! Plain and simple! It sunk into your mind and took root to spread its viscous poison throughout your body! If your sacred rules stopped others from helping you, what good are they really?!" he roars in disbelief. "I now realise what makes this stupid world so hostile, this stupid, mad world and its cursed mechanics! I now understand it and I *despise it!*" His tears are raw and red, like blood. A sob breaks from him as sadness overthrows his rage. "And I am so endlessly sorry for you, Christopher, that all that happened to you, and that there was no one there to protect you from it. That you were all alone in this madness..." The shadows disappear as he sinks to his knees. Sobs shake his hair out of order. "I'm sorry," he whispers, curling into himself. "I'm sorry if I scared you. Forgive me, I... I did not want to get this angry."

Although his knees are still like jelly, Christopher comes closer. He caresses Gyth's back from above as a sad smile ghosts over his face. It's not often someone gets angry for him instead of at him. And this is the first time it's eldritch wrath. It is vindicating in a way a human's succor could never be.

But hearing Gyth cry breaks his heart in two. His rough voice was made for sweet nothings and singing and laughing. Not this cruel sandpaper sound. "Don't beat yourself over the head for not saving that woman," Christopher whispers.

In a surreal reversal of their usual crying sessions, Gyth's fingers claw themselves into Christopher. Spreading into napped flesh across his shirt. He wants to believe him. But Christopher has got it wrong. Gyth is not irritated by not having been able to save her – that is normal, a guardian cannot protect everyone in this vast universe. It is one of the first lessons they learn.

No, the shame he hides is his lacking *want* to help her because she reminds him of a huntress. The notion is so very unnatural and new to him, and his irritation has scared Christopher, too, who cannot understand it.

A clarifying talk could bring them closer together again. But Gyth guards his tongue. If he told Christopher how his ancient nature has gotten chapped during his life with him, and how heavily he suffers under this insane knowledge, the poor human would blame himself for all eternity. Sinking into a purgatory of his own making, without any spell to help him resurface. His ground is too fertile for that sort of madness. Gyth will not allow it to happen.

Christopher's hands – those lovely, lovely hands – are soft around him. His voice is even softer: "Hey. Hot chocolate?"

Gyth sniffs. The banal thought does comfort him. Christopher's magic is that powerful. "Yes, please. A whole bloody pot."

Christopher's smile returns when he gets up. "Aye, aye. With extra pineapple juice."

Gyth gratefully squeezes his hand but cannot smile back. He watches Christopher leave into the kitchen.

So. His next step is clear.

He needs to actively press himself back into his guardian form. He has let this world warp his duty for long enough. He *is* a guardian, he thinks, that is his existence, and he will throw himself into this duty like he always has and shield himself from the impure thoughts born out of those twisted rules. Doing so will help him see clearer again, that's what he expects to happen.

And although the loneliness is suffocating him already, he is convinced it means he must get distance from Christopher.

For both their sakes, before he drives him insane and disturbs his rules of survival. He may not like this world, but it is Christopher's home. As a human, he is tethered to this dimension. That is both his biggest strength and his most tragic flaw.

And guardians do not prioritize.

It is Gyth's subtle but fatal fallacy to trace back his hesitation to help to a confused moral compass, instead of the warmth he experiences when he shares the hot chocolate at Christopher's kitchen table – a warmth so profound and all-encompassing it almost physically hurts him.

It is a feeling Gyth has no name for when it comes to himself. His guardian obsession clouds his judgement.

And Christopher – Christopher will experience Gyth silently slipping away from him soon enough.

The night is black instead of blue. Christopher's neck is craned on the pillow. That way, he can look through the window beside the bed. Black and pink, if you took Gyth hunting monsters into account. Pink flashes will light up the corners tonight and consume the horrors that try to eat people alive.

Somehow knowing that the universe, beyond all those clouds, is not gray calms Christopher down. The stars are burning bright. Nebulas and planets form the craziest structures. Shooting stars must be crashing through those all the time, and the exhausted cosmos would have to start anew. Must be a real hustle and bustle out there. No human eye could see it, and no telescope could ever photograph its entirety.

Ally has always wanted to go stargazing with him.

Christopher shifts to lie on his stomach, hugging the pillow. The streets outside are quiet. No cars or people laughing. Right, it's only Thursday. November 26 already. December is not even a week away anymore.

Feeling cuddly, Christopher slides his feet around beneath the blanket. Yes, he thinks, this will be his comforting lullaby for tonight: Imagining himself in an ugly Christmas sweater, beside a Christmas tree that Gyth and he have logged in the forest. Gyth would shape the fuzziest winter socks for their time by the fire – yeah, a fireplace would be nice. With stockings on top. Gyth would help Christopher build that. They'd look at their finished work proudly, and Gyth would sling an arm around him and kiss his coaly cheek.

With a song on her lips, Ally would play on the deep-pile carpet with her new presents. But her part of the dream distorts. When she stands up, the carpet is gone. The candles, so comforting just a moment ago, now float behind her. Her bare feet shiver on the stones – she is standing on an altar.

Christopher wants to put her back on the carpet. He steps toward her, his steps heavier than he anticipated. But when he says her name, she flinches, eyes wide.

Christopher stops dead in his tracks. "Hey, baby. Don't be scared. I'm here with you."

"No! You left me," Ally calls. "You left me alone with the monster!"

Desperation spreads in Christopher's stomach. "I'm sorry. I didn't mean to…" He swallows and takes heart – he always knew they would need to have this talk someday. "The monster was hurting me, too," he says.

"But only because you deserved it!" Ally calls, her small hands raised in fear. "If you behaved, nothing would've happened! Then grandma would still be alive! I want grandma…"

Tears stream down Christopher's cheeks, no matter how badly he wants to stop them. "Yeah. Maybe I deserve–"

He gags. He writhes, putting his arms around his seething torso, and sinks to his knees as he throws up. What he vomits is mostly fluid – clear and shimmering.

But it is stale, Christopher realizes in horror. It should be sweet, he's sure of it.

Ally's mumbles of fear snap him out of it. She's crawling backward on the altar. "Daddy, that's not good. You should've asked her first. She'll be angry when she finds out about all the dirty stuff you've been putting in your mouth."

Oh God – what *has* he been putting in his mouth? Christopher's naked legs twitch on the ground.

He's been sleeping with a monster. He has had sex with an ungodly abomination. It's been inside of him.

Once again, Christopher retches – his stomach feels like it's being pulled out of him on a string, through his thin throat and mouth, past his teeth and lips. Tears of pain mix into his vomit.

Ally is crying as well, shaking with fear: "She'll be so angry when she comes home… and sees what you've been doing with the body."

'The body'. That sounds wrong.

Christopher remembers who this fluid belongs to, this otherworldly honey. It is no abomination. His name is Gyth. And he has told Christopher something, something very important. His voice is hoarse but brave: "She has no right – this is *my body*…"

"Don't lie to me, daddy! Why are you always lying?!"

When he hugs his hurting torso now, Christopher can feel his heart tearing apart inside of him. "No… Ally!"

"I hate you! I hate you!" Ally stumbles backward, into the tunnel behind the altar. The darkness threatens to swallow her up.

In addition to those arrows piercing his flesh, Christopher's violent sobs weaken him further. But he still needs to get Ally out of here – she can't stay here alone. A cursed temple is no place for a kid. She'll get hurt.

But just when he wants to heave himself up, one knee after the other – he hears her scream of terror before it happens.

The scars on both his thighs split open. Tentacles spill onto the stone ground, covering it in blood, and taking with them flesh and fat and muscles, hairs, eyeballs, organs.

Christopher gasps, wanting to stuff the transmuting mass back inside of him. Something tells him he can stuff all that back inside of him. That universe spilling out of his body. "It's all right," he calls to Ally, grinding his teeth through the hot shame.

His plans are thwarted from the ankle of his left foot. Silver blades as large as hands cut him open, ready to sever all that excessive meat. Christopher yells in pain and fear alike. He kicks the blades away with his other foot. But that only presses them further into his flesh, tearing it through floods of blood.

Finally, with a last powerful cry, he kicks them into pieces. They splinter with shrieks – and from the wound, his foot twists, pinning him to the ground with broken bones. His leg, however, levitates, breaking his knee, heaved upwards against his mutating foot that eats away his skin, contorting his calves.

Christopher hisses through the pain, eyes screwed shut. "Ally?"

But her voice is far away by now. She is disappearing in the darkness of the temple. "You're the monster! You're the monster! Go away! Go away and die!"

That last poisonous sting of words pushes Christopher out of his nightmare. He pries his eyes open, opening his mouth for air and failing to close it. He screws his nails into the sheets. Yes, the sheets. It is dark but it is his bed. Right?

It smells like his bedroom. But he can't see anything. His foot, or what was left of it, tingles and twitches. As does his knee. Are his thighs still there? They can't be, he's so dangerously light. But he does not dare looking. Even if he did, he can't even move.

Christopher whimpers. Was Ally in safety? It was just a dream, right? But when he wants to call out her name, he croaks. He cannot reach her.

Reach him – where is that monster from the ceiling?

Where is Gyth?

Christopher can move his mouth, but all it does is tremble. He shakes with sobs and cries. Ugly sounds. Not meant for a lover.

Or a father.

Or a man. What kind of a man is he, so unable to control this body? The answer is evident.

MONSTER

HE IS A BAD MAN. Indeed, a bad person.

It is actually incredible for how long he has managed to hide himself from that truth. Now there is no sense in trying to shove it away anymore – he's a bad person.

He inflicts himself on others without consideration or respect. When have those things ever stopped him? He's troubled his schoolmates, his colleagues, his family, the community, and his lovers with his bullshit. He's even done it to the dogs, for crying out loud.

He's a bad father for leaving Ally like that.

He should've fought harder for her. After all, the divorce has not been filed with any crime. A simple divorce. His ex-wife has been right, she could've accused him of something and turned that whole thing against him. But she hasn't, out of the kindness of her heart. And how does he repay her for that?

He's a bad husband.

An ungrateful piece of shit. All those years, he has never appreciated what she did for him and to him. Being the sole person to rely on. Cutting off friends she deemed bad. Telling him what to eat, what to wear and read. What others would give for such a wife! He can't even wrap his head around that simple image. What they would give to be pinned against the mattress, to always be available whenever and wherever she wanted to have him. But in the end, his corruption has even destroyed his body. Her body, really. It was hers to have, like she always said. It was her responsibility to birth children, a divine duty which required a man. And he ruined it for her.

He's a bad lover.

So often he has left her unsatisfied. And without another child. It figures that he cannot build a family, with his own father having died so early. And his mother? She managed to do all of that alone. She fed him, clothed him, gave him a roof over his head. And how did he repay her for her troubles, all those decades?

He's a bad son.

What son would leave his mother without a bunch of grandchildren to rejoice in? What son would bother her with the hiccups of his marriage? Because that is all those were. No big deals, just his dramatic-ass ego. As always. He never was a good son.

Because what kind of son does not mourn his mother's death? It is inhuman, Christopher thinks as he stares against the ceiling. It blurs before his eyes as they fill with salt and tears.

He is a bad person. What kind of egomaniac doesn't mourn his mother? Or wife, divorced or not? What is a divorce, really? He is still hers. Joined before God. No earthly force can separate that bond. And only heavenly grace can help her heal after what he has put her through, just like she said.

His sobs are loud and raw in his throat. All of this points in one blatantly obvious direction. He is a bad person, and he deserves punishment.

And waiting for it to finally strike is part of it. Why should he have the mercy of a quick exit from this world? No, he is sure he deserves to suffer. A child could see that. He has been delusional enough to shove it away, too weak to punish himself, but the truth has always been there.

The cosmic plan is painfully, obviously, undeniably transparent.

The cosmic plan... A sob gets caught in Chris' throat, his eyes wide.

Of course, he thinks. It all makes sense now. Of course he feels inhuman. His emotions are violent, his desires disgusting, unfit for this world – because it isn't his world. It is true. Ally was right. He is the cosmic monster. One of them. Yes – how could something inhuman ever behave like a human, or think like one? Audaciously, he has dared to walk among them and inflict his pain upon everyone he ever touched.

It explains everything. Of course his classmates bullied him, they were only trying to stay safe. Of course his mother shut down his emotional eruptions, trying to destroy her. Of course he was unable to love, because monsters cannot love and always end up alone. He not only deserved all those things – it was the natural conclusion. It is how things were always supposed to be.

He sees Jeffrey Hobson, screaming as the monsters crash his car to devour him.

He sees Mary Ennington, terrorized by the monsters at her bedside.

He sees Allison Birk, crying in a lonely temple.

He sees – another monster. Brown and ink-black, though other colors shimmer over its countless appendages and organs. They are always moving, dodging bones or tendrils, or simply fusing with them. Causing static in the places that the five senses cannot comprehend. Everchanging, everlasting. Its eyes are manifold and sharp. Not dangerous, just attentive. And warm.

Christopher screws his eyes shut, fingers clawing into his pillow so hard it hurts. Gyth is a monster, too. Christopher will tear him apart not like a wolf but an eldritch abomination.

Gyth. His lover. Yes, the one who once saved him from his self-made hell.

Maybe they are the ouroboros. Doomed to make each other suffer for all eternity. Gyth is the guard dog sent by the universe to keep him in check. To hold him down –

To hold him. Yes, he held him. Christopher leans his head against the wet pillow and imagines it is Gyth's soft flesh. Warm and sweet with his honey.

He is real, is he not?

A single sob escapes his mouth, making him inhale. His room smells like always. These days, it smells of Gyth. Both his rosewood scent and that saccharine tentacle slime.

Gasping quietly, Christopher tries to sit up. Tentatively, as though looking was fatal, he glances over his shoulder.

The bed beside him is empty. The white sheets are crinkled from Christopher's tantrums, not heavy tentacles.

Gyth is gone. A few rays of sunlight fall through the holes of the blinders. Is it that bright outside already? Maybe that is just the contrast to the dark inside of here, Christopher thinks. His eyes have adjusted to it. But what day is it?

He has gone to bed last night, he remembers. And he has not gotten up yet. He has dreamt.

Oh, yes, he thinks. It was all a dream – everything.

He would think Gyth was real if it was in a dream. You always think dreams are real until you realize you've been sleeping, right? That's why he was so happy with Gyth. It wasn't real. Because he could never be happy in real life.

Gyth, then, wasn't the universe's guard dog. What was he?

Christopher sinks back into the bed. His body is boneless and without power.

But the sunlight keeps piercing inside.

He needs to go to work. Because, undoubtedly, if he has only dreamt of being with Gyth, then he has not been fired from the post office for real.

But how can he be sure?

He can never be sure. He'd need to call.

Christopher reaches to his left to grab the phone. His eyes fall to the clock – almost eight in the morning. What does the calendar say? November 27.

Christopher swallows. Why is it not September?

His raised arm jolts down onto the blanket. He hasn't been dreaming. If it is almost December, then everything he has thought a dream has passed in reality. Unless he has adjusted his phone calendar accordingly beforehand. Alternatively, he's been sleeping for two months straight, which – yeah, maybe. He has always been lazy. But he's also always been a dreamer.

Yes, he concludes. He must have been hallucinating. He has simply imagined Gyth. And other people's reactions to them.

That also explains their bigotry. He just thinks the worst of them, because he's a bad person. In reality, everyone would've welcomed him and Gyth, he thinks.

Ever the asshole, even in his own imagination.

Then, he concludes, he has been talking to himself. This entire time. And he's been jerking himself off, to all kinds of sick fantasies – of tentacles and eyeballs – instead of his wife.

Gyth, then, has sprung from his brain entirely, too. A gorgeous man, so kind and warm, with the voice of rockstar, falling for a troll like him? Yeah, he should've known it was wishful thinking from the very start. Even all those racist comments, then, have their origins in his twisted imagination.

All of Gyth's whispers, too. Every single touch of his…

His eyes follow the line of his arm and its unappealing hair, to his fingers. Solid. Human fingers. They *look* human, not monstrous.

And he can wiggle them. There, he has control.

But his thighs, hidden under the blanket right now, have split open just as easily as those everchanging shreds of flesh.

Gyth is a part of him, then. Not only real – but *physical*.

"Yes," Chris says out loud. This is it! It makes sense! His brain, in its efforts to shove away his monstrosity, has made Gyth up to distance Chris from his sick and evil nature. Outsourcing all that evil into a different person. But there is no fooling him now. The truth is out – it is inside of him. Inside of this body.

Chris smacks his lips, fingers curling against the blanket. He needs to act now. With the knowledge he now has, the moral thing to do is fight the evil. He can still do that, right? Like a human would. Like a man. Zest for action makes him brim.

If it is inside of him – and can come out, like it has done in front of Ally – he can sever it himself. Just like his dream has shown him.

He rolls out of bed, stumbling through the dark room. The corridor is brighter, with light from the kitchen falling through it. But that is not his destination. He won't sully the kitchen.

He needs to take a shower anyway; he's a stinking pig, he thinks. So, he'd do it there as always. Two birds with one stone.

The water is cold on his skin, making his hairs stand. But it'd be ridiculous to waste hot water for this. The razor trembles in Chris' hand as he looks down. He rakes his wet hair out of his face to see better, bracing himself.

His scars already show him where the monstrous parts erupted. All he needs to do is sink the blade back into them. Piece of cake.

Chris hisses at the pain, but the cool water soothes it. It takes the blood down with it. His skin fringes at the edges, burning hot.

No reaction inside his thighs. No counterattack.

Maybe it's deeper than that, Chris thinks. He hasn't cut deep enough. He drags the razor through the wound he just created, using his other hand to press it down harder. His jaw clenches from the pain. The slash gapes with blood. He uses two fingers to spread it, so that he can see inside.

It's nothing but red. The color of his fingers now, too. Of the majority of his hands, in fact.

Chris gasps. If the monster is still inside of him and got out just because he wasn't thorough enough with the extraction, that'd be really disappointing.

So, come on, his brain tells him. Be a little more diligent. There's lots of other scars to look into.

It takes forever.

His back screams at him for continuing to bend down like this. At least it still belongs to this body. In his mind, the legs have separated from it long ago.

When he's done with the right thigh, the shower's bottom half is red despite the water. But he works smoother on the left one. Practice makes perfect, Chris thinks. His head spins. He has lost a lot of blood, he realizes. When he's done, he should press a towel against the wounds or something. And bite back his pitiful hisses at the burning pain.

But, despite all of this – no tentacles or alien flesh to be seen. Oh, well. Wasted time. But maybe they have retreated even deeper into him?

He gasps at how red the towels look. They're just pieces of cloth. Those won't hold any monster back. He has now created several new exit points for it across his thighs – he should close them permanently. Just to be sure. Otherwise, it would be too fucking easy for the thing to break out of him now. How could he seal the wounds? He needs something tear-proof.

He stumbles on his way to the kitchen. Fucking dizzy. But he knows he has the cure-all stowed away in the drawer over the garbage bin. He is sure that'll help.

It must help.

Christopher's descent into madness is loud and terrible. It is a gaping abyss that screams in all the tones his body knows. But despite all this, it does not pierce the daylight.

Out here, Gyth is going about his business without any awareness of what transpires in 27 West Street. He has consumed two hunters already, who worked as a pair. From the eagerness in their flesh, he can tell they wanted to form a pack. It is easier to hunt with many. He can't let it come to that.

He has to admit it wasn't easy to defeat them. But he succeeded. There is no saying how many victims have been spared a painful death because of it. And that's all that matters.

Before he knows it, night falls onto Hillsburg. Strings of light and neon tubes illuminate the blue. From here, they're brighter than all of those stars above.

Gyth sighs.

He is on East Street right now. He has picked up the smell of another monster from here. When he finds it, he is surprised that is not a hunter, but a small predator – indeed, the same small creature has already rescued once in this dimension. By now they have learned to take on semi-solid shapes.

Two humans kick them around on the ground.

Gyth groans, folding himself back into a human form. "I'd ask you to stop," he growls as he steps out of the shadows, "but I doubt you foul pieces of shit would care to listen."

One of the humans opens his arms. "Yo, what the fuck, dude? Are you, like, the animal police? Animal cop?"

"It's dead already," the other one informs Gyth.

"I can show you," the first human says. "Here!" To demonstrate his case, he kicks the small animal against the nearest brick wall, where its furry body stills in the dirt.

A shudder crashes through Gyth. His human eyes widen, heat spreading in his body. He zeros in on the guy. It wouldn't take long for gravitational forces to compress his sorry ass into a singularity. Neat and tidy.

The human steps up to him. "What're you looking at me like that for? Hm? That racoon your little babygirl, or what, Crazy Hair?"

He reaches out to ruffle Gyth's curls, but he catches the wrist with ease, tilting his head as his jaw grinds forward. He's had it with humans and their quasi-hunter tendencies. "You are dead fucking meat."

Just when he says that, the other human starts screaming. Gyth lets go of the wrist and looks what the two are running from. The creature, with its fluffy striped tail, has grown spider legs. They saunter out of the shadows, looking at Gyth through black eyes.

"Hey, buddy. Sorry they woke you up."

They yawn, baring white fangs and a serpentine tongue.

"Good shapes. Spider legs are great," Gyth says – and sighs. He's talking to them again.

He closes his eyes and slumps down on the ground, crossing his legs. In the fashion that Christopher calls 'crisscross applesauce'. He blows a stray curl out of his face, resting his chin on his hand. "I shouldn't bloody compliment you. What are you doing here? This is no place for sleeping. This smalltown is dangerous."

The creature looks at him.

"You want me to take you home again?" Gyth asks, as if they could answer him. "I cannot keep doing that all the time, you know? It is much safer if you stay in your pack." He sighs;

he should hear himself talking. "But I'm the last one to tell you that. A guardian, always roaming alone."

The creature tilts their head – and emits an earthy, salty and sweet smell. Gyth would recognize it anywhere. They're imitating Christopher's scent.

His eyebrows rise in surprise. "You know him?" But just when he asks, he understands. "Oh, you mean to say – that I'm not alone. Yeah, I bet I smell of him by now." He chuckles. He likes that notion, smelling of Christopher.

But he sobers quickly, continuing with a tired smile. "But see, it is better if I keep doing this alone. Saving your tiny butt and such. Better not to interact with this mad world more than necessary. Left its cursed impact on me already." His brows furrow as he studies the little one – he can trust them, right? "That human who kicked you... I thought about hurting him. I had this – *impulse* to push him into a black hole. Never thought about something like that before. Except with hunters. But this..."

The creature coos. They lick their legs while eyes on their back pop up to look at the sky. Although they aren't communicating very clearly, Gyth thinks they're disagreeing.

They are. Not in a fashion of 'you're too damn dogged, it's not that serious, there is no such thing as a thought crime', like a human would upon hearing him. No, the creature is more like, 'What's a guardian anyway?'. But Gyth doesn't understand that.

"Of course I didn't do it, even if you would've liked it," he says. He follows their gaze into the night sky. This is the only time humans ever see the stars. By day, their closest star is too bright to make out anything else.

The human perspective can be tricky. And Gyth's attention is, too. Instead of the stars in the far distant universe, the clouds in front of them catch his eye. He could watch them endlessly.

Changing their shapes, wandering freely across the skies, transforming into rain and snow. Watering the earth ere ascending anew.

Everchanging. Everlasting.

"Maybe it is a page to take out of this world's book," Gyth muses. "That things can be real or not real after all." He shifts, whispering, "But I'd rather leave it all behind."

The little one blinks their oozing eyes at him.

"Yeah. Yeah, here I am, bloody wibbling, and you just wanna get home. I got it." Gyth raises a human finger, extending the spell against the air between them. His energy opens a pitch-black rift, crackles in this fabric of reality.

"There you go," Gyth murmurs, ignoring the cosmic winds trying to lure him back in. "Go back home."

The little one slithers inside slowly.

Gyth stands up after the rift closes. Somehow, his mind shows him Christopher's smile and lets him hear his 'honey, I'm home' jokes. His strange magic is still working its spells on Gyth despite their distance.

So now he, too, wants to go back.

What he finds when he gets there devastates him.

The strange smell and tinge of suffering in Christopher's home shape Gyth's first reaction: He's not alone.

The image of Christopher in bed, with a blanket shaking in his wet hands, makes the opposite abundantly clear. He *is* alone.

Blinded by his shock, Gyth cannot see the curse streaming through Christopher.

Instead, he hurries to the edge of the bed, whispering his name.

His blue eyes are wide. Not with adoration but confusion. Once he realizes who he's with, his breathing returns. "Gyth? Gyth..." He claws into him, trembling.

Gyth hugs him. The touch is limp, both out of consideration and confusion.

"Are you real?" Christopher sobs.

What a complex question – but Christopher needs no philosophical discussions now, Gyth reminds himself. He needs security. "Yes," he says, "I am here with you." And he says it as though they've joined.

A cry tears from Christopher's mouth. Now the dam is broken and gives way to his tears. His shoulders shake with every sob.

Gyth holds onto him. He takes in his hurting mind and body and everything in-between. One part in particular is different from the rest. Another nightmare? No, this time, it is… 'real'. Under his clothing, Christopher has hurt his own body yet again. It is emptier than usual, lacking blood and oxygen.

Gyth kisses his hair, trying to concentrate on what could've caused this. But he cannot think straight. His mind steers him toward different questions – Why didn't Christopher call him? Did he think Gyth would not come to him? Is this how far they have drifted apart?

Gyth shudders. "I'm sorry," he says, eyes stern with irritation. "I am here now, Christopher." He cups Christopher's head to make it rest against his chest. "Listen to my voice. Feel my heartbeat. It is the same as yours."

And Christopher can't help but wonder: Is it?

His hand feels like a barb as it attaches to Gyth's shirt, the muscles underneath it, and the organs under that. There must be organs inside of him. He's seen them explode in the past.

It *is* a heartbeat. It is beating in the same rhythm as his own. But is it the same? "Gyth?"

Gyth's hand and voice are as warm as ever. "Yes?"

Christopher presses his forehead against his chest, wanting to broaden this touch that heals so much. "Is the reason…?" he begins. But he struggles to put that blade of a thought into words. "The reason I never fit in... and always felt so alienated and alone and weak... because I'm not meant for this world?" He whispers before his voice breaks apart entirely: "Am I not human?"

Gyth cups his cheeks, his warmth cut with worry at how Christopher could arrive at this conclusion. This painful vortex he has been dragged down – Has the madness overcome him after all? So suddenly?

This is exactly what he has dreaded as soon as he had understood this system.

"Oh, Christopher."

Christopher meets his eyes. Red mixed with blue, crashing into brown. "Tell me. You can tell all creatures apart. Am I a monster?"

"Oh, Christopher, no." Gyth pulls him closer, into a hug. What to do? How could he show Christopher his humanity? Would that even ease his pain? What good would it be, if this world's madness infected him anew, perhaps as early as tomorrow?

If the next day, *he* got kicked around in a dark alleyway?

Christopher sobs against his shoulder.

Slowly, while caressing the back of his head, Gyth tells him, "The reason for you feeling alien is neither because you entered this world as a foreign body nor because you're prey. It's because its system is hostile. Its inhabitants have tried to cut you off. They made you feel as though you would not belong here, but that is not true." He pulls away to meet his eyes. The same color, the same wavelength, as the sky in daylight. Gyth sighs. "This is *your* world. And this is *you*, full of wonders and adoration, even if you cannot see them yourself." He caresses his cheek, his voice soft with regret. He had his priorities painfully, fatally wrong, he thinks in the belief that he could have prevented this nightmare. Ever the dogged guardian. "Forgive me, Christopher. Oh, forgive me, I should've been here for you much sooner."

Christopher screws his eyes shut, hurting, hurting, hurting. He didn't think his depression would get this bad. He feels safer now with Gyth. As he always does. And he wonders if that means he cannot be alone at all anymore.

While Christopher thinks this is solely his usual illness, it is hard to tell how much of it really is. Who could say how much of it is alien, planted into him, groaning with the curses of an ancient god? It is so intertwined, so adnate, that even Gyth cannot see it despite its size.

No, Gyth cannot see the forest for the trees. He is busy zeroing in on Christopher, his dearest Christopher. "It's all right. You're going to be all right. It may not look like it now – but you will be. I promise." He studies him. "Is there any way I can help you right now? Anything?"

Christopher is still crying. "Can you... I have..."

"Show me, if you cannot say it."

Oh, fucking hell. Christopher realizes he'll have to shift and pull away the blanket. He sobs at the loss of warmth. At the chill of the room air against his skin as he drags down his sweatpants.

Gyth's warm hands support him, and he whispers to him that it's going to be all right, but Christopher isn't so sure. This is humiliating. He feels eerily vulnerable right now, plunged into the poison of the past seven years. Guilt and shame stretch painfully through his lower body.

The silver duct tape strains across his thighs.

He wishes he didn't hear the shock in Gyth's voice when he says, "It's not so bad." Ever the soother, despite the bad lies. "I can take it off for you."

No bloodshed or tearing off chunks of flesh like Christopher has feared. Instead, a shimmering spell eats away the glue and plastic. Lingering on the wounds in a way that makes Christopher wish it would never leave. It's made of the same pink light that had once haunted him. Now it fills his bedroom with the warmth of a thousand candles.

Gyth is glad to be able to provide comfort to Christopher in this way. Still, the coppery taste on his human tongue is a cruel reminder of his neglect. He keeps telling Christopher that he will stay unless he'd send him away.

Christopher has no such plans, but the assurance that he can be alone if he wants to only adds to his comfort. With Gyth, he is not a prisoner. He sighs as he wraps his arms back around him. Rosewood smell.

He wishes he would've had this earlier. Not hours but years ago. Decades ago.

Gyth is *his* monster. There is no denying that now. Gyth is devoted to him in exactly the way he has once explained, in the night rain. He wants to be there for him. Protect him.

And he does!

But he is also a guardian, and the events of the past months have made it clear to Christopher that such a guardian is badly needed if humanity wants to keep on living.

That, plus taking care of a sick and lonely troll like himself? That's a lot to carry on Gyth's shoulders, even if he can multiply them. And so, later that night, when they lie close and warm, Christopher says, "You don't need to apologize for not coming home earlier. There are others who need your help."

"You needed it, too."

Christopher shifts, talking like he had any idea about these ancient principles. "Gyth. You can't save everybody. You can't. And you don't *have* to."

The words sink into Gyth. "I know. Every guardian knows that," he says truthfully, while only regarding the first part of what Christopher said.

Christopher has risen out of the masses. More prominently, more radiantly, than even at the beginning when Gyth has had to admit to himself that this one human has become special to him. He not only wants to protect him. He wants to be with him, feel with him, *join with him* –

That this desire of his was twisting his sense of duty is worse than simply prioritizing Christopher. It is so very unlike how guardians are supposed to be, in his view. They are alone! They must not tear between one protégé and all the billions of other creatures in need.

And yet...

He cannot help it. Although he tries to deny himself the glorious warmth that comes with their touch, tonight, too, he stays with Christopher. Always watchful. Always wary of both the silence and the chaos beneath it.

Is this the way he will be?

He comforts himself with the knowledge that what he has said just now has been correct: More than anything, he wants to help, and Christopher needs help.

Sometimes, with the right perspective, complicated things can be quite easy.

Gyth will stay with him no matter what. This is his decision. This is their wish. There is no saying what forces it would take to tear him away now.

WATCHER

THE DAYS ARE BLEAK and heavy. They weigh down Christopher's shoulders like an anchor, only it's not thrown out in the shallow but the deep sea.

The darkness is unyielding against him. Black walls. But at least he has a pink light to guide him.

Gyth is his anglerfish. He's the one who makes sure he functions. They eat together, shower together. Sit in silence. Lay in silence as they stare at the popcorn ceiling. Water seen from below, Christopher remembers. Watching a sea storm from below the surface.

The weather outside his flat is much gentler. On the first day of December, snow starts falling onto Earth as though to blanket it. It soothes Christopher's wounds like a bandage. He spends hours sitting in front of the window, Gyth embracing him from behind, just watching the snowflakes dance downward from the gray sky without a sound.

But the illusion of peace is fraud. When Christopher does step in front of the house, just to check his mail box, he finds slurs written in the snow on his car. On his mail box, smeared with black permanent marker, 'groomer'. And inside the mail box, beautifully made-up brochures for countryside conversion therapies.

He finds it tragic, that he planned on making a walk to the mail box his daily routine and now shivers just thinking about it. A microscopic hell right outside his place, connected to the macroscopic one of his hometown.

"I can get the mail for you," Gyth offers. "And see if there is anything from your boss." He stills the hand caressing over Christopher's hair. "If we find something like that bloody brochure again, we can burn it together in a fire," he says, trying to cover his anger with amusement and failing.

Christopher appreciates the effort. But he is too tired for adoration. Or anger, for that matter. He would've torn that brochure apart himself, but no. Too weak. He is utterly useless. Like a millstone around Gyth's constrained neck.

But that's not true, he tells himself. *Gyth likes helping you. He does this for you.*

Then why can't Christopher's thoughts finally break out of that vortex? His voice doesn't shake when he says, "I think I'm goin' mad."

"Not if I can help it."

"The thing is, I want your madness instead." Christopher slowly meets Gyth's eyes, warm and brown even in the dull bedroom. "C'mon. Change."

Gyth licks his lips. *His* madness, the one that meant death for Christopher's mother. "But would my body be comfortable to you right now?"

A pause fills the air between them. Christopher smiles at how the focus has finally shifted away from him to Gyth. "I appreciate your concern. It's sweet," he says truthfully. "But you gotta stop it. Seriously. Your body doesn't need to be 'comfortable'. It's your body. The truth is, whatever is the most comfortable to you is the most comfortable to me. Be yourself. I bet I sound like a broken record by now, but I am not scared of you and I'm not disgusted by you, Gyth. I'm scared when you're *hurting*." He pauses and looks away. "And any human shape is hurting you. And I don't want that. You soothe me either way, any way. Just by being you."

Gyth pulls his boneless body close to cuddle it. His curls spill around them both when he lowers his head into the crook of Christopher's neck, where it thinks. If fear is what makes a human's mind bleed, then what does Christopher feel towards him instead? What not only dodges his madness but transforms it into comfort?

Whatever the answer was, Gyth is grateful. "Thank you."

What a joke – "Thank *you!*" Christopher's smile fades as he buries his face in Gyth's transformations, dripping, vibrating, flickering. "Thank you…"

"It is marvellous how your heartrate calms down," Gyth's voice tells him from all sides.

"That's what you do. That's your thing."

Amusement laces Gyth. "If it's that easy…"

Christopher chuckles, hooking his fingers into the hot flesh that once was a shoulder. "It fucking is." The mass changes around him, meaty wrinkles caressing his skin. "Wouldn't have a difference from the start. With us getting discriminated anyway, you could've just approached me in your true form… without folding yourself into a tiny corset."

"And miss out on tasting things with my nose? Or experiencing sex? Hardly. Human shapes do have their advantages." Gyth's voice is an amused vibration against Christopher's body. All around him. Strings and shreds of flesh, adorned with eyes and claws and hairs and bones, floating, whirling, warming.

And things could stay like this, he finds.

Over the course of the next few minutes, Gyth finds creative ways to move below the ceiling. Over the course of the next few hours, he learns to secretly return the things and furniture warped by his otherworldly presence back to normal. Over the course of the next few days, he turns into Christopher's sofa and bed, because he feels safe enough to sleep on top of him. Always close to touch should a new nightmare pounce on him.

The apartment becomes their tiny little cosmos. One room after the other, all doors opened. That way Gyth can let his body drag all over the floor and through the air. A part of him in every room. Still not his entire height, but he can manage. It feels good to flow free once again, in this atmosphere.

Three rooms are Christopher's world now. One for cleaning, one for eating, one for cuddling. No upwards, no downwards. 'The ceiling is the limit.'

Christopher also reads on top of Gyth. But there are only so many books left on his shelf. Just like the TV started to show old FBI couple episodes anew, Christopher uses his time on Gyth's warming organs to reread his favorite novels. Sometimes he falls asleep while reading, sometimes he puts the book away on purpose to caress Gyth. Gyth enjoys their closeness and snuggles up closely to him, wrapping him in tentacles, threads and skin depending on how much contact Christopher desires.

He melts in Gyth's intimacy without the need for sex. Gyth suggests it anyway, once in a while, just as an additional activity to keep Christopher's hurting mind off the outside world. "Maybe I can help you unwind?" He gently nuzzles Christopher's temple.

But Christopher pulls away. His words are heavy as he prepares himself: "No... sorry. It's not you – I'm not in the mood."

Gyth strokes his weak shoulder. "That is all right. Don't apologise."

It's a short conversation, but Christopher clings into his eldritch mass anyway. Gyth shifts against his arms as he hugs him, crunching softly. It's a comforting sound.

Christopher has prepared himself for a discussion, at least an explanation or postponement, but Gyth warrants none. A fortunate waste of energy.

Books may run out one day, but affection doesn't. TV show episodes run out one day. Affection doesn't. But food does. One day, Christopher is out of options to eat. His body tenses in front of the fridge. "Only ketchup and BBQ sauce left. I've dreaded this day," he says, rubbing his face. "God… Is that my beard?"

"I'd say it is," Gyth trills helpfully and pops an eye in front of Christopher. It turns on its optic nerves to look inside the fridge. "Shall I go pay Stuart a visit?"

"I can't live on pizza," Christopher sighs. He gives Gyth a tired smile and starts a song. "Gotta go to the grocery store. The ol' supermarket." Although he does sing again – a beautiful sound, Gyth finds – he shivers.

"Old supermarket," Gyth repeats. "Outside."

Christopher closes the fridge. The light goes out. "Yeah." He crosses his arms, leaning back into Gyth. "Y'know, I used to sort the outside world into categories. I had places where I… didn't necessarily feel safer. But had something to do. The grocery store was one of them." The words linger on his tongue – he's never spoken out loud about this before. "More and more of those places vanished. But that one still stands." He meets the gaze of Gyth's eyeball. "I'm rambling. But you know what I mean."

"I think I do," Gyth says truthfully.

Christopher purses his lips and looks around with a grimace. "Then you also know that I'll need to put myself together nicely."

"Yes, I'll help you with that," Gyth chirps, riding on the humorous wave Christopher has sent his way. It helps ease his tension. It has made itself a home in his shoulders, his neck, his stomach.

Gyth encourages him to pick out his favorite shirt, even if it's "just for a trip to the supermarket". It's the one with short sleeves in pastel pink, the same color as the sky when the sun sets below Earth's horizon.

Christopher unpacks a new toothbrush. Gyth watches him curiously. He's observed humans use it before. But the bristles of Christopher's are very hard. "What does it feel like?"

"To wrush your weeth?" Christopher asks, giving him a look through the mirror. He immediately unpacks the second toothbrush in the box and holds it in front of Gyth with his free hand.

Gyth opens a mouth, as big as the mirror itself, full of white fangs. He shakes with prickling ripples when Christopher rubs the brush across them. "Oh?" he goes, almost choking on his peppermint toothpaste. "You're wicklish" – he spits it out – "You're goddamn ticklish?!" Laughter shakes through him, and through Gyth now, too.

He is lucky to be with Christopher. Continuing to unlock so many new things in him.

Christopher thinks the same when he sits on top of Gyth's fleshy body. "Lucky to be with you," he says, not minding how much the scissors shake in Gyth's tentacle, raised in front of the giant eye he has sprouted to zero in on Christopher's face.

"This is delicate work…"

"Yeah, trimming a beard is an artform," Christopher agrees, only half-mockingly. He is rather proud of his beard after all.

"I'm sorry, I'm gonna screw it up," Gyth sighs. "With these, at least."

"Then don't use 'em," Christopher suggests.

And sure enough, trimming a beard is much easier for Gyth when using sharp claws of his own instead of foreign scissors.

Christopher relaxes into his flesh, head tilted to give him better access – as if one strike with those fuckers would not mean certain death for him. He even chuckles, warmth blossoming in his chest. Lighting up when he presses a kiss to a thread of Gyth's flesh after a much-needed haircut, too. "Thanks, babe."

This is leagues better than having scissors in his own unstable hands.

Gyth just wants to hold them. Still them. Christopher's disquiet is hurtful, mentally and physically and everything in-between. Gyth grunts when he folds himself into his human shape. It's ridiculous how smoothly it works after fucking, in contrast to this pain, he curses. Very helpful.

"We'll grab everything real fast so you can change back soon," Christopher tells him on their way down the stairs.

Gyth unlocks and repositions his jaw. It's been a while. "Now that I have finally changed back into this amazing piece of arse? No way."

His comment does make Christopher's laugh return. It's all been very easy up until now. But now, Christopher is standing in front of the main door – bracing himself to go outside. His hand hovers over the door handle. Big and unsure.

Gyth softens. "I'm with you. All right?" He closes his human hand over Christopher's. It is not exactly a magic spell. But the effect does come close.

Outside, Christopher fills his straining lungs with the cool air. He doesn't flinch when Gyth sends the snow on his car back into the sky. He laughs at his "the coach is ready" joke he learned from some fairytale movie they've been watching. He drives carefully. He finds everything he needed from his shopping list. He gets Gyth a little sugar cane. He explains the upcoming festival and its massive decorations to Gyth. He tells the teenage cashier the dogs at Helping Paw are fine. He lets Gyth pay with the fingernail that became his credit card. He makes it back to the car. He arrives back home in one piece.

And he's ever so soft in Gyth's arms when they lie on his bed, on the wrong end, so that they can look out the dark windows left and right of the headboard.

Somewhen, the world outside goes to sleep, only to be shook awake with a winter tempest. The window frames one particularly close lightning like a painting.

Christopher's head is still against Gyth's naked chest. He caresses it with a loving thumb. Gyth's lower half, a gorgeous mess of tentacles and tendrils, curls around his sweatpants to warm him in return. Flowing soft and steadily. With every breath, his body eases.

Just like the candles on the nightstand, Gyth melts. The distant thunder is like a song.

"Today was good," Christopher says. "I liked going out."

"It was good," Gyth agrees. "Otherwise we wouldn't have gotten those lovely lights for the window."

Christopher snorts, a tired but amused sound as his eyes dart to their shopping snatch. "It's a dachshund Santa string of lights. For five dollars."

A tentacle waves in front of them. "I think it is a good light."

"Yeah." He sobers. The outside world is very dark already. And it isn't even seven o'clock. "We need to go visit the dogs sometime soon," he says. "I miss them."

His brain chuckles at so much naivety. *Making plans again already, are we, Mr. Suicidal?*

'Can you blame me?' Christopher wants to retort. The trip to the grocery island was so uneventful it gave him hope for a return to normalcy. Despite the fact that he hasn't eaten half as much as he wanted to tonight. Despite the fact that his knees buckled when he stepped out of his pick-up truck in the super-market's parking lot.

He'd give Gyth a handjob of gratitude, at least he feels like it. But he's too weak to even lift his arm.

"How about we visit Allison tomorrow?" Gyth suggests.

Oh... "Can't," Christopher mumbles. "Only on weekends." He shifts, waking up a little more, as though he was afraid of the night reaching in through the windows. "We had an un-contested divorce, so that my ex-wife could hold up the perfect image as much as she could. No lawyer. We agreed on paper that I pay minimal child support and that I'm allowed to see Ally on weekends."

"On paper? As a written contract?"

Christopher hums, still looking ahead. He wishes another lightning would light up the sky. "And then there's the un-written contract. And that one went a bit like, 'If I ever see you near my daughter again, I will destroy your life, you sick, sick man'."

Gyth caresses his hair. "Christopher..." His voice is better than any blanket could ever be. Christopher leans into his touch, closing his eyes to shut out this fight between the dark clouds and the stupid Christmas lights.

"Never answered your question about the rules," he an-nounces. "Whether or not I believe they're good. I don't. They hurt me and others like me. I'd be happier if I could live freely. I believe not following them would reduce damage instead of causing more. But living like that will hurt, too. What I've been trying to tell you, I guess, is that these ways are old, man. They're set in stone. Not that easy to erase. Or ignore."

Gyth's voice is simple and warm in his ears. "I wish I could shatter that entire stone."

Wouldn't that be nice, Christopher thinks with a weak smile. "Yeah. Amen."

But Gyth isn't done: "It is much like you humans to 'set something in stone', being so averse to change. But I don't think stones are that good to be written on in the first place. That must be quite hard."

Christopher snorts. "Please be an archeology professor."

"How?" Gyth's voice is laced with amusement.

But Christopher is tired. "I don't even know. Just talk to me about stones." And so, mixed with vanishing thunder, his lullaby consists of Gyth's wonderful body and voice wrapping him in fairytales of minerals, pressed together for millions of years, until eventually, they would form intricate shapes and colors – crystals, even…

Yes, even something as solid as stone had to change into what it is now – and it will continue to change in the future, too, many million years from now, broken, reassembled, reflecting the light around it…

Everchanging. Everlasting.

"You done?"

Christopher's head snaps upward. He's still in his bedroom. He recognizes the shapes. The man standing over his bed must be six foot one. Broad shoulders, dish-water blond hair. Blue eyes twinkling through the darkness.

It's himself.

"You done?" the man repeats, significantly more annoyed now. His eyes are wide behind the thick, dark-rimmed glasses. His old glasses.

But Christopher doesn't know what he's talking about. "What do you…" His voice gets caught in his throat – it grates and gurgles – his neck is suspiciously warm and wet, Christopher thinks, when he brings a hand up to it.

"I believe you haven't cut deep enough," the man singsongs before his voice drops about an octave. "I mean, look at you – what a fucking joke. Cutting your thighs? We both know you were afraid of cutting your wrists, arms and neck. Y'know, the places that would actually show others. No, instead, you tried to deceive them. Even though everyone has always been so honest with you!"

Not this again…

Christopher gasps, too hurt to tell himself off. His head rings. He wants to fight this. But all his body does is roll across the mattress, writhing to shake the pain away. It doesn't work.

The man steps around the bed. "Richard knew. Not many others. 'cause you didn't want them to see. You knew it was wrong to damage something that wasn't yours. Still you went through with it like a dirty little egomaniac. You wanted to go the easy way. And where has that brought us, hm?" He opens his arms in accusation.

Right, if he's Christopher – then he is in Christopher's mess, too. Christopher wants to tell him – but it hurts too much. The hand around his throat shivers when he gags. If only he could sit up straight…

If only his body wasn't so heavy.

The man lets his arms sink. "Yeah, that's what I thought. That happens if you don't take care of those monstrous parts. They grow and grow, and eventually, they'll consume us."

It's just like Ally said. Right? The memory blurs in the pain. Christopher shakes his head on the sheets, tears spouting, burning hot. There is only pain. "No…"

"What, 'no'?"

Yeah, 'what, no'? "It hurts," Christopher croaks.

"You wanna live? Then do something about it, like a man."

Christopher gasps. "What must I do?" he sobs. "Can you help me?"

"What? You think someone else will help you? No, you've sucked on the tits of others for long enough. You're finally going to have to deal with this on your own."

The popcorn ceiling above them looks like the entrance to hell. Christopher trembles. "Will I die?" That's it: "Will you – oh my God, boo-fucking-hoo!" the man yells. "Then you drop dead? So what! Two birds with one stone! Then at least you won't be *pestering* others anymore! Crying in a dog shelter at midnight? You wanna keep living like this?"

Christopher heart breaks when he answer, "No…" When has he last seen the dogs?

The man's voice – *his* voice – is just as much of a bark: "Then do what a man's supposed to fucking do! If someone hurts you, fight back! If something hurts you, cut it off!"

"Cut…"

"Yeah," the man says, stepping away. Blinking as he stares. "Now you have no other choice but to cut your goddamned throat."

But they're the same, right? He must know it will hurt him as well, right? Maybe he just needs a reminder. "It's *our* throat…" Christopher finally croaks.

Again, the man blinks. A sad smile tugs at his lips. He leans in closer, fighting to ignore Christopher's scared whimpers against his better judgement. Into his ear, he whispers, some-how comfortingly warm and icily cold at the same time, "It's not ours, now, is it? Keep it in shape. Keep it in proper care for her. She'll need to see it. She wants no stupid pain inside that you can't even take." His voice drops lower. "You know what she'll do if you do not obey."

A gasp escapes Christopher's throat, painfully close to his former self. "I will obey… But if I cut it – she'll see the scar."

"Yeah, you'll have to deal with that," he says. "You'll finally have to be honest."

Christopher gasps. And gags. "You're so scared. *We* are scared, me too. So much." He wants to comfort himself. But the words get stuck in his throat, again and again.

The man stands up straight by his bed, giving him a sad look from above. "The pain will only stop if you take initiative, Chris. You have to. Do it – please."

"Yes…"

His helpless voice claps through the darkness like a lightning. "Save us, please!"

"Yes! I will!" Christopher promises, blood splattering out of his throat with every cry. "I will! Just – look out for Ally, okay? Someone needs to look out for Ally. I'll do it, right away… I'll save us…!"

The bedroom brightens around him. Yes, it is brighter now. He can see the string of lights above the window. The dusty piano and lamp on top of it. The candles on the nightstand are almost burnt out. Small already. Won't be much longer now.

Back arching, Chris coughs – with that, his throat is uncorked. Pain floods his body from up there, bundled around his Adam's apple like a rusty nail in his flesh.

It burns, but in the way frost does.

He sits up. His hand, as it tries to steady him, touches something slick. It caresses him. "Christopher. Are you all right? Your sleep was uneasy."

Christopher knows that voice. It isn't his. It's like soft summer rain, warm and husky.

His eyes fall to the maze of meat and muscles that takes up the entire left side of the bedroom. With an occasional insect leg hanging in the air. And threads of flesh like spider nets. Eyes open from inside his body, dripping with clear fluids, before submerging again.

Gyth.

A voice that's older than Gyth's whispers to Christopher now. It's his own again. 'Don't ask him for help, all right? Don't bother him anymore. He's been helping you forever. It's about time you took care of things yourself.'

With that, Chris rolls out of bed. Overcoming his hurting throat, he whispers, "Just getting a glass of water." It's quiet, but he knows Gyth can hear him anyway.

The candle on the nightstand is almost out. So small already, only glimmering… If Chris waited a little longer, he could watch it go out.

But when Gyth gently squeezes his hand, he uses it as his cue to get up. He really should've acted sooner, he thinks as he makes his way through the dark corridor. But, hey, better late than never.

He has known it all along: He needs to cut out those mutations himself. He may have taped the wounds on his thighs, but the thighs were never the problem.

It's his throat.

It will tear open with a round hole from where his Adam's apple had once sat. Blood and flesh will spill out, before tentacles will claw the wound open from the inside. They'd descend from his brain right down through his throat. Or maybe they'd grown inside his stomach.

Yes, that makes sense. It's why he has no appetite. They're satisfied already. Almost ready to emerge. Already pushing against his throat from the inside, ready to pounce.

He'll give them no such chance.

Chris grabs the bread knife from the drawer below the cooktop. On the right side. That's where his mother has always stored it, too.

He may have fucked up before, but Mary will be proud of him for what he does now, Chris is sure. He'll choke it off, this monster – he'll cut right through it. He has no mirror here, but he doesn't need one. The pain tells him exactly where to position the ridged blade.

His arms tremble when he bends them. But this is foolproof. Not even an idiot like him could mess this up now.

308

Peace spreads inside of him. All he has to do now is grit his teeth and count to three.

Then he'll be free.

There is only pain.

He closes his eyes.

"Christopher." Oh, what now? It's…

It's that summer rain again. He knows the voice. He opens his eyes. The kitchen drawers are glowing pink. No, just reflecting the pink light. He turns his head around. Through the doorframe, a body of countless shapes melts into the kitchen. Slowly. Gently. Light flows from it, reflected in wet wrinkles and shining skin. Its voice is calm. It extends a tendril.

"Please hand me the knife."

Chris' face contorts in pain. It makes his tears fall. "It hurts…"

"I know it does," the steady voice says. "Hand me the knife, please."

Gyth – Christopher remembers his name. He reaches out. Lets his fingers slip from the black handle of the knife. They shake. And they can't stop, trembling violently, on and on.

"Thank you," Gyth says, softer than sunlight. The knife in his tendrils frazzles into a dark feather, floating to the floor.

A spark of panic rushes Christopher – no! He needed that! He needed it to save –

He breaks down, trembling against the hand wrapping around his throat. It's boiling like a frostbite.

"Make it stop…" he begs. But writhing makes it hard to talk.

Behind his wall of calm, Gyth is racking his brains about this strange pain. What is its source? It is really coming from inside of Christopher? "Let me take a look at you," he says, tensing everywhere. "Okay? I'll be gentle."

Christopher whimpers in pain as he offers Gyth his throat – a terrible, *horrible* sound – and then waits through it all.

Gyth opens as many eyes as he can. He lets his light stream through this dimension and the neighboring ones – he'll illuminate every last corner of the universe inside Christopher's body, if he has to.

There – green rushes through his mind and below, hiding, hiding... But guardians have their ways of detecting enemies. A tale as old as time. These ones hide in so many places Gyth has trouble keeping track. In every swallow breath, every sob, every tear and muscle spasm, tiny creatures rush and claw and bite through him, body and mind and everything in-between.

"What...?" Gyth reels from the realization, his words but a whisper. "Parasites." His voice shifts into a roaring curse – this is not the work of human depression.

How has he not seen them earlier?!

His eyes fill with disgust. These monsters have hidden themselves in-between all those other foreign influences inside of Christopher... They hid inside his illness for too long, battening themselves on him. Eventually, they would devour him in his entirety. Flesh and bones and soul.

Gyth wills his voice back to that of a human. "I need you stay still, Christopher, okay?"

But Christopher is off the deep end. He's heard what Gyth has said, and he can smell his panic in the night air, entangling with his own.

Parasites – he moans in pain. That image – his body, overflowing with bugs and spores, eating him and his brain away like a carcass, corroding even his bones –

"Oh God..."

Gyth shifts away from him. "I need to think."

"Consume them," Christopher presses out. "Can't you...?"

Gyth's tone is frustrated when he answers, "You saw what happened to your mother. I'll find another way."

Christopher gasps in desperation. His hands grow weak but not less tight around his throat. He cannot think about what was or what will be. There is only pain.

More to himself than to Christopher, Gyth says, "I won't hurt you."

"Gyth…"

Christopher's voice drives him mad with anger. He reeks with wrath against the ancient god who infected this helpless human, who has no idea, no capacity to comprehend what was happening to him, with his curse.

Gyth curls his flesh around, twists it in pain to stay in the moment. He is scared. Of accidentally hurting Christopher. And even if he didn't – in such a thorough consumption, Gyth would not be able to protect anyone else. Hillsburg will be on its own.

So much could go wrong. And Christopher has been wrong in the past.

But Gyth needs to help now, doesn't he? More than anything, he wants to save Christopher. One reason rises high above all others: He must save him because otherwise, there'd be no Christopher to be together with.

Gyth sinks down to his side, cradling him in his light and warmth. Tendrils twine around his limps. They tremble against his whipped pulse.

"I can try to do it slowly," Gyth offers. "Piece by piece. It will… take time."

Christopher shakes his wet head. "I don't care." His voice mutates into a high-pitched whisper. "Just… please."

Finally, Gyth takes him in. "I'll do my best."

Pink light surrounds Christopher. That pink light that makes everything so much softer and friendlier. He exhales. Resumes his breathing.

When he opens his eyes, they're still on a floor. Only it's invisible. Here, there's only Gyth's light.

And Gyth.

He's lying next to Christopher, eyes closed. Human eyes – he's in his human shape. Hair, T-shirt, nail polish… everything as it was. Except for the black smoke fuming from his back, spreading at the edges of his little pocket dimension.

Christopher grunts, trying to sit up straight. He is weak but manages it without hurting himself. "Are you all right?"

Gyth strokes his hand. "Yes. Just… concentrating." He gives him a smile, eyes still closed.

Christopher collects himself. His throat seems fine… The pain is gone. Reduced to usual levels. "Okay. Okay." He helps Gyth stand up. His lean body is surprisingly light.

"What can I do?" Christopher asks.

Gyth shrugs with a hum.

"What?" Christopher laughs, only half-relieved. Is this not more serious?

The sound pulls a chuckle from Gyth, one of the rough ones, warm and intimate. "You can do anything you want," he says. "You're in safety now, Christopher. We're in my world. In here, we can do anything."

"Okay. Hey…" Christopher shifts, inside and out, talking breathily. He's alive. "Thank you. Oh God, thank you." He cups Gyth's face, feeling his cosmic energy once again against the palm of his hands. Energy that can eat evil and light up the night. He would've killed himself without it.

"What would I do without you?"

At that, Gyth's smiles twitches. Without him, Christopher would've never been in danger in the first place – if it hadn't been for that one fateful hunt in the forest…

Normally Gyth would say it is his nature to help. Guardians rarely accept a thank you.

But this here… it feels wrong. Carving out the parasites. This consumption trembles in his bones, like laughter… Something is not right here…

What is happening to him?

Christopher stroking his thumbs across Gyth's beard brings him back into this dimension. "You're so strong, goddamn."

Taken aback, Gyth laughs – Christopher is tired but still trying to comfort him. To cheer him up, even though he is the one infected with parasites of Krysuldom the Dark.

His ancient and yet new storm is gathering already.

Looming. Always and never.

The realization spreads as sulphur inside Gyth's body: This won't end well.

But that has not happened yet, he reminds himself, solidifying. It is not now. Now is – Christopher. His lovely, dearest Christopher. And his happiness. That glow around him that Gyth loves so much. He exhales. However weak he is, and no matter how much weaker he'll get – no matter how badly he'll regret not seeing the cosmic winds again – he's determined to share these happy moments with Christopher before…

Before it all goes to shit, presumably. An inglorious end for a guardian, perishing while cleaning up a mess he himself caused.

But that's his future.

Christopher is his glorious, warm, joyous presence.

He falls – backwards, onto a round bed. One gigantic bed, Christopher finds as he looks around. It's the size of his kitchen. Soft as hell. Placed in a bright home, with fairytale gothic windows that reach from the shiny floor all the way up to the ceiling.

If there was a ceiling at all, Christopher muses with a smile. The pink world just goes on and on.

In this palace, Gyth overwhelms him with care. He comes walking to the bed with ten trays of breakfast on his tentacles. Though his eyes are closed – they always are these days – he is beaming with happiness.

Christopher covers his mouth. "Oh my God…"

"I *will* pamper you," Gyth lets him know, before parting his tentacles to lean down for a sweet kiss. He then places all the breakfast trays on the blanket as though they'd have a picnic. "I also have these for you," he adds, pulling a giant flower bouquet from behind his back.

Christopher's surprise gets lots in what follows. "Oh–"

The centers of each flower, none of which Christopher has ever seen in his life before, pop pink eyes and mouths. Gyth's voice is practiced but cute: "Whoops – it's only me!"

The demonic flowers laugh in high-pitched tones when he raises his hands to show they're just part of his body. Christopher snorts – and laughs. What a fucking dork.

Gyth smiles, happy to have made him laugh. "Do you feel better?" he asks, sitting down on the edge of the bed.

Christopher strokes his rearranging hand, dizzy with the smell of fresh pancakes all around. "Hell yeah."

Gyth nods. "Good. That's good. I will try and ease your pain as long as you're here. While part of me is gone taking care of the pain, you can wish for whatever your heart desires."

Christopher tilts his head, falling in love all over again. "It desires you." He pulls him in, kisses him, lingering – he has almost forgotten what it felt like. To feel Gyth's hot lips against his own, and his soft beard against his own.

Wouldn't it be nice – if it was always like this…?

Christopher pulls away, now dizzy with adoration, too. "Thank you so much." He inhales the sweet air of Gyth's world, mixing with his rosewood scent. And he wonders: "How much of this is real?"

Gyth lies down onto his back next to him. Christopher accompanies him, into the soft mattress.

"Hard to tell." Gyth squeezes his hand. "But I am here with you."

"I'd say that makes us real," Christopher smiles.

"You're the expert on that," Gyth says, voice laced with amusement.

Christopher chuckles as he tries finding the edge of this palace's magical ceiling. Someone unironically calling him an "expert" when it comes to telling what's real or not?

He rolls sideways, kissing Gyth's face.

They breakfast in bed. And then, finally, do that dance lesson Christopher has been wanting to have. Gyth doesn't do half bad for someone with his eyes closed. His body is pliant against Christopher's leading. Depending on how unsure or at ease he is, his hand tightens around Christopher's or gets gooey. With his sloth movements, he's the perfect partner for slow dancing.

Well, he's the perfect partner, period, Christopher thinks with a smile, nuzzling his temple as they sway.

"This isn't too difficult," Gyth finds, his husky voice all low.

"We'll see about that after we've stepped onto each other for the nth time," Christopher cautions mockingly. "Next lesson will be way harder. In high heels."

"I thought next was the drop," Gyth wonders.

"Dip."

"Yeah, whatever – this thing."

That's all the warning Christopher gets before Gyth sweeps him off his feet, literally. The entire room turns as he falls backwards, held by a bunch of soft tentacles wrapping around him. He gasps, but his shock instantly turns into laughter.

"Wow – wow, okay!"

"Like this, hm?" Gyth ask from above, kissing his nose.

Christopher is grateful that he seems to get better, too. At first, Gyth has been weak despite the refuge of his pocket dimension. Just when Christopher has been about to get a guilty conscience about this whole consumption thing, he has gotten the hang of it.

Seemingly, Gyth thinks ruefully. It is difficult to balance those cursed parasites and the presence. But he manages surprisingly well.

In no small part, surely, because of Christopher himself. He has great ideas for what they could do together, now that no one would stare or chase them for it.

Something that Gyth particularly likes is when his world takes on the shape of a bar, with its stage full of instruments and colorful lights. Christopher and the other men play music that vibrates inside Gyth's body, loud and shameless.

He loves it. And he loves singing to it. Truly, Christopher always suggests the most marvelous things.

Gyth has had no idea about what a human voice could do – swing on a melody, scream it, growl, whisper – and all to the vibrations of Christopher's guitar and the other heavy instruments. Gyth adores all the melodies he teaches him: the song about 'pouring sugar instead of pouring rain', the one about 'the seven seas of the fantasy realm', or the 'fifth mambo'. It's all loud and rough. Christopher likes it, too, Gyth notices. He always watches him from where he is playing on the stage.

Especially when he lets his hair fly in wild headbangs!

He also has that one special song for Gyth to perform – the one about the 'sweet alien from Transylvania'. Gyth loves that one, too. It's playful and, more importantly, shamelessly transgressive against so many rules Gyth has encountered. Over time, it becomes his favorite.

To be fair, this dimension's crowd goes wild no matter what they perform, but to Christopher, having this one approved seems more important. They cheer them on loudly – even when Gyth goes one step further.

He reveals his high heels from below the stage's shadows. He rips off his T-shirt to show off a lace-trimmed bustier, jewelry and glitter melting from his neck and ears...

The crowd goes crazy for him and his burlesque show – and Christropher is so, so, *so* in love with him. To watch him have such fun and listen to his heavenly voice while doing it – and finally getting to play an electric guitar once more! – all that is just perfect.

Well, it gets *absolutely perfect* when Gyth sprouts a tentacle to hold the microphone, so that he can clap his hands the same way the audience does – and they love it. Tentacle shadows twirl in the pink light. He transforms more and more, no longer strapped into his human corset. Why would he? In this world, anything goes. Happiness can be found in the weirdest corners. In the dog shelter they dream up. In the streets where they can hold hands. In that one lecture hall where Christopher watches Gyth push up his glasses and talk archeology and stones for hours on end.

"You see, stone" – Professor Gyth, in proper style with a white lab coat, knocks against a space rock on his lectern – "is quite hard to write on. And it is a very beautiful material, as opposed to paper. You'd think that those two reasons alone would suffice to keep you idiots from writing your bloody rules into stones, in your desperate attempts to lend them some sort of 'natural legitimacy'. My suggestion is thus very clear. Let me just pull up my presentation here... Shove your rules up your arses. Thank you."

Christopher's laughs come easy, now that he knows that Gyth is more comfortable in this tightrope act. The guy constantly has two irons in the fire. The only thing is, those metaphorical irons were now taking on the shapes of Earth beyond

Hillsburg. The pink light has been turned into more and more recognizable places. The park they were now walking in, hand-in-hand, isn't the real 1910s town park in Hillsburg with a pink sky painted on top. No, it is undeniably Gyth's world, full of its sweet scent and entirely empty of homophobia. It is a beautiful park. Tentacles curl around the lamps, cooing.

But when Gyth slips in the attempt to balance the illusion and the consumption –

What the hell is going on in West Street?

– he falters. Metacorporally and literally. Christopher sees Gyth stumble and reaches out to catch him. He's expecting to fall down onto the graveled path.

Instead, they land in pure pink light. Christopher shakes his head. The air is dense and his vision blurred…

"What…? Are we in a pocket dimension… inside a pocket dimension?" He turns around to look at Gyth, who's in a far too large, short-sleeved, pastel pink shirt, light blue jeans and white sports shoes. His face is without makeup but adorned with Christopher's rimless, angular glasses in front of decidedly inhuman eyes, large and pink – but wide open. Like an eldritch horror who has watched too much TV.

Christopher grins. "There you are. You're wearing my shirt. And – well, everything."

Gyth seems to have trouble closing his mouth. It's the cutest expression, making Christopher smile softly as he looks down himself. "What?" His smile dies. "Oh my God." He raises his hands to stare at black nail polish. "Oh, I'm – Jesus, your pants are tight – these are your pants, right?"

"Yes." Gyth's voice is ridiculously breathy.

"Jesus Christ…"

With a juicy sound, Gyth elongates his legs around Christopher to form a spooky mirror for him: black make-up, tousled hair, and an all-black outfit. And thinly rimmed glasses. They are definitely Gyth's, that explains the bad eyesight. Christopher's broad shoulders sink. "Oh, no. I look like a goth. Well, a poor man's goth. But still–" He yanks the T-shirt over his head – only to find he is wearing a lace bustier underneath.

"*Jesus Christ*, this–" Oh, he'd lie if he said he didn't feel sexy right now. He has never worn lace before, not even in his theater days. See-through, black, plus that shiny little ribbon… "This does look kinda nice, actually."

From behind him, Gyth gives him a hum so enthusiastic he almost chokes on it.

Oh, *that's* how it is? Christopher turns around. "You like that, huh? Me wearing your clothes?" And as he speaks, it finally clicks: Gyth doesn't have any clothes, he grows them directly on his body. "Because this is – this is all *you*."

The bustier's straps ripple, stirring.

Gyth stares like his lungs had stopped working – God, does he want to eat him alive?! "You look so different," he breathes. "But you feel familiar."

"It's more about me trying a new style then, hm?" Christopher turns back around. But the mirror melts away already. "Yeah, well–" He gasps, interrupted.

Gyth is on his knees behind him, mouthing at his lower back with his hands on his jean-wrapped hips, wandering to the front to cup his belly – the kisses are electrifying. But so sudden! And the tentacles go wild, they just absorbed the T-shirt by his feet, crawling feverishly.

"Gyth?"

Gyth's mouth widens in the curve of his back. Fangs the size of knives graze his skin, with a long tongue wetting it, circling the two little dimples above his ass. His voice is but a demonic growl: "Yes?"

Charmed by such fascination, Christopher snorts – but gasps quietly afterwards. The growl resonates in the bustier across his heaving chest. It should be too broad and large for this rag. But it somehow isn't. It's just right.

Christopher leans into the touch, laying his hands over Gyth's on his belly to squeeze them, gathering moisture. "Nevermind... Keep doing that."

They haven't done this in a long, long time.

Though his brain is already on its way out, Christopher wants to say how magical this must be, because if Gyth's clothes hadn't changed sizes, he would've torn them – and at that thought, the lace across his torso tears into oval holes, rough against his nipples. It moves, too. Just not as vigorously as Christopher would like. He slips two fingers under the bustier, making the fabric melt and curl around them timidly. Same with the glasses, they melt and caress his face.

He's literally had Gyth all over him! "Oh my God..."

The sounds alone make Gyth's touches grow slicker and wetter; he's dripping already, with all those juices that drive Christopher insane with their scent. "Oh, fuck..."

Gyth claws into the black jeans and shreds them like a fucking piece of paper.

Although he knows it's just more of Gyth's mass in this case, those mindless displays of strength will never not turn Christopher on. "Jesus..." Before Gyth can use his hands for anything else, Christopher catches one and guides it down to massage his dick. From the sound of it, the torn jeans just got liquefied.

Gyth is still growling. "Your butt was pretty in 'em. And this is, too." His hand twitches with arousal, hot even through the fabric of the underwear. "But I prefer them like this."

Christopher smiles, eyes closed. "Amen." He moans at the tongue sliding across his butt, past his smooth briefs – wait, they're panties?! "Oh, fuck." Christopher looks down, with a hand ghosting over his hip. Shiny panties with lace, in black, of course, soft against his skin and hair. They cling on him in just the right way, flowing around his cock and balls – *Gyth* clings onto him – starting to vibrate –

But just then, Gyth's tongue retreats. And with it, the panties, sadly. Christopher liked those.

"I am sorry…"

Christopher moans at his hoarse tone. "What?"

"I'll stop. Forgive me," Gyth growls, hands all tender on Christopher's hips as he rests his forehead against his lower back. "You told me you'd rather not have my tongue down here," he explains, stroking his inner thighs.

Christopher gasps. His heart grows three sizes – not literally, although it feels enormous in his chest right now. "I mean, y-yeah. Oral. On my dick," he stammers, screwing his eyes shut. "If you wanna eat my ass though…"

"Eat your…?" Somehow, Gyth's pause still sounds excited.

Christopher laughs breathlessly. "Yeah, well – use your lips and tongue on my asshole," he explains. And swallows – it does sound obscene to him if he says it like this.

Gyth's breath is frantic against his lower back. "You want that?" His voice is already swinging inside Christopher's mind, changing dimensions.

Christopher swallows. "Yes, please," he whispers.

The only warning he gets before Gyth melts against his lower half is a gasp, wet and hot. God, Christopher needs it bad. But more importantly: Are they going to do this standing up? "There's no place for me lean against."

Gyth is already busy licking and kneading his buttchecks. Almost in passing, he says, "Sit down on my face."

Christopher's voice is embarrassingly high. "What?"

"Sit down on my face," Gyth repeats, just as nonchalantly. He sinks down to lie on his back and guides Christopher on top of him.

His knees buckle already. "O-okay... Is that really okay? I'm a big guy."

"Exactly," Gyth growls.

Still nervous, Christopher chuckles, with his head thrown back to relax his shoulders as he lowers his body. That eldritch horror really is incorrigible. "Can't wait to be inside of me again, huh?"

"Damn right."

The largest, hottest part of Christopher's shame leaves his body with a sigh. He kneels above Gyth's face, or what once was his face, as black tendrils leave his fingernails to intertwine with his hands.

Oh, he loves this already.

He gasps when Gyth's dragon tongue – the one that's tiny in the front and thickens the longer it grows – ghosts over the rim of his hole, barely touching him. Still, he squeezes the tendrils that now reattach to Gyth's hand on his thighs, to hold him down as Gyth slides his tongue through his crack, all the way from his balls to his ass dimples.

He's so wet already that Christopher's balls drip with his saliva.

And who could blame him? This is Christopher's little hole right in front of him, puckering, salty, drenched with that lovely scent of his, surrounded by this supple flesh that's so easy to knead and part.

'I remember this part of you well,' Gyth growls into Christopher's mind. 'It smells so good... I can't hardly wait to finally taste it.'

Wishing he had imagined a shower beforehand, Christopher chuckles between his moans. "Then why not – *ha*... why not start tasting, champ?"

'More... build-up...' Gyth trembles as Christopher's heart picks up speed. He feels it pounding against the flesh spread across Christopher's skin – so thin, so silky – shuddering with every movement.

They both need to gather more energy first. And Gyth knows just what to do.

He splits his tongue so that it can reconnect with the piece of clothing that is his skin on Christopher's pectoral muscles. Once done, he shrinks the torn holes to close around Christopher's nipples, sliding them between the fabric. Christopher tenses under the touch – oh, he'll be so tight for him – just a little more patience…

Gyth uses his tongue to caress Christopher's crack, forming a sucker that fits perfectly onto the rim of his hole. He does the same on top of his two nipples – and starts drinking.

Salty and spicy energy streams into his body. As always, he isn't stealing it from Christopher but sharing it.

But Christopher's hum turns into a worried grunt. "Oh, fuck– oh – hey, I don't know if that's such a good idea. Like – down there–"

Equipped with a million other ideas, Gyth retreats, and with that, Christopher pushes his chest up against his two suckers. His moans are a symphony inside Gyth's mind. He streams around his pliant body, to feel him, and to collect his sweat – though it is decidedly more delicious in the heat right above him.

Gyth drools as his tongue circles around the sensitive muscles of Christopher's asshole. He'll find a rhythm with this bodypart just like he did with his tentacles.

Except now he has an entire mouth to swallow Christopher's ass with.

He squeezes Christopher's hand to signal him he'll start now. He slides through Christopher's tiny entrance with his tongue still small and thin. The thicker part of it retreats back into his throat, so that his mouth can dock onto that supple, lovely, sweet ass. Gyth opens wide, his spreading fangs shaking from arousal as Christopher moans above him. "F-fuck…"

Gyth is so horny he can't speak. Christopher's hole is just as soft and tiny as it was the last time he went into it. It seems long ago, and yet Gyth now knows the place like the back of his hand, as Christopher would say.

Speaking of hands, Christopher's are as lovely as ever, holding Gyth on his scarred thighs, fingers intertwined with his flesh as they start moving.

This is heavenly.

Christopher pushes his ass down ever so slightly, wanting to broaden this burning hot touch, before pressing upward again to meet Gyth's suckers. It's a rhythm so slow it should be illegal. It's the most blissful torture he has experienced in some time.

But still torture, with his legs tensing so hard.

Panting already, Christopher opens his eyes. He isn't even disturbed to see his own jeans and shoes under him. The white sport socks are drawn down, slack around Gyth's human legs, so that they reveal his gorgeous brown skin.

'You're so tasty,' he hears Gyth growl. 'Oh, I love your little hole so much…'

"Undoubtably – since you open that greedy mouth so wide," Christopher pants. Gyth's subsequent growl of pleasure vibrates through both their bodies, and suddenly, Christopher is much fuller. 'Damn right, I'm greedy.'

"You're so good," Christopher praises him, smiling blissfully as he closes his eyes – but only half in pleasure. He can only tense his thighs like this for so long. The pain is sharp already. "We need to… I need a break. I need to sit down."

'Sit down on my face.'

Christopher hisses – that again…

But Gyth is relentlessly gentle, his voice like honey. 'Sit down all the way.' He strokes a thumb over Christopher's hand, still intertwined on his thigh. The flesh on his chest grows higher to caress his face, comforting him.

All that care is overwhelming.

"Oh, fuck…" Christopher lowers his ass but stops in a sting of shame.

Gyth's voice is so sweet in his ears he might come from that alone. 'Just let go, Christopher. Sit down. Let me take care of you, yeah? I don't need air or breaks. I'll be your pillow.'

Something about the way he says that sends a surge through Christopher – maybe it's the trust, maybe the unabashed yet tender desire – and he sits down. The pain lingers just a little longer in his legs. And now, it melts away into pleasure.

Gyth's voice drops back into a needy growl, tentacles curling in excitement. 'Yes…' Finally he has Christopher's entire weight on top of his body, his ass in his mouth, his hole loose and relaxed, puckering now only under his loving touch instead of pain.

Christopher moans with trembling hands. Gyth's fangs are grazing both his back and his dick, sharp and yet tender. They send shivers down his spine – such a contrast to Gyth's hot, wet mouth, so soft – like a pillow, seriously.

He feels so ridiculously good his hips start moving on their own. Friction, he needs friction…

'Yes, very good!' Gyth encourages him.

Matching the rhythm of Christopher's hips, he sticks his tongue into him again. Its texture is rough, not overshadowed by its saliva. It pushes into him just right – just deep enough – just fat enough – retreating, circling his rim of muscles, then sliding into him anew.

Pleasure tingles in every corner of Christopher's body. When Gyth sucks harder on his nipples – *just rough enough* – he clenches his hole. This tight confinement pulls the most violent, thunderous growl from Gyth he has ever heard.

'Yes…!'

In comparison, Christopher's high-pitched gasps are a quiet joke. "Oh, fuck…"

'No shame, Christopher,' Gyth reminds him. Even his mental voice is hoarse – Christopher loves it whenever he's so far gone already, God, he's missed this. 'I adore being your pillow, Christopher, I really do… Your pillow and your clothes and your skin, *everything*…'

Another rough suck on Christopher's nipples makes him cry out. "Fuck!"

'Is that good?' Gyth wants to know, like he wasn't eating him out like a god. But Christopher's mouth is too slack to answer. Or his brain too fucked, who cares – he comes without having his dick jerked once.

Two smaller tongues from between the fangs on the front are ready and eager to catch his cum and lick it from his cock and thighs, while the big one down below curls inside his ass as Gyth's mouth starts sucking on his cheeks. Christopher can't help but grind against it, hands pressing into Gyth's. He is holding up Christopher's entire weight, hell, he must be getting squished under it.

Not that he seems to mind: 'Yes, yes, use me… *use me*…'

Christopher pants like he just ran a marathon, and the heat of Gyth's ever-so-eager voice inside his head is the first prize. "Oh God…" He gasps weakly when Gyth's suckers detach from his sore nipples, stroking him in the afterglow of his orgasm. His chest heaves with his breaths. Strands of sweaty hair fall into his eyes. "Oh… That was…"

"So delicious," Gyth moans.

Christopher nods, breathless. The orgasmic, shining colors of his mental eye vanish. But they aren't done just yet. "Now, come on. Let me kiss you back."

The rest of the half-bustier, half-blob of tentacle flesh leaves his torso, led by the split end of Gyth's tongue. This new tentacle slithers around his neck and to his mouth. Christopher holds it in both hands to press wet kisses to it. He raises it to flatten his tongue against it and licks it, all the way to the tip.

Below him, Gyth sighs and shivers.

Christopher takes him into his mouth then, sucking him off lovingly, always caressing his tentacle as he does. That Gyth always arranges his suckers in rows of two makes them perfect for fingering. Christopher rubs his fingertips into the sleek curves, humming as they close around him to pull him deeper. Some fucked-up handholding.

His name falls from Gyth's transforming lips like a prayer.

The transformation of his legs is decidedly less graceful. Christopher chuckles around the tentacle in his mouth.

The winding strings and shreds that once were human legs get tangled in Christopher's clothes, since they don't transform with the body. Still horny as fuck, Gyth tries to kick them off. "Bloody hell…"

'Would be easier if you just tore them apart,' Christopher reminds him with amusement.

"No, no, I got this," Gyth argues in a growl. He gets out of the wet socks surprisingly deftly, Christopher thinks, considering he can't even wink properly.

Then again, many *humans* can't wink either.

Christopher closes his eyes, reaching down to stroke Gyth's still-human shoulder. 'You're the best, you know that?'

"Am I?" Gyth utters. His breath hitches.

Christopher just hums, welcoming the bouquet of flesh coming his way. It's not like he sees it, but the sounds and the energy pulsating through the tentacle in his mouth tells him all he needs to know to catch them between his lips.

Gyth hums as he slithers into him. "How I have missed your mouth…"

'Missed you too,' Christopher sighs. He adores the different textures streaming against his tongue, teeth and gums. A dozen little touches. Some shreds are like jelly, others as hard and veiny as a cock. And all gathering Gyth's sweetness, that abundant honey, as he gets wet.

His hands grow restless on Christopher's thighs. He gives them a last squeeze before melting away, tearing, dripping.

He widens below Christopher, who's still sitting on top of him. He grows and changes, slithering against Christopher's balls, stroking his pulsating wrists as they move against the tendrils streaming in and out of his mouth. Eyes and teeth open across his body but roll right back inside, dripping with pleasure.

Some human bodypart must stay though – something must stay to generate more sexual energy.

A long hum vibrates around Gyth's tendrils when Christopher feels Gyth's cock throbbing against his own. He leans forward, grinding.

Gyth shivers as he expands and expands, blossoming under Christopher's care.

Christopher lets go of the tendrils in his mouth and lays down flat onto him. It's his entire weight of broad arms, thick thighs and beautiful hips below his small waist. Those hips, attached to such pretty legs, keep grinding against Gyth's cock, while his arms spread across Gyth's body as far as he can manage without hurting himself.

Gyth shudders with pleasure – he loves touching so much of Christopher at once. He's so happy to enwrap his long legs once more, something he gets to do so seldomly… Christopher always takes such care of him, holding him together, drinking from him when he thinks he's about to burst.

Christopher's large hands start kneading his flesh. They sink into it with all their power, before retreating and caressing him. It's far too much for him to grab at once, too fat, too broad from loving now that Gyth's body is so free. It yearns to stream into that pretty little mouth…

"Was I good for you, Christopher?" Gyth gasps. "Have I done you well?"

Christopher smirks around his tendrils – with them so sweet and wet already, this wouldn't last much longer. 'You fucking did, you marvelous devil. You always make me feel amazing.'

"Oh… my dear Christopher…"

Christopher falters. The desperation dripping from Gyth's voice is too thick even for sex. But he can't read his mind. What else…?

"I want to fuck your mouth, Christopher. Do you allow me to fuck your mouth?"

With that, Christopher aborts his previous train of thought. He'll learn the truth soon enough. For now, his sex-ridden mind is back in the moment. 'Have right at it.'

"Say if I should stop," is the last thing Gyth presses out before he goes nuts. Not only pound his tendrils past Christopher's teeth – his hot flesh grows around Christopher's waist to keep him in place as he bucks upwards, meeting the touch of his dick against his own.

'Oh, fuck, babe…'

Gyth grunts, another tentacle keeping their cocks pressed up against each other. But it's hard work when everything is so wet and slick. Short of melting already…

Christopher relishes the sounds they make together. As best as he can in this bouncing dance, he rubs buds of flesh between his fingers, grabs a handful, thumbs it, strokes it, and leans into Gyth's touch with his entire weight, loving how the flesh arches to meet him.

"Oh, now, Christopher, I'm–" Gyth's voice trails off into demonic growls of ancient tongues he can't understand. Body language is universal though.

Christopher unclenches his jaw and swallows Gyth's hot and fresh load as best as he can. Sure enough, he spills over, drenching their bouncing bodies in his sweet syrup.

And, God, the wet sounds of it all –

Christopher moans like he can't help himself. His nipples harden at the transforming flesh they're pressed against, now slick and wet, so wet –

The pink world turns – flies? – and sweeps him onto his feet.

Christopher flails, tries to regain his balance. He can see clearer again – his glasses are back, as are his clothes. He's back on the park path. Gyth is next to him, catching his breath in human lungs.

Christopher supports his arm. "You good?"

Gyth's voice is rough and low – and a tiny bit embarrassed. "Yeah." He tries pulling back the few tentacles that are still in his hair. "Just a… hiccup." He thumbs the corner of his mouth, looking past the pink sky above them. The rumbling is still out there…

What is going on in West Street? It makes keeping control much more difficult.

Christopher notices nothing of this. He just smiles. "One hell of a hiccup." He pulls Gyth close to kiss his cheek. And really, that's the best comfort, even if it's no explanation.

One thing this escapade has made them remember though is the beauty of their sexual intimacy. Now that they have rediscovered it, there's no holding back anymore.

Especially not for Gyth.

He turns into Christopher's briefs, he fucks him as the archeology professor on top of the lectern, or jerks him off in that giant bed of theirs. If Christopher wants, he kisses him senseless; if tells Gyth he'd like pancakes with his load as syrup on top, he more than happily obliges and touches himself until everything is covered lusciously.

"I'm sure it's best when it's fresh and warm, but by God, I would still bottle this stuff to stockpile it," Christopher muses.

It leads to them presenting a TV show that Christopher dreams up a pastel-colored studio for, complete with a bright glittery sign on the stage and an applauding audience in front of it.

"So, Gyth, what do you have for us today?"

"Well, Christopher, this is our newest product, one hundred percent organic, probably glutenfree, and we're very proud of it: Trio Tentacle Treacle."

"Wow! That's a mouthful!"

"It sure as hell is! So sweet it'll *drive you insane*."

Nobody tells them when it's an appropriate time or place, because here, they themselves decide.

But as time moves on, as it does, other things start factoring into those decisions.

Gyth needs to stretch his conscience from his togetherness with Christopher to the outer edges of his pocket dimension with increasing regularity. There, he burns the last of Krysuldom's parasites in the light of his consumption, to take care of Christopher's pain.

His own grows in every moment. And he soon learns it would be less painful to simply leave Christopher in this time. But that, in turn, pains him as well – he swore to never leave him again. But he has to admit that he would be of better help like that. Besides, they are still together in his world.

He explains the entire thing without mentioning the pain once. Christopher understands, needless to say. "That's okay. No need to feel bad about it, honestly. I'll think of something to do until you get back."

And he is right. Christopher's imagination is vivid after all. Here, he never despairs in his loneliness. Is it even true loneliness, if you know it will end soon?

Still, Gyth always hurries to rush back into his arms. Time looms over him, incomprehensible and dark in its vortex.

He'd much rather have Christopher hovering over him instead. And the worst part is – Christopher knows of his desire. Thankfully, not of his pain.

Right now, he is busy imagining his perfect workplace. It's one of his favorite pastimes. He means 'perfect' not only in what he would like, but what the rules would like, in all their hilarity and tailor-made clothing.

Society likes when men have huge offices, where they sit in their suit and tie all day and get work done by doing nothing, he thinks with a content smile, arms behind his head as he pushes his chair around on its rolls. His office towers above a skyline – New York City, maybe – with giant windows opening his view into blue skyscrapers under Gyth's pink sky. His own room is pink, too, though the furniture and office plants have colors from the usual world of Earth. They've bled into Gyth's dimension bit by bit.

When his phone rings, Christopher rolls back to his desk. It's a secretary, presumably. "This is your scheduled finance call, sir. You've earned one million dollars in the past hour."

Christopher snorts. "Thank you!"

"You're very welcome, boss."

He ends the call by pushing one of the telephone's fancy buttons, then spins in his chair with a big grin. It's a comfy chair, one with those shiny paddings that make you feel like sitting on a cloud. It adjusts to any movement or shift, back or forth, even sideways. It'd be a miracle to get back pain in this one, Christopher thinks.

He hasn't had backache for a while now. How could he, in such a comfy chair? It's almost too cozy…

Wait.

He could jerk himself off in here, just like in some cheap porno, and no one would know.

But his eyes dart to the phone instead. It gives him an enticing idea – something that he's always wanted to try.

He looks up at the ceiling, a smile tugging at his lips. "Hey, Gyth? No need to come over, just… talk to me, if you can."

Faintly, like soft summer rain, Gyth answers him. 'Hello, my dearest Christopher. What do you want to talk about?'

Christopher sighs at the cute greeting. He decides to drag this out a bit. That is how you do this, isn't it? "I don't know. I'm bored."

'You don't sound bored,' Gyth says, unmistakably amused. God, that smile in his husky voice is sexy…

Shifting in the chair, Christopher strokes the small bulge in his navy suit pants. "Am I this obvious?"

The fact that Gyth's voice drops about an octave lower is confirmation enough. 'Remember, you can imagine whatever you wish for.'

"That's the plan." Christopher closes his eyes, leans back into the puffy chair – and then, just as soft as that material, invisible tentacles crawl over him. That's how they would do it, right? He imagines them growing from the back, shy yet curious. His mouth waters. From behind, they'd crawl all over him, fat and soaked but soft nonetheless. They'd squeeze his pecs – he reaches upwards to pinch a nipple through his white shirt – then curl around his arms, direct them upwards to push him deeper into the pliant chair…

He loosens his tie, finally speaking again. "Is it warm where you are? Out there?"

It takes Gyth a while to reply. 'Everything I touch heats up.'

Christopher chuckles. "Ain't that the truth. I'm hot and bothered already." Warm clothes are annoying. He throws his suit jacket to the floor.

Gyth's tentacles would wander down to his pants, once he unbuckled them… He sighs, letting his imagination take the wheel. His belt is open quickly.

He trails his fingers down to it, like Gyth would move a tentacle. They'd be all over him. Christopher sighs. They'd be so firm against him…

"Oh, Gyth…"

Just when he wishes that Gyth would finally hold him down with his lovely weight, a jolt intensifies the touches. For but a second, Christopher could swear something real had slipped into the empty tentacle gloves of his imagination.

But it's over just as quickly – because someone knocks at the door!

The touch snaps away as Christopher jumps in his chair, packing his shirt and dick back into the pants. "One moment!"

Jesus, he's flushing already. So much for a shameless porno jack-off session. He'd sink straight into the earth if someone would've actually seen him like this.

He answers the door to an assistant, presumably. She's here to tell him how many dogs' adoptions they have arranged today and how successful their business is.

Christopher nods. "Wow. Nice!" He politely thanks her, with a hand on his hips. But since he finds it hard to meet her eyes, he looks to his right, a wall beside a filing cabinet.

A smirk creeps onto his face. The door closes, and before he knows it, he's thrown through the air, making papers fly and frames crash into the ground. He smiles, his chest pressed flat against the hard wall. "You won't pass up on any opportunity, hm?" He wiggles his shoulders against Gyth's powerful grip. He's not interested in why this is possible or how it works – he just needs it to work.

The power of imagination, huh?

Gyth is invisible – no, he's not even really here – but somehow still busy with Christopher's pants. Those wet tentacles sliding against his hands and thighs, throbbing with cosmic power yet still tender, couldn't belong to anyone else. It is an afterimage, softer, less defined than a real touch, but unmistakably *Gyth*.

"Welcome back," Christopher smiles.

'I'm not quite home,' Gyth whispers – God, even his voice is now clearer in Christopher's ear now – 'But I'll promise to take good care of you nonetheless. And myself.'

He crawls through Christopher's pants, moaning at the tightness through the fabric. His ass is supple and plump, that's the way he remembers it. He'd use a tendril to slide in-between his cheeks – then to stroke the rim of his little round hole –

Christopher moans into his wrist.

'Do you want me to take care of you, Christopher?'

Christopher just smiles – seriously, what a question. He has his ass stuck out already. "You can fuck me silly, thank you very much."

Gyth's touch pulsates against his hole, his voice already shaky from arousal. 'You want me?' He understood that phone sex thing already, huh?

Christopher swallows down all the impatient curses on his tongue in exchange for something sweeter. "Yes, Gyth. I want you. Do me. *'I want you now, I just can't wait no more, no…'*"

With a sigh that flows around him like a river, Gyth eases into him, fleshy and hot. Stopping his song, Christopher hums, his hips bucking like crazy already – it's less weight than he needs right now. He needs the real thing – but he'd lie if he said this wasn't somehow hot as well.

He wonders what Gyth has been doing when he reached out to him. Has he dropped everything, just for a quick fuck?

Christopher smiles, eyes closed in bliss. "Move, babe."

'Yes...' Gyth's voice is a demonic thunder, rolling down Christopher's back from the outer reaches of this plane of existence.

He fucks into Christopher through the dimensions separating them. Because the sensation is so faint, Christopher can't tell if it's a single tentacle or more. Just that it's gigantic.

He'd find it sexier if it was more. So, his mental eye shows him bouncing on a screw of three tentacles, twisted around each other, fattening so soon that only their very tips could thrust into him. "Fuck..." Gyth's pace is perfect as always, streaming into him quickly and pulling out slower. Christopher arches his back a bit more, so that his clothed nipples rub against the wall.

The office wall. This may be like phone sex, but he's still ten feet in the air, in a room with giant windows, for anyone to see.

It's not as unsettling as it should be – his cock throbs in his pants. Should he reach down and stroke it himself? It's not like he'd fall down. He's always safe in Gyth's grip.

Far beyond this plane of existence, Gyth is way ahead of him. He's been touching himself ever since Christopher's arousal has dripped from his faraway voice straight into Gyth's mind.

His body may be decaying, but as of now, it is still able to produce that lovely energy.

In his imagination, he pounds into Christopher with relish.

The bounces are so powerful Christopher's glasses are taking their leave. He smiles and asks, "You find me sexier with or without the glasses?" The distant growl he gets in return makes him shiver.

Gyth thinks of their bedroom in Christopher's home, their quiet mornings and not-so-quiet nights. He thinks of those transitionary moments when Christopher puts on his glasses or takes them off, those moments of change when he transforms into a different person – if only he could have that process forever, not the solid states... if only he, too, could change and last forever...

Gyth pumps harder into this pliant body, to shake it up. 'I like when they slide off your face...'

Christopher chuckles. "Oh, today's your lucky day. 'cause you're fuckin' me so hard." His mouth won't close anymore.

Gyth reaches around his body to stroke his dick and slides under his perfectly ironed shirt. Afterimages of a touch attach to his nipples and suckle – so sweet – but far too soft...

Another rumble from Gyth, and then Christopher gets pulled back by his hair. His spine arches, pressing his nipples harder against Gyth's transdimensional suckers, while the tentacles around his thighs reach higher to fuck into him deeper, rougher in this new angle. And just like that, he's held in place.

"Fuck...!"

Yeah, this is much better than phone sex, he thinks, melting into Gyth's touch.

Meanwhile Gyth is literally melting. He desperately tries to keep a semi-human body, *something* to produce sexual energy as he crawls along the edge of this dimension. He fails. By now, he's just some giant blob with thrashing tentacles and dripping organs all over him, somewhere in a cosmic ravine, struggling to keep himself together – but the grotesque view betrays just how wonderful he feels.

He's so glad Christopher has called for him. He hates how separated they are. He tells himself, as he plays with the tendrils curled around his cock, imagining they're the tight heat of Christopher's ass, that this here is better than being separated entirely. This is better than wallowing in the physical pain this consumption causes him.

Still, it's too little of a connection. It makes sex hard work. And those blasted parasites are a nuisance. A *cockblock*, that's the word. Eating away at Christopher first and now diverting Gyth's precious attention.

At least they can hear each other: "Oh, Christopher..."

'Y-yeah?' Christopher's voice is hot breath inside his mind. Gyth moans as his sides curl open – he imagines Christopher's flushed cheeks, rosy and round, so beautiful in contrast to his blue eyes, exhausted and half-lidded behind his gorgeously curved eyelashes – his white shirt soaked, his glasses falling off him – he wants to see him...!

As he's being fucked against the wall, desperate for friction, Christopher's nose bumps into an invisible mass from above. Moist and soft but not squishy. As best as he can while bouncing on Gyth's tentacles, Christopher tries tracing the shapes with his nose and mouth and does recognize them.

Above him floats an entire bouquet of eyeballs. Judging from the touch against his hands, that are flat against the wall, the mass must be at the very least four feet wide.

The real sight would've taken his breath away: almost two thousand eyes, arranged to watch him getting railed by their owner, all trying to catch just one glimpse at him, no matter their size or colors. But it's impossible – they are too far away.

Christopher uses the momentum of Gyth's thrusts to lick through the clusterfuck of eyeballs on their thin nervous strings. He flattens his tongue as they sink down, around his head. They tremble with pleasure.

"Can't keep your eyes off me, hm?" he hums. He catches two sweet eyeballs between his lips to suck on them. His own personal lollipops. Because of Gyth's rhythm, he pulls them down with him, before sending them upwards against – he bites down onto the optic nerves – not strong enough to sever them, if they'd been here for real, but hard enough for Gyth's liking. His tongue slides over the bumps of the irises, able to even feel the pulse of the little veins reaching to the nerves.

Gyth's husky moans echo all the way to him. For a few moments, Christopher can even hear the smile that his stupid pun elicited. He can *feel* it against his shoulders.

But then Gyth's thrusts into his stuck-out ass slow down. 'This is cruel, Christopher. This is too little a connection... I need to see you! I long to see you so badly...'

Christopher hums around his eyeballs at the high-pitched desperation – Gyth needs it bad. But, yeah, Gyth is allowed to see him in this state, he finds. That'd be fine with him. But how could you solve this problem?

Beating him to the solution, Gyth pants, 'Become my eyes, Christopher. Tell me what you look like!'

And though it is meant for Gyth to be sexy – that wording must be joining vocabulary, surely – it drives Christopher just as crazy.

'I'm... dripping with your sweet stuff. It tastes so faint, *God*, I wish you could pump it into me for real.' That's what he sends his way. He thinks a lot more – how much likes having Gyth both inside his mouth and his ass. How cute his tendrils are, trembling around his thighs and fingers. How masterfully he sucks and tugs at his nipples – how insane it is that he is down for this –

Gyth's reply is one desperate moan.

Christopher opens his eyes, leaning back further to be able to look down at himself. 'I'm... curved in your grip. Mouth full. Sweaty as hell. With my fingers spread. Just like my legs.' He *does* find that sexy, actually – formulating this description somehow makes him desirable to himself on a whole new level. He's forced to look at himself and put it into words. 'My glasses are on the floor, my clothes are ruined,' he continues with a smile of adoration around Gyth's hot eyeballs, tilting his head. 'You're ruining them, babe.'

Invisible tentacles stroke his face as Gyth pulls out of his dripping mouth, nuzzling his head.

And Christopher knows what he wants to hear: "You're so good to me."

Three quick, hard thrusts. 'Am I? I want to do you good…'

"You always do, darling, always."

Gyth pulls him closer, fucking him harder. Christopher gasps as his smile fades – he speaks in swallow breaths. He is going to be one sore mess, without being even a little bit stuffed. "I just wish… I wish I had your gorgeous eyes back inside of me…"

Gyth's voice is a desperate growl in his ear as all tentacles yank him closer, fucking into him passionately – so fervent despite their distance – unleashed. 'What fucking good is it if I can't bloody feast on the inside of your *tiny-little-fuck-mouth*–'

Christopher interrupts him with a chuckle. "Woah! *Ha*…"

It helps to will himself away from the orgasmic edges he was just pushed onto, together with slowing his own restrained movements. He needs to laugh this off, or else he'd come here and now – holy hell… Good thing this fuck is so much work.

Just as suddenly, Gyth's grip loosens, caresses him. 'I'm sorry– I'm sorry,' his usual husky dream-voice says. 'It's difficult to balance my consumption – and this entanglement–'

Christopher just smiles. 'Entanglement'. "No worries. I know you aren't like that for real. Even though you could be, with me as your little toy. Makes it hot." He swallows – he still needs Gyth back inside his mouth. He wants to come with him inside. "Eyes? Please?" he begs.

'But I cannot see your mouth…'

Christopher moans, rolling his head as he nears the edge. "Hmm, yeah, that sucks…" He smirks weakly. "Too bad I don't have any other holes… that you haven't checked yet…"

Like a gust of wind, Gyth twirls him around. Now his sweaty back is pressed against the wall. Tentacles slither out of his ass. Christopher whines at the loss of weight and pressure inside of him; it truly is cruel to be so terribly empty when all you want to do is come. Precious friction is so rare this time!

But then Gyth pushes something round against his hole. 'Breathe, Christopher.' Carefully, he inserts it through the dimensions. It is wet and slick, thins, and then another ball follows. It's thicker than the first.

Oh, shit. A guttural scream escapes Christopher as he realizes what's happening. "Fuck!"

'It's not working…' Gyth whines.

Christopher tries to smile as he holds onto invisible flesh, fingers digging into thin air. "Too bad, h-huh? It was worth a try."

Gyth gasps, at his end. 'I'm sure – you look – so pretty… so pretty, my dear Christopher, my dearest Christopher…'

Christopher can't help but moan at that. He is a sentimental guy, and he never gets tired of Gyth calling him all that.

Especially not now that Gyth is inserting eyeballs on a muscle string into his ass.

Christopher tries to steady his breathing, burning up with pleasure. His mouth waters. Once he's full, Gyth pulls his eyes out slowly – and back inside again. It burns and caresses him in all the right ways. He is beyond grateful that the transdimensional connection does convey the eyes looking around inside of him, twitching gently. Still, they need to try this one out for real someday.

Below him, invisible tentacles search for Christopher's glasses, as though they were looking for a lost contact lens. Putting them back on Christopher's face is a mess, but the imaginary image only makes Gyth growl in need. He must be huge already.

He broadens further inside Christopher's ass, blossoming with the voice of an angel – and fucks into him fast and hard, with a fucking eyeball tentacle, making him bounce like a helpless piece of meat to finally, *fucking finally* break through that cursed threshold – God, those sounds! Could they travel the dimensions, too? Can other monsters hear how thoroughly, how *madly* Gyth makes love to him? How many needy whines he keeps pulling out of him?

He's close to crying. "Oh, fuck… Gyth…? Gyth, I'm…"

More tentacles rush past his torn-off buttons, below his shirt, to suck hard on his nipples, taking their turn, each trying to get a taste of him, and down below, his pants get shredded, freeing his bouncing cock, steadied only be the thick tentacles sucking on his balls.

Good thing he can't see it, or else he would've burst apart.

Christopher comes hard, in an explosion of colors and static. His orgasm is relentless, fueled by Gyth and his sped-up movements. His head is dizzy – he'll sully the office carpet with his cum, he fears. It'll rain down from up here, all the way down.

Only he didn't spill into thin air. When Christopher opens his wet eyes, still flushing in the heat of his orgasm despite the slowed movements, Gyth's image has materialized in front of him. He's gigantic, moving every moist bodypart of his, shimmering in all colors in the wrinkles and veins of his flesh, glistening tentacles curling hungrily.

342

It's so short Christopher thinks he's dreaming. His eyes flutter close when Gyth comes flying toward him, into his mouth, to kiss him rough and hard. With his nose squished and his arms getting raised like this – Gyth pins him to the wall by his wrists – all he can do is rolls his body in the last waves of pleasure, trying to breathe, trying to return to reality.

When it's all done, wet flesh rests against his forehead. Christopher opens his eyes: Gyth's lower half, all tentacles and tendrils whirling and slithering around, dragging all the way down to the blurred floor, is sticky with his tiny bit of cum.

Gyth's moans echo in his head. It's clear he wants him to take a breather, but his helpless growls are quite obvious, although not as faraway as before. Christopher raises his head, nuzzling the pulsating flesh in front of him. It hardens under his hot breath. Gyth forms a little bud. Two.

And to Christopher's right, a lamprey mouth emerges from a hungry tentacle. He smirks, fucked silly. "Let's see who does it better, beasty."

He hums in relish when Gyth presses himself against him then, pinned nicely in place. He's heavy and hot, though not as hot as his body usually is. Oh, well, it's just not the same when it's transdimensional sex, Christopher thinks as he sucks on Gyth's nipple. Beside his head, the lamprey tentacle bulges with its contractions. Gyth moans, pressing his fleshy tits harder into himself and Christopher. His voice sounds as though it was melting. "Can you… can you use your…"

Christopher obeys before his wish was even fully articulated. He bites down hard to into Gyth's skin, humming at how it tenses and shivers and drips. The vibrations travel through Gyth like an earthquake. "Y-yes…"

Christopher's own nipples, though sore from Gyth's earlier ministrations, harden between their grinding bodies. He's still horny – or once again, rather.

But his contest against the lamprey beast is still going on. He bites down again, then pulls away to flick his tongue against the semi-human nipple, nuzzling it gently, then taking it into his mouth anew. The flesh he buries his hands in is deliciously juicy already. Two desperate suckers appear, again, for him to finger. And when he sucks now, he can finally taste Gyth's honey in all its sweet glory.

But that must mean that he was really –

"Oh, Christopher…!" Gyth presses him so hard against the wall that a cry of pleasure vibrates in Christopher's stuffed mouth. It's suffocating – but in a good way. He thrusts his hips to provide Gyth with more friction as his gigantic body orgasms, spasms, spilling tentacle slime everywhere. His honey soaks any part of Christopher that has been dry until now. It gets everywhere, runs down his throat in thick threads and drops, and smells so, *so* heavenly.

When Gyth pulls away, breathless and shuddering, Christopher uses the space in-between them to take a breath. His head is still spinning from sex. He caresses the tentacle beside him. He smiles as he slips his freed fingers into its lamprey mouth, grazing its sharp teeth and powerful muscles. "You wanna suck on my fingers, or–"

The room spins. Gyth whirls him upwards, all the way to the high ceiling – and kisses him.

Though Christopher is taken aback, Gyth doesn't use the opportunity to slither into his mouth. He only meets his tongue once Christopher regains his senses and kisses him back, wet and sweet and – lingering. Tentacles and tendrils cup his wet cheeks. But they don't rush. Don't demand anything, despite the intensity.

Their kiss persists.

Gyth pulls away a little, taking in Christopher's warmth. How foolish, to have wasted time apart when they could have had this instead…! He dives in anew, and Christopher welcomes him just as tenderly as before. As always. His heart is pounding against his ribcage. His fingers curl against Gyth's flesh and tongue, as soft as always.

Always and never…

Christopher is absolutely breathless. He opens his eyes, heart skipping a beat – and not just because of the height. "You came here for real."

Gyth traces his slanted glasses with a gentle tendril. His giant eyes are round and soft, with just a tint of melancholy despite being closed. "Didn't want to miss out on dessert."

With that, a tongue emerges to lick them both clean. Happy trills escape him when Christopher kisses him again. Inside his mouth, his salty semen has mixed with Gyth's honey.

He smiles, his arms deep inside Gyth's flesh. "We do taste amazing together."

Gyth's voice is warm, something that no longer applies to his body. "We…"

Together, entangled and commingled…

Gyth just kisses him again, before slipping away. This pain is eating him alive.

He thinks he can hide it from Christopher. Stay with him in paradise for a little longer. Bathe in his warmth without pain.

But nothing lasts forever.

They share a moment with the illusion of Allison. Christopher's imagination builds up a cozy room. It is red from the fire in the wall, not blood. Instead of copper, the air smells of cinnamon and oranges. And it glitters.

They sit beneath a lush, green tree full of lights.

"Merry Christmas, daddy! And Gyth!" Ally hugs them, one after the other. Christopher laughs, but he can no longer deny that Gyth is looking weak, despite his eldritch form. His movements are more erratic yet slower, his touch colder.

Ally doesn't mind the silent chaos. With a smile, she reaches out her tiny hand to caress threads of Gyth's flesh.

Christopher mellows. "Merry Christmas, baby. You good?"

"A-o-kay!"

Gyth's voice is warm as always, just quieter. "That is good to hear, Allison."

Christopher shifts besides him, then turns to Ally. "Hey, what's your sweater made of?"

She giggles. "This?"

"It's the best fabric for any Christmas sweater. It is called *fleece Navidad...*" An echo extends his song.

Farther than he can know, beyond this world's thin walls.

Ally rolls her eyes but joins the song anyway. Watching through closed eyes, Gyth hums along. Even sways to the music, just like them. He loves Christopher's singing voice. He loves when he's at peace.

Christopher adjusts Ally's braids. "We'll sing together sometime soon again, hm?" he says. "How's that sound? With a piano and all? I just gotta get it tuned." He gives her a smile.

For a few seconds, Ally's brown eyes are frozen. The only sound in the room is the cracking of the fireplace. And then: *"Can you hear me?"*

Christopher snorts. "Always. You've got the loudest voice."

"Dad, can you hear me?!"

Now he falters. Is her concerned voice dropping into that of... an adult? He frowns, looking to Gyth for help.

Countless eyes twitch behind his lids, concentrating. He gasps as he spreads his muscles to stabilize the dimension, but it doesn't work. The room slips from his grip and shakes.

Oh, he mustn't fall now...! Do not lose control!

Ally continues calling out like Christopher was miles away instead of right in front of her: *"Can you give me a sign? Dad?"* Her voice nears a kid's as she raises her small hand, uncanny, before dropping deeper again in a dozen echoes. *"A sign? It's Allison."*

Christopher's breath hitches. Gyth can't help him now. "Yes," he sighs, fighting to not lose eye contact with his kid, no matter how unsettling it is. His skin crawls when he answers, "Yes. You're Allison. You're my baby Ally."

Whispers dance in the distance. *'Everchanging, everlasting.'*

Christopher's hands cling to what he thought was a Christmas rug. In a flame of hope and confusion, maybe foolishly so, he asks, "Ally? Are you... are you here?"

A grin spreads on Ally's face. She whirls around and throws a fist of triumph in the air. *"Yes! I knew it!"* She screams of joy in countless echoes. *"I knew it! Dad?"* She sticks out her tongue, eyes fluttering – and her voice returns to a child's singsong, just as the room stops shaking. "I knew it!"

"Ally?" Christopher breathes.

"Yes, dummy, I know," she snarks, grinning wide.

Relief floods Christopher as he laughs and hugs her. "Ally..." She's less real now that she was back to being an illusion inside Gyth's world. Before, she has felt just as real as him and Gyth.

She groans mockingly. "That's my name!"

"Yeah, yeah, it is." Christopher holds her close. He doesn't care if his voice is shaking. "Don't – don't scare your old man like that."

"I will – on Halloween!" She roars like a lion.

Christopher caresses her arms when he pulls away. Then he looks up at Gyth with a sigh. "Same goes for you."

Gyth curls over the rug slowly. "She's fine. We're all fine."

Christopher tilts his head. "You are?"

"Yes, me too," Gyth lies.

Christopher closes his eyes. He exhales and strokes Ally's forehead. "We're gonna be fine. We're all right, baby." No matter how real she might've felt now, she is an illusion. Gyth is with him for real. He swallows and turns around anew. "But you're not fine." Carefully, he reaches out to caress Gyth's cold body.

It exhales weakly.

Christopher nods and whispers, "It's okay." He pulls Gyth closer, hugs him, as he understands. This struggle, this constant fighting, has weakened him so, so much…

Christopher buries his face in his wet flesh. "I'm sorry, Gyth. Let's go somewhere nice. Hm? Let's go…"

The blood is loud in his ears. But the longer he listens, the more it sounds like the rushing of the ocean. Wave after wave it crashes against the shore. No, wait… it's a forest. Tall trees rushing in the wind. Not an illusion this time. Just a wish.

Christopher tilts his head, rests it against Gyth. "I'm sorry that this mess is so exhausting for you. I can only imagine how debilitating it must be to keep all those illusions up."

Gyth's voice is soft but trying to be strong. "Don't apologise. You didn't ask for those realities. I chose to gift them to you."

"You didn't have to do that," Christopher says, rubbing his forehead against his skin.

"I said I'd pamper you." Gyth's husky words are not without amusement.

Christopher smiles. "You did."

Slowly, Gyth adds, "Besides… those 'illusions', as you call them… they're not what's sapping me." It doesn't sound like a lie. "Then what is?" Christopher asks.

"I am not entirely sure. I'm… scared a bit, to be honest."

Christopher swallows. "Well, I'm with you. All right? We're together. That's what counts. We'll figure it out together."

He raises his head. Around them is a fall forest now, rushing with colorful leaves and black twigs. The trees are alive, branches intertwining playfully. Bees with giant eyes buzz through New England asters. And hundreds of wildflowers that Christopher cannot name. He doesn't know if they have real-world equivalents besides the faces and tentacles they sprout. But they are all beautiful and swaying in the wind.

He doesn't sway. Just sitting in the grass, next to Gyth. He is more aware of his own body these days. But at ease.

The sky above them is pink as always, with fast changing clouds galloping over their tiny glade.

He can be there for Gyth. Just like Gyth has been there for him, when he was in pain. No demands. No conditions. Just togetherness.

Christopher feels sappy but doesn't care about the implications. He hasn't tried to be a perfect man for a while now – the perfect American, the perfect son, the perfect lover, husband or father. He has no role to play with Gyth. With him, for once, he can simply… be.

No pain weighs him down anymore. It is his turn to take care of Gyth.

He sighs, inhaling this world's sweet air. The rushing of the trees does sound like the ocean though. And their swaying in the wind makes them look like algae…

"I haven't taken you to the sea yet."

All of Gyth's eyes are closed. "Hm?"

"Maybe in here. Or on the other side." Christopher turns his head to give him a tired but happy smile. "I have a feeling you'll like the coast. Has been ages since I've been there. Remind me to take you there as soon as… all of this is over. You deserve a nice little road trip."

"Not much longer now." Gyth shifts, curling around his hand. Then he asks, "Do you like the sea?"

Christopher looks fondly at their intertwined extremities. Beige fingers against brown and pink and black tendrils, shining golden in their wrinkles, flowing slowly like glittery sand in an hourglass. He says, "Something tells me I'll like it better with you. And with Ally, and a rescue dog, maybe. I like everything better with you." He caresses Gyth's flesh over his hand. When he looks up at him, seagulls cry in the distance. "I love you. You know that?" He grins, surprised by how easy it was to say that. It came very naturally.

Gyth trills quietly. His shy movements speed up ever so slightly.

Intrigued, Christopher grins at him in adoration. He wishes he had eyes to lock his with, to share the joy that spreads within him now that he himself really understands what he just said. "You know that?"

"Yes," Gyth smiles. "I know now. I could've known earlier. It tints the air around you." But his voice is weak. And now the smile fades from his breaths. He shifts, fleshy flower petals opening up to the sky, no matter how hurtful – he braces himself for the vortex.

"What's wrong?"

"He is coming," Gyth says.

Christopher frowns. "Who?"

"The one who sowed his nightmares into you. Not much longer now…"

Pink glitter streams from Gyth's body as he stretches it toward the sky, like a cursed water fountain. He's bleeding, Christopher realizes in horror. "Hey. Hey, hey, what can I do?"

"Nothing," Gyth says, his voice the colors of sad smiles and regret. "It is not your fault, Christopher. I want you to always remember that."

Below them, the grass dies.

Whatever happens, be there for him, Christopher reminds himself. To calm Gyth, he rests his head against his body, not caring that it showers him in blood, the blood that attracts the monsters from under the bed. He doesn't care. "Listen to my heartbeat," he whispers, glancing at the sky through blinks against wet eyelashes. Bright, sickly green mixes into its fuchsia tones, swirling like liquid.

He shivers, holding on tighter. It's getting cold.

Terrible waves crash into Gyth. This cruel discrepancy between them tears him apart.

All he has wanted was to protect Christopher from the knowledge of what came toward them. Death, death, death, from the time vortex looming over them.

But Christopher has been right. They do not have time together anymore. Gyth comprehends it now, time. At least in parts. It always, without question, eventually runs out. It is a terrible lesson that he has finally learned.

He spreads himself across the small world.

"Christopher..."

OVERCOMER

AS FAR AS HE remembers, Christopher hasn't fallen asleep. And yet, he wakes up, on the floor. It is the gray linoleum of his kitchen. But the cupboards, the table, the doorframe – everything is warped. Like a funhouse mirror.

He holds his head. Takes a breath. Goddamn, this isn't Gyth's world. But it can't be his world either. That world doesn't smell like sulphur. Does it?

Christopher heaves his body upwards. It's raining outside. From the sounds of it. It matches the veins and vines across his apartment. Like an ancient rain forest. A jungle of furniture and architecture instead of plants.

He is barefoot, he notices, when he steps into something wet. Blood. Christopher looks himself down. No stains on his clothes. It's not his then, but Gyth's.

The puddle leads outside of the kitchen. Over the corridor. By the time the traces reach the bedroom, the deep red has turned entirely fuchsia. Christopher pants at the sight.

It ends in a pile of meat, pooling around it. It's only about the size of a laundry mountain but still too much to take in.

Wrinkly and wet flesh heaves and sinks slowly. It is illuminated only by the gray daylight through the rainclouds outside the windows. A lone tentacle curls on the floor, as if trying to return its tip to the pile. Weak static flashes up and disappears just as quickly. From a pore, a human eye drips away, landing the blood pile below with a quiet splash. It stays there, wide with fear but too paralyzed to change.

When Christopher hurries around the pile, he recognizes the tendrils spiraling toward the ceiling – they're hairs.

On the other side of the pile, two human heads drip from the flesh. Dark beards, soft edges, but distorted in fear. One of them has its mouth torn wide open, jaw dislocated as the flesh melts away. The second one is still alive. Twitching at least. And its brown eyes meet Christopher's.

Panic widens Gyth's face. His voice is but a demonic rasp, just when Christopher wants to lean down and help him stand. "Don't… Poisoned…"

Mentally, Christopher is kicking himself. Physically, he's struggling to even stand still. He stumbles against the piano in the corner. "No… no, no, no." His head heats up, his toes curl in fear.

This is real. This is what's left of Gyth – he is poisoned, in the real world, from *his* parasites.

Christopher's hand is trembling so hard he can't even cover his mouth with it. "Oh God… oh God, what do we do? What can I do, Gyth? Gyth?"

His cry echoes with ripples in the floor. Just like back at the dog shelter.

Floors can't do that, Christopher reminds himself – and walls don't fold down onto him, and furniture can't yell, and daylight doesn't pierce skin –

A guttural scream is the last thing he hears before the room overtakes him. He slides down the toppling floor as though it was a sinking ship. Bones crack and fluids spill. And then a hand takes his. It's warm and rough with claws and slick with blood – but Gyth holds onto him.

Christopher closes his eyes as the tsunami swallows them. Whatever has overtaken them – it's suffocating him. It's hard and cold. Sometimes he thinks he can identify things from his apartment by touch, a polyester blanket, a sleek ceramics mug. But each sensation is gone just as quickly.

Just when he thinks that they would just spend eternity falling, his back hits a surface. It's icy and wet, engulfing him – water. Christopher flounders to return to the surface, even though he isn't sure it would provide him with something breathable.

Still, he kicks and shoves the fluid away, clenching Gyth's hand in his. His scarred lungs fill with air and sulphur. But it's warmer than the water.

He coughs, hurling Gyth upwards. A scream erupts from his body, covered in cuts. He heaves himself upwards. Like ice, they're able to stay afloat. Only Christopher can't see any floes. It is dark on this ocean. There are stars in the sky, shining in rainbow colors, but they're faraway. And just as clear in the towering waves around them, as though it was their destiny to crash into this ocean one day, trapped.

It's not an ocean, Christopher thinks. It can't be.

He shudders.

If he's feeling like *his* body is falling apart, what must Gyth endure right now? "Gyth?" His voice comes out weak and distorted, and his eyes can't focus on the semi-human body beside him.

Oh, this cold will vaporize his brain.

Still, Christopher holds onto Gyth when the water curves beneath them. A wave crashes into them, covers them in pitch-black starwater.

The storm rages on without mercy.

Christopher grunts, holding onto Gyth. If they could make it to the top of a wave, somehow, they'd be able to look for an escape from up there. There must be a way out of here, right? To the top? From where they had fallen?

But the universe is dark.

'Christopher...' Gyth's voice is swallowed by another wave.

"I'm here," Christopher gasps, pulling him closer with all his power. "I'm here! Let's go!" He tries pulling them uphill – upwave – bare feet trembling in the icy cold. Each labored breath is like a knife in Christopher's lungs. He grunts, pain spreading all throughout his chest. He loses his footing, stumbles, and pushes Gyth upwards to keep his lump of a body afloat.

How will they do this, Christopher wonders, if the poison prevents Gyth from changing his shape? Will he just... suffocate...?

Screeches ring in Christopher's ears. From inside the wall of starwater in front of him, arrows shoot past him. Or are they –

'Save them,' Gyth rattles in his mind. Christopher looks down. The small things, oblong and with countless fins, are living creatures. About a dozen, caught up in the storm. They shift and transform in the water, dark eyes twitching with fear.

Christopher blinks. "I'll come get you," he calls, coughing violently as soon as he speaks. Holding onto Gyth, he slides down the wave, covering his weak body as the water crashes over them.

A weak tentacle curls around the little creatures.

"Hold on!" Christopher calls. But his feet have lost their balance for good. His eyes burn with the starwater and his lungs with the cold that spreads across them anew.

At least the small creatures can cling onto them. They shriek and click so loudly that Christopher fears for his ears. The only good thing about bleeding through them would be the warmth of his blood amidst this freezing hell.

"We need to get to the top!" he yells. He curls his arm around the creatures, hissing at their fangs and claws tearing through his skin in the waves' chaos.

But it's without use. The next wave topples them, and Christopher loses what he held in his other arm, no matter how often he reaches out again. "Gyth!"

A boom shakes his bones, and the sea spray no longer cuts through his face – the storm dies down. The sea of stars is dead quiet. And before him, on the still surface, towers Gyth. His lower half is a mess of bleeding and twitching tentacles. From it grows a human torso, bent over, with arms stretching as far as a room, cracking, shivering as they expand their thin fingers in this grotesque shadow of a human shape. His head hangs down, with grunts of pain falling from his mouth like cursed fruit in this distorted otherworld. But then, a familiar sound: "Christopher…"

Christopher stumbles, kneeling in the water in front of him. He reaches out to touch him, to comfort him, still radiating warmth. "I'm here," he whispers. "Hey, I'm here."

The little creatures whine behind him.

Gyth tries to free himself, but his arms and fingers are stiff like branches of a tree. "I'm trapped. I cannot move." The stars on the surface below him shine in a constellation. Like a net.

Christopher nods, lips shivering. "Okay. Okay, doesn't matter. I'll carry you." Whereto, he doesn't know. But he'll do it. "We'll be out of here before you know it." He lifts one knee to steady himself, then hugs Gyth to pull him upward – but all it does it tear a scream of pain from Gyth.

His trap works harder now, lines flaring up brightly, cutting into his unchanging body from below. He tries to breathe through his cries, but it's useless.

"I'm sorry!" Christopher's eyes rapid as he lets go of him. "We'll find a way. It's okay, we'll get out of here!"

Gyth's human face distorts. "Christopher – I'm sorry I could not protect you."

Oh, hell no. "Hey. Hey, this isn't over. Stop saying things like that." Christopher caresses his cheek, trying to think. But he's distracted by his own hand, unmoving now, too. He is freezing to death.

Through all the pain, Gyth lifts his heavy head. Framed by those beautiful curls. And tears. His eyes are without hope.

He dreads what comes next. That which will happen to Christopher, and to the little ones, and himself. His body is stagnant. Unchanging.

But deep inside of him, there is something that still moves, yearning to spill over. It is steady and yet in flux. Just like he himself once was. The incorrigible, stubborn, bright warmth amidst the darkness that he only now comprehends.

Christopher's blue eyes are on him.

"I love you," Gyth whimpers. It is but a drop of his heart, not nearly as powerful as it deserves to be. As it *longs* to be. "I love you so much, Christopher."

Christopher stares. Trembling. And then –

The sea roars and rears up behind him. He doesn't stumble, but it's not flying either. Cold flesh closes around him, flaring up with sparks of impossible heat. He gasps, raised by what he now understands is a giant hand. It turns him around to reveal a creature as high as a skyscraper rising from the sea of stars, distorting it anew.

The stormy waves make a terrible return, impossibly loud. Lightning strikes around the creature's green and moldy body to illuminate it. A man's body, at first sight, but dripping with threads of scaly flesh, with tentacles melting from its face. With eyes as terrible as watchful as the night. Ancient and merciless.

Over all that noise, even over Christopher's screams of pain, an otherworldly voice speaks – or a dozen different voices overlapping? "Tiny incubator. Tiny piece of human filth. Spinning a net, a net, a net with a guardian…"

Despite not having much power left, Gyth calls out, "Let him go! It's me you want!" But his words die and he coughs up blood.

The little ones scatter to hide behind him.

"Oh, but this is it! The hideous veil that has shrouded the guardian from this one's reach." The giant turns Christopher toward itself, lifting him up higher, further from Gyth. "This here is the source of that peculiar energy, so steady and adamant."

Its colossal eyes drip and shriek, flaring with interference that Christopher's brain cannot comprehend. He whimpers.

This is the monster Gyth has been afraid of.

It roars and whispers at once. "Tiny human. At any moment in time, billions and billions of forces are tearing at the cosmos. It is so cold. It is so hot, with radiation that melts away your body, mind and everything in-between. Even your nearest star, engrained in your atoms, will kill you. It is screaming into the void. And yet, over all that noise – *you*." It actually sounds intrigued when it asks, "Is your mind tearing already? Or did you have more fun as an incubator for this one's divine parasites?"

Below them, Gyth forces out a guttural scream, trying to fight the restraints of his trap.

The sound cuts wounds into Christopher's heart – he screws his eyes shut. But the noise remains.

The monster's grip around him shifts. Images penetrate his mind, flaring up, dying down, forcing him to watch. "The guardian is in pain. Do you see?" It laughs, though a shadow of confusion flickers through its voices. "All this pain, if only it weren't for this – this human…"

"Don't listen to him! Christopher…!" Gyth's voice cuts over the noise as beautifully as ever. But it's not strong enough.

I'm trying, Christopher wants to reply. I'll find a way to get us out of here. But all he can do is focus on breathing, to try and block out the pain of the monster's grip around him.

The voices lower: "Look at how he is now lying to you. All this pain… and the departure from his eternal duty… You did this. You filthy fucking piece of worthless shit." They slow down, forcing the images of Gyth's bleeding body into Christopher's mind. "You have kept a guardian from the one thing that gave his existence meaning. He is in pain because of you. You are the burning lens of his destruction. Only you, only you, only you."

Christopher thinks, that's the way it has always been. Isn't it? He fucks up everything he touches.

Only… he hasn't made Gyth bleed. He hasn't put him in a trap. He hasn't poisoned him.

No, they've been *happy* together.

Christopher pants hard as realization washes over him. "I'm not doing this to him."

The voices echo: "You are! You are!"

"No." Fighting against all that pain, Christopher opens his eyes, craning his neck to face the monster. His words pick up pace – this is a fucking hunter – this is one of the fuckers that Gyth has been dealing with all this time, just gigantic. "You are doing this! You're hurting him, let him go! Piece of shit!" He may not be wearing shoes, but he's still a big guy, he doesn't need them. He kicks away the flesh that holds him, squirms in its grip to try and free his arms.

How foolish! Impertinence!

The monster yanks him closer, flaring up green and wrathful now that its madness has failed to infect him, in spite of the careful preparation of his soil. It tightens its grip, pressing his hands in-between two fingers, behind his back. Christopher can't fight the image that visualizes what happens – a thin, long needle of a bone pierces through his hands, binding them together, stuck.

He screams, his breathing only heating the pain.

"Stop it!" That is Gyth's voice. The small creatures join his protest, yelling, shrieking amidst the universe's roar. The cacophony of hell.

Blind with pain, Christopher pants when his bones crunch and break, screaming when his elbows crack and invert. He's getting squished.

Gyth sees it all. Through tears, he begs, "Stop this! Please!"

The vortex' otherworldly voices intensify. "A plea, a plea, a plea so silent in this universe! So meaningless. Your body may hurt, guardian, but this one knows that the pain of seeing this human *crushed* will torture you even more." The voices soar into high-pitched amusement before tumbling back into roaring depths. "I'll crush your little human whore the way you didn't dare."

Gyth has barely power left to even sob. "No…!"

One hundred yards away from him, one hundred lives away from him, Christopher screams of pain. Oh, if only he wouldn't feel any pain right now! If only he was allowed to pass out and die in Earthly silence…!

But Krysuldom the Dark grants no such mercy. What would be the point if he did?

"The human's life will end not in *consumption*…"

Around Christopher's compressed body, a spell forms. Floating sigils in a green circle, as distant voices whisper magic and doom.

He must understand, Gyth realizes in horror. The way Christopher's helpless eyes meet his, he understands what is happening to him, as Krysuldom's hand guides him the heaving center of his stomach.

You and me...

"He will meet death by joining!" Gyth's voice and his body and his mind and everything in-between strain to escape his trap. "No!"

This can't be the end.

Oh, but it is!

All he has wanted to do was to protect Christopher – his dear, dearest Christopher – only to now watch him die as his remains fuse with Krysuldom the Dark. Stretching. Tearing apart. Disappearing in his galactic mass, unable to stop the cruelty, unable to comprehend despite his wide blue eyes.

His beige and red flesh mixes into terrible greens as thunder shakes the universe.

"Filth! How incompatible we are, human! I will swallow you up!" Krysuldom delights in this power. Oh, yes, he savors it. It is always the best part. And this time, it tastes so very deliciously of that pesky guardian's demise.

Indeed, this is victory! This is glory! He can now feel that human's dimension in his body, every tiny human on Earth, ready for him to devour them.

His stormy sea dies down... and the stars are dull and cold and silent. As they are supposed to be at this distance.

All alone, the guardian sobs in his trap.

Satisfied with his deed, Krysuldom leans closer to sneer into his face. "Filthy little guardian nuisance. Too hurt to go home. Too weak to fight back. Too lonely. Is no one rushing to your rescue?" He laughs – but falters when he hears the guardian wasting his last powers to sob a spell.

No, not a spell... Just a name. Over and over again...

"Your mind is still with the human, the human, the human who is not here anymore," Krysuldom notes. He nears the grieving guardian, water dropping into the depths. "This one is full of curiosity. How does it feel to be sucked into the abyss with him? Even though you're still here, still here, still here?"

Oh, but what is he doing right now? This is no fun, with that pest ignoring him. "It is no matter," he states coldly. "You have failed in your duty. You must wonder if your entire existence was without purpose, you useless fucking louse. What meaning does your existence have if you cannot even fulfill the duty you have bestowed upon yourself, guardian?"

What a bold fucking question, Gyth thinks bitterly, considering that Krysuldom planned on him wanting to protect Christopher so much that he swallowed his poison – he's so full of shit, all hunters are.

'Guardian'... the last construct. The last stone to shatter.

Gyth won't honor this fucker with any more attention.

"Always changing, changing, changing, until the human changed you one time too often..."

Gyth's head rolls from the tentacle trashing it. "Think of all the poor creatures that died in the light of your consumption! And those you willfully neglected to save this one human! Too busy having your tits sucked to do what you've always prided yourself on doing. Your conscience is spilling over with the blood of your victims!"

Is it? Gyth remembers how he has protected Ally and Christopher with his deed. Right now, his conscience is spilling over with *love* – his only regret is that it has come to such an end. It has been anything but inevitable.

But he doesn't regret loving.

Now, he does raise his head to glare at the darkness. "Change is not disgraceful, bitch."

"Then why is the human whore gone?" Krysuldom booms.

Gone… Gyth shuts his eyes close, as a human would. Despite knowing it would neither shut out the world nor ease his pain.

"Too torn to answer! Not in body but indeed in mind. And everything in-between." Krysuldom sheers off from him. "It is no matter, filthy slutmeat. You have lived, have lived, have lived among humans. You must know that when this one tears your lonely body into pieces now" – he rips off the branch that has become Gyth's right arm, spilling human blood instead of his own – "you will not endure much longer. And your failed existence will come to an end. You will die alone in this human cage, cut off from everything you have ever known! You will fade into nothing – always and never. The very last change for you to undergo."

Gyth is crying through the pain. Slowly but surely, it carries him away. But he lets it all happen.

The other arm ripped off, tearing open his side, more and more… He must be spilling all of this precious body into the universe. But he can only assume. He cannot see, he cannot hear. But whatever happens to him, he'll let it happen. He does not want to spend his last moments despairing over his agony. He just imagines being held. That once sweet place…

Oh, how divinely glorious indeed! Krysuldom feels the trembling fear of humankind inside of him. Fear of their bodies. Their souls. Their reality.

That is Christopher. He shivers in this all-encompassing terror that tries to erase him once again. It has happened to him before. Just slower.

This is too fast. He is *thin* already, and thinning further…

Is he even real? Has he ever been? Has he lived?

He must have, because he remembers a touch. You can't touch if you aren't real. He remembers this touch… and a look, through warm, brown eyes – meeting his.

His eyes, shining like molten skies.

That is him. And he remembers Gyth and he remembers his words. Not only has he lived, he has lived as his own person. In his own body that could touch Gyth's, with his own mind and emotions. And his own power.

With it, he needs to get Gyth away from the monster.

Christopher is now acutely aware of his body, despite it being stretched inside another. It is already reduced to shreds and atoms. But it is *his*. He can feel it. He knows it. Eternally, intimately.

There is no cosmic plan. There is no baggage holding him down.

There is only him.

A blue eye opens inside the flesh.

In the midst of his play with the semi-human tentacles, Krysuldom's giggles stop. The guardian falls over, thrown off-balance in his ripped body. But still unable to move. So, the trap is working. Then what is it that's derailing right now?

Krysuldom's throat bulges and hurts. He throws his head back, groaning. Something's in his throat. His body wants to throw it up, but he seals his lips tight.

Christopher tears them apart. He screams as he crawls out of the mouth. It is useless trying to shrink it, his hands always find a way.

After a few moments of emergence, he fuses back behind the scales – it is painful – but that tactic of confusion doesn't work, not anymore. Christopher can tell his parts apart from those of Krysuldom. He can't make him forgot those anymore.

Steaming, fuming, Krysuldom sprouts countless giant eyes. Anything to look for the tiny whore!

Christopher kicks one out from its gooey inside. The universe's coldness chills against his skin. But every second this thing is busy fighting him instead of Gyth is a success.

Screaming over the loss of his eye, Krysuldom tries caging him anew. His voice booms through the vortex of time. He will cage the pest, he will hunt it, as he has always done! Always and never! He will not be killed by his own joining!

But nothing, neither bones nor flesh nor organs, can contain Christopher. He always gets away, crawling out further every single time. His hands shovel a way through the meat, scales and slime. His head follows, then his torso, his hips, his legs –

Eventually, he has his entire body back. It is his, and it steps out of the goo with a scream.

Yes, it is a scream, Gyth notices. It's Christopher's voice. It mixes with the excited shrieks of the little ones, jumping up and down the waves.

His bliss is weak. But still strong enough for him to smile. "Christopher..."

Yes, it is him. Stumbling over the gray remains of the body of Krysuldom the Dark. Looking back on it with wide eyes, as though surprised by his own power. Panting. And saying, "You should've practiced that swallowing." He stumbles, bare feet making their way over the starwater.

He rushes to what's left of Gyth. With the sea so still, he realizes it's a physical trap. He tears away an icy star from the shimmering constellation in the water beneath Gyth, and the entire net dissolves.

Gyth rolls to his back, wheezing, breathing again. His body struggles to take in air. And to change. But he can do it. It forms and absorbs the torn-off limbs and reassembles itself to heal.

His movements cause ripples in the ocean. It returns to its wavy state. Krysuldom's body sinks into it like a ship.

But that's behind Christopher.

In front of him, he cradles Gyth's shapeless form with a frostbitten hand. Gyth is twitching, covered in slime and sticky blood. But he manages to hug him back. Christopher, himself now covered in blood instead of clothes, closes his eyes as his naked body, too, resumes breathing. Resumes crying, relieved by the knowledge that they're both alive.

He can feel the water pooling around his legs. And he can hear Gyth saying his name, and sighs. "It's over. It's all right."

Around them, the small creatures assemble silently, their dark eyes big and questioning.

Christopher breathes hard. They saved these guys too, right? "And you? You all right? Yeah? Okay. Okay." His head returns to Gyth's, still holding him. This is right. This is good. They're in safety now. The storm has passed.

He sniffs. Looks around. And with the light of those distant stars, a terrible realization dawns on him.

"How can we get back?"

Below him, Gyth is crying. "I'm too weak…"

Christopher returns his eyes to him. Only to see that acid is streaming from Gyth's eyes. They close, dripping away. "I'm sorry…"

Christopher wants to caress him for comfort, but his hand shudders with the shock. "Don't – It's all right. You'll be fine. Hang in there."

Hang in there. All I need is time. Time to think…

Christopher looks around. There is nothing around them. No point of reference. No planets. Just a darkness with stars like holes in a ceiling, suggesting light but not warming them. And in this state, they still can't move. If someone else was out here, they could never reach them before Gyth –

He has to do *something*. He has to try. Finally, Christopher calls out: "Hello? Anybody? Help!"

The small creatures trill and coo next to him.

Though it is hard to do through those shudders, Christopher is certain that this is the right thing to do. If they can't get to safety, safety must come to them. "Help!" he calls, louder now that his throat is burning with whatever was in the air out here. Trying to fixate the horizon. And then realizing he should look at Gyth instead, as long as he still can.

"We need help! My friend is… is dying – Help, please!"

No light. No wave. No sound that calls back.

He whispers into the vastness when he realizes they're alone. But they can't be, right? They're not alone in the universe.

But maybe they are in this plane of existence.

"Anybody…?"

"I'm sorry… Christopher…"

Christopher snaps his head to look at Gyth, nodding. His flesh is not moving nearly as much as it should. And it's cold.

"It's all right. I'll stay." He strokes a lifeless tentacle, cradling it to stay and not fall off.

Like he had any idea how to deal with this!

Christopher curses himself and the darkness. Will he freeze to death? Or fall apart like Gyth? Or will he maybe even die first, leaving Gyth to suffer alone for eons before he, too, would finally perish?

He swallows it all down. "What's important is – that we stay together now." He rocks Gyth gently but still shivers. "I'll stay with you. Okay? Just look at me. Just listen to my voice…"

Gyth broadens below him. "Yes…"

A sob shakes through Christopher. They'll stay here forever. He will stay here forever and never return to his world. Because he stays with Gyth. And the ones they saved. Is that fine? To never blink against the sun again?

Christopher sobs anew and starts rocking him. His tears pour onto Gyth's closed eyes. Instead of talking, he should hum a melody, he thinks. A lullaby.

No one else hears it. No one else is supposed to hear it. This is their song now, their melody.

They're together now. And that is good.

They're alone.

And then… they're not.

The small creatures start shrieking, but Christopher only looks up when they scatter away. They head for the horizon. It rips open with a pitch-black rift that moves at its seams, as though the night sky was falling into it. Golden lights burn from inside it. Flames, dots, stripes – Christopher can't make anything out. It is only when a large tentacle makes its way to the starwater that he understands another monster is coming through.

For a second, or maybe a century, Christopher thinks he's sealed their fate by crying out for help. But the small creatures don't sound frightened. On the contrary, they seem to communicate with the big one.

It sends out a louder call through what looks like a trunk. Roars and clicks and trills and melodies – not unlike Gyth's whale song and yet profoundly alien.

His eyes puffy from crying, Christopher inhales, pulling Gyth closer. He still looks weak. But there were still lights pulsating beneath his naked flesh.

Another creature follows the calls through the rift. And a second – or is that one giant thing? Christopher can't tell. Though their shapeshifting is less lush than Gyth's, it is hard to describe the shapes of their large bodies. He can, however, make out the same whirling shreds of flesh and flickering static when the creatures crawl closer across the waves. They trill gently, opening big eyes, swirling with stars, to look at Christopher.

They seem friendly enough.

He gasps when tentacles unfold from Gyth's body, using his last ounces of strength to reach out. "He needs help," Christopher croaks. God, he hopes they would understand.

Circles of dancing sigils appear above Gyth. Golden and orange and purple, all looking like shades of each other. He drifts away, into their embrace. And then he himself trills pink sigils into existence.

They're communicating.

Hell, they're friends, Christopher thinks. Gyth has friends out here, he realizes as Gyth's body transforms softly, without rash movements or breaking bones. His human torso rises from the mass, beautiful arms stretched out in the light.

His face is without expression – without pain, too.

Christopher may be short of air, but he can still call out to the creatures through their silent flames. "Thank you. Thank you for helping him!"

Golden eyes stare at him closely, blinking. A proto-human voice echoes across the waves. "Dear one… Reverse…"

"She likes you." That was Gyth, full of tears. His expanding hands connect to his fellow creatures, and now his gorgeous face does break into a smile. "She means to thank you for your gratitude." He looks up fondly, glowing. "For all that we do."

Christopher's eyes widen – Guardians!

They continue to communicate in trills, clicks, songs and thunder as they surround Gyth, holding him close as he heals in their maelstrom of light.

They scold him for getting into such trouble. They welcome him back in their midst.

Gyth lights up with them in pure, warm adoration, transforming in their spells. In here, he can feel their friendship as physical warmth against his body. And their anxieties, too. Goosebumps, as Christopher has taught him. They're the same insecurities he has, the same doubts.

But there are even more fears. Or rather, memories of them. They have been scared for him after that desperate cry for help, relieved now that he'll survive, rejoicing… His joined ones.

'You always think you're alone! But you never are!'

'We always knew where you were.'

'You had a brightness streaming around you, relentless and adamant. Wait 'til you see it.'

Love, Gyth realizes. More specifically, Christopher's love, entangled with the one shining from within himself, mixing – a beacon, a quasar in the universe for those who see it, and a shield against enemies.

'This is you.'

He blossoms with emotions. Widening, shining brighter, just like a sun. 'Thank you…'

Below him, Christopher witnesses his beauty. He's still kneeling in the water, swallowing a knot. He smiles. Who said the cosmos was ugly and cruel? Well, maybe it was, and he just didn't see it anymore. Maybe it is not peaceful. But then again, even something as mundane as a tempest isn't. And still he likes to watch the lightnings burst through the clouds.

Drops of light fall into the starwater and illuminate what is below. Giant creatures course through this ocean. Christopher watches their shadows from the surface. Watches them travel and light up.

With the next sparks and drops, Gyth sinks down to him, floating tendrils curling back into his human body. He comes to a halt in Christopher's arms, warm and breathing. Christopher supports him. He's still weak. But alive.

A travelling shimmer eats away the dried blood from their bodies. Then the creature of golden light opens a rift behind them. Well, not so much a rift. More like a rectangle, back to Earth. To their bedroom.

"Go." A large tentacle nudges them both into the right direction.

Christopher sighs and hugs Gyth to hold him tighter. "C'mon. C'mon. Let's go home." He stops, looking back to the others. While their sizes aren't the same, each one is about as big as a mansion, distorted by his human vision but undeniably there. They seemed to have given them their blessings, right?

"I'll take good care of him. I will," Christopher promises. With a bit of an unsure smile – where do you look at an ever-changing eldritch creature without it being rude? – he offers, "Come visit us, maybe? Sometime soon?"

The reply he gets are otherworldly growls, so deep and luscious they shake his bones.

"Okay…" That does things to him, all right – they should leave already. "Okay."

Beside him, Gyth chuckles. That sound, as they step over the threshold, is accompanied by faraway songs. They swap the water beneath their naked feet for dusty laminate flooring. And then, the waves and silent flames are gone, as is the sulfuric air. Instead, sweetness spreads between them. Their breaths return.

Collapsing on the bedroom floor, Gyth and Christopher hug.

FINDER

Somewhen, Christopher pulls away from Gyth to look him in the eyes. From below thick brows and dark lashes, they smile at him. God, Christopher has missed this look. He sighs when his hand caresses that soft beard without shaking.

He's been so cold… But that is now all over.

"Are you okay?"

Gyth nods, taking his hand in his. "Yeah." He strokes a gentle thumb over Christopher's knuckles.

Christopher chuckles when their gazes drop. "We should probably get dressed."

"Yeah," Gyth giggles. It's the same rough sound, soft around the edges, that has enchanted Christopher all that time ago. He's overjoyed to hear it's back. He wouldn't know what to do without it anymore.

With a grunt, he gets up from the dirty floor. His wardrobe is open on one side – his clothes have collected just as much dust as the rest of the room. He sighs, rummaging through the internal drawers. They don't open as smoothly as usual. The metal rails are wobbly.

Behind him, juicy splashes announce Gyth growing some clothes for himself. The sounds make Christopher smile.

He finds clean underwear, his spare pair of sweatpants and, deep down in the closet where the dust couldn't reach it, a fan shirt of his last trip to Broadway, one of the cheap black ones with some lyrics and the musical logo slapped on top as a print. It did, of course, still cost a fortune, but he had thought it was worth the money as a souvenir. It's smelly but better than being naked. He pulls it over his head.

"This is, what, ten years old now? And I've not worn it once." He sighs, turning back around. "Well, I guess I did defy gravity. So today seems apt."

Gyth smiles at him from where he sits on the floor, barefoot. The rest of his clothes are the same as always, black jeans and bomber jacket. And glasses.

"Ah, right..." Christopher looks around. They entered Gyth's pocket dimension in the middle of the night, right? So, his glasses must be on the nightstand. He does find them there, gives them a quick clean with his T-shirt and puts them on with a grin. "There."

His smile does fade when he realizes how chaotic everything looks right now. Rain forest architecture, still. But also *so* dirty and dusty. You can't even look through the windows anymore. It must be daytime, because warm light does get through. But the bedsheets are gone. And there are dark spots on the ground where the bedroom floor meets the corridor. And while the smell isn't alien, it's not exactly pleasant.

"This place looks abandoned."

Gyth's eyes follow his look around. Then they meet his again. "But you aren't sad," he observes.

Christopher exhales, smiling at him. "You're right. I'm not. C'mon now. Let's go outside and see what this is all about."

"All right." Gyth takes his extended hand, warm and rough.

Much to their surprise, the door isn't locked. And anyway, where are the keys? Gyth does chuckle, but he needs help to walk down the warped stairs. Christopher supports him. The staircase is in a sorry state, too. In fact, the whole building seems to have become a ruin. For some reason, lots of electronic waste lies around, cables and monitors that Christopher has never seen.

Outside, things are just as weird – except for the blue sky.

The weather must've cleared quickly, because the sidewalk is still wet from rain. A mixed weather day.

But no parked cars block Christopher's view when they step outside the house. He pulls away to exchange a look with Gyth, who is just as clueless. The entire street has been emptied to make room for tents and more tech stuff. There is a commotion of people in white protective clothes, and scientists, all running around the wet street and talking and –

"Oh my God."

He knows that voice. Blinking, Christopher turns around. Up the street, he sees a young Black woman in a dark blue coat with a faux fur hood, sporting brown corkscrew curls. She is the only one to see him, to stare right at him. A bunch of papers fall from her hands, onto the glistening asphalt. Through tears, her high-pitched sob gets through to him: "Dad?"

For a second, Christopher is reigned by disbelief. But it doesn't last long. "Ally?" His bare feet move on their own.

He storms toward her, into a hug. Ally clings onto him, on the tip of her toes, to hold him close, her voice pressed out through all her tears. "Dad…!"

"Ally…" Christopher pulls away. Cups her cheek – not that of a child. "You're all grown-up."

With a hand on his face, as if to check that he was indeed real, she replies, "And you look so young."

They laugh for a moment, but she's still sobbing. Her eyes are just as kind and sparkly as they were when she was a kid.

But she *is* a kid. Isn't she? Or...

"It's been... years, hasn't it?" Christopher breathes. He nods, more to himself than her. "Obviously."

Ally, too, nods, rapidly so. "Fourteen years, five mouths."

Christopher swallows. Was he gone for that long? Now that he understands, his overwhelmed eyes fill with tears as well. "I'm sorry I couldn't be there for you. I had no idea what was happening, I..."

Ally just nods, her chin furrowing from crying as her rapid hands hold onto him. "It's okay. It's okay. I knew you were still there, I knew it. I knew it! I was looking for you. I called for you. I knew you were here, I knew it for sure when I heard you singing."

Her adult voice – Christopher now remembers: "I heard you, too." You reached out to me through all those different dimensions, all that chaos, and it worked, he wants to tell her.

But neither of them knows how to say all that. In fact, they don't want to speak for now. They just hug again, teary-eyed. And they won't let go anymore.

"I heard you," Christopher repeats. "It's gonna be all right. Now everything's all right."

In the distance, Professor Mikaela Wong laughs in relief. "Well, that's something!" She fails to hide her bitterness. "Almost compensates for the loss of my anomaly. Hey, don't fucking clear that shit. Leave everything as it is. I'll go think of something to tell the board."

"An anomaly?" Christopher pulls away from the hug with a chuckle. This is a whole-ass scientific operation.

Ally nods, wiping away her tears. "Yeah. The Shimmer. Disappeared just two hours ago. An energy field. Pink light,

UV radiation, all sorts of weird molecule transformations, deadly transmutations…"

Christopher's eyes focus. "Are you hurt?"

Ally shakes head. "No. Not a scratch, after all this time. As by a miracle."

Ah, yes, 'a miracle' – Christopher turns to look at Gyth, who gives them a weak smile from where he stands.

Christopher's heart widens. Thank you, he mouths, losing a few tears as he does. Even in his time of pain, Ally has always been safe. He gestures for Gyth to come closer, then looks at Ally again and guides her in his direction to meet him halfway.

"You… you remember Gyth?"

Gyth raises a hand to greet her. "Allison."

"Yes. Hi!" Ally wipes away her tears and gives him a bright smile, straightening up. "You were in many of my theories. Not all of them. I couldn't remember your name."

They laugh, before Ally breaks into tears yet again.

She's been alone all this time, Christopher thinks as he offers her another hug. He has missed his child growing up. Missed the crucial years of her life, when she would've needed a parent… But she still looked for him. She missed him, too. And now, they were reunited. That's what counts. "We'll start anew," he says, eyes screwed shut. "A whole new start."

Ally just sobs into his shoulder. "Yeah. Yeah…"

They cry again when she, after explaining how she had been adopted by the Rodriguez' when being declared an orphan, shows him a photo of a drawing she made of them together, for Christmas fourteen years ago. It's the two of them by the dog shelter, as happy stick-figures. Together with a big husky, a one-eyed chihuahua, and an old mongrel. Ally tells Christopher how she researched all the dogs from his time at the shelter with the old staff and that all their best friends – Chief, Pebbles, and even Shelly – got adopted.

Christopher tears up. Not just because of the dogs and their happiness, but also because he can't make head or tail of the device Ally used to take that drawing's photo.

They just cry a lot, in general, for the next few hours. But they beam just as much.

"You're at MIT!" Christopher exclaims in the back of the FBI car. "I'm so proud of you, baby. Oh, is it – I probably shouldn't call you that anymore, should I?"

"It's fine!" Ally assures him. "It really is, I don't mind."

"Okay. Okay, but, man – MIT! I mean, it figures. You've always been sharp."

"Thank you. It was a lot of work, still."

He is thrilled they're talking about this. "I'm sure, I'm sure. So, how is it? Did you make many friends?"

"Yeah! The people there are so sweet. I live with two friends in my dorm. They supported my every whim with the Shimmer. Even though they found it weird. We called the building the Hillsburg Haunted House. And I have been dubbed Creepy Ally."

Gyth leans forward in his seat with a round mouth and even rounder eyes. "Like that agent in the FBI show."

They laugh.

"Exactly!" Ally calls. She goes on to tell them how interesting physics are and how great life on campus is, that she is on the baseball team and so on. This time, Christopher cries not only because how happy he is to talk to her again, with the brightest grin on her face, no less – but also because she has managed to build a life for herself.

He may have been gone, but she still turned out okay. Things turned out a-o-kay.

Ally is the first to leave the back of the car. Christopher now turns to his left – he can't believe his luck. Not only is he reunited with his daughter – he also has Gyth.

His darling monster.

He can't help himself, he reaches out and squeezes his hand. "Thank you for protecting her," he whispers.

Gyth smiles and melts his hand into a bouquet of tentacles, slinging around Christopher's hand to hold it closer. "It was a mutual effort," he says. "Allison wasn't afraid. She may have been scared of the future, of what would happen, perhaps – but not of me. It spared her from the madness."

Christopher looks down, tearing up again. "I can't believe I got to see her again."

To comfort him, Gyth curls a tentacle against his cheek.

It makes Christopher think. Was Ally just not afraid because she doesn't know of Gyth's true form? "Do you want her to know the truth?" he asks. "Not now, I mean, just... someday?"

Gyth smiles at him. "Someday. When we're all ready. She deserves to know."

They have a few more stops until their arrival at the FBI compound in Salem, near the coast. When Christopher and Gyth are once again alone in the back of the high security car, they learn that 'someday' could be sooner than they knew, if they weren't being careful from now on: Gyth feels something crawling up his back. He snaps a tentacle at it, pulling the stowaway to the front.

"Oh, for fuck's sake – you – bugger."

Christopher leans closer. Trapped in a fleshy tentacle, one of the smaller creatures from the star ocean blinks at them through large eyes. It thins its body to escape Gyth but stumbles over its flimsy spider legs in the process, falling flat against his chest. And deciding to stay there, trilling happily.

"Are you serious?" he asks it.

Christopher tilts his head at the familiarity between the two. "Is that...?"

In a low voice, Gyth explains, "One of the smaller pack monsters. This one's a clown, the one I've told you about before. They've been following me *forever*."

Christopher snorts at the expression. "Okay." He grins at the small bundle of flesh and black eyes. "Hey there, little buddy." He wiggles a finger at them but decides to pull away still – just because they have the size of a bunny doesn't mean they're just as harmless. That said, if they're a shapeshifter like Gyth, they could teach them to look like a pet, right? So, the logical question to consider is: "Can we keep them?"

Gyth thinks about it, but not for terribly long. "Why not?"

They try to think of a name for the little one, since they still have time. FBI transfers take forever, apparently.

The questioning takes even longer. But it entertains Gyth to no end: "All right, so I learned that my two favourite agents weren't 'real', *but* I did get to meet another team that was almost similarly competent and friendly."

Days later, all three of them are dismissed. Four, if you count little Ashley, but the FBI didn't notice them. For the better, probably – certainly!

They take a stroll along the coast. Its massive cliffs fall down stoutly into the rushing sea. But the grass is green in the May sun. The air smells of salt. And peace.

Ashley soars over them, hidden in a group of seagulls heading for the white clouds in the sky, traveling and changing in the sea breeze, just like the grass below. Christopher sighs. He'd lie if he said he wasn't melancholic to be here without Shelly, Chief or Pebbles.

But Ally and Gyth comfort him. And, wow, the sea air does wonders for his airways.

"It's just like the regency novels," Ally jokes. "'Sent to the sea for your health'. Just as true nowadays."

"*Indeed,*" Gyth sings, making them all laugh. His converse smile has turned into a grin, now that his comments could bring two people joy instead of only one.

Christopher smiles as they make their way across the grass. It's not Cape Cod. But it's beautiful anyway.

Soon, Ally takes her leave. She waves to two people uphill, calling to them over the rushing of the sea. "My friends are here. I'll take the bus back to Cambridge now."

Christopher gives her a smile. "All right. We'll join you as soon as possible, hopefully."

"We're only allowed to leave once the FBI and their colleagues issue us new licences for driving," Gyth adds helpfully.

Ally frowns. "I hope it won't take too long. Especially for your UK one." She smiles. "All right. I'll see you guys in Boston then."

Christopher nods. "Yeah. Bye-bye."

Ally hugs both of them. She then leaves to meet her friends uphill but turns around when Gyth calls after her: "Oh, Allison, by the way – cool hair."

She grins at him from over her shoulder, head tilted to show off her afro puffs. "Thanks, I did it myself!"

Gyth smiles back – she really hasn't forgotten him.

They wave goodbye.

And then, Christopher and Gyth are alone once again. Walking. Gyth holds Christopher close as they near the edge somewhere. Christopher leans over it to watch the waves crash white and blue against the rocky cliffs. The ocean glistens in the sun, though it is clouded from time to time. The wind out here is stronger and cooler than up-country. Further up north, there is a white lighthouse watching over everything.

But Christopher just wants to stay here.

Gyth is warm by his side. He gently embraces his waist, curling a soft tentacle around it. When he turns his head to watch the sea, the wind blows the hair out of his face so that the sun shines onto it, dripping gold into the brown of his eyes. "I am proud of us. For still being here. Krysuldom's curses could not work their power on us," he says, looking at Christopher anew. "Especially not on you, who he had thought would be such easy prey." He strokes a thumb over Christopher's hand and whispers in awe. "I only had an inkling of that immense strength lying dormant inside of you. Once again, it saved me. *You* saved me."

Bliss widens Christopher's smile. "I never could've done all that without you. If that shit had gone down just a little earlier in my life, I couldn't have..." His smile weakens as his gaze drops to their hands.

The last few days have been a haze. But not a painful one. He's not the same... is he? "Gyth? After everything that happened, am I... still human?"

Gyth turns to stroke his cheek. "To the core." He nods and swallows, a crease forming between his eyebrows. "To your very core."

The words sink into Christopher, slow and adamant. He smiles, closing his eyes in peace. "Water and oil, hm? I don't know. I feel like part of him will stay with me." He gives Gyth a questioning look. "And you? I heard what he said to you."

Gyth thinks about that. After a pause, he says, "While it is true that you have changed me, most of what he said was bullshit." He smiles at Christopher's chuckle. "He was mistaken. You changed that everlooming question in my mind – it no longer revolves around what 'a guardian' wants," he whispers before giving Christopher a devoted look. "I learned to love. In all its facets. Wonderful and terrible alike. You taught me love and allowed me to share it with you. It is not only change. It's the greatest gift I have ever known."

And what to say to that, Christopher wonders.

He pulls Gyth into a hug, melting against his body. His sigh trembles. "I love you."

Oh – Gyth rejoices. Christopher has really caught that lonely drop of his heart! He pulls him closer, bathes in his presence, eyes closed, heart blossoming to curl around Christopher's. "Oh, I love you, too! Ardently and endlessly."

With tears of joy in his eyes, Christopher snickers and pulls away. "That's some… costume drama shit right there. As fuckin' always. 'Taught you to love', heh."

Gyth engages him in a smile. "You have. You changed me." Even slower, blinking, he says, "We changed each other." His smile returns, shier this time. "In effect, it is as though we had joined after all."

Christopher gives him the cutest smile – oh, Gyth thinks, he is so wonderful when he's at peace! "How so?"

"To join brings out the greatest strengths of the other."

Christopher smiles back and caresses his human arms. "How about we try it for real then? Hm?"

What? Gyth's eyes widen, then blink. He draws in a shallow breath. He is more than content with having Christopher in this way, symbolically connected – but to be presented with the opportunity to join after all…

"I'm not afraid," Christopher says. "Not of you and not of the universe. Or myself."

A tear falls from Gyth's eyelashes when he whispers, wind in his hair and courage in his heart, "Then I wish to join with you, Christopher."

Christopher raises Gyth's hand to kiss his knuckles. "Okay. Okay…" He gives him a smile before they kiss. He thought their lips would be chopped by the sea salt. But every touch is just as close and soft as always. He holds onto Gyth's hand when he breaks the kiss to look him in the eye. He remembers the spell.

"*You and me…*" Otherworldly chants whisper beneath his voice, mixing into it and carrying on in the wind. "*From me and you, taken and given and…*"

"*…found,*" they say in unison. "*A part from me – now no more parted.*" And with that, they join, the parts of them now no more parted.

This is right, Christopher thinks. After all this time, he feels at home in his body. A home he can now share. He is as close as ever to Gyth; both tremble in the magic. But they hold onto one another, mastering the balancing act.

It starts with their minds. They reach out, synapses connecting like gentle threads. Memories flicker and coo. It tickles, just a bit.

Christopher sucks in a breath, twitches. But his hand doesn't. He raises it between them, still holding Gyth's.

At their raised fingertips, they're physically connecting. Christopher stares as he moves his index finger back. Gyth's follows suit, melting closer into his in the movement. It doesn't hurt or even tingle. It's like they've always been a part of each other. Brown and beige skin twirls at the points of connection like water. Like galaxies.

'This is it,' Christopher thinks. No, that is Gyth –

His eyes snap to his. Theirs.

How strange, to see oneself from the outside without a mirror. Strange and beautiful.

Christopher sucks in a breath before leaning in. When he kisses Gyth now, they merge at their mouths. Then their entire faces. Like a wave flowing back and forth, their bodies melt into one another. Their hands steady them, then sink into the flesh like everything else. Their nervous systems branch and intertwine. Clothes tear apart as their body widens, broadening with love. It grows toward the open sky. They can see it so clearly, and far beyond it. Is it up? Is it down? It is no matter. Trills vibrate from deep inside their organs. They bubble with bliss, sigh and brim with euphoria as their flesh whirls around them, growing and growing.

Right now, Gyth feels as anchored in Christopher's world as ever. To join Christopher means joining his dimension and to see the nearest star as a sun in the playful sky, shining bright in her light. Giving life instead of destroying it. It is his bloodstream, his heartbeat, so powerful – so steady and adamant. Relentless, stubborn just like he.

This – this is what 'real' means to Christopher. And to his colorful mind, that is now his as well.

This is the ground Gyth touches. But Christopher feels like he's flying.

He can now see the everexpanding edge of the cosmos in Gyth's memories, with his eyes – with all its horrors and its beauty. What looks like destruction is the bedding of something new. Everchanging, everlasting.

And he hears the song that floats above it all. It is spooky but beautiful. Familiar by now. Familiar since hundreds of millennia. Cradling him on in this dance.

And to think that all of this is just what he feels from where they're standing – Christopher cannot wait to fly through this universe. He has Gyth by his side, around him, inside him. He could move through the dimensions like air – when he reaches out, he can touch the waterfall of light. It is pouring onto Earth. To the bugs at the bottom of the ocean, the birds building nests, the fumes of volcanoes, the leaf cells that transform sunlight into oxygen, sugar and colors – and he is overflowing.

With love! Love for this world –

Gyth's love, too – their love –

This universe is vast. But so are they. And they're one.

They wish you could see it, too. Wouldn't you like to see it? What we are?

We... are.

KEEPER

After the events of May, Christopher and Gyth move to Boston. Ally lives here, too. Or rather, across the river. It takes less than an hour to walk from her dorm at MIT to their new place in South End. She likes visiting whenever her schedule allows, seeing how she continues to work for Professor Wong even after the Shimmer's disappearance.

This future is kinder than Christopher would've thought. Gyth tells him part of it is because he has put his foot down – few hunters dare enter this dimension now, after the destruction of Krysuldom the Dark through a guardian and a creature now known as the Artifact: the man who made himself.

Gyth likes listening in on the transdimensional rumors. Gossip flourishes whenever he checks in with his fellow guardians and their missions. Earth is now his very own area of operation. Smaller than usual. Overseeable. But the bigger hunting grounds are now protected by entire groups of guardians, as more and more join the cause.

And this floating rock… It is Gyth's home now, here, by Christopher's side. Gyth drops him off by his doctor's office where he goes to therapy, and by the dog shelter where he found a job. And listens to his occasional complains about being unable to adopt one of the animals, seeing how Ashley still needs to learn what and what not to eat.

Over time, Ashley grows into their dog though. A small, wire-haired monstrosity with lovable black eyes. They bring Christopher much joy with their crazy grimaces and antics. Trips to the sea only work with intensive behaving practices from Gyth, but eventually, they figure this out as well.

It is heaven on Earth to walk along the beaches with Allison and Ashley, as a little family. The summer water is every bit as blue as Gyth has imagined.

Allison also helps with retrieving personal items from 27 West Street. For Christopher, it is an excellent possibility to spend time with her and talk about the past. They stand in corners, looking down at photographs and whispering quietly. How it would've been her right to move on and forget about the whole thing. About how she tried but was unable to.

About why the hell there was a canopy-less canopy bed in this apartment, which causes them all to laugh. "You know what? I'm not actually sure, it was just in here like that when I moved in!"

Allison inherited her father's watchful eyes, Gyth finds.

On a more practical note, Christopher also considers the dusty upright piano a personal item. After Gyth and he (but mostly Gyth) have put it down on the truck they rented for the occasion, he wipes sweat off his forehead and puts his hands on his hips. "Great. Now all I gotta do is get it tuned."

The MIT students who accompanied them stare in awe. "Wasn't that heavy?"

Gyth turns to them and shrugs.

They return back upstairs where Allison wanders through the warped apartment. Gyth stills and smiles at her. These rooms have once been their entire world. Christopher's treasured home that he couldn't have possibly lost. And yet, now that everything is empty and abandoned, the rooms seem brighter. Flooded by sunlight. The alien distortions invite humans to see familiar shapes in them, the same game they sometimes play with clouds. It contributes to that sunlight.

Or maybe that's Christopher after all. He retrieves the black high heel shoes from the wardrobe and, after a brief moment of consideration, slips into them. His legs stretch and his back straightens – and his chin is higher than before. "Fits like a glove," he grins.

"For your feet," Gyth says absentmindedly. He only focuses on Christopher when Allison beams at her father: "Oh my God! They're yours? How can you walk in those?"

"Second nature," Christopher shrugs and spins, like it's no big deal. "Your dad was a theater kid back in high school."

Ally quirks an eyebrow at him. "You're telling me it's like riding a bike?"

Gyth looks on calmly, leaning toward her to explain, "It's more like rearranging your insides with every single movement, lest you fall flat on your face."

Christopher snorts, hands on his hips with a grin.

"No, he's right!" Ally protests with an equally big smile. "Gyth gets me!"

They laugh, but Christopher is quick to swallow his grin. "I mean, it's easy to learn with the right technique."

"And what's that?"

Christopher walks in synch to his words: "Step by step."

Gyth laughs brightly, but Ally's grin is undercut by her eyeroll. "Oh my God. You two really are a match made in heaven."

"Why do you say that?" Gyth straightens with a struck of self-awareness, licking his lips.

Ally rolls her eyes again, smiling. "You like puns and he makes dad jokes. Twenty-four-seven."

With his signature slowness, Gyth replies, "Well – he is a dad."

The statement makes Ally pretend to hit him. "Don't encourage him!"

"Don't sue me for my dad jokes, I have a license!" Christopher calls in faux desperation. These plateau shoes add more than a few inches to his already tall back, but he doesn't mind. He's missed wearing them.

It does not escape Gyth's attention that the madness-inducing system of Hillsburg is as good as gone in their new environment.

Christopher thrives in this new life in Boston and its gay-friendly neighborhoods. There is something about finding friends who are gay as well and seeing them almost every week. There is even a band he can join. Soon, all his favorite songs blast through their go-to bar, sometimes even accompanied by Gyth's amazing voice.

Their closeness doesn't go unnoticed, except for its otherworldly nature, of course. But Gyth refrains from picking up that one expression – 'other half' – to refer to Christopher. They're two wholes after all. He prefers the phrase that Christopher sometimes uses, the 'late night double feature'. That one also comes with its own song.

However, Gyth can't deny the appeal of the image: the two of them separating in the middle, face-to-face, threads of flesh hanging from their disconnecting bodies in the aftermath of their joining as their bones and nerve systems resort.

So sometimes, when someone asks, Christopher is indeed his 'other half'.

That is also the term Gyth uses with his fellow guardians. Once in a while, he and Christopher slip away into their dimensions for a day or two, to check in with them on mission details or simply to chat. Gyth adores explaining the marvels of human bodies to them: from wound healing over organs sharing senses to sexual pleasure. He only shares what he and Christopher have agreed upon beforehand, which Christopher greatly appreciates.

He usually kneels under moving flesh during these chats, hands on his thighs with a polite look around. It is during one of these get-togethers that he learns Gyth's friends have no names, since their eldritch language doesn't require any – which makes Gyth's obsession with *his* name even cuter, in his opinion.

'As a human, you get to choose a name for yourself. But not just one. You can get called many names, depending on the other person and the relationship you share with them.' Gyth translates his conversations and the guardians' intrigued reactions into human language.

One time Christopher has asked him, "Does your name mean somethin' specific in your language then?" Gyth has replied, "No, I simply liked the sound of it." And they've both smiled.

Other chats are decidedly more awkward.

"…That is a good question, actually. Christopher?"

To meet Gyth's eye, Christopher looks away from the black static he's been watching on one of the guardians. "Hm-m?"

"Is sex with me unexpected?"

Christopher straightens his back and blows up his cheeks, staring into the nebulous distance. "I mean, yeah. But that's part of the appeal, I'd say."

Gyth translates his answer while Christopher looks on politely. He soon turns his everchanging body toward him anew: "They would like to know what the most surprisingly pleasurable practice was for you until now."

"Um… surprising?" Christopher looks around, exhaling. Anything to ignore the watchful eyes and swirls all around him. "Biting, I g-guess? And having it a bit rougher, in general, y'know. And – oh, there was one that time where I came embarrassingly fast…" He pinches the bridge of his nose, eyes screwed shut. "The, uh, brain-fuck?"

Gyth curls two giant tentacles over his rolling eye. "Oh, *yes*, that one was *good*, wasn't it?"

"Yeah. A literal and metaphorical brain-fuck," Christopher murmurs. Even shier, he adds, "You can explain all that to them, if they wanna know." He blushes hard when he thinks back to that wiggly gray matter under his hands, squeezing his helpless dick between the two organs – then again, it doesn't feel all that weird to talk about those intimacies when he's in the company of people whose genuine answer to such madness is an almost scientifically detached 'Ah, interesting, good for you'.

For talk that doesn't include any eldritch sex, they have their friends in Boston now. Friends that Gyth, thankfully, embosoms just as much as Christopher does. He loves inviting them to pizza and paying with his fake credit card.

In general, he likes living as a human when it's not dictated by those godforsaken rules. He adores singing to Christopher, only topped by singing *with* him. Some nights, they would dance through the rain post-band sessions, reckless, only to kiss like crazy when they got each other out of the wet clothes afterwards.

Pouring rain can be good, Gyth finds when he smiles at the ceiling in those nights. He now knows that rain makes the Earth grow, just like the sun. It takes time. Time is neither good nor evil. It just is. And then, beauty unfolds from inside its stream.

Stuart is older when they see him again in his home in Philadelphia. Ally has arranged a meeting since he was overjoyed to hear that her father has reappeared. Beside his wife and son, they also meet his daughter Darleen and her wife Gabriela here, two lively women in the same short-sleeved, over-sized shirts that Christopher likes to wear so much.

They laugh a lot over their coffee and cake in the distinctly 1980s living room. Gyth adores the sofas' floral patterns and tries to trace them across the fabric while stroking Ashley in his lap.

Christopher watches him with soft eyes.

Darleen picks up on it. She puts down her coffee cup. "Look at you two. Oh, Jesus. There were times when I thought I was the only queer person in all of Hillsburg."

Christopher nods and gives her an understanding smile. "I know the feeling." He only realizes what he says when the words have already left his mouth. But Ally just smiles at him from the third sofa. They haven't talked about everything yet. But they will.

"That's why I moved away years ago," Darleen recounts. "Trying to get through in New York City. And before you know it, you land in the arms of a beautiful Puerto Rican, and you meet her loving family…"

Gabriela laughs. "Puerto Rican and Italian."

Her wife lights up. "That is the greatest combination, let me tell you! Her mamma is the craziest woman you ever met! Makes a mean arrabbiata sauce and one hell of a garlic pizza."

Everyone laughs when Stuart touches his chest mockingly, like it pained him to hear there were other great pizza bakers in the world. He is in his late seventies now but still energetic.

"What's your family like?" Darleen asks Gyth. "British Jamaican?"

Gyth shifts on the sofa as Ashley climbs onto the backrest. "Not exactly. It's hard to describe. It is kind of a hotchpotch."

"Oh, oh, I get that."

"A what?"

"A confused mixture."

"Ah, thanks, honey!"

"I had a loving home," Gyth smiles. "As I have now, with Christopher."

At that, Gabriela sighs in adoration. And maybe Christopher would've, too, if he wasn't busy tracking Ashley's journey from the sofa to the rubber tree by the bookshelf. They unfurl a large tongue, many times longer than their own body, to lick across the leaves. From what they've eaten before, this entire plant could very end up as their afternoon snack. They're lucky it's in no one's line of sight – yet.

Just when Christopher wants to call them away, Stuart gets up with a groan. "I'll be right back. I forgot my medicine. Again!"

Ashley's ears perk up as their tongue streams back. With a lighthearted bark, they follow Stuart to the kitchen.

One exchange of looks with Gyth is enough for Christopher to get up. "I'll come with you."

'Look after the little one,' Gyth gestures to him, sent over transdimensional waves in addition to his hand movements.

'What do you think I'm doing?' Christopher gestures back. 'I can do it.'

Christopher's hands twitch in a series of 'the hell you will, I'll take care of it while you keep talking to these wonderful people'-gestures. With that, he's out of the living room and into the kitchen. There, Ashley visibly surpresses their desire to climb up the door frame and instead slithers across the tiles. Just when Christopher reaches down to grab them, their body splits into tentacles to escape his hands.

"I always forget that damned medicine," he hears Stuart say. He hums to signal him he's listening when he is actually busy getting a hold onto the little devil –

"So many pills to take…"

"Yeah. The wonders of medicine."

"Wonders my ass! I now take pills against the side effects of my other two pills. Can you believe it?"

Christopher glares at Ashley when they curl their entire spineless body around a table leg. "Yeah, it's – it's unbelieva-ble." He will *not* get down on all fours just to catch them.

"You bet it is," Stuart sighs and turns around.

Christopher raises his hands, ready to redirect his attention literally anywhere else, but Stuart's gaze has already dropped to the floor. "There you are, little Ash. Come to Uncle Stuart."

Christopher takes the deepest breath – only to watch a tiny terrier jump up Stuart's cords with a wagging tail. A regular dog's tail.

"Who's a good girl? Who is a good girl? She is a girl, right?"

Christopher's eyebrows rise as he shrugs, trying to think of something to say other than 'they're a shapeshifting eldritch monster with no idea of such concepts'. But anyway, Stuart is already back to patting their little head. "A good one you are! Yes, a good one…"

Christopher softens. This is nice. Just – everything.

This kitchen is filled with early summer's sunlight. It bathes the culinary herbs on the windowsill. Basil, thyme, oregano, all in pretty little ceramic planters. The closer one steps, the clearer their scent of Mediterranean gardens and food.

He and Gyth should get some, too. Their new kitchen has a big window after all. He can hear his laughter coming from the living room. Soft but rough around the edges. As always.

Christopher stops daydreaming when those sounds mix with a stifled sob. Behind him, Stuart is covering his face.

"Hey…"

Stuart's back is bent and his eyes slack. Suddenly, he looks very old. "Chris, I… Do forgive me. I just…" He shakes his head. "I just can't believe you're back."

Christopher's shoulders relax as the emotions sink in – Stuart is honestly worked up about this. People did care he was gone just like that, didn't they? Ally and Stuart, too, and maybe even that cashier that always asked how the dogs were. Maybe even his old friends from before his marriage.

Although nothing of it has happened through his fault, Christopher feels sorry for the old man. He should sit down. Christopher pulls up a chair, but Stuart dismisses it.

"I mean, Ally, she never gave up!" He hums enthusiastically to hide another sob. "But I thought you was – with all that's happenin' to you people, and all the theories Ally had of hate crimes and all…" His high-pitched voice trails off. "I thought you was *dead*…"

Ashley whines by his feet.

Christopher steps closer to rub his arm. "Stuart, you're part of the reason I'm still here," he smiles, "together with Ally and Gyth. I really mean that. Friendly faces have been very rare. Thank you, honestly." He swallows, remembering that one talk they had about cocky teenagers calling him names and how Stuart would have none of it.

A secret island, in that rundown, eclectic, romantic little pizza parlor.

"I owe you a lot," is what Christopher settles on. Stuart nods at him. They hug.

The world is kinder, Christopher thinks as they sway, shedding a tear or two. It is kinder, now that he is kinder to himself as well. No such things as 'that's gay' or 'punish yourself'.

And where those thoughts still overcome him, Gyth is right by his side to help him understand they are not important. He instead encourages him to speak to his therapist about it, and for now, to go to that little bakery down the street, and that new bar that opened in South End, and go order that Piña Colada Deluxe, and to phone Ally, and come sit with him in the sun for now.

And the best part, about all of this, everything – is that Gyth stays. He has the entire universe at his feet. But every day, he chooses Christopher.

Sometimes, it's almost too much to bear.

Like on that one Saturday morning. Christopher comes home from his run to the bakery. It's perfectly close for spontaneous breakfasts of croissants – "Your partner is European, right? He told me the other day that he has never tried some before!" – and delicious pancakes.

Christopher slips out of his sports shoes next to Ashley. They still sleep where he left them, by the shoe rack, in what looks like a new contender for the most uncomfortable sleeping position ever. But they're snoring just fine. They're just like a real dog in that regard.

A sweet smell reaches Christopher's nose then. And it's not coming from the kitchen.

He follows it to the bedroom and its opened door.

Lying on his back, Gyth is spread out on the white bed in a naked human body, drenched in the light of the morning sun falling through the windows. He has sprouted two eyeballs with pink irises. They are connected to floating red strings of optic nerves and blood vessels where his nipples once were. His brown muscles strain and tense, shifting in his writhing movements. A wrist twists on the sheets as his other hand rubs two fingers across the right eyeball.

The lack of a ball sack allows a free view of his ass as well as his erected cock. It bops softly against his abs, curved so very beautifully between his spread legs.

Christopher's lips fall open in a shocked smile. "I'll be in the kitchen," he whispers. "Sorry to intrude. Didn't mean to stare. Should I close the door?"

The shy apology pulls a moan from Gyth as he strokes the eyeball. He lets go off it in exchange for a thick tentacle that grows impatiently from his hips but still crawls slowly, flaunting. His head rolls to the side. "Oh, no, Christopher, don't. Please stay – I didn't know… that you'd be back so soon…"

Oh, all right? Christopher steps to the bed's footboard and puts the bakery bag on the drawer with a chuckle – even after all this time, that cheeky fucker is still a bad liar.

"The nipple teasers are still recharging. So I took matters into my own hands." Gyth smiles into the sheets as he works his tentacle in unison with the eyeball, milking them for their sizzling energy with his long, slow fingers. "But now that you're here… Do you like what you see?"

"What a question." Christopher tilts his head, only half-chastely. "And how about you?" he asks, although Gyth's eyes are closed. The ones in his head anyway.

The eyeball not dripping in Gyth's hand floats toward Christopher on its threads, flesh growing longer and thicker until it is right in front of him. He uses two fingers to lift it lovingly, gazes into it, black and pink against snow white and red veins. His mouth is watering and still won't close.

"What an eye catcher you are," Gyth lets him know.

Christopher laughs at the old joke. Soft with adoration, he retorts, "Look who's talking." Carefully, he turns the eyeball to face Gyth. He deserves to see his show from the outside.

And his eight toes do curl at that, bones cracking softly.

With his sweet eye so close, Christopher finds it too hard to hold back. He nudges the eyeball from behind to turn it, then licks across it with a flat tongue.

He can actually feel the iris widening under his touch.

Pleasure surges through Gyth's writhing body. A high-pitched ring travels through the room, descending into a horny trill. "*Ha…*" He moans, rolling onto his back when his torso arches, pressing into his own touch.

The croissants can wait, Christopher finds. "Maybe I'll just have *you* for breakfast?" But his amusement slips away in favor of desire when he closes his hungry lips around the shivering eyeball on his fingers, humming in relish. His groin tenses. His other hand comes up to cradle it, sugary slime dripping down his fingers – Gyth is so wet already…

"Your mouth is bloody gorgeous," he drawls, smiling at the ceiling as his movements still. "This… makes me look maximally uncool, huh?" He exhales. "I meant for it to be much cooler. A bit of a sexy surprise. For the pancakes."

Christopher chuckles at the notion that he could ever find this display 'uncool'. "In the mood to cover them in your stuff? Good idea. I'd like that, too. Or…" He grins, then bites his lip as he sways, all sweet himself as he looks over the eye to meet Gyth's human gaze. "We could waste it all right now," he says. "If you wanted to."

Gyth smiles back at him through half-lidded eyes. "You'd really have me right now? Before breakfast?"

Christopher turns away like his jeans weren't already painfully tight. "Unless you prefer it before lunch? Or, y'know, whenever."

Gyth's puppy dog eyes go wide with indignation. "That is the stupidest…" – he wills his mouth to stop – "Will you move your pretty arse over here alread–" And he gets cut off when Christopher jumps to the bed. It creaks softly as he settles on top of Gyth, smiling into their kisses.

Chuckling, he pulls his big T-shirt over his head and laughs when a tentacle makes quick work of his jeans' fly, while another squeezes his ass. "Oh, this is how you do it, yes? Luring an innocent man into your den just like that?" He puts his glasses away, wiggling out of the pants to free his body.

Gyth's reply is without any edge because his smile is too wide already. His eyes close as he embraces Christopher with warm arms. "*Our* den."

Through the softest smile, Christopher replies, "Yeah. Ours." He trails kisses along Gyth's ear, jaw and neck, further down to his collarbones that already ease like jelly under his lips. His hands travel along his sides, caressing the sharp edges of his heaving ribcage and slim waist. Marveling at how his heated skin turns wrinkly and wet as it grows into tentacles and shreds that just soak everything they slither across.

Christopher stills his fingertips against two suckers, circling their delicate roundness, before curling them inside for some tender caresses. They close around his fingers yearningly.

His cock is burning between their shifting stomachs. With the eyeball nipples melting into hungry, hair-thin tendrils of white, pink, red and black, Gyth tries to give their waves a rhythm. "Christopher…"

Christopher sighs into the crook of his neck – this voice will never be anything but music to his ears.

Gyth's heavenly moans intensify when Christopher slides out of his suckers to guide his own dick to the orifice Gyth has prepared down below. He eases into him through the slime, stilling in the beloved heat. He's not entirely erected yet. But Gyth loves to feel him grow inside of him.

His breathy kisses are proof of that. "Oh, Christopher… *ha*…" He looks up through starry eyes, like a hundred pinholes that let the universe's light stream through his darkness. "Am I tight enough for you? Am I?"

"You go as tight as you wanna, babe," Christopher murmurs, wrapping his arms around his waist and tentacles to hold him closer, squeezing Gyth's cock between them and burying his face in his neck. It helps with propping up his ass.

Gyth gets the hint. He reaches around them with a pair of soft tendrils. They curl against the supple flesh of Christopher's cheeks, kneading them gently. "Yeah?"

Christopher just hums. He settles further in Gyth's embrace when he slides into him, slow and thin, just to be careful. "Breathe," he reminds him, his melting hands all gentle on Christopher's back. Ironically, since his own breath hitches when he stills inside of Christopher – he can feel their squished cocks throb against each other through his skin.

Oh, they're so beautifully locked in place...

Christopher heaves himself up, just to look down at the gorgeous soul that is his darling monster. He smiles, caressing his temple with disbelieving fingers. His dark curls pool so beautifully around his head, so messy around his sweaty face and parted lips and half-lidded eyes, that it's almost too gorgeous to look at.

Heads over heels in love, Christopher sinks into him. Moans vibrate through their kiss as his dick slides deeper into Gyth. Riding on that same wave, Gyth pushes himself further past the rim of Christopher's hole, retreating in just the same way as him, before pushing back inside his soft heat.

Their rhythm is slow and warm. Everything's easy with a bit of slime. Their pecs rub against other, pressing firmer every time nipples slide against blossoming tendrils. Christopher shifts his body, rolling his hips at the same time as spreading his legs, to deepen their touch. Gyth extends smaller threads to caress his balls, to squeeze them just when they're locked together once more.

"Oh, you feel so good... What's that song? *'Do me... like you've never done before...'*"

Christopher moans into his shoulder to block out the faint slowjam playing to him from beyond this dimension. "If you sing to me now, this is going to be over real soon."

"Then I won't," Gyth chuckles, low and warm. He caresses Christopher's back with flat hands. But sloppy sounds signal Christopher Gyth is unfurling more and more tendrils. His legs drip away, splitting into brown tentacles that crawl all around them, holding him close, attaching their gentle suckers in all the right places – especially when they find a way between their wet chests, to suck on his nipples.

Christopher tilts his head, sighing shakily as Gyth's changes vibrate around his engulfed cock – God, this is paradise…!

His voice is all dry when he whispers, "Let me suck on you, too. Hm? On your head?" He smiles, nuzzling Gyth's beard.

"Oh, yes, please do!"

Christopher leans down, caressing Gyth's face to stroke curls away from his left eye. Such a beautiful eye, hidden behind his closed lid, twitching, pulsating.

He gives it a kiss, harder than it needed to be, just to pull another one of those agonized sounds from Gyth. It is accompanied by a squeeze around his dick and a helpless tentacle slap against the mattress.

"Oh, Christopher – don't tease…"

"Never," Christopher lies. By now he knows what drives Gyth insane. After a lick across the curve of his eyebrow, he nibbles at it with coy teeth. Retreats against Gyth's wishes, just to repeat his ministrations on his cheekbone.

It melts beneath his touch.

"Oh, you bastard…!"

"Tut-tut," Christopher chuckles, as if he didn't enjoy the nails digging into his back, crunching in their claw transformation. He shakes it off, trying to regain his cool and going in for a slow bite. Hard at first, then gentler. His tongue is met with so much liquid honey that Gyth squirms, messing up their rhythm. "Please!"

Christopher surpresses a laugh – he knows that he's close to what he wants. So, innocently enough, he asks, "What?"

He earns his reward instantly: Gyth tightens around him. "I said…" A bunch of tentacles erect around their connected bodies like eldritch pillars, pulling Christopher impossibly close, burying his cock deep inside Gyth's flesh while the tendrils in his ass curl and twist like hell.

Gyth's voice snaps into that fast and demonic growl that, as always, turns Christopher on far more than it should: "Suck my eye out of this fucking skull before I melt your brain into a *bloody piece-of-fucking-goo!*"

Christopher shudders, hips thrusting into poor Gyth who falls right back to his usual dreamy self, hands and tentacles all helpless across his back. Gone is their slow pace from before. "Oh, shit, Christopher…!"

He wants to retort something clever or at least something sexy. He really does. But now, Christopher simply succumbs to the hunger that has broken loose inside of him.

With his hips picking up speed, his hands hurry to Gyth's face, fingers spreading the soft skin around his left eye as best as they can in their quickened rhythm. It opens like a human's would – for now, at least. It's like legs falling open.

Christopher sinks his mouth onto it thirstily.

Gyth broadens inside his ass, crying out in pleasure when Christopher sucks on him.

He relishes the sweet taste, mixed with salty tears that are undeniably still human. The eyeball trembles beneath his tongue, shaking when he sucks again, opening the lid wider with his fingers stretched above and below it.

Gyth's tentacles are trashing and throbbing like sin incarnate. Christopher buries himself deep inside Gyth's ass when he finally scoops the eyeball out with his tongue, freeing it from the restraints of its not-so-bony socket with a meaty sound. He savors the round sweetness in his mouth for a while, feels it pulsate with pleasure.

Gyth gasps below him, desperately trying to hold him closer. His cock twitches madly between them.

So now, the real fun starts: Christopher rolls Gyth's eyeball around in his mouth for a bit, sucking on the thin string of nerves and veins, making sure he can hold it there, before he sinks his mouth back onto the eye socket. It's soft and wet with all sorts of juices, mixing into one another as he drinks from it. Salty tears, sweet honey and hot blood, growing firmer as it transforms into flesh.

Christopher hums. His right hand slides down to cup Gyth's cheek and stroke his beard. Gyth intertwines his fingers with helpless threads and shreds.

If his mouth wasn't busy milking this head, Christopher would've smiled. He moans around the flesh streaming into him. Truly, once the eyeball was out the way, there was no stopping Gyth. Tentacles trash around their bodies, curling themselves deeper into Christopher's ass as he sucks more and more of Gyth into his mouth and over his chin. The hot flesh trembles and changes around the eye inside of him before spilling over, dripping down both their faces, messing up their beards.

What was that about brains turning into goo?

It could be smoother though, Christopher thinks and bites down once more. Gyth is always wetter and slicker after a few well-placed bites. His orifice is already a hot mess.

Helpless moans and splashes fill the room. God, the bed must be dripping by now. The air is so saccharine already…

Christopher stops sucking to rest his head against Gyth's, ripped open and gorgeous in his hands as they rock into each other. A breathy chuckle falls from his lips when what once masqueraded as a brain curls upwards to stroke his cheek. "God, I love you. I love you so much."

"I love you," Gyth presses out as his reply, bucking upwards with what's left of his hips.

Christopher grumbles into his hair. Gyth writhes beneath him. Around him, really. So many shreds and tendrils and tentacles stroking his back, sliding around, rubbing his nipples with their cute little suckers…

Once more, Christopher rearranges himself, just to catch Gyth's mouth in a kiss. Though their tongues dance briefly, wet and so impossibly hot, it doesn't last long.

Like a flower, Gyth's head blossoms, opening itself in large, gorgeous petals of flesh and organs. They pull Christopher in. He kisses what he can get a hold of, his hips taking up speed.

Gyth's husky voice derails into a shower of praises and whispers inside his mind.

They're nearing that longed-for edge.

Christopher grinds his hips down with a needy grunt, a sound that would've left him incredibly embarrassed in the past. It repeats itself, higher in pitch and desire, when Gyth returns to sucking on his nipples – God, they're so sore by now, so wet – but nothing feels better around them than those soft tentacles and their cosmic pulses, which take so much care of him. This is their perfect place, where they can take in his crazy heartbeat.

By now, he's pure friction. Just movement and waves and colors and moans. He *needs* to come… together with Gyth, preferably. That always feels best.

"Oh, I love you," Christopher presses out anew.

The tiny room shakes then, giant tentacles and other limbs stretching out into its corners as they try to balance their bodies and deepen their touch, making the bed creak dangerously.

"I love you, too, I love you…" Gyth's growl is all-encompassing, like the thunder of a summer storm, vibrating through their rocking bodies. Breathless, Christopher reaches out to stroke a spider leg by his side. Spots an unoccupied lamprey tentacle. Curls two fingers to slide them past its fanged mouth, feeling its powerful throbs, deeper into Gyth where eyes open up, connected on so many levels…

The tentacles on his chest twitch. "I want to share your heart, Christopher," Gyth whispers. "And be inside of it."

Christopher moans against his hot flesh. "I'd like that, too." He smiles blissfully. Gyth is already in his heart metaphorically. But that's not what he means right now – they haven't done this in a while. Joining before an orgasm.

Gyth is already trembling, willing himself to slow down inside Christopher's ass despite every inch of his body screaming at him to do the opposite. "And into your mind," he adds. "To melt into your beautiful mind and body and every in-between…"

When Christopher kisses a tentacle now, he is at peace. "Then come into me. I wish to join with you." He almost comes from just saying it. But he wills himself to still just in time. Breathing.

Gyth speaks the spell in his own voice now. The fact that he's too horny to even bother with the translation, just chanting his otherworldly melodies, growls and clicks, is too much for Christopher to handle. His vision turns pink. Hot flesh engulfs him, streaming into every corner of his body, to milk all of his sweet spots for that beloved energy. And so, they merge as their climax nears – broadening – spilling over –

Their nervous system is a pulsating, spiraling mess, exploding in bliss. Entangled voices whisper their sweet nothings, gasping when meat thrusts past teeth and bones against softer flesh, again and again. Throbbing kaleidoscopes swirl behind the interferences of the human mind, surpassing it to enfold their beauty in unforeseen dimensions. Their slowjam song swings through it all, like silk.

In-between his own desire, heavy and sweet, Gyth can taste Christopher's – fluffy and salty and familiar and his – just for a brief moment, before they blend entirely, to break free and share their energies.

Their one orgasm has the force of two now, shaking them wonderfully as their body cries out in pleasure, screaming to the stars. Flesh pumps and heaves, steaming the windows, crashing the furniture that they'll have to repair yet again.

All worth it. All for this joint moment of primordial freedom and bliss and love.

This is *their* time.

They lie close afterwards as they calm down, shuddering in shreds and nets, flesh and nerves alike. Sighing. Separating through smooth touches and heavy breaths on this wet bed. Wasted. Even after moments and moments of detangling, they still haven't figured out when they each start and end.

But the one hurrying from the demolished bed is very clearly Christopher – oh, they're two again.

What about breakfast?

Gyth blinks against the ceiling. Ashley is barking. At the doorbell.

In one jump, he flies from the bed to follow dear Christopher, who is already by the apartment door. From behind his broad shoulders, with an extended tentacle to hold Ashley back by their spiked collar lest they should melt through the half-opened door, Gyth asks, "Password?"

"Shut up!" Christopher hisses through a laugh. He opens the door just wide enough to hide their naked bodies. "Yes?"

It is their elderly neighbor from next door, her frown as deep as ever. "Hello."

Christopher's voice drops to a serious tone in an instant. "Good morning, Ms. Leblanc. Can we help you?"

"You better. I am pretty certain that when I came home just now, there was a giant octopus squished against the window glass – and I have questions, young men."

"Um…"

Her eyes narrow. "You do not play with food."

Gyth chimes in to tease Christopher: "It is so considerate, Ms. Leblanc, to remind my partner of that important rule."

His reward is a shady sideglance over Christopher's naked shoulder.

But their neighbor is already backpaddling. "Well, it's all the same to me," she says, pretending to not be charmed by his accent. "This is a free country. You can do whatever you want. But at least draw the curtains – there are people in the streets. Have some decency."

"We will do our best, ma'am," Gyth tells her with gravitas. "I'll teach him some manners. Have a nice day."

Christopher is short of losing it as he politely closes the door. "Yes, goodbye!"

As soon as it clicks shut, they both break. Christopher is laughing so hard he has to lean against the door. Now that it's closed, Ashley has lost interest in it and goes back to sleeping by his shoes like a tiny sandbag, and that only makes him laugh harder.

When his eyes meet Gyth's, he calls out "You!" in sarcastic accusation.

Gyth tilts his head and uses a raised tentacle to clutch imaginary pearls.

"*You* wanna teach me manners?!" Christopher asks, striding closer to hug his waist.

More tentacles peel off Gyth to sling around Christopher. "*You* should be putting these in your mouth, young man!" His funny voice trails off into giggles when he adds, "On the kitchen table…!"

Lit by the joyful morning sun, they bark out more laughs in their embrace. After all, they both have an inkling that 'decency' is a long shot for them by now. But make no mistake: they like it very much that way.

APPENDIX

The information on this page is an addition to the trigger warnings in the beginning and will spoil parts of the story and its characters. If so desired, please consider the following warnings before your read:

- sex with human organs, particularly eyes (oculophilia and more specifically oculolinctus; all performed on a non-human character)
- biting kink (odaxelagnia)
- great amounts of tentacle fluids / ejaculate, as well as "cum play"
- child conceived through rape (in the past and not between the main characters)
- temporary fake death

On these characters' sexualities and gender identities

The two main characters in this book are queer, and they've done their utmost to bake their queerness into the story's themes. As the author, I do not dictate whatever personal reading you have for them beyond that. I am aware that knowing what exact kind of representation they're dealing with is important to many, including the queer authors themselves. I am also aware of discourse on social media going back and forth about queer characters' specific labels.

However, firstly, I am not comfortable with that sort of authority. Transformative fandom culture has been my home for many years now. If attaching specific (micro)labels to this novel's characters beyond the umbrella term 'queer' is affirming, interesting, or simply fun to you, go to town. You do not need my permission.

The second and more important reason is text-bound. The term 'queerness' incapsulates vagueness, intangibleness, weirdness, and transgressive rule breaking, as well as resisting assimilation into a cis-heteronormative system. It serves the story's themes in exactly that sense. What follows here are simply my own thoughts on Christopher and Gyth that you can take with a grain of salt, or not.

Christopher exploring his queerness means a great deal to him because his homophobic surroundings and internalized homophobia have meticulously suppressed it until the events of this book. While he loves his eldritch darling in any shape or form, Gyth presenting as masculine when out in the streets is crucial to Christopher's healing journey, which is why the gendered aspect of their relationship is important to him in that regard.

You'll find Gyth on the other end of this spectrum. He doesn't care all that much for gender. Hell, the guy barely understands the concept of time. If you sat down and tried to explain human genders to him, his head would explode (possibly quite literally).

In the end, whichever way you read these characters – they are queer!

Author's Final Notes

At this point, all I have left to say is thank you. I'm delighted you chose to read my book and sincerely hope you enjoyed it (and that it reached its intended audience, haha!). Parts of it have been painful to write, from exploring my own abuse history and queer identity to trying out a quasi-omniscient narrator who puts into perspective what is real and what is imagined by the poor characters. Hence the many filler words. It was a personal choice – but still…

But overall, it has been quite therapeutic and great fun to craft this little project, in English no less, which is not my first language. Needless to say, I take full responsibility for any typos, faulty vocabulary etc.

Seeing how "Far Beyond The Moon" is my debut novel, a review or rating online would really help me out. Or tell your friends, old-school!

Also, how many song titles and references have you found? I've written "Far Beyond The Moon" as a love letter to the cheesy and gory body horror movies of the 1980s. You may have found some homages to those and other fantasy and sci-fi shows, movies, books, and anime in here.

Lastly, be kind to yourselves.

And please, should you ever catch a glimpse at any other-worldly shimmers – keep your eyes peeled.

/

Milton Keynes UK
Ingram Content Group UK Ltd.
UKHW010641150124
436059UK00004B/238

9 783756 862832